GANTLET

A Love Story

Lee Travis

PublishAmerica
Baltimore

© 2003 by Lee Travis.
All rights reserved. No part of this book may be reproduced, stored in a retrieval system, or transmitted in any form or by any means without the prior written permission of the publishers, except by a reviewer who may quote brief passages in a review to be printed in a newspaper, magazine, or journal.

First printing

ISBN: 1-4137-0142-6
PUBLISHED BY PUBLISHAMERICA, LLLP
www.publishamerica.com
Baltimore

Printed in the United States of America

Chapter I

Love

It all started in the poetry class where he sat spellbound by the whirling colors in her long, rust-colored hair and the strange softness of her voice. After class, in the hallway, he reached out his hand to her.

"Hello, R--, ah, I mean, Miss Brockton. My name is Ja--Jason Adams."

She took his hand with her fingertips, looked up and smiled at the grinning, muscular man with blond hair and squinted eyes.

"How do you do," she smiled, "but my name isn't 'R' it's 'Russet' 'cause of the color of my hair. It's a nickname my father gave me when I was a little girl because he said my hair was red-orange-brown."

"Like the color of caramel apples?"

She looked up at him.

" Well, it is natural color--not store-bought--if you know what I mean."

He looked. Natural or not, her hair had been styled in swirling layers that fell like a waterfall of red wine alongside her oval face. Her cheekbones were high, her lips full and red, and her pinkish skin had faint freckles hiding just under its surface.

Jason kept grinning, shuffled his feet side to side, and tried to think of something intelligent to say to his classmate.

"Do you like men poets?"

"I like men poets. I'm sorta a Tomboy. One of my other favorite poets is e. e. Cummings. I adore his poem, 'since feeling is first'--do you know it?"

He grinned.

"Since feeling is first, who pays any attention to---"

She flushed and completed the line.

"--the syntax of things, will never wholly kiss you."

He laughed and quoted from the next stanza.

"Lady I swear by all flowers. . . ."

Her lips parted, her eyes glittered.

"My God! Are you married?"
He looked at her left hand.
"No. Neither are you."
"Do you like women?"
Jason threw both hands up in the air.
"Hey, I *love* women, but I'm way too young to be married. I'm just 24 years old!"
"Just kidding, Mr. Adams--just kidding."
He threw his hands out, palms up, before her.
"Mr. Adams? Name's Jason. And how old are you?"
"I'm 21.'
They stopped at the top of the stair well.
I can't let her go, Jason thought, and put his hand on her shoulder.
"Do you like boogie-woogie?"
She peered up at him, and raised her right eyebrow.
"What's that?"
"Just wondering what kind of music you liked."
"I like good music. Music that is good. And?"
Jason set his jaw.
"I'm not just a graduate student. I moonlight playin' boogie-woogie and rock'n roll piano to pad my pocket. Now, do you dig—like--boogie-woogie?"
"I don't know what boogie-woogie is. I like the lyrics of country and western songs, and I like to listen to semi-classical music--light kind of stuff, you know."
He reached his fingertips over to her far shoulder, turned her towards him, scowled, and emphasized his words.
"*You don't know what boogie-woogie is, do you?*"
"Ok, I'm a little naive–a small town girl in the big city--."
"Ann Arbor is hardly a 'big city,' Russet. New York is a big city, not Ann Arbor."
"You're from New York?"
He kept both hands on her shoulders.
"New Jersey. Now, do you want to learn about 'woogie--I mean, by hearing it played? I'm playing tonight downtown at 'Flick's.' It's on Fourth Street. I play until 1:00 in the morning. I'm subbing for their regular piano player."
"Why?"
His grin radiated warmth at her.
"Why what?"

She found herself on the edge of the giddy kind of laughter that happens when there's magic in the air. Jason, to her, was new--so different from any of the boys up north who all smoked *Camel* cigarettes and worked on their trucks and motorcycles and fished and hunted and talked football and swore a lot. Jason seemed totally different, from another world, and she was at a loss exactly what to do with him.

She giggled.

"Why why? I thought you were a graduate student in the English program—like me?"

"I am. I'm also a hack boogie-woogie—and rock n' roll--piano player."

She shook her head and sighed.

"Oh my, you are a weirdo, aren't you?"

"Yup, a 'ww'--wacko weirdo."

She laughed and held her book of poetry in both arms before her stomach the way one cradles small infants.

"You're not making sense at all."

"S--so, are you coming down?"

"I'll think about it. I've got just a ton of stuff to read, you know."

"What the hell, drop it by and get some boogie-woogie indoctrination Ok?"

Her batty fellow student befuddled Russet, she admitted to herself. But she was also charmed by him, so, driven and drawn, she decided to go to Flick's for drinks and to hear him play boogie-woogie piano, whatever that was, and find out more about him. She sat herself in a booth near the back of the dimly-lit room, at an angle from the bandstand where she saw Jason's face glowing yellow in the beam of the spotlight that also shone on the bassist and the drummer

The trio finished the set with a very fast piece called "J's Boogie" that Jason said he'd written. A symbol crashed, and the lights on the bandstand went out to the audience applause.

Russet sipped at her glass of Crême de Menthe and waited for Jason to discover her, which happened almost immediately.

"Well, hello, my fellow student," he said.

"Fellow?" Russet said, laughing, and nodded towards the seat opposite her in the booth.

He sat opposite her and let his eyes languish on her face and her long hair resting around her neck and shoulders. His words hung loosely in a vacant space somewhere in the back of his mind.

"I—I mean, what other word---?"
"Associate scholar?"
"Colleague?"
"As it may please you, " Russet said, and unconsciously fluttered her eyelashes.
"Or companion student in the illimitable universe of words?"
Russet faked a muted high-pitched screech like that of a teenaged girl meeting a rock star.
"Wowsie! A wondrous word wizard. Can I please have your autograph?"
"*May*," Jason corrected.
"I beg your *pardon*," Russet laughed, and winked at him.
Jason looked straight at her.
"Oh, pardon, fair princess—what mayest-- ?"
"Quiet, Minstrel--."
Relishing the silliness, Russet lit a cigarette and blew a large, lazy smoke ring across the table at Jason who grinned, took a bite at the smoke, laughed, clasped both hands together before him and shook them in the air.
"Alas, alack, I am a peasant, a starving artist, lady, I must beg--."
"Ok, wizard of words," Russet laughed, her head cocked, "you're wacky and you can play that thing, but--?"
"But?"
"—but can--"
"But can what?"
"But can you dance?"
Jason saw the interest he had hoped for sparkling in her eyes.
"When?"
Russet looked at him over the rim of her glass. She felt giddy, not from the drink, which she had only sipped once, but from the strange intoxication of just being with him.
"To your next tune. Your drummer is headed back to the stage."
Jason grinned and kept his eyes on the most beautiful women he'd ever met in his life.
"He's going to the john."
She shook her head and looked towards the bandstand.
"He's at his drums."
Jason looked over this shoulder, and handed Russet the paper napkin from his side of the table.
"Here. Write your phone number on here, and we'll talk about dinner--

later. 'K?"

She took the paper, wrote down her telephone number, and handed the napkin back.

"Maybe . . . if you play a song I can understand."

Jason put the napkin in his pants pocket.

"Name it."

"A song I can understand, I said."

"How about a blues?"

Russet's face soured.

"What blues?"

Jason grinned at her over his shoulder as he headed towards the bandstand singing "Just Say I Love Her."

Jason fell asleep thinking about Russet—her laughing brown eyes, her husky voice, her glowing smile, her lilting laugh, the delicious way she smelled, the way her warm hand felt on his. He wanted to hold her against him, run his fingertips through her lustrous hair, nuzzle her at the base of her neck, nibble gently on her ear lobe, and kiss her soft lips.

He telephoned her the following morning and they agreed to meet that night for a dinner the next weekend at The Pad, a restaurant and night club in Russet's apartment building on the north campus of the University.

The restaurant was on the ground floor of the apartment building, and looked like a bachelor's swanky apartment, with abstract cubist paintings mounted on the dark walls, thick pile carpeting, and heavy ruby-red drapes. The ground level dance floor was to the left from the front door entrance, and had a slightly raised bandstand featuring a black baby grand piano highlighted by an overhead pencil spotlight.

To the right from the entrance there was a raised level of the bar, two steps up, with an oil painting of a partially clothed woman above the lines of glistening liquor bottles. Facing the bar was a small dining area looking out over the campus in the dark valley below.

Jason walked through the front door 15 minutes early. He wore his best charcoal-gray sports coat with a pale-gray turtleneck, and dark blue pants. He had shaved twice without once nicking himself, had patted on some Old Spice after-shave, and had brushed his blond hair until it shone.

"Reservations for Adams, for a table near a window," he said to the dark-haired hostess, who cooed that her name was "Rebecca, your pad playmate," and led him across the room to his table. Jason sat down, lit a cigarette, and studied his floating smoke trials, his heart pounding.

Russet appeared at the table a few minutes later, on time. Her red hair was pulled up on a stylish bun; she wore a low-cut reddish-brown cocktail dress with an expensive gold necklace; and smelled of "My Sin" cologne.

"You look absolutely lovely, especially for a poet," Jason said as he stood and ushered her to her seat.

She fell forward in a half-laugh.

"Jason Adams, I swear--you make no sense! What am I going to do with you?"

Jason counted one finger at a time, with his tongue lurking in the corner of his mouth, and his eyelids drooped lasciviously.

"Well now, let me see, one--"

Russet moaned, shook her head, looked up towards the ceiling, and muttered something about "Dear God, let . . . " that Jason couldn't hear.

Their waiter was a distinguished-looking older black man with a round face and white hair dressed in a tuxedo. He introduced himself as "Mr. Ellis, at your service," and they ordered two draught beers. Mr. Ellis vanished into the now milling crowd, reappeared with their beers, and dissolved back into the noise and shadows.

"To poets, poetry, boogie-woogie and graduate school," Jason said as he raised his glass to her.

Russet met his glass, and beamed at him.

"To poetry and boogie-woogie."

Russet put her glass down and scowled. She raised her soft voice against the chatter of voices and bursts of laughter around them.

"When you play piano, are you concerned about every note and how every note relates to the note preceding and the one following and the whole collection of notes?"

Jason leaned forward, shook his head from side to side.

"Can you ask that again--three times very slowly in 4/4 time?"

She stared at him, a faint smile playing on her lips.

"You heard me, wise guy."

"Well, essentially, yes."

She frowned at him.

"Then your music is a kind of poetry without words?"

"More or less, but in time--meter. With rhythm. Drums. Bass. Other instruments."

She smiled to herself.

"Aha. Now, it makes more sense to me. Next time, I'll be a better listener when I hear you play."

Jason's stomach warmed at her words-- *next time*. He raised his glass in the air, and waved it slowly back and forth.

"Aha! Signs of budding sophistication. Now, the difficult questions. I'm from the east coast. Mainly New Jersey. Where are you from?"

She smiled at him. He noticed for the first time that there were dimples in both of her cheeks, and he was entranced by this discovery.

She kept smiling at him.

"Lake Michigan. My parents have one house in the Pellston woods and one right on Lake Michigan. It's really beautiful. You can sit on the front porch at night and watch the naiad moon undulate through waves, embrace her lover, and slip back into eternity."

Jason's fingertips trembled as he lit his cigarette.

"Do you always talk like that--I mean, in images?"

She blushed.

"Not always. But I write a lot of poetry. Did I embarrass you?"

He took a deep drag on his cigarette.

"No. Threw me. I've never met anyone who did that--I mean talked like that."

She laughed and pointed her finger at him.

"And I've never met anyone who played boogie-woogie piano and studied literature. We, sir, are a puzzling pair indeed."

Jason was simultaneously excited and afraid. He sat back in his chair, and tried to look casual and relaxed.

"That remains to be seen. You say your parents live up north. What does you father do?"

She glanced briefly around, and leaned forward over the table. Her soft voice was low, and hard to hear.

"My father? To make things more impossibly weird--my father is an accountant for the mob. What does your father do?"

Jason stared at her: *the mob?*

"He's dead. A hit-and-run driver killed him while he was being a hero helping some woman whose car had run off the road. The police said he was dead by the time his face hit the ground. Just like that–like apoplexy–a blood clot that just kills you, bang."

She grimaced.

"How old was he?"

"Fifty-two. It was just before Christmas, about three years ago. I was 21, a junior in college, when my mom called me and told me dad wouldn't be home for the holidays. Left a huge hole in my stomach, like a small grenade had exploded there."

Her face crinkled; her brow furrowed; her eyes moistened.

"That's horrible. I mean, losing your father like that."

He bathed in the compassion of her eyes.

"It was a nightmare. Suddenly, part of me just wasn't there anymore."

She kept her gaze on his eyes.

"Are you Ok?"

"More or less. Thank you."

She sat back.

"You're welcome. By the way, you don't have to translate for me. I know what apoplexy means."

Jason let himself relax and thought *good—we're playing again. I'm not too good at this serious stuff.*

"Translate? Who translated? I defined, Miss Loveliness."

He grinned at her.

Mr. Ellis delivered the two small salads that they had earlier ordered to their table.

"Do you like lobster?" Jason asked as Russet took her bantam glass pitchers of vinegar and oil and dribbled them over her romaine lettuce. She looked up briefly and went back to her salad preparations.

"I've never had it."

"Huh? How old are you?"

She kept her gaze on her salad and the glistening dressing.

"Twenty-one."

"And you've never had lobster?"

She glanced at him.

"Never. I'm a mid-west girl--we don't grow lobsters out here, you know--don't you?"

Jason gulped his beer and fought an unexpected laugh in his throat.

"Of course I know that. I'm a hot-shot easterner--remember that, if you would."

She smiled to herself, and reached into her purse for a cigarette.

Jason reached across the table and lit her cigarette for her.

"So, you've tried boogie--wanna try lobster?"

She blushed and looked up at him over his hand.

"Are you trying to corrupt me?"

He looked deeply into her eyes.

"Yes--absolutely."

She shrugged her shoulders, raised both eyebrows at him, put her cigarette on the glass ashtray between them, and started to eat her salad.

"Fine. I'll have some lobster, then, Lovelace."

He waved to Mr. Ellis, ordered their lobsters, and turned to her.

"Lovelace? The vile seducer of Richardson's 19th century novel?"

She put another imaginary mark in the air.

"One and the same. Remember that I've got you pegged, Mr. Piano-Player-Word-Wizard."

When their broiled Maine lobsters arrived, Jason moved to her side of the table next to her. He guided her hand.

"Here, you just pull it apart, thusly, and the tail meat comes right out, see? Then, you cut off a piece and dip it in the drawn butter here, and *voila*."

She took a bite, and looked at him out of the corner of her eye.

"My God is this good. Do you have any other gourmet surprises lying in wait for me?"

"Plenty. But, can I ask you . . . ."

"What?"

"Did you like the blues tune?"

She fiddled with her lobster and dipped another piece in the butter.

"The song you played for me?"

Jason took a slug of his beer and felt dizzy.

She turned her head and smiled at him.

"It was beautiful--very beautiful."

Jason returned her smile.

"And so, I--I--I daresay, are you."

They finished dinner sitting next to each other, and were cleaning their hands in the warm, lemony water of the finger bowl when Mr. Ellis appeared.

"Coffee?"

"Yes, please," Russet replied, and reached for her half-smoked cigarette.

"So," Jason said as he clicked his lighter for her and moved his leg against hers, "you're from Michigan?"

"Right. I told you. My parents live up north."

"And your father?"

"I told you. He's a rich accountant."

"Rich? An accountant who's rich? You're putting me on."

A shadow fell across them.

"After dinner drinks? Dessert?" Ellis smiled as he served their coffee.

"Ever had Bananas Flambé?" Jason asked and pointed to the dessert menu.

Russet sighed.

"Here we go again. No. What are *they*?"

"They're bananas with cream and brown sugar, flamed in brandy. A wonderful invention of, I believe, the French."

He felt her thigh stiffen against his leg.

"Sounds awfully rich."

He turned his head towards her.

"Because of the cream?"

She did not return his gaze.

"No. The brown sugar. I didn't tell you, but you should know. I'm a diabetic."

Jason's stomach went hollow. He had no idea what "diabetic" meant. He let his leg stay against hers and shrugged.

"Oh. Well, that's fine with me. I don't know much about diabetes--except that it's got something to do with sugar, right?"

She smiled to herself and patted his hand.

"Well, right, something like that. So, I guess I'll just skip desert this time, if you don't mind?"

He nodded.

"I don't mind at all. Look, the band is going to start any minute now. Would you like to see if the Word Wizard knows how to dance?"

She turned in her seat, looked him flush in the eyes, and beamed.

"Lead on, Lovelace."

They walked, hand-in-hand, to the dance floor.

"I dance to the words and the rhythm," Jason said, as he put his arm around her.

"Just move, I'll follow," Russet murmured as she stood on her toes and put her head next to his, "Just move against me, guide me."

The tenor saxophonist played the first three notes of Errol Garner's "Misty." Russet nestled her hips flush against Jason and as they danced he traced the curve of her spine with his finger tips, let his thigh slip lightly between her legs as he twirled her, and held her hand tightly in his. She felt as light as a flower in his arms, and no matter which way he moved, or how intently he whirled her around, she was there, against him, the way a summer breeze embraces every nook and cranny of the earth. To Jason, as they floated on the undulating waves of the music, it seemed that by a miracle until that moment totally unknown to him, they had somehow, right *then*, fused and become a strange dance never before seen or known on the face of the earth, and he fell suddenly, and hopelessly, in love.

There was a long saxophone cadenza, and without a moment's hesitation, oblivious to all around them, they kissed, hungrily tonguing each other's mouths, lost to the world.

The pianist began the introduction to the next song, a shuffle beat version of "Kansas City," and awakened them.

Jason kept his arms around her, found his voice, and said, "Wanna try another dance with me?"

She licked at his ear and kept her hips flush and hot against his.

"Only if you'll promise to come upstairs with me to see my apartment."

He bent his head down and whispered in her ear.

"Now?"

She rubbed her forehead under his chin, and then looked up at him with one eyebrow slightly raised

"*Now.*"

"To?"

Her smile was naked desire.

"To? Don't you remember? You promised more gourmet surprises."

After that night, they went out for coffee together before their classes at the University; they studied together and went out at night and drank beer together; they spent nights together in her apartment; and they talked together for hours in her apartment about literature, about poetry, about music, and about surviving graduate school.

A year went by.

"What are we doing to tomorrow night?" Russet asked one morning over coffee at the two-seater table in her apartment kitchen.

"Hmm. Let's see. Tomorrow is--Thursday. I'm not playing. Ok--making love again?"

She sighed.

"Is that all you think about?"

"No. I also think about what I'm going to have say in my seminar an hour or so from now; I think about how the hell I'm going to get all my papers written; and I think about making love with you."

She smiled at him, the bemused way mothers bless an arrant child.
"In that order?"
"No."

Russet stood, rinsed out her coffee cup in the kitchen sink and turned around.
"In reverse order, right?"
Jason grinned.
"Well, what else is there to think about that's important?"
She planted both hands on her hips.
"Here's something else for you to think about. You promised that we were going out to dinner tomorrow night. . . on you. Remember?"
'Is that all you think about? Restaurants?"
She pointed her index finger at him and lowered her voice.
"And promises. I think about promises. There's something we've got to talk about. . . but not now."
"Something wrong?"
She squinted at him the way ministers scowl at parishioners.
"Not now. I've got to get to class and to the library and get a paper written for Monday-- tomorrow. Ok?"
"You look serious. Is there something wrong?"
She grabbed her books and walked towards the door.
"Tomorrow night, Jason, tomorrow."

The Frontier was made in the style of a log cabin on the outside. Inside, there were fireplaces in every room and walls decorated with farm implements, old muzzle-loading muskets, and reproductions of Remington pen-and-ink drawings of galloping horses and rampaging buffalo.

Russet was dressed in a fluffy pink sweater, and was coolly polite and distant on the drive and throughout dinner. Jason had come straight from class dressed in his button-down long-sleeve striped shirt, and kept fishing for whatever it was she wanted to talk about and Russet kept saying "please eat and let's enjoy ourselves."

Finally after their coffee arrived, she said: "Why are we eating here?"
"It's new and different. I thought it would please you."
She tilted her head down and stared at him from underneath her eye brows.

"Do you know what today is?"

Something wiggled in his stomach.

"Sure. Today is Sunday."

She stared at him with her jaw set.

"What else?"

"Well, let's see. It's not your birthday. That's month's away. It's not Christmas or any other holiday that I can think of, is it?"

Russet glowered at him and the cast down her eyes.

"Yes, it is."

"A holiday?"

"Sort of."

"Is this one of your jokes on me? An IQ test or something?"

Russet shook her head.

"Jason, damn you, *think*."

He lit a cigarette and racked his brains for the answer she was looking for, and felt hopelessly stupid like he had often felt in high school calculus class when an answer or procedure escaped him. The wiggle in his stomach turned into an unmoving rock.

"I'm sorry, Russet, I seem to be missing the point."

"Excuse me," she snarled, dropped her napkin down on the table, and strolled away.

Jason waited for her return, stymied. He searched his memory for some promise he might have made to her in jest, or for some promise made in earnest that had come due that night, and could recall nothing. *What was wrong with him?* He was insanely in love with her; he thought about her all the time--her witty mind, her laughter, and her madcap, voracious sexuality. She had become and was his whole world. The rock in his stomach slowly grew heavier and the skin on the back of his neck was cold and prickly when she returned.

He stood as she sat down and reached out towards her.

"I'm sorry. I give up. I can't remember any promises I made that have to do with this specific date."

She sighed. Her face was expressionless.

"There weren't any damned promises, Jason, none. Forget it."

He reached for her again.

"Look, I want--."

"Forget it. There's something else I want to talk to you about."

He stood and reached out to her.

"Russet--I'm flabbergasted. What the hell is all this--."
She lit a cigarette, took a drag, exhaled, and looked off towards the ceiling.
"Sit down."
He obeyed and looked over at her.
"'Look, Jason, we're both young. We have a lot of our lives to live. There are many, many, beautiful women out there . . . much more beautiful than I am . . . and maybe you ought to find one of those beautiful women out there that you could really love and care about."
The rock in his stomach exploded; the inside of his head spun like a child's toy top.
"What are you talking about, Russet? I don't give a damn about anyone else except you."
Her face soured. She looked off into space.
"What am I talking about? Commitment! I'm talking about us shifting back and forth between your place and my place and about us kissing and screwing and going our separate ways, and. . ."
"And?"
Her face twisted into a wrinkled sheet of pain.
"About you forgetting that tonight is the anniversary of our first date."

Within weeks, they were living together at Jason's rented home on the northwest side of town. It was a post World War II ranch house with two small bedrooms, an unfinished basement, and a study. Jason appropriated the study for his use, and Russet took the extra bedroom for her study, share and share alike.

The living room had a sliding door picture window that faced west out into a shambles of a back yard with a wilderness of weeds, wild flowers, anemic maple trees and large rocks. There was a small porch just outside the window, accessible through the sliding glass door.

The furniture was a motley combination of used furniture he had picked up at yard sales and used furniture stores. A brown three-seater couch and small coffee table faced the living room sliding picture window and a black standing lamp stood at one end of the couch. A faded blue easy chair sat at the other end. Jason's brown Wurlitzer piano was against the right wall of the dining room, and there were reams of his music stacked on a wall shelf just above the piano. Opposite the piano, at the other end of the living room, there was a four-tier metal bookshelf with books Jason had arranged meticulously by color, height, and subject matter. On the top shelf there were three German beer mugs and a glass jar full of loose change.

When Russet first saw the living room she made a face, laughed, and hugged Jason.

"Oh, Jason, its darling. The decor presents a picture of perfect poverty . . . just right for broke graduate students like you and I."

He cocked his head.

"*You* and I? I'm the broke one, not you. Remember, you've got a rich father and all that stock he gave you to use to pay for your graduate school."

Russet bowed her head, and walked around the room, chuckling softly to herself.

Jason had raved to Russet about a six-foot Steinway Grand piano he had played in a local music store. A week after her introduction to their new home, without his knowledge, she had gone to the music store, bought the piano for cash, and placed in the center of the living room one day while Jason was in class.

When Jason opened the front door that night he thought for a moment he had wandered into the wrong house. He was about to back out when Russet suddenly appeared, dressed in a low-cut, black cocktail dress.

"Know how to play 'Just Say I Love Her,' piano player?"

Her eyes sparkled, and she stood arms akimbo with her hips thrust forward, in the stereotypical pose of a streetwalker.

He stared at her.

"What the . . . I thought that . . . ."

". . fate had abandoned you to a worn-out Wurlitzer?"

He looked at the polished, black grand piano sitting in the middle of the living room. Deja vu. It looked uncannily like the beautiful grand he had played at Knight's Keyboard a few weeks ago.

"Where'd the piano come from?"

She smiled at him Cheshire cat.

"Knight's Keyboard."

"How'd it get here? You didn't rent it, did you?"

She grinned at him.

"I didn't rent it."

His jaw dropped.

"You bought the Steinway?"

She blushed; her eyes sparkled.

"It didn't walk in here by itself."

"You're dead-flat incredible," Jason said, "You're just incredible. But--"
She glowed.

"Why? When I heard you go moony over the damned thing I got damned jealous and decided I'd much rather have it here where I could supervise the affair and, when necessary, intervene."

He shook his head back and forth like a pendulum on a grandfather clock.
"But. . . ."

"You can't stop me from adoring both what your hands do to it and me, can you?"

His head felt light; his mouth was dry; his eyes were moist.
"But. . ."

She moved up against him, grabbed him by the crotch, and gently pulled him down the hallway towards their bedroom.

"You can play her for me later, right now, I want you to play me."

Months passed.

To Jason, Russet was sheer magic. Not only was she lovely to look at and smell, she was endless fun and laughter and was passionate beyond anything he'd ever dreamed possible. Together, they seemed psychic. She read his mind. She finished his sentences--and he hers--and most of the time they somehow both knew intuitively what each other was going to do before it actually happened. She was precious, his dream-lover, his *liebestraum*.

And he wasn't going to lose her.

She was clothes shopping with a girl friend that day—usually an all-day venture.

He had the time to set their future together in motion.

He called the Department of English to confirm what his dissertation chairman had promised the preceding week. It was true--he, Jason Adams, graduate student and piano player, had miraculously received an appointment as lecturer in English.

That meant a salary.

Money.

He went to the basement and checked in his hiding space above the rafters. The engagement ring was there inside its red velvet-lined box. He had used his $300 savings as a down payment on the ring in the hope that his appointment as lecturer would come through.

Now, he had a job, he had a ring. Did he have the guts?

He came upstairs, sat down at the Steinway, looked at the single-stone ring, and thought: *I have never loved any woman the way I love Russet. Oh, I've screwed them, laughed and played with them, but for the most part I was always self-consciously aware of who I was and what I was doing with those women: they just were, like actresses in a movie scene I was somehow an actor in. With Russet, she is the reality; the reality of being with her is me--the two realities are indistinguishable, and time simply doesn't exist in our world when we're together. She's precious to me--far more precious than this diamond ring.*

He had made his decision. She loved romantic poetry, romantic novels, and romantic movies. He was going to give her a romantic night she would never forget. He went down to the local hardware store early that morning, came back, and proceeded to change all the electrical switches in the house from 'on/off' switches to dimmer switches in every room, including the bathroom, and put dimmer switches on extension cords to all individual standing lamps as well.

It was three o'clock. Time to get to work on a gourmet dinner.

He washed and pared the potatoes, put them in the refrigerator in ice water, and sliced the tomatoes. The cookbook was very specific; and he followed instructions dutifully to make the Bordelaise sauce for the steaks he'd bought. He set the sauce aside on the stove. He then filled a circular Lazy Susan with an assortment of appetizers--garlic toast triangles, oysters packed in olive oil, sliced Swiss cheese slivers, cucumbers in sour cream and minced onions. He washed and set aside some sprigs of parsley to garnish the dinner. He wrapped the Lazy Susan tightly in tin foil, refrigerated it, and calculated that the second Russet drove in he could unwrap the appetizer tray and have it on the diner table before she got out of her car.

At 5:30 he filled a glass vase with fresh wild flowers from the back yard, put the ring in his pocket, and watched for her car to appear outside the little picture window in the dining room--which it did, on time.

Russet walked in the front door dressed in her red-burgundy three-piece business suit and laden with packages, stopped, and stared at Jason.

"It smells good in here. What in heaven's--."

Jason had dressed in his best blue pants and white turtleneck sweater.

"Welcome to Chez Adams, my love," Jason grinned as he took her packages from her and waved his arm towards the Lazy Susan and the flowers on the dining room table, "your repast awaits."

She half-grinned and half-frowned at him.

"Ok . . . I give up. What horrible thing have you done that's consuming you with guilt?"

Jason puffed out his chest and puckered his lips.

"Nothing. I stand before you as innocent as childhood itself."

She cocked her head.

"Ok--I'll try again. you've been reading an Agatha Christie murder mystery, and you've been inspired to create a new culinary murder plot--'The Case of the Roasted Redhead?'"

Jason kissed her lightly on the cheek.

"My love, your wonderful poetic imagination is getting the best of you."

He waved his arm towards the Lazy Susan.

"Here, have a seat, and select the appetizer that best suits your exquisite fancy whilst I open our vintage bottle of red wine."

"You're *impossible*," Russet said, and sat down.

While she nibbled on toast and oysters, he threw the steaks into a hot skillet alongside the cooking sliced potatoes and the pot of minted peas. A few minutes later, he brought the steaks along with the potatoes and peas to the table decorated with parsley spears.

"*Voila!*" he announced--a sugar-free, fat-free, repast!"

Throughout dinner she tried to guess what plot Jason was hatching but his lips were sealed until he served them coffee. He stood, clasped his hands before him, and lowered his head.

"*Mea culpa*. I admit that even I, your vile seducer, have had enough of this torture. The secret--the news--is I got the lectureship. We're filthy rich."

Russet leapt to her feet, stood on her toes, embraced and kissed him.

"I *knew* it! I *knew* you could do it--you're so brilliant."

He squeezed her to him and let her hair tickle his cheek.

"And don't forget formerly broke," Jason said, "that counts equally with brilliance in this game. But—wait. There's another, a matter--a, ah, something else."

She stepped back from him, holding his hands, and cocked her head.

"What?"

He led her into the living room and sat her down on the sofa, facing the picture window.

She reached for the light switch on the lamp to her right on the end table. He grabbed her hand.

"No. Wait."

"It's dark in here."

"It's part of--a prelude to--the atmosphere. Sit here, in the dark. I'll be right back."

"Jason!"

"Sit, dammit. I have another surprise for you. You'll love it."

He went around the house and turned the lights down with the dimmer switches, until each individual light glowed softly in the darkness and cast faint, yellowish shadows in each room. He came back to the living room, where Russet dutifully waited, and flicked on the wall switch controlling the lamp by the end of the sofa and the two other standing lamps in the room.

She looked around herself at the transformed living room.

"Wow, it looks like Hong Kong Harbor at night. Those lights look like those little Sampan boats floating ever so slowly around, each of them softly lit from inside. Why all this romance, Jason? Is this the surprise?"

It was time to act.

The world became a dream for him. Everything was unreal and at the same time more real than reality itself. He knelt down before her, and wordlessly handed her the boxed engagement ring.

She stared briefly at him, and then looked at the present. Her fingers trembled as she opened the tiny lid and uncovered the diamond. She took the ring out, held it with the tips of her fingers and turned it so that the light from the dimmed lamp played off the facets. She brought the ring under her chin, took a deep breath, looked him straight in the eyes, and winked.

"Are you asking me to go steady?"

He laughed despite himself.

"Huh? I'm asking you to *marry* me."

She smiled and caressed the ring with her fingertips.

"Marry? Isn't that rather serious stuff?"

"Hey! I've spent the whole day preparing for this and. . . "

She raised an eyebrow.

"Just a day?"

"Jesus Christ, Russet. I asked you a. . . "

"—a question."

He remained on his knees before her.

"That's right. A question. Will you marry me?"

She looked down on him, pure bliss glowing in her eyes.

"Marry you?"

He reached both arms out towards her.

"Goddammit, Russet--."

She laughed, jumped up from the sofa, and shouted.

"Yes! Oh, yes, yes, yes! I will marry you--if--"
Jason got halfway up from his knees.
"Now what? If *what*?"
"If you catch me first." she laughed, and ran off down the hall to their bedroom.

They lay in bed side by side, looking at each other.
Her brown eyes were laced with circular bands of green and flecks of bright yellow. The interplay of colors and designs fascinated him.
"You have lovely eyes."
She smiled and snuggled her hips against his.
"So do you, you lecherous Lothario. But they seem to change colors--how come?"
He tossed his head to the side.
"Oh dear, you've seen right through to my treacherous soul."
She tugged lightly on his ear. Her voice sounded girlishly young.
"Sure. Tell the truth. Why do they change color? Is there something wrong with them?"
"No. They're blue-green. Their color changes depending on what color clothes I'm wearing, the weather outside, and God knows what else."
She looked up at him.
"Hmm. Next question. Where'd you get that scar on your chin?"
He ran his index finger down the center of his cleft chin.
"This? French and Indian Wars. Irate Indian, wielding a ferocious tomahawk, as I recall it."
She tapped him lightly on the chest.
"Oh boy. I want a straight answer out of you, Sir Lecher. The jagged scar under your chin."
He ran his fingers through her disheveled hair, and bent over and kissed her lightly on the forehead.
"The truth?"
"The truth--no dramatic b-s crap."
"Ok. But it's boring."
She sat up in front of him with her legs crossed under her and pulled the sheet loosely over her naked breasts.
"So bore me."
He sat up and faced her.
"I was in, I think, about fourth grade. I went to the top of a hill that ran

down in front of my house, got on my two-wheeler bike and, half way down the hill, stood up on the seat."

"And?"

"And let go. The bike crumpled into a steel pretzel under me and I hit the pavement, chin-first, whack. Just like that. That's why I wear the goatee—to cover up the damned scar."

Her smooth face soured, like she had just smelled vinegar.

"Why the hell did you do *that*? And don't give me any baloney about 'just being a dumb kid' and garbage like that."

"The goatee? I just told you."

"No! The insanity."

"Do you really want to know?"

"Of course I do. That's why I'm asking, dummy."

He froze.

"I don't honestly know. It had something to with my rage at the world about something that happened to a kid named Brian, and something about my father and mother and what had happened to Brian, but I don't want to remember now. Do you love me and my scar anyway?"

She pulled him back down on the bed next to her and put her head on his shoulder.

"I love you, scars 'n all."

He wrapped his arms around her and kissed her on the cheek.

"I love you, too, more than I ever dreamed I could love a woman."

Suddenly she sat up and turned her back to him.

"Dammit."

"What's wrong?"

She looked away, out the bedroom window into the night.

"Some day we'll both be old, you know."

He sat up behind her, and stroked her hair lightly with his fingertips.

"How the hell did we get from loving scars to being old? I mean so what? Everyone gets old."

"And dies."

"So? We'll grow old and die together. I want to grow old with you, and be the sexiest old married couple in the annals of human history."

"Jason. We're not married yet."

"Huh? Of course we're not married. I just asked you to marry me after dinner."

She frowned.

"You're right. Dammit. Excuse me. I'd better grab some orange juice. I'm feeling a bit shaky. . ."

"After that rich dinner?"

She smiled to herself, bemused by his adolescent innocence.

"No, my love--after all that exercise."

They went to sleep, woke up, and the next day drove off and got married in Ohio.

II

Months passed, crammed with texts read and papers written late into the night.

It was Sunday morning. Jason, dressed in his navy-blue bathrobe, sat at the Steinway fooling with chords, a cigarette smoldering in the ashtray on the piano top. Russet came in dressed in her silky, white nightdress, leaned on the black piano top to his right, and handed him a folder of bound papers.

"I've written some poems about us. . .well, you," she said in her soft and breathy voice.

"About me?"

"Yup, that's right, Jason. You heard right. They're called 'Pretty Bewildering Dreams, or, Poems You Have Inspired'."

"You're kidding."

"Nope. Wanna read them?"

She handed him the folder. Inside, she had written, alluding to the e. e. Cummings poem 'since feeling is first.' "To the man who *has* wholly kissed me."

He blushed.

"No one has ever written me a poem, much less a book of poetry--ever. No one."

She leaned over the piano and traced a line down his cheek with her fingertips.

He cradled her chin in his hand.

"No one has ever loved you the way I do. . . nor will anyone ever love you the way I do, Russet. Remember that."

He held the poems in both hands the finicky way one holds a fragile glass, and looked up.

"Do I read these now?"

"No. You don't have to read them all now. As a matter of fact, I'd prefer you took your time with them to feel them through. Why do you ask?"

He put the book of poems on the piano bench next to him.

"Because I want you to listen to this," he said, and played the slow rock ballad he had spent weeks composing and several hours finishing the previous day.

The ballad was a rock 'n roll portrait of his love for Russet. The meter was slow; the chord structure spare, and the words simple, like "Love Me Tender."

Her lips parted and her eyes moistened as she listened.

"What's it called?"

"It's called 'Song: For Russet'."

Her eyes lingered on his, and searched within him.

"It's haunting. You wrote that for me?"

He flushed.

"That's because you're beautiful. We're really a pair. You write me poetry; I write you bluesy ballads. I love you very, very much."

She looked intently at him, and then looked down, seemingly lost in the wonder of what had just happened between them. She looked up at him.

"Let's talk."

He raised his right eyebrow.

"In bed?"

She shook her head.

"Right here."

She went out to the kitchen and returned with two cups of coffee.

"Thanks," he said as he took the cup from her at the piano, "I love you."

She leaned on the piano top near him.

"I love you, too, dammit, and now I want to talk about that love of mine, of yours, of ours. I've been thinking for days now about our love after I wrote those poems to you. And got scared."

He covered the piano keys and looked at her.

"Scared? Serious?"

She looked directly and unblinking into his eyes.

"It is."
"What is 'it'?"
She walked around the piano, and sat next to him.
"Our marriage is a beautiful dream--but it isn't going anywhere."
He wrinkled his face.
"Huh? Are you kidding? I mean, you just gave me a book of poems, I just played a song I wrote for you. . . what do you mean?"
She glowered at him.
"All we do is study, write papers, go to class, go out to restaurants and nightclubs, dance, play, party, and make love."
He half-grimaced and half-frowned at her.
"And write each other music and poetry. Russet. Not going anywhere? Are you kidding?"
Her face was gray and drawn, the way faces look at a funeral.
"No."
He raised his voice.
"Then what's wrong? What in heaven's name could be missing from our lives?"
She focused intently on his eyes.
"Don't you want children?"
The back of his head tingled and he felt himself blush. He put both hands on the keyboard cover before him and looked away.
"Haven't even thought about it. I mean, I thought that was down the road--after we both got our degrees, had good jobs, had our own home, had. . . "
She put her hand on his shoulder and forced him to look at her.
"Forever to love and live, right? The romantic dream? Forever fucking in the Elysian fields of eternal pleasure? No noisy kids and no financial agonies? Jason, you're a dreamer."
He put both hands on his lap.
"Well, like I said, I just hadn't thought about it. It just didn't occur to me. I guess I've never thought of myself as a father. I mean, it just hasn't occurred to me."
Russet smiled to herself.
"Sonnets from the Portuguese."
"Huh?"
His normally soft voice was suddenly strident.
"It's a reference to a fragment of a poem about what men don't think about when they fall in love. Never mind. Do you want to have children? I

want to have your children. I'm sick of being on this damned birth-control pill."

He frowned and looked straight ahead. His stomach was a vast cavern.

"Hey, wait a second-- that was our deal, wasn't it? That we'd both get our degrees before we had children and then we'd take turns working and staying home to raise the kids--a true '60's partnership, right?"

She grabbed him under his chin and forced him to look at her.

"That's the dream. But it's going nowhere now. Children?"

"I--I don't know."

She stared at him.

"You're not committed to our marriage?"

He caught her look and then stared at the piano top.

"Huh? I'm committed for life. I can't imagine being with anyone else."

She rubbed his back and he turned to her.

"With any one else in the clouds, you mean. I'm talking down-to-earth stuff, my love: a home, a life together, children. Yes or no. Do you want to have children with me?"

She looked terribly vulnerable when she asked the question, like a hungry child pleading to be fed.

The look floored him.

Discussion closed.

He cupped her head in his heads and kissed her forehead.

"Of course I want children with you."

III

A few months later, Russet came bouncing in the front door at dinnertime and walked over by the piano where Jason was playing 'Angel Eyes'.

"Listen to these changes that I've used as substitute chords--very bluesy, no?"

"Sit down" she beamed.

"I *am* sitting down."

"Then stand up and sit down."

"For cryin'--."

"Ok, I'll sit down."

She sat down on the piano bench next to him, still grinning. He looked at her. She looked fine, dressed in her usual pale-brown blouse with the hint of red in it.

"What it is?"

"Guess."

"You got an 'A' on your James paper?"

"Wrong. Guess again."

"You've fallen in love?"

She beamed at him like a radiant sunrise.

"I *am* in love--with you, dummy."

"I give up."

She moved her breast against his arm and rubbed his back.

"I just came from the doctor.

Jason jumped in his seat.

"Doctor?"

"Doctor."

Jason's heart palpitated.

"And? Is something, ah--"

"Nothing's wrong,"

"'Then---?"

"I'm *pregna*nt."

Jason's stomach went suddenly light like a helium-filled balloon. He searched her eyes.

"You *are*?"

She bobbed her head up and down.

"Two months. Almost two months. I can't believe it. I'm due sometime in early January next year."

His jaw hung open. It was difficult to talk sitting in mid air.

"I'm ah, ah--astonished."

"Astonished? Why?"

He shook his head.

"I don't know."

"Down to earth from the romantic clouds?"

"Maybe."

She pulled him off the piano bench to the nearby couch where he had sat her down and proposed to her two years earlier.

"You didn't believe I could get pregnant because of my diabetes?"

"Hell, no. It's not that."

She rubbed his back.

"Then, what it is?"

He looked straight ahead out the picture window.

"I don't know. For some crazy reason I guess I've never even thought of myself as a father. Makes no logical sense. No man in my family has ever been anything except very fertile. But me? A father?"

"Your father's dead, isn't he?"

"Yeah. Told you. Killed at age fifty-two."

"That's awful young to die."

"He was killed in an accident, remember?"

"But your mother is still alive, right?"

"Yes, but my mother and I don't get along."

"Why?"

"Beats me. She's a terrible moralizer. Very fire-and-brimstone Christian."

"Too bad. I guess she and I will not see exactly eye to eye."

"My Dad would have adored you."

"And your father got killed. I know you told me a long time ago, but I can't remember.

Jason rested both elbows on his knees and leaned forward.

"Being a hero, plus cigarettes and booze. Dad died intestate--no will--and it took almost two years and $200,000 in attorney fees to settle his estate. I got a whopping $60 a month in social security survivor's benefits while I was getting my master's degree at Wesleyan University."

"Then you came out here in 1963 for the doctoral Ph.D. program, the year we met?"

"Yes. That's why I was so broke when we met."

She rested her hand on his knee.

"Do you miss him?"

"God, yes--and no. I adored him. He was my hero when I was a little boy. He could do everything. And did everything with me. He took me fishing with him, taught me how to row a boat and bait a hook and throw a baseball and how to plant peas and the names of animals and trees and bushes and how to--."

"And what happened?"

Jason slumped forward and dangled his arms between his legs.

"Then, when I was about eight or nine years old, he started traveling around the world solving engineering problems. I rarely saw him, and when I did see him, he was my demon. He was always drinking something– a beer, a martini–always telling jokes and being the life of the party at home, always fighting against this dumb idea and that dumb idea, and always going off to different states and different countries. Then, out of nowhere, he just got killed before he and I could reconnect. How can your hero be your demon too?"

She rubbed his back.

"So, that's why you're afraid of being a father?"

Jason felt a chill down his spine.

"I'm afraid I'll blow it. I'm afraid of the crazy part of my father I have inside me and of the hole in me that was supposed to be the completed world of him and me. The other part of him--the part I remember from my childhood--I adore, and want to be like that part."

Russet smiled.

"That why you wanted to be a teacher--no travel?"

"Yes. And I wanted to be a teacher to finance my piano playing. Teaching's steady work; playing piano isn't. So, the plan was--is--I can stay put, make money, play the piano, and avoid always being away from home. Too many bad memories of that gig."

She leaned her head against his shoulder, and the sweet smell of her clean hair somehow calmed him.

"So--."

"So, there's this place of agony and emptiness–a dark place inside that you avoid with your wit, learning, flashy piano playing, and your flair for the dramatic?"

He looked straight ahead towards the sliding glass door.

"Something like that."

She rubbed his back.

"So, do you want to chance the job as father to our child? You just sorta said so."

Jason held his hands together between his legs.

"Whew. Scary. A big job."

"Looks like you've got the job."

Visions of his father teaching him how to plant seeds on their little family farm and hitting a baseball and the feel of his father's strong arms lifting him up to see a robin's nest flashed before him.

"Sure. Of course I do. I mean, I sure as hell will give it all I got. I love you, Russet, I love you and. . . ."

She laughed and hugged him.

"Whoopee. How about some splendid cheap wine to celebrate?"

He smiled at her and stood.

"Your wish is my command. Will do, my love, will do."

Jason went to the store. As he drove, he felt dizzy about the unknown future bearing down on him and then was suddenly swept up in a nameless terror--what might happen to the baby inside her if she had an insulin reaction?

The first insulin reaction he had seen her experience had happened about a year ago and it was unreal. They had come in from grocery shopping, and were putting the groceries away. Suddenly, she threw down a bottle of shampoo on the table. Her face turned blood red and contorted like a mad dog and she screamed.

"Goddamn you. You fubble forgot the ducking marfules."

He thought she was kidding.

"Huh? We don't eat marbles, for Christ's sake--at least not on Saturdays, and today is Saturday, my dear."

She screamed at him and started to cry.

"I'm telling you. You forgot 'em, dammit. It's so goddamn sad. Dandelions."

"What the hell are you talking about Russet?"

She looked down at her feet, and started to sway.

"Up yours, you bladdat, this is--."

She began to shake like she had just come in from being outside in frigid cold. He suddenly realized that what she had once warned him about was happening, and he rushed some orange juice to her from the refrigerator.

"Here, sit down," he said, guiding her into a dining room chair.

Her hands trembled violently and Jason held the glass to her lips. He watched her struggle to drink the rest of the orange juice she held in her trembling hands. Gradually, the shaking subsided and, finally, stopped. She looked glassy-eyed drunk for several minutes, and then looked up. Her eyes were bloodshot and soaked in tears.

"Thanks . . for . . . the . . . help . . .I hate this unforgiving disease--I hate it."

Later that night, they had talked about the insulin reaction, and how it had been unusual for her to have such a powerful seizure.

"What causes them?" he had asked.

"Imbalance in my bloodstream. I had too much insulin in me, and not enough carbohydrates for the insulin to eat."

"Can't we stop 'em?"

"No. My pancreas is all screwed up and sometimes goes berserk. Just kinda lifeguard me and shove a candy bar down my throat when I go nuts like that, Ok?"

He felt the cold shadow of her sickness suddenly grab his bowels, never to leave again.

"One lifeguard coming up," he replied.

At the store, he bought an extra half-gallon of orange juice as well as the bottle of wine, and went back home to quietly celebrate the beginning of a new chapter in their lives together.

IV

The next week they went to see her physician at his small, file-littered office at Women's Hospital. Dr. Marsh was a thin man in his forties with thick glasses, salt and pepper hair, a stiffly formal attitude, and a pinched way of pronouncing his words with barely a movement of his thin lips.

"There is no medical reason," Dr. Marsh said, "that a female diabetic cannot have a normal child. As a matter of fact, to date we have never lost a diabetic mother's child or the mother here at Women's Hospital."

"But there are some risks, aren't there?" Russet snapped, cross her arms across her white blouse, impatient with Dr. Marsh's cool medical distance.

Dr. Marsh looked up at the ceiling.

"There are of course more risks during a diabetic's pregnancy than in the pregnancy of a person without diabetes. But the odds are with you so long as you follow the diet we will prescribe for you and do exactly whatever else it is that I advise you to do. It looks like you might go full term and have a normal birth."

Jason's heart pounded in his chest.

"Can I be there with her in the delivery room?"

Dr. Marsh sighed, apparently irritated by Jason romanticism.

"Yes."

"Can I hold her hand?"

Dr. Marsh's jaw set.

"Yes, of course you can hold her hand, Mr. Adams."

A corner of Jason's stomach howled in terror. He fought it in his usual way, with his offbeat humor.

'Can I drink beer and smoke cigarettes and watch?"

Russet poked him in the ribs, and Dr. Marsh went busily back to a pile of papers on his desk as they left, seeming relieved to return to his mundane world.

Russet and Jason went about their lives, watching Russet's stomach swell, uneventfully, day after day. Then, about six and a half months into the pregnancy, the first sign of danger appeared. Various measurements of the ovarian metabolic count were uneven. Dr. Marsh decided to hospitalize Russet to monitor the diabetes during the remainder of her pregnancy.

"This stinks," Jason moaned when he heard the news as they had their morning coffee at The Java Joint, a small coffee chop with an open grill and brown two-seater booths where they had often met before classes for years.

Russet shrugged. stirred the cream into her black coffee, and pointed her spoon at him.

"Hey, moron, this is about our baby. And, besides, I'm the one who's going to be stuck in the hospital with no one to pick on."

He grinned at her and pretended to be wounded by the spoon.

"Ouch!-- a bona fide heroine before me."

She threw down a gulp of coffee.

"Up yours."

"Sorry."

Jason went to his and Russet's classes, and brought Russet her homework assignments. They saw each other every night in a bland hospital 'visitor' room with red plastic chairs and tan folding card tables and machines from which people brought candy bars and crackers filled with peanut butter.

"We could sneak into that closet over there," Jason said, and pointed to a closed door next to the fire-engine-red pop machine.

Russet sighed, looking pathetic and pale wrapped in her drab hospital gown.

"It's probably locked."

Jason set his jaw.

"I can check it out."

Russet sighed again.

"Don't bother, Samson."

"Why not? It's been days--."

"Because there's no way to do it. I'm too fat," she said, and patted her swollen womb through the off-white gown.

Jason grinned at her, and stroked his chest through his charcoal-black sweater..

"You're pregnant, for cryin' out loud."

She puffed out her cheeks and looked like a chipmunk with a full mouth.

"Fat. Bulbous. Obese."

Jason stroked his goatee.

"Hmm. Pregnant. Very pregnant."

She pointed her index finger at him and pouted.

"And you did it to me, you over-sexed cad."

Jason planted both hands on his chest under his sweater.

"*We* did it to you. It was a unanimous procedure of unmitigated lust."

She whispered.

"Hmm. Sometimes I hate logic. Your logic."

Jason pointed at her nose.

"Ha. Gotcha."

As the weeks passed, Jason's misery grew. He went to his classes, wrote his papers, and played the piano for hours. It wasn't just the unfamiliarity of going through a pregnancy, it was that Russet's pregnancy seemed fraught with dangers that Jason's fertile imagination made into monstrous insulin reactions and teams of masked, white-cloaked emergency doctors bent over the dead body of Russet, shaking their heads in frustration and failure. "We've lost her--we've lost her," they murmured in Jason's ongoing nightmares.

There was no end in sight. The ordeal would last forever.

Early in the morning of late November, the alarm next to his bed went off at the same time the telephone rang.

"Hello?"

It was an unfamiliar woman's voice.

"Mr. Adams?"

"Speaking, barely."

"This is the head nurse at your wife's ward. Could you get here to the hospital, please?"

"Is something wrong?"

"Please just get here. Doctor's orders."

The atmosphere in the white hospital room was as thick as cotton . The room smelled of rubbing alcohol and Ivory soap. There was one bed against the wall with Russet in it. She had IV's in both arms. Her face was pasty-white, and the whites of her eyes were gray and glistening. Dr. Marsh's face was a blank mask. He wore a black bow tie under his white surgeon's coat, and stood, a stone statue, looking like a funeral director, on the other side of Russet's bed.

Jason walked in, kissed Russet, held her hand, and looked at Dr. Marsh.
"Why the IVs?"
Dr. Marsh's lips nibbled at his words.
"Control. We're carefully controlling the insulin and carbohydrates."
"What's wrong?"
Dr. Marsh's face was expressionless.
"The Estriol count has dropped significantly, and hasn't come back up yet."
Jason stared at Dr. Marsh.
"What's that mean? What count?"
Dr. Marsh's words sounded dull and metallic, like the sounds of a manual typewriter.
"The Estriol count is a measure of the placenta function. The count tells us how well the placenta is feeding the fetus. The count is down."
Jason looked down at Russet. She said nothing. He looked at Dr. Marsh.
"Is that dangerous?"
"Possibly."
"How long has the count been down?"
Dr. Marsh consulted his chart.
"About two hours now. A decision has to be made about the birth "
Jason's body went hollow. Suddenly, there was nothing inside him--no stomach, no bowels, no heart, no lungs. Just pure, ice-cold air.
"When?"
"It must be made now."
Jason glanced at Russet, and then turned to Dr. Marsh.
"What are the odds of the baby living if we do nothing?"
Dr. Marsh's face was as blank as the wall behind him.
"Fifty-fifty."
Jason looked down at Russet, then back at Dr. Marsh.
"What are the baby's odds of survival if we get it out of there now?"
Dr. Marsh's face remained an impervious blank.

"Fifty-fifty. The decision is up to the two of you."

Decision? Fifty-fifty? What 'decision'? Jason anguished.

Jason looked down at Russet. Her lower lip trembled and her eyes were teary.

Plead with her, Jason's empty gut said.

"It's your body, you know things, can feel things in there that I can't--."

She gripped his hand, her lips quivered, and her eyes pleaded. She said nothing.

"You're afraid to make the decision?"

She said nothing. Her pupils were dilated and at the dead center there were pinpoints of black, abject terror—the frozen look of a person staring straight at death.

Jason ears buzzed and his hollow stomach felt like a damp cavern. He looked straight at Dr. Marsh.

"Can she think clearly with all those drugs in her?"

Dr. Marsh did not answer.

Russet kept looking at Jason, pleading.

Jason thought: *it's up to me. I'm the only one in the world who can make this decision.* He swallowed hard, and dove into the blackness.

"Take it outta there--now."

Russet's hand relaxed.

Dr. Marsh's tone of voice was matter-of-fact.

"We'll have to do a cesarean. A natural birth is too risky. Labor could take too much time."

I thought you said it was 50/50 either way, you bastard, Jason thought, but said nothing. Jason sat on the edge of Russet's bed and held both of her hands. They looked at each other and lightly kissed, but did not speak, paralyzed by the unknown future pulling them forward.

A few minutes later several people dressed in white gowns with surgical masks over their faces flowed into the room. They turned Russet on her side in the bed, gave her an injection in the buttock, lifted her onto an operating table, and rolled her out of the room. Jason went with them and held Russet's hand right up to the operating room door where Dr. Marsh was putting on his white operative cloak.

Jason squeezed Russet's hand.

"I'm going to be there with her, right?"

Dr. Marsh shook his head.

"No."

Jason glared at him.

"Huh? You said I could be with her for the birth of our child. Why the hell not?"

Dr. Marsh tied something behind his back.

"Not for a cesarean. Hospital rules. Sorry."

Jason was enraged. He stood, arms akimbo, and snarled like a rabid dog.

"Hospital rules? Swell. Who the hell makes these so-called rules? This is downright idiocy. I'm her husband--this is patent horse-shit."

Dr. Marsh pushed open the swinging door into the operating room, paused, and looked at Jason.

"Fathers sometimes get in the way. They have been known to faint."

Jason's cheeks burned.

"That's bullshit."

"Those are the rules."

The attendants pushed ahead.

"Chin up," Russet mumbled, and disappeared behind the swinging doors. Jason shouted.

"I love you! I'll be as near as I can be. I'm here for you."

Jason turned to Dr. Marsh again.

"You *sure* I can't be with her?"

"Absolutely not. Hospital rules," said Dr. Marsh's muffled voice from inside the mask, and he vanished behind the doors.

Jason went into the white, hollow waiting room with a couple of other expectant fathers. They sat together, smoked one cigarette after another, and rarely spoke.

"Christ," Jason said, breaking the silence, "They're cutting my wife wide open in there without me there to protect her--what happens if a stupid scalpel slips and she bleeds to death and the baby is killed by some jerk surgeon?"

"Easy, buddy," said one of his companions, a man with a craggy, pock-marked face, "They know what they're doing--this is my third time around. She'll be Ok."

"You hope."

"I hope."

Two hours later a masked nurse stuck her head in the door. "Mr. Adams?"

"Yes?"

"Your wife has given birth. Both she and the baby are doing fine. Please come outside."

Jason followed here and paced around in the hallway. A door down the hall opened and a nurse rolled out a baby in a cart with translucent plastic cover. She looked at Jason.

"Mr. Adams?"

"Yes?"

"Here's your son, dad. Congratulations."

Jason looked down. Inside the plastic bubble there was a baby wrapped in off-white swaddling clothes, a baby whose hair was a curly, reddish, mess, and a baby who was blind-folded and kicking and screaming piteously. *Ohmygod*, Jason thought, *he's been born blind. Those bastards fucked it all up and I wasn't there to stop them.*

He whirled towards the nurse.

"What's wrong?"

"With what?"

"With his eyes."

The eyes above the white mask were expressionless.

"Nothing. The blindfold is there to protect his eyes from the bright lights."

Thank God, Jason thought, and bent over the screaming infant and was mesmerized by its miniature human shape, its jerking movement, its piercing noise, its miraculous life.

He turned to the nurse.

"Does he have all of his parts?"

"He's perfectly normal."

Jason's gut ached for the trapped child. He reached out to the nurse.

"Can I *please* hold him and give him a kiss?"

"No."

Jason bent over the carriage and clenched his teeth in fury at the nurse, and thought: *"Don't you understand? He's so damned small and helpless. He's scared, he's frightened, he's terrified. He's my son. He's counting on me. He needs my help."*

Jason looked up at the nurse.

"Just once? Just so he can feel me touching him and feel safe?"

"No, not now. We have to clean him up, get him some diapers, do some tests, and treat him for jaundice."

Jason's spine suddenly became rigid and cold, an icicle.

"Jaundice? What's that?"

"All premature babies have it. Nothing to worry about. Go see your wife.

She's down the hall in Recovery."

"Can't I just--just touch him? Just once?"

The nurse shook her head and wheeled the cart away.

"No. Go see your wife."

Russet's hair was matted in dark, roan-colored, clumps. She smelled of anesthesia and rubbing alcohol. Her eyes looked yellow, and her voice was hoarse and barely audible.

"How are you feeling?" Jason murmured as he leaned over the steel rack at the edge of her bed.

"Poofed. Didwa--?"

"He's beautiful." Jason whispered in her ear, and held her as best he could as he leaned over the cold steel railing. "He's a beautiful redhead, like you. I love you, go to sleep now, my love--thank you, thank you, thank you."

The next morning at home the air smelled different, the bathroom floor beneath Jason's feet was unusually solid, and his face in the mirror looked new and strangely unfamiliar.

"My God, it's *real*," he said to his reflection as he shaved, "You are now a different person: for Christ's sake, Jason, you're a father. Holy shit. This is enormous. This is an emergency. There are things for you to do, and do now. Lots of things to do. People to call. Things to buy. Diapers to buy. Bottles. Soap for babies. Health insurance to up date. Russet and the baby to see at the hospital. Food to buy--God. Hundreds of things to do."

Then, it hit him.

My life has changed--forever. Nothing will ever be the same again. It's a totally different world. How the hell do I be a father? How?

At the hospital, Russet and Jason went over names in a book the hospital provided for new parents. They spent several hours, picking and rejecting various names.

"How about Jason Adams II, Word Wizard?" Russet said, grinning to Jason, but somehow terrified of choosing a name that would offend Jason, be the wrong name for their son.

Jason felt naming his sin was a serious matter. A very serious matter.

"I don't believe so. There are several reasons. He's brand new. There's no one else like him in the world. It is paramount that he has a name different from the name of anyone you or I know or have ever known. This is important stuff to me, you know--major important stuff. Big."

In the past, Jason thought, *fathers always named their sons 'Jr.' or 'The II' or 'III'. I can't do that to him. He's got to start out with a fresh, clean slate, nothing and no one to live up to, no family name except his last name. Russet probably thinks, because he's a boy and I'm his father, that I'll expect her to cave in and let me do the naming as the patriarch. I won't do that to her.*

He smiled at her.

"Any ideas?"

Russet sighed and grinned to herself.

"Ok, Mr. Word Wizard. I give up. You name him--he's your son."

She had read Jason's mind again. His grand plan of mutual objectivity had vanished.

"How about 'Ellis Brandon Adams'?" Jason said a couple minutes later. "I don't know and have never known anyone with those two first names."

"And we'll call him?"

"Brandon."

V

Jason went to his Department Chairman, explained what had happened, and within days found himself teaching an extra entry-level course in Freshman English at the University.

Three weeks later, Russet and Brandon were home. Brandon was on a twenty-four hour bottle-feeding schedule. Russet fed him during the day while Jason taught, and it fell to Jason to do the night feedings, which he dutifully did for the four months preceding a miraculous night he would never forget.

If only Brandon could say what the hell it was he wants, Jason mulled, looked down at his son's tiny hands, and shifted his arms around Brandon. *All I have to do is to be patient with him, and gradually lead him, step-by-step, through the intricacies of understanding the language--one syllable, one word, one sentence, one paragraph, at a time.*

For the preceding months Jason had talked all night, non-stop, to Brandon, knowing full well that even when he was awake, Brandon probably couldn't understand the meaning of one word that Jason said. Nonetheless, he talked to Brandon about the works of Ernest Hemingway. About the plays of Shakespeare; about the novels of D. H. Lawrence: Linguistics; the greats of rock 'n roll piano; cereals; communications theory; about anything and everything--all to a sleeping miniature little man who refused to acknowledge a single word his father said.

"I might as well be speaking French, or German, or Spanish, or Russian, or pig Latin to you," Jason said, laughing out loud, "but what the hell, I've got to stay awake--so what does it matter? Maybe just the sound of my voice is communicating something? Maybe there's a kind of non-verbal communication level in just the tone of my voice? A kind of non-melodic wordless hum that may mean something to you, something that you may someday return to me transformed into the form of a real word?"

At least I am trying to communicate with my son, Jason thought, *That is something that neither my father nor mother ever tried to do with me. My mother talked down her nose at me in quasi-moral clichés: "look before you leap," "don't count your chickens before they've hatched," "the early bird gets the worm," "takes one to know one." On and on. And my father would sip at his martinis and nod his smirking approval in response to the clichés. After a while I just stopped listening to their crummy clichés, and merely tuned them out.*

I do not talk down to my students, Jason thought: *never.*

He looked down at his left arm at his cradled son. *What, if anything, is Brandon dreaming about?* Jason wondered, *What kind of world does he perceive he's living in?--if he has any idea at all he's alive, if he has any perceptions at all?*

It was frustrating, a hopeless feeling sometimes, different from, but ironically much like what he had felt like long ago trying to communicate with his parents or now with his apparently deaf and dumb Freshman Composition students. He sent carefully sculpted messages to them all, and got non-answers back, as if the telephone line between them was somehow dead or blocked by static of some sort, or as if he was talking to blank stone walls, and not sentient human beings.

There were noises, but no meanings, exchanged.

"You, my son, are going to learn how to listen to and speak English correctly. I have forbidden anyone at all to talk 'goo-goo baby talk' to you on the grounds that English is a tough enough language to learn as it is. I won't allow anyone to make it any harder for you than it already is. I'm going to teach you the meanings of words and sentences and paragraphs and how to speak and write clearly. I'm going to see you through your 'no' stage, teach you the 'ABCs' and how to count to 100 and how to spell your first, middle, and last names, and how to accurately crap-detect all the bullshit words the world throws at you. You're going to be a master of the English language, and never be swindled by anyone's phony words, by God. Never, never, will you be fooled by some charlatan television show or crummy commercial--no, not you, my son."

That's where Jason wanted Brandon to get to. But how to get him there from where he was? Brandon's world for four months, Jason guessed, had been essentially mostly black invaded now and then by impertinent hunger pangs; the sharp, spasmodic internal pains of colic; sudden bowel movements and wet diapers; indecipherable and inexplicable noises such as words, door bells, alarm clocks, the radio and television, running car engines, dish washers, and bird songs. A world of stunningly bright lights; gigantic hands turning him over, lifting him up, putting him down, washing him, changing him, dressing him; a microcosm centered on the life-giving nipple of the small baby bottle.

Most of the time Brandon's eyes were closed, even when he was awake and feeding. He seemed totally impervious to the language spoken to him, totally untouched by Jason's very existence, and totally unaware that Jason was alive--much less that Jason was his father.

"I'm your daddy, Brandon, I'm your daddy, and I love you," Jason said softly, and repeatedly, in the early morning silence.

"I don't honestly know how to do this daddy job, but you don't know how to do the son job, either, now, do you? So, I guess we're both in roughly the same boat, aren't we?"

No response to the question.

"I can empathize with you," Jason said, "but you can't empathize with me. Hell, you don't even know I exist as a person."

Brandon's lips tightened for a second, and then relaxed.

"You're living in a world of Titans, aren't you?" Jason said, and wondered how Brandon could possibly figure out how to get away from, or want to leave, his enchanted post-womb world of almost continuous sleep, of being fed, cared for, washed, dressed, cooed to, and coddled. Some kids, autistic kids, someone had once told him, seemed never to want to join the real world. They withdrew mentally from the world, and became psychological hermits living in a silent cocoon they construct for themselves. Other kids, like some of his students, grew up physically and then drifted into the linguistically garbled world of LSD, speed, cocaine, marijuana, and God knew what other drugs, and wound up just as tranquilized as the sleeping baby in his arm.

Jason looked down. How he loved that speechless, warm, being, loved his tiny, microscopically perfect hands, his Lilliputian, beady little eyes, his puffy cheeks, and the wisps of bright red hair on his dwarfish scalp.

The sky outside the kitchen window lightened. Jason yawned, smiled down at Brandon, and became suddenly terrified of what the unpredictable world of reality might hold in store for the innocent child. He picked him up, held him close, and patted Brandon lightly on the back.

Brandon stirred and made indecipherable noises.

"Getting a bit hungry? Wanna chat about it?" Jason said, laughing. He reached over on the table for the bottle of milk sitting in the bottle warmer, and put a drop on the inside of his forearm to test its warmth. He rested Brandon in his left arm, facing him.

"Good morning, my son. I'm your daddy, in case it's slipped your mind."

Brandon gurgled something nonsensical and then his tiny eyes suddenly popped wide open. He looked Jason straight in the eyes, and fixed him with the terrible, frozen concentration of people meeting unexpectedly in a foreign land.

Jason returned his son's fierce gaze.

Brandon smiled toothlessly at Jason, looked him in the eyes again with savage, searching intelligence glowing in his beady little eyes, flapped his hands, smiled deliriously like a madman, and said.

"Da-da."

It was not a question. It was a *statement*.

Suddenly, all time stopped and was put on hold, forever.

"That's me," Jason replied, once he'd overcome his astonishment, "that's me, I'm your daddy."

He carried Brandon down the hall to where Russet was sleeping and tried to wake her up.

"He knows who I am." he declared as her eyes half opened, "he knows I'm his daddy."

"Uh huh," Russet mumbled, and went back to sleep.

VI

Two months later, in late March, at Russet's insistence, they drove up north to Mason for Brandon to meet his grandparents.

"Not too much further, Brandon," Russet murmured, and held the irritable baby to her warm breast.

Jason glanced over at her. She was dressed in a beautiful, gold-green Spring jacket that contrasted strikingly with her long, shoulder-length red hair, and, for a brief second, he tried to write an opening four bars with lyrics about the lovely colors of the lovely woman sitting next to him—but got back to the business before him.

"You sure you don't want me to hold him for awhile? You've been doing that duty for all the way up."

Russet looked at him and winked.

"Alas, alack, the slings and arrows of subjugation mothers must endure."

Jason groaned.

"Enough drama, Mother Mary. So, once again, why the hell are we killing ourselves making this Odyssey?"

"My father demanded to see you with Brandon," Russet said as they crested the top of a long hill overlooking a lush valley of pine trees bordering on Lake Michigan. "Because I had talked so much about you as a father he wanted to check me out about you."

Jason glanced over at her and returned his eyes to the road ahead.

"Check you out about me? Hell, he and your mom met me after our wedding, remember? What does that have to do with me and Brandon?"

Russet adjusted Brandon's sky-blue blanket and looked over at Jason.

"Remember? He also wants to see the trust fund you wrote for Brandon."

"Right,. But what does that have to do with checking you--me--out? Are you kidding me again?"

Russet laughed.

"Nope. 'Check me out.' It's sorta a game he and I have played for years. It started with me telling him fibs about the fish I'd caught while he was away, or stories about how I'd fixed the car engine while he was away. It was a game we played, a kind of mental 'tag.' At any rate, he's gonna see if

I made up the stuff about you feeding Brandon and the way you talk to him as if Brandon could understand you. You're sometimes hard to believe, you know. My dad's kinda tough--he doesn't believe anything until he's 'seen for himself,' remember? He's going to play the game with me to see if you're as real as I wrote you were and knowing him, he's going to fall head over heels in love with Brandon."

They started down the hill. Jason glanced over at her.

"How far and how fast?"

She pointed straight ahead with her free hand.

"See that drive down there with the boulders and the iron gate? Turn right in there."

They went through the gate and around a long 's' shaped paved driveway and stopped at the back of a tall, shingled home where there was a silver-gray Lincoln Continental parked in front of a double garage door. The house was, Jason calculated, at least four stories tall, and looked like some kind of fortress. There was what looked like turrets at the corners of the roof and the windows were encased in wrought iron. A shoulder-high wall of boulders, Jason reminded himself, surrounded the property, so the idea of a fortress house was in keeping.

"How old is this house?" Jason asked as he took their overnight bags out of the back seat and Russet got out with a sound asleep Brandon in her arms.

"I think it was built sometime around the 1850s. All the inside is made of solid iron support beams, polished oak and shaped stone, and I vaguely remember workmen constantly swearing about being 'miners' when they put in the wiring and the plumbing years ago. I was very little then--I mean, this was years ago."

Russet, Brandon, and Jason went through the brass-plated front door into a long hall with a carpeted wooden floor, passed a series of framed original landscape paintings on either side of the hall, and into an expansive living room shaped like a half moon. In front of them there was a room-wide picture window that looked directly out across a rock-strewn shoreline on to Lake Michigan, where birds flew over the incoming whitecaps. The furniture was arranged in a semi-circle facing the picture window and a large, polished wooden coffee table, at which a bald Larry Brockton sat, wearing blue overhauls, smoking a cigarette.

Mary Lou Brockton, a diminutive, dark-haired woman, dressed in a nondescript blue dress and also wearing glasses, stood by him with her left hand hidden behind her back and her right hand hanging lifelessly by her side.

To Jason, there was something fragile about her, as if she was ready to give way under the slightest pressure, like the dried skeleton of a dead bird, or a house of cards.

"Mom, Dad," Russet said, and cradled Brandon before her, "may I introduce you to Ellis Brandon Adams. Brandon, this is my mother and father."

Russet lowered the baby for her parents to see.

Mary Lou Brockton smiled civilly and silently nodded. Larry Brockton studied Brandon, grinned, fanning crinkles everywhere on his wizened face. He looked Jason steadily in the eyes, stood, and shook Jason's hand with the iron grip of a blacksmith.

"Welcome, pop. I hear yer' ready on speakin' terms with the Little General, here?"

Jason returned Larry's crushing handshake, and held his own against the older man.

"Well, in a manner of speaking--."

Larry held the handshake, and grinned.

"Good grip, by gum--here, have a seat. Mommy? Can you have Jenny get our company somethin' to wet their whistles 'n a bite to eat?"

Mary Lou nodded and vanished. An old woman, her white hair done up in a bun, appeared out of nowhere, and politely asked what Russet and Jason wanted to drink. Russet took Brandon away to change him, and Jason sat at the table before the picture window.

Larry lit a cigarette; Jason followed suit.

"Wanna play poker after supper" Larry asked Jason.

"Sorry. I'm not really a gambler."

"Cribbage?"

"Sorry. But I do play bridge."

Larry frowned, and then grinned. His eyes sparkled.

"You play all those fancy things--Gorin and them others."

"Yes."

Larry slapped the top of his leg.

"Well, I don't. Just common-sense poker bridge. Wanna be ma pardner 'n give 'er a try? We can get inna game later after Jenny brings us supper, eh?"

Jason grinned and thought: *No bullshit with Larry. Everything right straight down the middle. I can see why Russet loves it when I'm straight with her.*

"Sure, I'll give it a shot--why not?"

"Fine," Larry laughed. He reached down into his overall pocket, and slammed a wad of bills on the table between him and Jason.

"How about a dollar a point?"

Jason stared at the pile of bills. They looked like they were all hundred-dollar bills, and the stack was a good two inches tall. Larry beamed over his thick. bifocal glasses.

"There's my stake. 'Bout two grand, I reckon. Now, put your money where your mouth is, friend."

This is a test, Jason's gut said.

"Thought we were partners? Share and share alike?"

Larry laughed, and his eyes sparkled as he scooped up the money and put it back in his pocket.

"Right y' are, right y' are, pardner."

The two men grinned at each other, dragged on their cigarettes, and sat silent.

Russet returned with Brandon, and Jenny brought in a pot of coffee and a spread of crackers, cheese dip, and cut fresh vegetables—cucumbers, celery, radishes. Mary Lou remained standing by Larry, stared at Brandon, and said nothing. *There's something wrong with her,* Jason thought, as he contemplated Mary Lou's expressionless eyes and blankly smiling face, *there's something missing in her.*

"So, what do you have to say about your grandson?" Jason said to Mary Lou.

Russet frowned at him.

Mary Lou put her fingers before her mouth.

"He's a--ah, a very pretty baby. Very pretty. Yes, indeed, pretty."

"He's a boy," Jason snapped.

"Supper," Jenny announced from the kitchen door, and they moved into the adjacent dining room for a meal in which Mary Lou served, but did not look at, Larry. There was a rigid formality between them, what seemed to Jason a silently understood code of behavior, like a once blithe dance, somehow frozen into a motionless ice sculpture.

The next day, after lunch, Larry sent Russet, Brandon, and 'mommy' out to 'ta go shoppin' or sumthin,' and sat down across from Jason at the living room table. Because of his advanced emphysema, Larry had difficulty walking, and had to struggle to catch his breath after he'd sat down. He looked out over the slate-blue lake, picked up a half-smoked *Cool* cigarette butt from the ashtray, lit it with a paper match, and looked at Jason.

"Ya got a fine boy, there, pardner, fine."
"Thank you."
"You lov 'im?"
"More than life itself--certainly as much as I love his mother."

Larry took a puff of his cigarette and sucked the smoke deep into his lungs. He turned, looked out over the lake again, and returned his gaze to Jason.

"Got that trust fund paper with ya?"

Jason handed him the sixteen-page trust document and looked Larry straight in the eyes.

"I put this together from a whole bunch of sample Trusts I got from banks and attorneys, but this trust is radically different from all those."

Larry fingered the document and frowned.

"Why?"

Jason took a breath. He was ready for the question. He had rehearsed the answer.

"They stunk. They were designed to make the banks and attorneys rich and had nothing to do with protecting Russet and Brandon in case something happened to me. I wrote my own trust. It covers all the usual contingencies of taxes and last expenses, but it also provides monies far into the future–if, that is, Russet survives me. I also provided for contingent beneficiaries and custodians in the event, God forbid, Russet and I somehow get killed simultaneously and Brandon survives. If that happens, there'll be money there for him for whoever is taking care of him."

Larry's nicotine-stained grin was grisly, a skeleton.

"Good."

Larry put on his bifocal spectacles, ground out what was left of his cigarette, opened the stapled pages, and read.

As Jason waited, he fought waves of comparisons between his dead father and Larry. They both had been born in the early 1900s; they both were fierce individualist's; they both smoked cigarettes, and Russet had said that her father had once been a two-fisted drinker and a hellion like Jason's father.

Thirty minutes later, Larry looked up and grinned.

"It just like tha damned one I writ myself, darned close."
"You can't see anything wrong with it?"

Larry glowed.

"Nope. Not one durned thing."

Jason received the stack of papers back from Larry

"Do you mind if I take a look at your trust?"
Larry scowled.
"What for?"
"To see if my trust doesn't conflict with yours in some way?"
Larry grinned and shook his head.
"Nope. No problems there, by gum. None. They's purty much tha same."

Mary Lou, Russet and Brandon returned. Larry lit another cigarette. He beamed at the sleeping Brandon, patted him lightly on the head, and announced.
"Well, we menfolks got the little whippersnapper here all taken care on. Time fer sum cards?"

The afternoon was spent playing 'poker' bridge, as Larry called it. The team of Jason and Larry did not get the best of cards, but managed to bid and play the cards they did get well enough to thoroughly trounce Russet and Mary Lou, who seemed not to communicate at all.
"One no trump," Russet opened.
Mary Lou fidgeted with her cards.
"Dear me. One no trump you say?"
Russet smiled happily.
"One no trump."
Mary Lou squirmed in her seat and stared blankly at her cards.
"Dear me. I will, ah, just have to pass."
Russet's jaw fell.
"Mother. One no trump is a demand bid. It's an invitation to game. You can't pass unless you've got a bust."
Mary Lou lowered her head and brought her cards up under her chin.
"Dear me. Little old me is just not good at numbers, you know, just not good at numbers."
Brandon stirred in his crib next to Russet, and started to cry.
Russet looked down at him and reached into her bag for a bottle.
"You're hungry, aren't you little man?"
Mary Lou stared at Russet's fingers and pointed towards the dining room.
"Don't, ah, wouldn't you prefer to, ah, there's some, ah room . . ."
Russet glanced at Jason, stood, picked up Brandon, and sneered.
"Oh, of course, Mother. I'd forgotten your rule about avoiding reality at any cost."

That night after dinner Larry and Mary Lou showered Brandon with gifts, and the next day Jason, Russet, and Brandon drove back to Ann Arbor.

As they got back on the highway, Jason looked over at Russet

"You and your mom don't seem to see eye-to-eye the way you and your dad do."

"Never have. She told me her goal in life was to be totally inconspicuous, and that was the goal of all women and it should be my goal, too. I told her to go to hell years ago."

"She's totally different from your dad?"

"Totally. Night and day.'

Jason looked straight ahead.

"I really like your dad. He and my dad would have *really* hit it off."

She patted Jason on the knee.

"I love him. It's clear he really likes you and loves Brandon. Did you see the way he looked at Brandon when Brandon smiled at him?"

"There's good times ahead for our son and his grandpa, Russet--lots of times ahead, I bet."

She smiled and hugged Brandon.

"You bet. How about getting together with them again at Christmas?"

And so they talked and planned their futures together with Larry all the way home, having no idea that their lives had been forever altered by a man who was doomed not to live long enough to see Brandon ever again.

VII

Then Russet's disease made its merciless reality known.

Russet had hired Cecilia Adlar, the wife of a graduate student, to care for Brandon during the day. Three months after the visit up north they dropped Brandon off at Cecilia's to be cared for while Jason taught at the University and Russet did library research for her Ph.D. dissertation. Earlier that morning she had complained of a sharp pain in her chest which she had passed off as "probably heart burn or indigestion, or something dumb-ass like that."

They sat in the car in front of Cecilia's apartment building, ready to head off to the University. Jason looked over at her and felt instantaneously queasy.

The whites of her eyes were a peculiar gray color, as was her normally pink-colored skin, and he sensed trouble looming before him in the day, the way experienced sailors sense a storm brewing on the far horizon of a clear sea.

The decision was clearly his to make.

"Look, Russet, we're only four blocks away from the Emergency room at the University hospital. I'm going to leave you off there, and teach my classes. If everything's Ok, just call the English Department, leave a message where you'll be, and I'll come get you, alright?"

"Alright, but--you're being your usually over-dramatic hero type--."

He pulled over in front of the double Emergency Room doors, reached across her, and opened her door.

"No 'buts.' That's the plan."

She nodded and forced a grin, said "Alright, chief," and walked through the swinging doors past the gurneys in the hallway, into the hospital.

A few hours later Jason went to the English Department to get her message as per the plan; but there was none. He called the hospital.

"Hello, this is Jason Adams. I left my wife off at Emergency earlier today, around 9:00 this morning, and she was supposed to call and tell me where to pick her up, but she hasn't."

"What's her name?

"Adams--Carol Adams. Her nickname's 'Russet'.

"Just a moment."

Jason lit a cigarette and waited.

"Mr. Adams?"

"Yes?"

"She's in Intensive Care."

The air around him went ice cold.

"Intensive Care? Why the hell--?"

"You'd better get over here."

In the hallway outside of the Intensive Care Unit the doctor, a young intern named Waliwolski with pasty skin and curly brown hair explained what he thought had happened.

"We are reasonably certain that an artery in your wife's left lung is blocked by a blood clot."

Jason gulped down the ice cube in his throat.

"Is she going to be Ok?"

Waliwolski fiddled with the stethoscope hanging from his neck.

"She's being monitored. It's a serious condition."

"What's wrong?"

"Looks like a pulmonary embolism."

"How serious is that?"

The doctor looked away.

"Serious."

Jason got to her bedside in the freezing-cold Intensive Care room. She had IV's in both of her arms and an oxygen mask on her face. Jason was racked in despair: *Jesus, Russet, for God's sake fight it.*

"I'm here, Russet," he said close to her ear, "I love you."

Her eyes wandered toward his voice, looked blankly at him, and closed.

Jason panicked and was about to scream for help when he saw she was still breathing through the oxygen mask. He watched her breathe for a few minutes, then backed helplessly away.

"She didn't recognize me," Jason said to the attending physician by her bed.

"She's heavily sedated. She's not out of the woods yet, but we think we'll be able to save her."

Jason's hands went ice-cold. His lips felt rubbery.

"*Save her*? What can I do, doctor?"

The doctor scratched a few notes on his pad.

"Go home. Come back tomorrow."

Russet remained hospitalized, in what to Jason looked like terrible pain, for several days in the Intensive Care Unit at the University Hospital.

"What could have happened if I didn't force her to come here?" Jason asked the Intensive Care doctor. He shrugged and toyed with his stethoscope.

"Hard to tell."

"Give it your best guess."

"She could possibly have died."

My God, Jason thought, *She's the most brilliant person I've ever known--why the hell didn't she know something serious was wrong with her? Or did she know and not want to admit it like some 19th century type frontier heroine? Or does the disease itself hide itself from its owner?"*

And all of a sudden, the mindless nightmare of the disease that inhabited Russet's body and mind became a fiend that was to torment Jason's life and consume hours of his thoughts as he struggled to understand, explain, and defeat its indifferent destruction of the woman Jason loved, and the mother of the son Jason loved more than life itself.

VIII

It was a summer that Jason was doomed never to forget. At Dr. Marsh's suggestion, in the summer of 1970 they went up north to Harbor Grove, Michigan, to Russet's parents' cottage, for Russet to recuperate and regain her strength after her embolism. The cottage was on the shoreline of Burton Lake, about six miles long and two miles wide, shaped, from the air, like a crescent moon.

The cottage was paneled inside with unstained pine boards and smelled faintly like a pine forest. There were two small bedrooms to the back and a cramped bathroom with a shower and a tub across the thin hallway from a storage room that contained the upright refrigerator. Towards the lake, there was a small kitchen and a dining table by the front windows. In the middle of the square front room, there was a plaid sofa facing a huge fieldstone fireplace made, Russet explained, "by a wonderful alcoholic Indian man."

Behind the cottage, attached to the garage, was a furnished room with its own bathroom. Nandini Pillar, a student from one of the graduate courses Jason taught, lived in that room and cared for Brandon part of the time during the day so that Russet could recuperate and not put any physical strain on herself chasing after her rambunctious son.

Summer teaching jobs at the University were reserved for the senior staff, so to make money Jason played piano in Ann Arbor with his band at Galaxy West, Friday through Monday nights, and commuted the 240 miles from there to the cottage in Harbor Grove. He stayed Tuesday to Friday, swam with Russet and Brandon, or took them for rides around the lake in the 18 ft. outboard motorboat that came with the cottage. Sometimes he and Russet shot pool at The Lake Bar, a tavern three cottages away, or they went out to a restaurant called The Olden House down the road near Mason for dinner and to listen and dance to a jazz trio.

It was a time, Dr. Marsh had prescribed, for them to "rest, relax, and dream of a better future."

Jason sat at the edge of the placid lake and let his eyes wander down their boat dock out to a raft some 25 yards off shore. It reminded him of the raft in Little Sebato Lake in Maine, where he had gone on vacation with his parents one summer when he was about five years old. They had stayed in a pine-board cottage with faded furniture and old magazines that smelled faintly of mildew. The kitchen had a wooden ice box lined with sheets of steel that a man delivered a block of ice for every two days, usually at about the same time a raccoon appeared at their back door to be fed the preceding night's table scraps. The ground around the cottage was padded with a blanket of brown pine needles from the sugar pine trees that surrounded the cabin, and smelled clean and almost antiseptic..

The memory lulled, and terrified, him.

Little Sebato Lake was a short walk away from the cottage. One day Jason and his parents went down to the sand and dirt beach for swimming and a picnic. There were another 10 or so people with their kids on the beach that morning, seated on multi-colored beach blankets with picnic baskets and sunglasses perched on their noses. All the kids wore bright red life jackets except for Jason. He was too big for that kind of little kid stuff, he had convinced himself that morning.

Some 30 yards offshore there was a wooden raft riding on oil drums and anchored with a thick rope to a block of cement on the bottom of the lake. He had taken swimming lessons that winter at the YMCA and felt it was about time he joined the older kids who were laughing and jumping off and climbing back on the lazily bobbing float.

"Can I go out to the raft?" Jason asked his mother.

She scowled and shook her head.

"It's too far. The answer is 'no'."

His stomach sank. He turned to his father, and tried again.

"Can I go out to the raft?"

His father wasn't a good swimmer. His swimming lessons had been of the sink-or-survive 19th century variety where, as a boy, he had been merely thrown headlong into a pond and learned to thrash his way from there to land.

"Think you can make it?" he answered and gazed out at the raft with his hand shading his eyes in the early morning sun.

"I think so," Jason had answered, although secretly he knew it was a long swim.

"Ok. Give 'er a try," his father smiled, patted him on the butt, and added, "I'll be watchin' ya."

GANTLET

Jason waded into the water, right up to his chin, and measured the distance to the raft. It didn't look that far, and there were other kids swimming out as Jason gauged his courage and what looked like the short distance between him and the magic pontoon raft.

He started swimming, and kept swimming for a long time before he paused and looked again: unbelievably, the raft hadn't moved. The lake water splashed into his eyes and caught in his nose. His arms ached, and his legs seemed heavy, like anchors. He summoned his resolve and kept swimming, kicking his leaden feet, flailing his heavy arms, and fighting his fatigue. A thousand strokes later, he looked up, treading water. The raft still looked to be miles away. His feet turned into granite blocks; his legs refused to move; and he knew he was sure to drown.

"Help?" he gagged towards the shore. As all hope of staying afloat plummeted inside him, out of nowhere his father's strong, athletic arms suddenly materialized and grabbed his armpits and hauled him to the safety of the shallow water near the shore. He left Jason standing in the shallow water.

"There," his father said as he walked away through the water in the direction of their blanket, water trickling off his broad shoulders and down his muscular back., "Better do a little more practice. If at first you don't succeed, try, try, try again. Ok?"

Jason followed his rescuer back to the blanket. Jason's mother looked down her short, chiseled nose at him. Her nostrils flared and her eyes squinted fire.

"You foolish daredevil. *When* are you going to get some common sense? If it weren't for your father you'd be *dead*."

Jason awoke from his reverie and looked out at the Burton Lake raft. *My father saved me: is that why I became a lifeguard? God knows I pulled enough kids out. Kids. Always kids or drunken old men. Never some luscious 36 x 24 x 36 lady. Always foolhardy kids.*

He watched Brandon play in the shallow water a foot or so away. Brandon squatted down, slapped at the water, watched as it splashed into the air, then stuck his hands down in it, giggled, and bounced up and down at the water's edge.

"Fun, isn't it?" Jason said.

Brandon squinted in the bright sunlight, and smacked the water again.

"Come 'ere," Jason said, and reached out his arms, "would you like to learn a little bit about how to swim?"

Brandon ignored his father and was instead intent on fishing up something floating in the water before him between his legs. He leaned forward and picked at it with both hands and then, when it repeatedly tried to slip away, cradled it in a pool of water caught between his open hands. The thing settled into one hand and stuck there. Brandon picked it up with the fingers of his other hand, and put whatever it was straight into his mouth.

"Whoa," Jason said, stood, pried upon his son's mouth and took out a piece of wood. "You can't understand everything about the world by eating it. There are better ways to learn."

Brandon looked up at his father, smiled, and went back to splashing and fishing things out of the water.

An hour or so later, Russet and Nandini, dressed in summer shorts and halter-tops, appeared at the shoreline.

"Jason," Russet said, leaning over, "How 'bout some coffee? Can I talk with you about something inside the cabin? Nandini will watch Brandon, Ok? It won't take long."

They went inside and sat down at the dining table for a cup of coffee. Russet looked over the table at Jason. Her eyes were watery and red around the edges, and at the center of her pupils there seemed to be a sharp point aimed at him, like the tip of a stiletto.

"This place is full of ghosts. I had a horrible nightmare last night."

He shrugged, looked carefully at her, and decided that while she seemed upset she was not in physical pain.

"Sorry."

"Will you help me understand it?"

"I thought we were going swimming with Brandon?"

"Nandini can take care of him."

She stared at him again.

"Please."

"I'm a piano player and English teacher, not a psychologist."

Her eyes bulged. The skin on her cheeks and temple went rigid.

"Please. I want to talk about it."

Her voice was tremulous and cracking at the edges.

"You're really serious, aren't you?"

"Jason--I'm really serious. It was a horrible dr—nightmare. Horrible."

Jason sipped at his coffee and wondered. *Since the embolism she seemed to have changed. She hadn't been as quick and witty as she had been before, and seemed somehow dreamy, off in another world, for weeks.* He tried to back out.

"This seems somehow weird to me— I mean, this dream interpretation stuff."

Russet waved her hand in the air.

"I'm weird. Are you going to at least listen about the nightmare?"

"Well, Ok, I'll do my best, but all I'm going to do is hear you out and ask questions, Ok?"

"Ok. That's fine."

Something is definitely wrong, Jason thought--*is she on the edge of an insulin reaction? Or something worse?*

He sat back and took a drag on his cigarette.

"So, what was the nightmare about?"

Russet took off the new eyeglasses she'd gotten because the diabetes had made the preceding ones useless, and put them down on the table. She glanced over her shoulder at the lake, turned back to him, and shrugged.

"I know this sounds really weird, but I think it was about me being buried alive--I seem to remember I was being buried alive. I was in this kinda box, and kept screaming for help, but no one came--I was trapped."

Jason grimaced and tried to smile.

"This isn't one of your cute jokes on me, is it?"

She scowled at him.

"No. This time I'm not pushing you around. And I'm not having a reaction and I'm not drunk. This is real."

So is this the madness you fall into when you're getting sick, Jason thought, watching her hands to see if they had started to tremble like they always did before an insulin reaction.

"Ok. So, tell me about the box. But I gotta tell you, all I'm gonna do, really, is ask you the kind of questions I ask myself when I'm trying to figure out a story, or a poem, Ok?"

"Ok. I think I was inside it."

The air around them suddenly thickened and felt damp.

"Inside what?"

"The box."

"This is in the dream, right?"

"Right."

"Inside the box? How big was it?"

"Small. Very small."

"About the size of a shoe box?"
She shook her head; her hair hung straight down in the thick air.
"No, bigger."
Jason drew several boxes on a piece of loose scrap paper on the table.
"About the size of the inside of a child's wagon?"
"Yes--no, bigger, a big, small, rectangle."
"Small enough for a child to fit in?"
"Yes--I think so, about that big."
"What color was it?"
Russet put her head in her hands.
"Brown, I think, the color of wood."
Jason saw a funeral parlor.
"Could you smell anything like flowers?"
"No."
"Could you hear anything?"
She lit a cigarette and frowned.
"I--yes, I heard people talking. There were voices in the dream."
Jason drew some stick figures around the boxes on his paper.
"What were the voices saying?"
"I don't remember--they were muffled, far away, eerie."
Jason felt like he had stepped onto another planet, a place he had never been before, and struggled to keep himself in balance. It was the world of the mind---someone else's mind--with hidden traps, strange places, unknown forces, terrifying monsters. He was an explorer in an alien world where the air now felt as thick as maple syrup..
"Did you recognize the voices?"
"I don't know--wait--I think one was my father--and there was a woman's voice, too, but I don't know whose."
"What were they saying?"
"I don't know."
Jason scratched his head and felt queasy.
"What else did you hear?"
"Sounds--sounds like a car makes on the highway, you know, the dull roar of wheels rolling down the road. This--analyzing dreams is frightening."
The air now seemed to have thinned and was easier to breathe.
Jason saw three pictures in his head, like a rebus puzzle, and drew them on his sheet of paper. He put a "plus" sign between each picture and an "equal" sign at the end.

"Have you ever been in a car with your father, another woman, and a small, brown box, on the highway?"

Russet smoked her cigarette, then suddenly looked across the table at Jason. Her eyes were wide, and her mouth hung open, the look of someone who has just recognized a ghost for who it really is.

"My God. I just remembered driving to Detroit with my father, perhaps his secretary, and a little coffin in the back seat of the car, a child-sized coffin that contained the dead body of my brother, Terry."

Something horrible happened, Jason suddenly thought. *Something horrible happened, so horrible it's still there, alive like a demon in her mind.*

"How old were you when this happened?"

Russet was slumped over in her chair, looking like she'd been clipped across the back of the head.

"About seven I think."

"And after you got to Detroit what happened?"

She frowned and took a deep drag on her cigarette.

"We went to this place that had lots of big slabs of stones sticking up from the ground and then over to a hole in the ground and they stood there talking."

"Who's 'they'?"

"My father and some man, an old man with a big nose and a beard."

"Then?"

"The man and my father picked up the box."

"The box?"

"The box Terry was sleeping in, and they put it into that hole in the ground, and--."

Something went 'pop' in Jason's mind. He shook his head, looked at the sketches on his paper, and jerked forward over the table towards her.

"Hold it. You just said that Terry was '*sleeping*' in the box--did you hear yourself say that?"

Russet stared at him. Her eyes were wide and unblinking.

"It just slipped out. I didn't mean it, I mean, I meant Terry was dead in that coffin."

Jason shook his head. *There's something insanely rational about this insanity,* he thought.

"Yes, you know that now. Then, at age seven, you didn't."

Her brow furrowed.

"Do you mean that--."

"Go ahead."

"I can't figure it out. What do you mean."

Jason's heart pounded in his chest.

"I mean that it appears that you apparently thought Terry was alive in that coffin when they buried him that day in Detroit."

Russet looked at him. Her face went white.

"Oh my God."

Jason perched on the edge of his chair.

"'Oh my God' what?"

"I think you're right. There's the terror of the nightmare. My brother was being buried alive like in some gruesome Edgar Allen Poe story."

Jason took a sip of his coffee and heard Brandon squeal somewhere behind the cottage and Nandini say something to him. Jason reached across the table and touched Russet's hand.

"You were just a little kid, and that's why you probably thought Terry was alive when they buried him."

"And that's what the nightmare means?"

"Shit, I don't know--I'm a rank amateur at this stuff—far worse than playing piano."

She put both of her hands around his.

"It's pretty awful. Thank you for helping me."

"You're welcome, but I'm not certain I'm right."

Her face was still white, although some color was faintly returning to her cheeks.

"It feels right to me. Too damned right."

They sat and drank their coffee for a few minutes. She saw a frown on Jason's brow.

"What's bothering you?"

He felt a sharp pain in his gut, like the kind of unreal frenzy he had felt years ago when he'd heard his playmate, Brian, get hit by that car. Jason had watched him scurry down between the parked cars, and disappear from sight. There was a screeching noise like a cat makes when its tail is pulled. and then a dull 'whump'. and then silence. Jason ran to a black car stopped in the middle of the street where an old man with thick eyeglasses was bent over a bundle of something.

"He'll be Ok, won't he?" the man rasped, and then quickly looked back down towards the crumpled thing at his feet .

Jason stood by the man and looked. Brian was on his side. His face was white; there was a driblet of blood at the corner of his mouth, and his mouth looked like a thick piece of rope. Brian's eyes momentarily looked at Jason, went glassy, like marbles, and then just stared blankly straight ahead.

Jason rose, and began to pace back and forth between the table and the stove in the kitchen, a few feet away.

"How did Terry die? What caused his death?"

Russet walked over to the stove and poured herself another cup of coffee. "Want some coffee?"

"No. Anyway, how did Terry die? What caused his death?"

"I don't know. I just remember him being sick--really sick. My mother never talks to me about Terry's death. It is somehow a forbidden topic. Goddamn her, anyway. I never ask her about it."

Jason felt a pure, straight line materialize down his back.

"Both of your parents know what caused his death, don't they?"

Russet stared at Jason. His eyes were intense, piercing.

"Yes, I guess, but daddy's too sick with his emphysema to ask him. It might upset him too much, and might even kill him. I love him too much to be that cruel to him this close to the end."

"Then there's your mother. She knows, right?"

Russet shook her head.

"Jason. You're out of your mind. She's not going to tell you the truth--she *never* tells the truth. Shit, she has no idea what the truth is. I have never, ever, been able to talk with her about anything. She avoids everything. Hell, when I had my first period and pleaded with her to tell me what was wrong, all she kept saying was something about me being a 'good girl, not to worry'. When the diabetes hit me when I was about eleven, all she said was that I needed to 'eat a little chicken noodle soup' and everything would be 'just hunky-dory.' It was always my father who helped me, not her. You're not going to get a thing out of her. Why bother with her?"

Jason stopped pacing, lit another cigarette from the one burning in his fingers, then stood still, immobile, a statue.

"Why? I hate bullshit. I guess I'm just the kind of guy who has to know the 'why' of things unknown. That's the way I am--period. I hate lies that hurt people I love. And this lie about your brother's death–if it is a lie–is hurting the hell out of you. Didn't you say once that there were some papers about Terry's death somewhere in that other back bedroom?"

"I think so."
Jason walked towards the hallway.
"Fine. Let's go look."

A couple of days later Jason got Mary Lou Brockton into his car on the pretense of taking her out to the cottage, drove over to the side of the road a couple of miles from the cottage, stopped, and turned off the engine.

Mary Lou panicked.

"Why are we stopping? I thought we were going out to the cottage for me to have a little visit with the little darling?"

Jason lit a cigarette and looked straight ahead through the windshield.

"We are. But first, Russet had a nightmare about her brother's death the other night, Mary Lou, and I'd like to ask you some questions, if I might."

She fidgeted with her pince-nez and smoothed down her plain brown skirt.

"Poor Russet. But she is getting better all the time, thank God."

Mary Lou's trying to wiggle away, Jason thought.

"Once again. Your son's death. I know this is a delicate matter, but do you remember what caused it?"

Mary Lou shifted in her seat

"Oh, dear me, that was so very long ago, and I don't have the very best of memories— 'out of sight, out of mind'—you know."

"Try. Where was Larry when Terry died?"

"Dear me. That was very, very, long ago."

Jason looked straight ahead and didn't move in his driver's seat.

"Try again, please. This is important."

Mary Lou looked straight ahead.

"Oh dear me. Let me see. In Detroit, I believe. His office was there because he did the books for the Detroit business people."

"You mean the Detroit mob. The Mafia. Right?"

"Well, ah, perhaps yes. It's hard to remember that long ago, you know."

"Didn't that bother you?"

"Not that he was doing the books for the mob."

"But it bothered you because?"

"Just that he was away, so very far away, in Detroit."

"And you were lonely?"

Mary Lou began to fiddle with her hands, as if she was washing them in a sink.

"I had two tiny little tots to care for, all by myself alone."

Jason kept his gaze straight ahead through the windshield. His hands were frozen on the steering wheel. His cigarette dangled from his mouth. His biceps flexed as he squeezed his hands.

"Two babies? I thought Russet was then about seven years old?"

"Well, two little tikes, two bundles of joy, you know."

Goddamn her and her clichés, Jason thought, *I had enough of that kind of run-around shit as a kid, and I don't need any more of it now.*

He took his cigarette out of his mouth and turned his head towards her.

"So, what happened with Terry? Russet said he got sick--terribly sick. How?"

She looked out her driver's side window.

Jason knew she was hedging, knew that she was not too cleverly trying to hide from him behind dainty clichés. He felt the fury rising in his chest.

"How old was he?"

"About a year and a half."

"What happened?"

She avoided his intent stare.

"I don't really know. I was just visiting the neighbor next door to the cottage."

"And?"

"I put him down on the floor, and he started picking up little pieces of dust or something and putting them in his little mouth, you know."

Jason saw Brandon picking up the piece of wood from the water and putting it into his mouth.

"And?"

"Well, I don't really know, but my neighbor screamed at me--."

Mary Lou looked out her window and fiddled with her hands.

Jason glared at her.

"And? What happened?"

"And she said 'don't let him play on this floor'."

Jason carefully controlled his fury at her stalling and supposed poor memory. He went cold inside and heard himself talking like a prosecuting attorney.

"Why not? Why not play on the floor?"

"Oh dear, I don't know if I can. . ."

Jason glared at Mary Lou, then turned his gaze straightforward.

"What the hell did your neighbor say?"

"Dear me, something--I think I can vaguely remember now--it was so long ago--age, you know, it plays tricks--something about 'It's just been sprayed with something--it could hurt him?'"

"Sprayed with what?"

"Oh, I don't know, one of those little bug chemicals like DDT, you know."

Jason spit his cigarette out of the driver's window and lit another.

"Did you pick him up from the floor?"

Mary Lou shivered faintly.

"Dear me, I can't really remember, you know. This is horrible, you know."

"Did you pick him up right away—yes or no?"

"Maybe not right away."

"Why?"

She fidgeted with her pince-nez and cleared her throat.

"Ahem. I guess I knew Larry'd come home if something was wrong."

Here it comes, here comes the damn truth, Jason thought.

"Why did you want him home?"

She sighed, and looked out the window to her right. He voice cracked.

"Larry was having a--an affair with his secretary. I found out about the affair. Someone told me, I seem to remember."

'Seem to remember,' Jason thought, *this woman is trying to squirm her way out of a nightmare crime.*

"So you put Terry down on that floor hoping to hurt him?"

Her head bowed. Her voice was choked.

"I--I, I just wanted to make him a little sick, you know so that Larry would come home, that's all, you know."

Jason felt nauseated.

"No I *don't* 'know' dammit. *Why?*"

"I told you. So that Larry would be forced to come home."

Jason felt rage rising hot and unstoppable in his chest.

"Why the hell didn't you just call Larry, and tell him that you wanted him to come home?"

Mary Lou did not answer the question.

Jason pushed open the car door, grimaced, and lit another cigarette.

"What happened to Terry after you put him down on the floor?"

"I told you. He played with some things, some little dust things--I don't know what--and put them in his little mouth, like little babies do, you know. Then, a few minutes later, he suddenly started shaking a little."

"A little? How bad?"

"Pretty bad."

Jason bit his lip.

"Was he having convulsions?"

She shrugged her shoulders and looked straight ahead.

"I don't know. Perhaps. I don't know what convulsions really are, you know."

"Perhaps? What did you do?"

She sounded like she was about to sob, but no tears came.

"Of course, I naturally took him straight to the hospital, and called Larry."

"What happened?"

Mary Lou looked out her window, and shuddered.

"Twenty-four hours later, Larry was home, and 48 hours later, Terry was dead."

Jason slammed the car door shut.

"Of what? The cause of death on the death certificate read *Spinal meningitis. We found it in the bedroom next to ours at the cottage.* That wasn't true, was it?"

Mary Lou Brockton wiped her eyes and said nothing.

"That wasn't true, was it?" Jason repeated.

Mary Lou said nothing.

"Ok, let's try this. Did Larry drive to Detroit with a woman, Russet, and Terry's dead body in a coffin?"

Mary Lou looked straight ahead and caressed her pince-nez.

"Yes."

"Was the woman Larry's secretary?"

Mary Lou looked straight ahead and continued to caress her pince-nez with both hands.

"Yes."

"And that's why you didn't go with Larry and Russet?"

Silence.

"That's why, right?"

Silence.

"Right?"

"Yes."

Jason sat back. It was clear. Russet's nightmare now made sense. He looked over at Mary Lou.

"Sorry to have put you through all this, Mary Lou. I just had to know."

Mary Lou's eyes were wide with panic.

"You're not going to tell poor Russet, are you? I mean, in her condition, you know, this might, ah, cause, ah, problems?"

Jason said nothing.

He seethed in silence, took Mary Lou back to her home in Mason then returned to the cottage. He met Russet in their kitchen and told the story her mother had just told him

Russet wrapped both arms around her stomach, and looked sick.

"My God. This is horrible. My own mother killed my own brother?"

"Might be. God, do I hate deceptions like this done to little kids."

Russet cocked her head.

"Deceptions? What little kids?"

He put his hand on her shoulder.

"You. I think you've been cruelly deceived about the true cause of Terry's death. And now that I have some idea of what really happened, I'm terrified. If what I suspect is true about what your mother did--I don't want her anywhere near Brandon."

Russet leaned against him. He put his arm around her.

"Why not?"

"She terrifies me and Brandon puts things in his mouth."

She put her head against the base of his neck.

"I don't understand."

He let go of her and walked over to the kitchen table.

"I'll explain after I make this call."

Jason picked up the telephone.

She went over to the couch, sat down, and lit a cigarette.

"Who are you calling?"

"I'm not done with this bullshit, dammit. I'm calling 'Poison Control' over in Echo Springs, and I'm gonna ask them if DDT could kill a one-and-one-half year old child."

"Poison Control--" a female voice said at the other end of the line.

"Hello. I'd like to ask you a rather weird question."

"Go ahead."

"What I'd like to know is whether or not DDT that had just been freshly sprayed on the wood floor of a cottage could kill a small child."

"How old?"

"About a year and a half old."

"It would depend on the dosage, whether or not the DDT was pure or had been diluted."

"Suppose it was pure?"

"Well, DDT doesn't get through the skin very easily. If the child ingested it somehow, the child would probably start vomiting right away."

"Could there be convulsions?"

"Yes. And breathing failure as well if the DDT was undiluted."

"You're saying the stuff could kill a child?"

"It's possible."

"Thank you very much."

Jason got a beer from the refrigerator, and sat down next to Russet on the couch.

"This is a nightmare about a nightmare. I think your mother killed Terry--killed her own son because she thought your father had been unfaithful to her."

Russet shuddered and turned to him. Her eyes were full of terror.

"Like Medea in *The Golden Fleece* who killed children so horribly?"

"Like Medea, only worse. At least Medea was an honest child killer. I think your mother killed your brother by some kind of an accident-on-purpose, damn her."

"On purpose?"

The insides of Jason's head whirled like a merry-go-round.

"Christ, I honestly don't know. That's the problem with her. I can't figure out when she's telling the truth, part of the truth, part-lie-part-truth or some other ghoulish combination. Talking with her is like trying to relate to an empty hole in space. But whatever it is with her, I don't ever want you to leave Brandon alone with your mother–not ever."

Russet looked ill and grabbed Jason's arm.

"Jason, this is insane. It's unreal. Sometimes--times like now--I'm terrified that I'm going insane. The problem is--and I know how weird this must sound--I'm having trouble trusting my own mind now. It's really impossible to explain, except that sometimes I think things and know I've thought things, and they seem right, but at the same time I sometimes just can't trust my own thoughts. Sometimes I know it's the diabetes--know after it happens it's the diabetes--but sometimes, like right now, I just don't know anymore. It's almost as if my own thoughts and feelings are traitors, or potentially traitors, to me, if you know what I mean."

He patted her hand, not like a father, but neutrally, like a friend.

" I've seen what happens to you when you have a reaction. This isn't about a reaction--it's about a nightmare and something that really happened. But whatever you mean, in the case of Terry, your mother, and your nightmare about the little box, your thoughts seem to have been right on the point."

She half smiled, the sides of her lips curled downward at the edges.

"It feels weird, believe me, it feels totally unreal. Who's going to believe it? I mean, what people would really believe it?"

Jason sighed.

"What people? Who knows? Most people have so little knowledge of themselves that they believe just about anything anyone tells them, the way blotters soak up ink of any color."

IX

Jason officially received his. Ph.D. in 1970, and was given a one-year teaching appointment at the University of Michigan. Their lives settled into a comfortable pattern. He taught the academic year 1970-71, and Jason, Russet and Brandon again spent the summer of 1971 at the lake front cottage in Harbor Grove. Jason got another teaching appointment for 1972, Russet had almost completed her dissertation, and that summer of 1972 they again headed up North, where Jason had secured work as a pianist in Webberville, fifty miles away from their cottage, at a high-priced restaurant called The Waterway.

The restaurant had been built next to the canal leading into the Webberville Bay so that diners could watch the sailboats pass as they ate dinner. There was a bar at the other end of the restaurant from the dining rooms and the cocktail lounge where Jason worked.

He played at a piano bar made from the stained and polished rudder of a sunken Great Lakes ship. The piano bar sat about ten people, and by mid-July Jason had established what he thought of as a group of petitioners who came almost every night to hear him play their requests, and whose enthusiasm for his music he fantasized would secure his place as the house pianist at the Waterside for years to come.

"Gonna play 'Satin Doll' tonight, Your Honor?" asked Harry, the bearded, retired corporate attorney, and inveterate Duke Ellington fan.

"You got it, counselor."

"Can you play 'Begin the Beguine'?" Harry's wife, the romantic 'Lil' with the shoulder-length black hair and heavy mascara, asked, sipping at the dregs of her double Vodka martini.

Jason laughed and played a riff.

"The whole 64 bars?"

She smiled seductively at him, slack-jawed, and looked for the waitress to get a refill.

"Yes. I love it. It's so romantic."

"How about 'Cow-cow Boogie?' Jerry Crane, a dentist, said, laughing. Jerry was always fashionably dressed and easy with his money. He put a ten dollar bill in Jason's glass tip mug situated in the middle of the piano bar top and pointed the thumb of his right hand upwards.

Jason kept playing and nodded his thanks.

"I'll play it just before I take a break. Ok?"

"Do you know 'Amapola'?" an old man with a grisly salt-pepper beard asked, toying with the empty shot glass next to his draft beer.

"I think I have the music for it. I'll check on my break. Ok?"

"'Angel Eyes'? 'When Sunny Gets Blue'? 'Lush Life'?" Alex Turkin, a jazz enthusiast with thick bifocal glasses and a shaggily moustache, grinned and requested his three favorite tunes, as he did virtually every night

Jason ended his tune and wrote down the requests on a pad he kept on the piano.

"How about 'Don't Get Around Much Anymore'?"

"You got it, Harry."

"How about 'You Don't Know What Love Is'?" Alex asked.

Jason smiled inwardly.

"I know it. Boy do I ever know that tune."

One night the place was dead, and one of Jason's two bosses, Dick Willams, a short, handsome man with dark hair and brown eyes, came up to the piano and said.

"Hang it up. Come with me, I've got something to show you."

Dick took Jason down the road to another nightclub named Barney's Pub in downtown Webberville. It was packed, wall to wall, with a noisy, milling crowd. An older man with a gray handlebar moustache wearing a pin-striped suit and bowler hat was seated behind a spinet piano, puffing on a cigar, cracking foul jokes, and playing "sing-a-long" tunes.

"See how he does it?" Dick asked, dollar bills in his eyes. "That's what I want you to do for us at The Waterway."

"I'm a rock 'n roll, boogie-woogie and jazz pianist, Dick," Jason replied, "I don't really do sing-a-long, and I don't tell dirty jokes or insult customers. It's not my bag."

Dick's brown eyes clouded.

"Bag?"

"Style."

"But you could do it if you wanted to, no?"

"Let me think about it."

Jason and Dick went back to The Waterway Inn, Jason got in his red VW bug, and drove the 50 miles back to the cottage. Russet was still awake when he got home.

"Hi," she said, "you look like hell. What's bothering you?"

"Christ, Dick--one of my bosses out at The Waterside--wants me to play sing-a-long piano."

She frowned.

"You?"

"Yeah, me."

"Will you do it?"

Jason leaned against the kitchen stove and lit a cigarette.

"I told him I'd think about it. But I think I'll refuse. There's something hokey about sing-a-long stuff, something about it that makes me feel, well, spooky, some kind of a sell-out. I can play the tunes, of course, but I just don't want to do it. Bores me stiff, that stuff."

Her forehead wrinkled.

"You sure? After all, it's work, isn't it?"

"So is being a male prostitute. Look, Russet--do we have any beer?"

She touch him lightly on the chest.

"I think so. Why?"

"I think I just want to grab some beer, take the boat out into the middle of the lake, ride along in the channel, and think about this mess."

She rested her weight on one leg, jutting her hip to the side the way fashion models sometimes stand. She raised one eyebrow and ravished him with her eyes.

"Can I tag along to make sure you're not screwing fish on me?"

He grinned and looked her up and down.

"Dressed like that? You'll get cold."

"You'll warm me up. Can I come along?"

"Well, sure--but, wait, what about Brandon?"

"He fell asleep in Nandini's room, on her couch--he's fine."

"Well, grab the beer and come along. I'm not sure what kind of company I'm going to be, but what the hell."

They rode out towards the middle of the lake, some three-quarters of a mile away, and turned off the motor. It was a clear, moonlit night, still faintly warm from the blistering heat of the day. The lake was silent as if time had vanished back to the beginnings of life, except for the sounds of the water lapping lazily against the hull of their boat and an occasional fish breaking the surface.

Russet popped opened a couple of beers and handed him one. He took a hearty swig, and felt the cool brew pour down his throat into his edgy stomach, calming it.

"Listen, Russet. It's so silent, so peaceful. I feel better already."

The night air embraced them in shadows, leaving only sounds and shadows.

"So, what are you going to do, dear Jason?"

He draped his left arm over the side and ran his hand back and forth through the cool water.

"I think I'm going to speak with George, my other boss. Argue that 'The Waterside Inn' is far too classy a joint for that kind of mindless crap, and that I have a business disagreement with Dick about the quality of the customers at the restaurant."

She raised her beer can in the air, off to his right.

"Salute! Sounds like a good plan to me. I'm all for you defending your integrity."

What? Jason thought, *no witty barbs?*

He glanced sideways at her.

"You support me?"

"Sure do, always have. Give 'em hell, my hero, give 'em hell. I support you all the way. Always have been your cheerleader, right?"

She's playing, he mused, *she's playing with me. She must be herself again. Wonderful.*

"Except when you try to beat me playing pool."

"Yeah, and I did it once."

"Once."

She touched his arm.

"And I almost beat you swimming in from the raft."

He laughed.

"Almost. And that's being supportive of me?"

"Keeps you on the straight and narrow, dummy."

He turned to her and laughed.

"Except when you try to beat me in 'Yahtzee' to force me to do lowly unmasculine things like changing diapers and doing dirty dishes."

"Yeah, and I beat you once in 'Yahtzee' after I figured out how you were cheating with the dice."

Jason grinned and toasted the night sky.

"Cheers. Hey. That's skill, not cheating."

"I beat you, fair and square."

"That you did. Most assuredly."

God this is fun, Jason said to himself, *just like the old days.*

Russet stiffened next to him.

"Wait a second. You didn't let me win, did you, you sonofabitch?"

He shrugged and looked at her in the darkness. Her red hair looked almost black, her freckled skin, alabaster white in the moonlight.

"You're beautiful when you call me names."

"Thank you. I meant it."

A soft warmth rushed up inside of him.

"I love you, Russet."

She turned her face towards him, and smiled.

"I love you, too, piano man. Wanna make love?"

The back of his head went stiff.

"Here?"

"That's where we are, isn't it?"

He tried to catch her gaze in the dark night air, but couldn't.

"How? This boat isn't exactly a cabin cruiser, you know. Hell, knowing us, we'll get energetic, forget what we're doing, and probably tip it over."

She laughed.

"So what? We can both swim. I've got my Red Cross Life Saving Badge. You're a former lifeguard. No sweat."

He moved over and rubbed her back through the sheer nightgown.

"You always want to make love in the craziest of places."

She curled her back around under his touch.

"Like where?"

"Like under the boardwalk in Atlantic City."

"Well, it was better than on the beach among all those people that night."

"Like in the woods."
"We were the only ones there."
"You thought."
"I thought."
"Like in the car, when I'm driving."
"Yeah. That was fun."
"It was diabolic."
"It was diabolic fun, then."

Jason laughed so hard he fell forward into the steering wheel.

"Holy spamoly, woman. You wanted to screw in the movies, too, right in the middle of dozens of people. So, now, you want to make love here, in the middle of the lake, in the boat?"

"Yup. It's your fault."
"Whatdaya mean, my 'fault'?"
"For being so damned sexy."
"Is that all you think about?"
"When I'm around you, yes."
"Ok, Jezebel. How?"
"Look straight ahead. Don't peek."

She stood, went around behind him, threw several of the square flotation pads they carried in the boat on the bottom of the boat behind him, and arranged them in a row. She came up behind him, laced her arms around him, and started to unbuckle his belt.

"I still don't see how we--."

She laughed.

"Hi-ho silver. Finish taking off your pants, come back here with me, and I'll show you how."

X

That night on the lake was a rarity.

Day-in, day-out, Russet struggled with the disease consuming her body, and Jason saw the struggle, as was his tendency to see many things, as a challenge. They returned to Ann Arbor and Jason went to work on the problem.

"Maybe it's something we're doing wrong with your diet," he said to her one day. "Let's go see the nutritionist at the hospital."

She shook her head and made a sour face.

"It's not going to do any good."

"Can't hurt. Let's give it a try. Ok?"

"As you wish, Jason. But I'm telling you, it won't do any good."

The nutritionist recommended a strictly-controlled, measured, daily diet, and gave them a chart listing what Russet could, and could not, eat, with specific measurements of exactly how much of each food group she was allowed on a daily basis. At home, they sat at their small dining room table, and Jason studied it.

"Hey, Russet, look at this: coffee is 'free.' You're a coffee-holic, so that's some good news right off the bat."

Her eyelids drooped.

"I've known that since I was 14 years old."

Jason looked back at the chart, with its tables of foods and amounts to eat in ounces and teaspoons and minute 'dashes' of salt and sugar.

"Pepper is free."

"But salt isn't."

"You can have some salt. And, so far as I can see, you can eat just about anything else."

She sighed.

"Except for lobster; barbecued spare ribs; sweet and sour shrimp; fried eggs; bacon; sausage; ice cream sundaes. All the good stuff."

Jason went out into the kitchen, came back with a couple of cups of cold coffee, gave her one and sat down next to her with the list before him, his hip touching hers.

"Let's look at that list again."

She lit a cigarette, sipped her coffee, handed him the sheet of paper, and said nothing.

Her depression about the food list gnawed at and desperately annoyed him. Jason studied the regime carefully, and underlined those items he knew she liked. Then, he saw what seemed to him to be the solution to her depression.

"Every system has a flaw. We can beat this bastard."

She glanced at him and then looked away.

"I said we can beat this bastard – we can beat it."

She turned her face to him, her head cocked.

He pointed to 'herbs and spices' that he had underlined in the 'free' column.

"See? All we have to do is figure out how to combine various herbs and spices to simulate the tastes of the forbidden foods like butter and vegetable oil and salt."

She puffed on her cigarette and glowered at the wall.

"I hate cooking. You know that."

It was a challenge. Jason knew how to handle challenges.

"Fine. I'll do the cooking."

She shook her head, and looked over at him with at look that said "you're a nut, you're dead flat wrong, but I love you anyway, dear jerk."

"Ok, chef, tell me this. How are you going to simulate the taste of salt?"

Jason looked at the 'free' column, grinned, and said, "Garlic. It's free. I'll just substitute garlic in recipes that call for salt beyond the allowable daily amount. It'll work, trust me."

And Jason's plan worked. After a few gustatory disasters, the food he prepared following that discussion of the list usually turned delicious and within the prescribed diet.

But the diet did not control the diabetes, which seemed intent on relentlessly going uncontrolled. Russet had repeated insulin reactions, most of them minor and easily stopped with orange juice, but nonetheless repeated unpredictably and for no discernible cause.

And, at age 28, her eyesight also seemed to be going bad. On several occasions, she jerked her hand to one of her eyes and swore under her breath. Jason saw a couple of these sudden twitches, at first thinking that perhaps a piece of dust had gotten in her eye. Then, one day in their bedroom, he figured out that something else was going on. She was dressed in the expensive, tailored gray business suit her father had given her to impress whomsoever she wished to impress—that day, Jason.

"You look gorgeous," he said, to loosen her up. Then : "what's happened to your eye?"

She emptied the contents of her purse on her side of the headboard, looking for, and finding, her cigarette lighter. She kept her face directed towards the wall.

"Nothing. There just seemed to be a kind of little dark spot that appeared and then went away."

"Went away totally?"

She said nothing.

Jason sat down on the bed and touched her on the elbow.

"I think we should check out this mysterious dark spot that does, and doesn't, go away."

'"When?"

"Now."

They drove to Ann Arbor to Woman's Hospital. Dr. Marsh sent them to see a specialist in diabetic ophthalmology, Dr. Reimer Wolostein, a man in his 60's with florid skin and snow-white hair. He put in eye drops then inspected her eyes with his diagnostic equipment. Afterwards, he sat them down across from him at his office desk.

Dr. Wolostein's voice was baritone, rich, compassionate.

"The dark spots are the result of tiny blood vessels breaking in the eyes. The condition is called diabetic retinopathy" he said.

Russet said nothing.

"Can it be helped?" Jason finally asked when the silence grew too heavy to bear.

"Perhaps. We can seal those tiny vessel breaks with a new laser surgery technique I have devised. It's painless, and takes about 30 minutes or so to perform."

Jason looked at Russet, whose eyes were watery and red from the eye drops.

"What do you think?"

She squinted in the direction of Dr. Wolostein's voice.

"How permanent is this fix? Does it cure it?"

Dr. Wolostein folded his hands together across his chest.

"Sometimes the results are rather permanent,. sometimes not. But without the procedure your eyes will remain clouded and make it difficult for you to see clearly."

Russet looked back and forth between Jason and the doctor.

"Will I be able to read?"

Dr. Wolostein looked at Russet.

"Can you read now?"

"No."

The surgery was performed and for days afterwards Russet could see clearly again. Then, another group of tiny vessels broke and another surgery was performed. Her eyes cleared up for several weeks. Then another group of blood vessels broke and there was another laser surgery.

To prevent any further incidents of the hemorrhaging, Dr. Wolostein told Russet she was "not to engage in any strenuous activities that involved lifting heavy objects."

"Such as what?" Jason asked.

"Oh, heavy bags of garbage, vacuum cleaners, large bags of groceries," Dr. Wolostein replied.

Jason scanned their daily life.

"What about a wiggling baby boy?"

"Baby boy?"

Jason touched Russet's hand.

"Our son."

Dr. Wolostein shook his head.

"I would advise not."

Too many doors were closing. Challenges met, one after the other, turned into defeats.

Jason waited until Russet had gone to classes and called Dr. Marsh.

"What can I do to help her? What different things can she and I do to stop all these damn things from happening to her?"

There was a long pause. Jason could hear Dr. Marsh breathing.

"You mean she doesn't know? They didn't tell her?"

Jason stomach felt suddenly sour.

"Tell her what? Know what?"

Dr. Marsh paused. Several long seconds went by.

"That the probability is that she's going to die by the time she's 40. . . early onset juvenile diabetics just don't make it beyond 40."

Jason's stomach went to cold air.

"You're kidding."

"No. I'm afraid not."

"Are you reasonably certain of this?"

"Yes, I'm reasonably certain, medically certain."

"I don't believe you. That's not what you told us before we got married when we came in to see you about the odds of us having kids. You said that if she took her insulin, stayed on her diet, and took it easy, she'd live to be 85. Don't you remember that?"

"Yes, I remember that meeting. We did not know then what we know now, and what we know now is that it is highly unlikely that she'll live past her fortieth birthday. I'm terribly sorry, Mr. Adams, we doctors aren't exactly infallible."

Jason's head suddenly ached, as if it had been rammed against a wall.

"Are you sure you're sure?"

"Yes."

Jason's voice cracked.

"Will you tell her that? I can't tell her. I mean, I'm her husband, you're her doctor. Will you tell her what you just told me, so she knows?"

"No. Not now. The time to tell her has come and gone."

"Which was?"

"In the hospital, after your son was born."

"That would have been unspeakably cruel."

"That was the time and place. There, we could have monitored her reaction, and sedated her if necessary."

"But dammit, she should know--she has a right to know."

The phone went dead.

Jason and Russet and Brandon drove back up north. All that summer he kept to himself what Dr. Marsh had told him, wrestling with a hopelessly brutal dilemma. If he told her what Dr. Marsh had said, it would be a vicious blow to her heart. If he didn't tell her, he was left to live alone with what seemed to be cancerous secret eating away at him every hour of every day into their future.

But was it the truth? Was she really doomed?

He didn't know. He went out for a walk down the dirt road behind their cottage, and thought.

Is this what love is all about? Keeping truth from the woman you adore and love more than your own life? Lie to Russet? Bullshit. She knows me too well, sooner or later she'll sense that I am keeping something from her and nail me for it, Once, she smacked me right across the face for keeping something from her, pow, just like that, right in our bedroom. She's brilliant and exquisitely sensitive. She'll surely sense that I have some sort of secret, and might even think I am having an affair or God knows what else. The cowardice of her doctors has left me with a nightmare, and I don't know what to do.

He went back to the cottage and, coward that he then was, played dumb.

"What's up?" Russet asked.

"Nothing," he replied, and took Brandon for a ride in the boat.

Finally, one rainy night in late August, as he ate his dinner before going to work at The Waterside Inn, the agonizing dilemma tortured him anew, and he was sobbing like a lost child. When the tears subsided, he racked his mind: *I can't go on with the sham I've become. I'm not being straight with her. I am, in effect, lying to her by omission. The way out of this quagmire has to be to reverse the situation: what if the shoe was on the other foot, what would I want her to do?*

The answer was inescapable. *I would expect her to tell me the truth. And I had to tell her the truth. It was her life, she had the right to know. She had the right to ask Dr. Marsh questions, so that she could make reasoned decisions regarding what she wanted to do with whatever time she might have left to her.*

He knew what he had to do.

Jason drove home from work that night through pelting rain, slowing down the drive home by 20 minutes.

Russet was sitting at the dining table in her ruby-red bathrobe, smoking a cigarette and drinking a cup of coffee.

"Hi," she said, "Where've you been? Play any 'sing-a-long' Liberace?"

He looked at her, and felt the way men must feel moments before they confess to having an affair and asking forgiveness.

"No. Remember, George agreed with me on that issue. The weather delayed me."

He walked around her, sat down on the couch and faced the empty, ashen fireplace.

"I've got something to tell you, Russet. Here, have a seat next to me."

She walked over, sat down to his left, saw the red rims around his eyes, and frowned at him.

"What are you so upset about?"

He felt her warmth next to him, and smelled the clean fragrance of her shampooed hair.

His mouth went dry. He forced the words out.

"Before we came up here this summer. . ."

"Yes?"

"I--I called Dr. Marsh."

"Why?"

He glanced at her, then looked back into the ashen fireplace.

"I wanted to ask him if there was something I--we--could do about the insulin reactions and the other diabetic stuff, how to stop them from happening."

He felt her stir next to him.

"And?"

Jason's neck and throat hurt as he spoke. He kept looking straight ahead. He stumbled over the speech he had rehearsed dozens of times on his way home through the pelting rain. He looked straight ahead, and then turned to her.

"I'm so sorry--I don't want to tell you this, but I've, I've just, I--I have to. It's not right. You have a right to know. But Dr. Marsh wouldn't tell you himself, so. . . ."

Her eyes narrowed.

"So? Tell me *what*, Jason--."

He looked down at his empty hands and bit his lip.

"He--he told me that there was nothing we could do. That they should have told you after Brandon was born, in the hospital."

She stiffened next to him and raised her voice.

"Who's 'they'? Told me *what*?"

Jason put his head in his hands.

"'They' is the doctors."

She shouted.

"*What the fuck were the doctors supposed to tell me*? Come on, Jason, you're being cruel to me."

His voice cracked.

"I don't want to be cruel, I--I don't want to hurt you, Russet, I love you so."

She leaned over towards him. Her voice was calm, coaxing.

"If you love me, you'll tell me, so--tell me."

Jason took a deep breath, turned, and looked her straight in the eyes.

"Dr. Marsh told me that--that there's nothing we can do about what's happening to you, that--that it will get worse, that, that you won't make it past your fortieth birthday, that the diabetes will kill you before then."

She froze, shuddered, and then broke down sobbing.

Jason was horrified by what he had done. He sat next to her, feeling her shuddering warmth against him, then slumped over and waited for her to scream at him and call him names for being a callous, cruel asshole.

"How long have you known?" she asked when she had stopped crying.

Her eyes were rimmed red with tears. Her elbows rested on the top of her legs, and her arms dangled like broken wings between her knees.

"I don't know--a couple of months, I guess."

She hung her head.

"Ohmygod. You poor guy. That's what I figured. I thought I knew something was bothering you this summer, but couldn't trust my mind at all to figure it out."

"You did? I tried not. . . ."

She looked up at him.

"You poor man--keeping that inside you all that time, making love to me--making love to a dead woman--pretending that everything was just fine."

He got down on his knees on the floor before her and stared up at her.

"You were crying for me?"

She shivered and looked nauseated.

"It must've been horrid for you, knowing that, touching me, kissing me, a diabetic dead woman. Horrid. Revolting."

He reached towards her.

"You're hardly a dead woman, Russet, and you're anything but revolting."

She gagged. Her tongue hung out of her mouth, then vanished.

"Horrid. Nauseating."

Jason reached and touched her knee.

"Will you call Dr. Marsh tomorrow and get some facts from him? I probably misheard him, and got something all screwed up, you know."

"No."

"I probably got it all wrong, Russet."

"No. I've been afraid this was happening."

Jason stood and looked down on her, then knelt down again on the floor between her legs.

"I thought Marsh told us the diabetes didn't affect your longevity?"

"He did. That's what I thought, too. I guess it looks like I was wrong--dead flat wrong."

"What are you going to do?"

"I don't know."

She put her hands on his shoulders, and then encircled his head and pulled him to her breast.

"Thank you for telling me. It was very gutsy of you."

Her breast was soft against his ear. He felt her chest rising and falling as she breathed. His voice cracked.

"Russet, I'm sorry, I'm so damned sorry."

He was racked with guilt and petrified with terror of the future. Jason shuddered and broke down sobbing on her breast.

Russet somehow knew all that he was feeling and, in her soft voice, comforted him, the way a loving mother soothes an ailing child.

"There, there," she said, and rubbed his back, "thank you for being straight with me. It must've been God-awful for you. Horrible. Sickening. You poor man."

XI

They returned home to Ann Arbor. As the days went by, Jason worried constantly about Russet--about her driving a car with Brandon in it and suddenly having an insulin reaction and crashing the car, killing them both, what might be her short life, and about what had become her almost total inability to care for Brandon.

It was no longer advisable for her to lift Brandon into his high chair or into his car seat. She couldn't wrestle with Brandon on the floor and instead sat by to watch Jason play with their increasingly rambunctious and mobile son. Sometimes she could see well enough to read the label of a jar of baby food, sometimes not. Sometimes downtown she could see if the traffic light was lit red or green, sometimes not.

"Bzzzzz" Jason buzzed as he made the spoon with baby food into a dive-bomber, piloted it into Brandon's open mouth and mopped up the excess from Brandon's chin.

"You're a nut," Russet said, "You're going to make him into a madman."

"Bzzzzz," Jason retorted, and fed Brandon again, "Like father, like son."

"Alas, alack," Russet moaned, "The poor child's future is bleak, I fear."

It was the opening Jason was looking for.

"Speaking of the future, I talked with Dr. Wolostein today. He said that there's a school for the blind we can visit--just in case these laser surgeries don't, ah, always work as well as they – we hope for them to work."

Russet smiled at Brandon and patted him on the head.

"I'm not going blind. I just have these annoying blood vessel problems."

"I said just in case."

Russet got up, and walked past him towards the bathroom. "No. And that's final."

She refused to talk any more about the school. It was a forbidden subject. Her eyes continued to get worse, particularly her right eye, which had a kind of blank, flat look to it, like it was made of brown plastic. The insulin reactions kept coming. She kept drinking beer and smoking her Kent cigarettes as if there was absolutely nothing wrong with her. She had terrifying dreams and nightmares she awoke from screaming, in a cold sweat. The nightmare about being buried alive had never gone away, and Jason was in despair for her.

He became deathly afraid of making love with her, terrified he might somehow hurt her eyes, or something else, and she would get sick and die in Intensive Care. It was horrible to see her suffering, watch her dying, right before his eyes, to feel trapped in the grizzly truth like he was in a straightjacket.

Life had become unreal.

Jason called Stanley Weinberg, a psychotherapist in Ann Arbor Jason and Russet had consulted early in their marriage about Jason's terror witnessing the first insulin reaction and his ensuing anxieties about feeling sometimes more like her parent than her husband.

They had seen Stanley on and off for a couple of months, both individually and as a couple, and Jason had learned that sometimes there are things in life that no one can control– including how one's spouse behaves.

In their last session with him some five years earlier, Stanley had said, "You are not in this world to live up to her expectations, nor is she in this world to live up to yours. Just live and let live."

Following that advice, Jason had reasoned that playing the role of her parent was no longer possible, but he had more insidious choices before him now. Things were no longer in the normal range. If he just let Russet be, she might die and leave their son motherless and him alone in the world. He had to do something. He needed to talk with someone good at understanding feelings, and that man was Stanley Weinberg.

Stanley was a short man in his mid-forties with unruly curly hair he rarely combed. A full professor of clinical psychology at the University, he was married, had three children, and characterized himself a something of a rebel in the Psychology Department. He adhered to no particular 'school' of psychology and had once told Jason that the secret to being happy was simply "making the right choices."

"Long time no see," Jason said. "It's been what? Four years?"

"Five years, I believe. Have a seat," Stanley replied, pointing to a legless, blue chair opposite another legless, brown, chair, which Stanley took. Stanley's office, like his hair, was unruly, and had piles of student papers strewn about the floor. There were travel posters and a single overhead light.

"How's your son?"

"Brandon's just fine. Happy, healthy, almost three-year-old kid."

"How's Russet?"

"That's what I'm here about. She's really sick. I can't seem to do anything about it."

"I'm not a medical doctor, Jason."

"I know that. This is about me."

Stanley shifted in his chair and looked intently at Jason.

"You're confronting some truths in yourself, finally?"

"What do you mean, 'finally'?"

Stanley took a deep breath.

"The truths you just couldn't see before your marriage. Then, you were absolutely cock sure you could figure out a way to beat her diabetes, that you and Russet would live together for centuries in connubial bliss and die together in each other's old and shriveled arms."

Jason shrugged.

"She told me she'd live to be 85 and Dr. Marsh told us both that, years before we got married."

Stanley rested his chin on the knuckles of his right hand.

"And you *believed* it?"

Jason shrugged and threw his open right hand in the air.

"Yeah, of course I did. Why would she lie to me about something like that?"

Stanley leaned back and put both hands under his chin.

"Because all she's ever wanted to be is normal, not sick, not diabetic."

Jason felt a wave of cold air lap at the back of his neck.

"She's lied to me?"

Stanley shook his head.

"No. She lied to herself."

There was a moment of silence as Jason tried to fathom what Stanley said.

"And I believed her?"

"Yes. You believed her wish to be normal. You wanted her to be normal and thought if things didn't go quite as planned you could help her be normal."

"So, she didn't really lie to me?"

Stanley thought for several seconds.

"Not really. You loved each other. The love made you lie to each other."

Jason massaged his forehead, and felt the cold air settle in his stomach and form a solid block of ice there.

"She's been given a death sentence."

A line ran across Stanley's forehead, then disappeared.

"What do you mean?"

"Dr. Marsh--her physician--told me last summer that she wouldn't live past age 40--that her kind of diabetes would kill her by then."

Stanley scowled.

"Did you tell her what he said?"

"Yes."

"So, she's been told the truth."

Jason put out his cigarette in the ashtray and took a deep breath.

"It was awful when I told her."

"I'm sure. Now, how do you feel about her so-called 'death sentence'?"

The block of ice in Jason's stomach did not move.

"Sick. Trapped. She dying everyday, right there in front of me. I can almost see it happening."

"And you still love her?"

Jason felt tears begin to well up in his eyes and gritted his teeth.

"There's not much of her left to love."

"What do you mean?"

Jason wiped his eyes and looked at Stanley.

"You remember what she looked like?"

Stanley half smiled and tossed his head slightly.

"Yeah. A gorgeous, vivacious, redhead. Incredible smile. Hard to forget her."

The ice block was now lodged in Jason's throat.

"Her hair has lost its color, Stanley--the red and the orange highlights are gone. She's getting gray hairs here and there. Her teeth are rotting and falling out. She's only 32. She can't see well in either eye now. She keeps having those goddamned insulin reactions and winding up in the hospital."

Stanley's lips barely moved.

"Sounds hopeless."

"Hopeless?"

Stanley studied his client.

"Hopeless. Do you really believe there's anything you can do for her?"

"I don't know. I keep on trying to help her; and I keep on failing. I'm afraid all the time--I'm afraid of getting a call at work from a hospital or a doctor--I'm afraid to come home because I don't know what horrible thing might have happened to her during the day that she did nothing about--I'm afraid of her being alone with Brandon, having an insulin reaction, not being able to help herself and dying right there in front of him. I'm just plain afraid all the time, Stanley."

"Sounds like you feel that you have to care for her night and day?"

Jason thought for a few minutes.

"Feel? Hell, it's a reality—I *do*."

"You can't--no one can."

Jason lit another cigarette.

"You're telling me that there's really no way I can live my life without ignoring Russet in the bargain."

Stanley did not move.

"What do you think?,"

"And what that means--if I ignore her--is that I'm afraid she'll--she'll most likely wind up in the hospital, and me in there with her. There's no way I can win."

Stanley thought for a few seconds. His eyes were steady.

"That's right."

"Then what can I do?"

"Maybe you'll have to think about choosing between Russet and Brandon."

Jason slumped forward.

"Jesus Christ. What the hell does that mean?"

"It means you're going to have to choose just how much there is of you to give to her and how much of you there is to give to Brandon, and what's going to be left for yourself. Think about it. I'll see you next week."

At the next session, Jason reported that things were unimproved.

"She got violently sick to her stomach last Saturday. I had to rush her to the hospital. She's still in there. Some kind of kidney and bladder infection. I'm taking care of Brandon myself. She kept denying that anything was wrong. I don't know--it's insane--it's almost as if I've got to rescue her not from the bad guys, but from herself."

Stanley was silent. He looked at his hands, and then up at Jason.
"You can go on trying to save her life, but it's going to cost you yours."
"Huh? I'm not risking my life at all."
"Think about what I said. Just think about it."

By the next session, two days later, a sleepless and unshaven Jason had made a decision that he was certain would please Stanley.
"I don't want to give up. I want to, somehow, gently shock her into a realization that she has to choose to do a better job of caring for herself. If I am successful, and she makes a commitment to her health, and gets it back again somehow, then. . . ."
Stanley folded both hands under his chin.
"Jason, sometimes there are some things you just can't change."
"I'm hoping she can somehow be saved, damnit."
"Are you looking for a miracle?"
Jason gritted his teeth.
"I'm going to give it one hell of a shot. I'm gonna lay it on the line."

Jason went straight home that day in late October. Brandon was playing with Nandini, hammering wooden pegs into a toy pegboard in the living room and Russet was drinking coffee in the kitchen.
Jason told Russet that he wanted to talk with her in their bedroom.
"We'll be out in a couple of minutes, Nandini," Jason said.
Russet sat down on the bed and looked up at Jason. Her eyes were cloudy and blood-shot, her skin sallow. She seemed frightened by the meeting he had called.
"You said you wanted to talk."
"Yes."
"Are you mad at me?"
"No, not really. I just want to talk with you."
"What about?"
"About our lives. Us."
She frowned.
"Ok. What about us?"
Jason gritted his teeth and delivered his ultimatum.
"I want you to make a choice to make a commitment to caring for your diabetes. Make it a kinda career job, like your dissertation. I know that if you choose to do it, you can and you will."

She stared at him.

"And if I can't?"

He pulled out the trump card, a bluff to drive her into action.

"Then we'll have to talk about splitting. I'm asking you to choose to make a commitment, now."

She continued to stare at him.

"And if I can't choose?"

That question wasn't in the script Jason had rehearsed. He tried to buy time to think of an answer.

"Then, I suppose--."

Tears welled up in her eyes.

"I flunk, right?"

Jason shook his head.

"No. That's not what. . . ."

"Shape up or ship out, huh? You're kicking me out."

He put both hands out, palms raised, to her.

"Huh? You didn't hear me right. I didn't say anything like that. Do you want something to eat? Some orange juice?"

She slumped over. Her voice was low and soft, barely audible.

"I was terrified this was going to happen. I knew it. I could tell it by the feel of it. You're just dumping me, you shit. I've seen this; I've had nightmares about this. How could you do this to me? How? Why?"

Jason shook his head, thinking *I can spike her coffee with sugar*.

"Whoa, slow down. Do you want a cup of coffee?"

She leaned her head towards the bedroom door, to her left.

"From the beginning. It was right there to see, to touch, even to contemplate."

He moved to sit down next to her; she shifted over towards the other side of the bed. He reached out to her.

"You're not making any sense, Russet, I didn't say anything about dumping you. That's not what I said at all. You're not listening to me."

Her eyes flashed at him. She jumped up from the bed and rushed out of the bedroom past Brandon and Nandini out the apartment door with Jason trailing helplessly behind saying . "Russet? You've got it all wrong. Russet!"

XII

She didn't come home that night. Or the next. Or call.

Jason taught his classes, and graded student papers, cared for and played with Brandon. He periodically called the hospital and the police in case something had happened to her but there was no news. He thought of going around town to various bars and nightclubs he knew she liked, but decided instead to stay home with Brandon and to wait for her to call or come back.

She never called.

He was sick with worry and despair, and was lost in a maze of dead-ends. He hated himself for delivering his 'choice' ultimatum to her, and felt wretched about what she must have suffered because of it. *You ego-centered asshole*, he berated himself, *you fucking asshole. You should have checked to make sure her sugar was Ok before you opened your damned mouth–asshole.*

Late the third night after she left, around 11:00 p.m., there was knock at the apartment door. Jason went to the door and opened it cautiously.

It was Russet.

She had snowflakes in her hair and on her brown trench coat. Jason was simultaneously dumfounded and relieved to see her.

"Well, hello. How. . . . "

Her face was downcast.

"Can I stay the night?"

"Of course you can. Come on in."

She took off her trench coat, slapped off the snowflakes and hung the coat up in the hall closet.

Jason was painfully cautious abut what came out of his mouth. He tried to be nonchalant.

"Been shopping?"

"No, job hunting."

"Job hunting?"

"Yes, and I got it. I'm going to be an editor of a journal at the University."

He looked at her mouth. Her lips were moist, and not dried and cracked like they were when she was sick. He smelled no alcohol on her breath.

"Congratulations."
"Thank you."
"Do you want some coffee? Are you Ok?"
"Yes to both. How's Brandon?"
"He's fine. He's asleep in his crib. Do you want to see him?"
"Later."

She went into the kitchen, poured herself a cup of black coffee, and sat down with Jason at the kitchen table. The right side of her face was partially hidden behind a now prematurely gray lock of once red hair. She avoided his gaze.

"I've thought it through," she said, without looking at him.
"Thought what through?"
"What you said."

Watch your mouth, see if her mind is back to normal, he thought.
"About what?"
"About us splitting."
"Hey. I said no such thing. I was talking about a choice I wanted you to make."

She looked off somewhere away from him.
"I've made my choice. You've rejected me. Don't lie about it. Don't try to protect me. I can figure things like this out by myself and I just can't take it because it's just not fair at all to be deceived by someone you love. I can't stand the nightmare of living with a duplicitous man I can't trust day-to-day, whose love comes and goes willy-nilly. I'm leaving you."

Jason sat bolt upright.
"Jesus Christ, Russet, I didn't 'reject' you. All I said. . . ."
She kept her head down.
"Was that you wanted me to chose to leave you."
"What? You're making no sense. I said nothing of the sort. Somehow, you totally misheard me."

She gazed at her coffee.
"There's nothing wrong with my ears. I've thought it through, and it's too horrible. I've made the choice you wanted me to make and I'm getting out of this and leaving you to save myself."

He reached out towards her.
"You're making no sense, Russet--I mean, sometimes the dia. . . ."
"I'm perfectly balanced. My mind is working just fine in every way."

Bullshit, Jason thought, *reason with her, talk some sense into her head.*

"If you leave, where are you going to stay?"

She turned her head, and looked at him.

"I've found an apartment. You keep this one with the Steinway and the memories."

Jason returned her look. Her right eye was totally blank and sightless.

"Hey, look, all I meant by what I said was. . . ."

"I heard what you said, damnit. I thought about it. I knew it was going to happen someday. I've made my decision."

Jason shook his head. He felt ill.

"Hey, sweet Jesus, Russet--we can fight it, whatever it is."

"I've made my decision."

Jason panicked. *She's in a reaction,* he thought, *her mind's all fucked up. Try to keep her here before she does something stupid again.*

"Do you want some orange juice? A coke?"

She stared at her coffee.

"Stop being an asshole. I've been perfectly balanced all day."

I've got to find her, got to make some kind of contact with her in reality somewhere, he thought.

"How are you going to live?"

She turned her head away from him.

"I told you I got a job. But I don't start until sometime in late August next year. Will you give me some money to live on until then?"

"How much?"

"A couple of thousand should do it."

Down to earth, bring her down to earth, Jason thought.

"That's not enough money to live on between now and August next year."

"I've got my stocks. This is just for the time being."

Try again, Jason counseled himself.

"Ok. But--will you promise to keep seeing Dr. Marsh, and go have your diet checked and see Dr. Wolostein? My insurance will cover you, remember?"

"Yes, of course I'll do those things. I can take care of myself. Thank you."

Ok. At least she knows she's got to take care of herself and get better, Jason thought, *I'll humor her; I'll give her the money. Maybe I can pull her more down to earth in another way?*

"You're welcome. What about Brandon?"

"He can stay here with you, for the time being, until I can buy him a crib and other things for when he's with me at my apartment."

Nothing made any sense anymore. *She's really going to do it,* he realized, *and there's nothing I can do about it.*

"And we'll share him, share taking care of him?"

"Yes. Of course."

"Are you sure about all this?"

Her face remained turned away from him.

"I'm sure. I can't do it to you."

"Do what to me? You're not making any sense, Russet. Let's talk about it."

"No. I'm exhausted. Let's go to sleep."

"Don't you think we should. . . ."

"No."

They went into the bedroom. She took off her clothes, went to their dresser, put on her off-white nightdress, got in bed with Jason, lightly kissed him 'goodnight' on the lips, curled around him, and fell asleep on his right shoulder.

The next morning they had coffee and doughnuts together in the kitchen. Her hair was washed and brushed; she was dressed in her gray business suit from the preceding night. Jason had splashed water on his face and brushed his hair, but was unshaven and was wearing his blue bathrobe.

Jason took a deep breath.

"How are you feeling? I mean, last night I was worried that. . . . ."

She sipped noiselessly at her coffee and lit a cigarette.

"I'm fine. I'm a grownup, remember. I remember everything. Do you remember about the money?"

I could refuse to do it, he thought, *but if I don't someone else will–her mother, her father, or one of her friends.*

He went to his desk in the adjoining room, wrote the check, and returned, feeling miserably at cross-purposes by what he had just done.

"Here's my check for $3,000.00. Is that enough?"

"Yes. I think so. Quite enough. Thank you."

She put the check into the wallet in her purse.

Jason lit a cigarette.

"Did you say 'hi' to Brandon?"

"I didn't want to wake him."

Jason blew a wobbly smoke ring across the table.

"How are your eyes?"

She looked at her fingernails.

"I can see well enough to do my work."

Jason stood.

"Do you want more coffee? Another doughnut?"

She shook her head and stood.

"No. I'm leaving now. I've got to get to the bank then go buy Brandon some stuff."

She went to the hall closet, and put on her trench coat.

He stood in the hallway and watched her.

"Do you want a ride to campus? I can get shaved and dressed in a second."

"No, thanks. I'll walk. I'm perfectly fine."

She moved over to him, stood on her toes, and kissed him perfunctorily on the lips, the way relatives kiss each other at family functions.

"Good-bye," she said, turned around, and Jason watched the faded red hair of the woman he adored walk out the door.

You'll be back, he thought, as the door clicked shut, *we're not finished with our story, we're just not finished.*

Chapter II

War

Russet did not come back to the apartment, or call. As time passed without a word from her, Jason felt adrift, like an empty bottle cast into the sea. He tossed and turned in bed, desolate and scared. He sensed that sooner or later, something was sure to happen. She would call; she would write him a poem; she would walk in the front door. Something

Without her to share care of Brandon he needed money for babysitters and the quickest way to get that money was to play piano.

A month after Russet left he went to talk to Jim Kally, the owner of The Falls, a dimly lit jazz club and restaurant, with dark, cavern-like walls. Inside the entrance there was an artificial waterfall dropping down a rocky cliff into a pool of swirling water strewn with dozens of nickels, dimes, quarters, and pennies. Just past the waterfall, there were two-top tables with enclosed yellow candles arranged in a semi-circle around a black baby grand piano.

There was one table by a small wall next to the waterfall where years before Russet and Jason had talked in the candlelit darkness about dreams of their future together as the falling water danced beside them. "Will you still love me when I'm old and gray," Russet had asked, sipping her Crème de Menthe, raising an arched eyebrow.

"Only if you go to bed with me tonight," he had retorted, knowing full well she would.

Jason glanced at the table by the waterfall, felt the back of his neck go numb, and then walked past the table and its memories to the bar. He told Sally, the blonde bartender with a low-cut dress displaying ample breasts, that he wanted to talk with Jim, ordered a beer, sat down, and waited in the cool darkness. Someone came up out of the blackness and Jason, sensing trouble, turned cautiously around and looked up into the florid, rugged face of John MacDougle.

A friend of Russet's, MacDougle was a tough guy, an ex-professional hockey player, and his eyes were watery and red. His nostrils flared and his jaw quivered as he pulled his right hand back next to his cheek. He glared at Jason and snarled."How cudya do that to her? You son-o-bitch."

Jason's gut went cold. He watched the poised fist and did not move."Do what? To who?"

John kept his right fist cocked next to his face."Throw Russet out wish no money an' a baby in her arms, you bas-tard."

Jason turned around, stood slowly, and inched his right hand up in the air in a "stop" signal."Hold it. I did no such thing. Let me buy you a beer–here, John, have a seat, Ok?"

John lowered his fist and stared at Jason, who ordered a beer from Sally and pointed to the barstool next to his. John paused, waved in place like an underwater weed, then sat down. John rocked back and forth in his seat, and snorted as he breathed. His face glistened with sweat and he reeked of beer and tobacco.

"John," Jason said when the beer arrived, "do you really *believe* that I would do that to Russet?"

John slurped his beer and wobbled his head from side to side. "That's what I heard."

"Do you believe it?"

John fumbled with a pack of matches and lit a cigarette. "Well, wash your story?"

Jason looked at John, but John ignored him and looked straight down at his smoldering cigarette. Jason spoke slowly and kept his eyes on John. "Hey, she slept on my shoulder our last night together--honest. When she left the next morning, she left with my check for $3,000 in her purse to live on until her job starts in August. She left our son with me."

John studied his cigarette ash and then turned his watery eyes towards Jason. "That true?"

Jason looked him straight in the eyes. "That's the truth."

John sensed that Jason was telling the truth—he just looked and sounded like a guy telling the truth, "Wonder why they says that?"

Jason moved a fraction of an inch closer to John."Who's 'they'?"

John shrugged."Oh, yanno, folks. Can't figure why they's says shat."

The conversation got stalled. Jason bought John a couple more beers, patted him several times on the back, and talked a little hockey. They parted 'buddies,' as John put it. Jason left The Falls without talking with Jim, who never showed. Better to pour beer in that frying pan of John's crazy story before it ignited and exploded, Jason reasoned as he drove into the sun-drenched parking lot behind his apartment and was amazed to discover Ariadne Brown standing in the middle of the lot.

She was dressed in a bright red-print business dress, had a cigarette in her mouth. Her pallid green eyes bulged at him.

He looked out of his open car window,"Well, hi, Ariadne, what in god's name are you doing here?"

Her jaw was set. She cheeks were glossy with sweat. She spoke through her teeth. "Where the *hell* have you goddamn been? I've been trying to get you."

"Get me? Why?"

Ariadne leaned both hands against the driver's door, squinted her eyes in the afternoon glare. "Listen to me."

"I'm listening, for Christ's sake. What the hell is going on?"

Ariadne sucked on her cigarette, blew the smoke out through her nose, looking him straight in the eyes."Listen. Russet attempted suicide last night."

"*What?*"

"She called me, said she was killing herself and needed someone to care for Brandon--she sounded shit-faced drunk and said she had taken about a 1000 mg. of Nembutal. So I right away called the police and Dr. Jonathan Clays--he's been taking care of her diabetes--and then flew over to her goddamn apartment."

Jason's head swirled. His mouth tasted like nickels. "Jesus H. Christ. Unbelievable—did---."

Ariadne leaned forward against the car, her face flooded by sunlight. She scowled. "The police had to kick in the goddamn door 'cause Russet had dead-bolted it. There she was, face-up, half-naked out cold on the goddamn floor, with hypodermic syringes strewn all over hell 'n gone along with a bunch of dead Boone's Farm wine bottles."

Jason had a sickening, nightmare picture of hypodermic needles sticking out of Brandon's mouth and rivulets of blood dripping down his tiny jaw onto his chest. "My God--where the fuck was Brandon?"

"Asleep in his crib."

"Was he Ok?"

"Yes."

Jason shut off the engine and looked up at Ariadne. "Why the *hell* did she try to kill herself?"

Ariadne shaded her eyes with her left hand."There was a suicide note to you in her goddamn typewriter and a folder on her desk with her journal saying how you'd 'rejected' her. "I gave you everything and you rejected me," she wrote. I read it while they were hauling her out."

Jason got out of his car. He leaned his back against his sun-warmed car next to her. "Calm down, Ariadne–can you calm down?"

"Shit. Yeah, damnit. Ok."

He stared at her. "Ok. A suicide note to *me*?"

She inhaled her cigarette and nodded. "Yup. You."

Something quietly rose up in Jason's gut and then fell suddenly like a bird killed by a bullet. The world had become a bizarre Fellini art film where tennis was played without rackets or nets, where up was down, in was out, where nothing, absolutely nothing, made sense. He kicked the ground with the heel of his shoe. "Bullshit. I never rejected Russet. The only thing that's rejecting her is her own body. Where's that suicide note and the journal?"

Ariadne shrugged. "I picked it up and the goddamn journal and put it away in her desk."

The sun burned into the back of his neck and across his shoulders. Suddenly, he saw himself in court asking for custody of Brandon and offering the suicide notes and journal as evidence that Russet was insane and unfit to be Brandon's custodial parent. He looked at Ariadne, his eyes calm and blank, the way doctors look when asking delicate questions. "Can you get them—the suicide note and journal--for me?"

Ariadne shook her head and mumbled. This was serious and confusing stuff. Maybe legal stuff and the stuff of friendship and loyalty to friends and what other people might think. "I--Russet's my friend, you know. It's her private stuff--I can't really--."

Jason touched her shoulder. "Hey, look, that stuff is important--it might be important for something—like a custody hearing or something. Brandon's important too, you know after all, he's just a defenseless kid."

Ariadne inched away and looked down at her feet. She pinched her full lips together, "I don't think that I really--I mean, she's my friend, the morality--I can't cross that line, you know. I mean, I know Brandon's important, but Russet's my friend and—and what will people think, after all, she's Brandon's mother, you know."

Jason looked off towards his apartment building across the parking lot from them. Ariadne was fudging, gutless, tangled in hackneyed moralities. His hand shook as he raised the lighter to his cigarette. He turned to Ariadne. "Speaking of Russet, where is she?"

Ariadne shrugged and looked at her feet. "They took her to the goddamn hospital and pumped all the booze out of her stomach. She's Ok, I guess."

He swung around in front of her and touched her on both shoulders, "Where's Brandon?"

She cringed under his touch and looked at her feet. "At Russet's apartment with a baby-sitter."

Jason moved away, opened the car door, and got in. "I'll go get him. By the way, did any one tell you I had thrown Russet out in the middle of winter with no money and a baby in her arms?"

Ariadne half smiled and looked up towards the now orange-lemon sun coating the trees and the sky . "Yes."

"Who?"

"I, I, just can't--you know--."

"Anonymous character assassination, huh?"

Ariadne kept her eyes raised to the heavens. "Rumor. What people say."

Jason looked up at her, inserted his ignition key, and sneered. "Do you always believe what people say?"

Ariadne threw her hands up. "I felt that they were probably goddamn bullshiting a little."

Jason hit the dashboard with the heel of his fist. "It's a dead flat lie. For cryin' out loud--it's just plain ridiculous, like some stupid kids' cartoon."

"They seemed pretty sure."

Jason felt the contempt rise, like a column of burning gas in the middle of his chest. "Yeah, sure of Santa Clause and the Easter Bunny. What utter nonsense. *Me*? Throw her out, penniless, with a baby in her arms? It's pure crap."

Ariadne looked down at him. Her eyes had softened. "Why don't you just call Russet and ask her if she knows about it?"

Jason shrugged and started his car "In the hospital? To hell with it. It won't make any damned difference right now. Anyway, I've got to go get Brandon."

Ariadne looked off over the top of the car and shrugged. "Good luck."

A week later the phone on the night table next to Jason's bed rang him out of a dead sleep. It was Ariadne.

"Russet has goddamn done it again. This time she slit her wrists."

He sat up beside his bed, snapped on the light, and stared fuzzily at the shadow of himself on the wall. His voice was hoarse. "I tha-thought she was still in the hospital?"

"She got out."

He shook his head and looked around for his cigarettes. "Jesus. She's really fucking lost her mind. Who told you--how'd you learn this?"

There was a pause. He heard her take a deep breath. "The grapevine at the University. It's reliable, well, pretty reliable for assholes."

He found his cigarettes and lit one, trying to torture himself awake. "You're still a teaching fellow there?"

"Yes."

"At least this time I have Brandon with me."

"Good. I didn't know. That's why I called. Sorry if I woke you up. Talk ta ya later."

Why the hell is Russet doing this shit? Jason agonized, *Why? What the hell is she doing? Drinking herself to death? Or is it the goddamned diabetes doing her in? Or both?*

Three weeks later Russet insisted that she was well enough to care for Brandon. Since she had gone back to work--Jason called her several times at her office to verify this--he found no logical basis to prevent her from having Brandon with her. It was a hopeless dilemma. Jason's experience with her diabetes had taught him that if it was anything, it was treacherously unpredictable and any improvement was likely more illusion than reality. On the other hand, it was possible--it was always possible--that something unforeseen and miraculous had happened in her body--some kind of spontaneous remission of the diabetes like what sometimes happens with cancer--and that Marsh's prediction of an early death for her had been a horrible error.

"Look for the silver lining." One of his parents' clichés echoed in Jason's mind and he went with the hope that this time the change in her health was to be permanent, a change that would clear her muddled mind and bring her back to the wonderful woman he had fallen in love with, married, and who gave birth to their son.

One of these days, he dreamed, *she's going to call and say she loves me and wants us to get back together again, and this whole unspeakable nightmare will be a thing of the past.*

For a while, life went on. Russet and Jason both worked at the University, Jason as a teacher, Russet at her job as an editor. Jason also played piano at two separate clubs--'The Falls' and 'The Penthouse'--to make money to pay for baby-sitters for Brandon when Jason taught at the University. He taught on alternating days, so that the care of Brandon was divided between Jason,

Russet, and day-care providers. Every other day Jason picked Brandon up from Russet's apartment at around 1:00 P.M. From there, weather permitting, he took Brandon to the 'Mandermetz Park,' a park and playground up the street from Jason's apartment, and stayed there with him for the rest of the afternoon.

The women who came to the park with their children didn't once say a word to Jason. Indeed, they seemed leery of any interaction with him, always keeping their eyes averted and their backs turned to him. *Maybe I get the looks,* Jason thought, *because of my goatee? Or is it because I am the only man in the park? Impossible. There's got to be other men who take their kids to the park--aren't there? Where are they? Why weren't there other men there teaching their kids how to face fear?*

Jason looked down at the tiny Brandon. "Want to go down the slide?" Brandon looked over at the gigantic yellow contraption, back at his father, squatted, and picked up a pebble underneath the wooden picnic table. Jason touched Brandon on the shoulder. Brandon took his father's hand and Jason led him to the base of the slide ladder and looked down at him. "Stay here, I'll show you how it's done." Jason climbed up the steps to the top of the slide, and purposely went recklessly whooshing down.

"Wheee!" he yelled, and Brandon looked intrigued. He moved towards the bottom of the slide where his father had come to rest, and stopped. Jason stood, and put both hands on Brandon's bantam shoulders. "Here, come on. I'll help you climb the ladder. Come on--it's not too high."

Jason wrapped his hands around Brandon's lower back. Brandon inched up the slide steps one at a time, and froze at the top, staring down the long, shiny lane that ended fearsomely far below. Jason put his face next to the side of Brandon's head.

"Ok, tell you what. I'll go down to the bottom to catch you. Wait here. Ok?"Jason climbed down the steps, ran to the base of the slide, opened his arms, smiled broadly, and cooed. "Come on. Come on, Brandon. I'm here for you. You won't get hurt--I promise."

Brandon hesitated, inched his feet over the top step and on the slide. Then down the slide he came, wide-eyed, mouth agape and Jason caught him gently, like a lightly thrown pillow, just before the bottom. Brandon looked up at his giant father, giggled, then ran around to the slide ladder, climbed, and came down again, and again, for the next five minutes until the boredom sat in.

He stood at the bottom of the slide, pointed, and said. "Wanna go sings?"

"You want me to push you on the swings?" Jason translated.

Brandon's head bobbled up and down like a bouncing ball. "Bes."

"Yes?" Jason translated, attempting to teach pronunciation.

"Bes." Jason took his hand.

"Ok, come on."' Jason lifted Brandon onto the swing seat, put the iron safety bar across his middle, and pushed, first gently, and then with greater force."Wanna go higher?"

Brandon looked down at his father, who seemed somehow smaller, and nodded with his lips pinched together. "Bes."

Jason pushed. "Higher?"

"Bes-bes-bes." Jason pushed. And pushed. And pushed. He gave Brandon the ride of his young life. As he swung, Brandon looked down between his legs and squealed "Eeeeee-" then "-ah"—as if he was a rodeo cowboy riding a bucking bronco.

What word is there for this feeling? Jason asked himself as he felt the light weight of Brandon's body touch against his hands. *What word? Bonding? Togetherness? Pure love? No. The right word is all of them in a flash blended together and married forever in a squeal of happiness–Eeeee-yah!*

"Eeeeee-yah," Jason yelled, and pushed his son on the swing, "Eeeeee-yah!"

"So, what'd you two Olympic athletes do at the park today," Russet quipped when Jason and Brandon arrived. Her skin had the peach-rose color it always had when she was well. Her hair, while not as cranberry red in places as it used to be, had a healthy sheen to it.

"Sheer magic," Jason grinned into her one good eye.

"Go sings." Brandon shouted. He hugged his father's leg and pointed up in the air. "Sings."

Russet laughed and mussed his hair. "You went high on the swings?"

Brandon nodded vigorously, and pointed at the ceiling. "Sings."

"You mean swings," Russet laughed.

"Sings." Brandon nodded, again pointing to the ceiling. Jason grinned down at his son.

"You're learning the language--we just have to try to translate your language into ours."

"Brilliant, absolutely a brilliant observation," Russet said, smiling at Jason.

"Don't I ever know. By the way, I'm not S-I-C-K any more, so you won't have to worry about me caring for B-R-A-N-D-O-N, Ok?"

He searched her face and one good eye, looking for some magic. He waited for her to say something about getting back together. But she looked away, down at Brandon. Jason's stomach felt sour. He put on a smile. "Great. Happy to hear that. Hey--if you want to, you know, it's perfectly all right with me if you visit me while I'm playing piano and bring him along. Might be a treat for him."

Russet patted Brandon on the head, hesitated, and looked away. "I'll think about it. I'm pretty busy these days, you know."

"Work?"

Russet hated herself for lying, but did so anyway—as she had been coached to do.

"Work."

She's ashamed about that stupid suicide note, he thought, and tried to catch her good eye. She kept looking down at Brandon. Jason persisted. "And, oh, by the way, do you know anything about the utterly insane story going around town that I threw you out in the middle of the night with no money and Brandon in your arms?"

Russet lifted Brandon into his child's seat at the table, looked across the room, ignored the pebble that had suddenly formed in her stomach, and raised an eyebrow at the wall opposite her. "What?"

"That's the story."

She scowled and busily tucked a white cloth napkin into the shirt under Brandon's chin. She did not look at Jason. "I have no idea of who might say such a ridiculous thing." She sounded like she was telling the truth, but she made no eye contact with Jason.

For the first time in his life with her, he did not know whether or not he could believe her. His heart ached. With a sudden rigid certainty, his hopes of getting back together with Russet suddenly seemed as hopeless and illusory as was the futile wish his father would one day suddenly reappear and ask him to go to a Yankees game again. Jason was wracked with uncertainty about the damning story. The next day he called Ariadne to see what he could find out, and inched his way towards asking her what she knew.

"Hi."

Ariadne was sick of the soap opera. "Russet doesn't talk with me any more, Jason."

"I thought you two were buddies?"

"She doesn't trust me any more–not after I told her that I had told you about the goddamn suicide attempt. It's almost as if she's dividing the world up into two camps: those friends who will cover her ass and people who won't. I guess my ass is in the latter group."

"Along with me?"

"Along with you. You can't trust her any more, Jason."

Right here, Jason told himself, *right now. Go to the source of that asinine story.* "Sorry. That leaves a kinda big hole for me. I wonder–that story about me--. "

"Huh? You still stuck on that bullshit?"

"Never mind. "

The line was silent for a few seconds. Then Ariadne spoke. Her voice was soft, sensual, and laced with tears. "Is there room there for a woman?"

"Room where?"

"In that big hole. In your life."

The telephone receiver went sweaty in Jason's hand. "Who've you got in mind?"

"Little old me."

Jason shook his head. "You're married, Ariadne, and so am I."

"You're separated, and have been for over a year, Jason. And I'm not goddamned married for much goddamn longer."

"Huh? You and Ralph have been married for what? Ten years? What's wrong?"

Ariadne started to cry.

"What's the matter--he having an affair on you?"

"Yes."

"Huh? How do you know?"

There was a long silence. "He told me, the son-of-a-bitch-bastard."

"Since when? I mean, you two seemed so happy. . . ."

"Things ain't always what they goddamn seem to be, sweetie. I've known for years, but I thought I could somehow win him back. I can't. I give up. He moved all of his shit out yesterday. Will you come over here and be with me--kinda hold my hand? Please?"

"It's kinda late."

"Please, Jason, for God's sake, *please--*."

A woman who needed him? "I'll be right over."

"And would you bring a goddamn bottle with you?"

"Sure. What do you want? Scotch?"

"Oh, I don't give a shit. I just want to get smashed on my goddamn ass with some one sweet like you and kill the pain."

Jason never did ask Ariadne about the melodramatic story. The timing was always all wrong. They got hopelessly drunk together and bemoaned the sad state of their lives and the world in general, swore eternal friendship and fidelity, and passed out sitting across the room from each other in Ariadne's apartment.

The uneasy peace between Jason and Russet continued. In the fall of 1972 Brandon slept alternately at Russet's apartment then at Jason's apartment. There were no arguments; no fights over money, no disagreements over when and where Jason would see and be with Brandon. At times, Jason continued to delude himself that he and Russet were merely living apart for an indeterminate time before a miraculous reconciliation happened and thereafter they would go on together, as they had dreamed and planned years before. Then the world changed again.

At Christmas when Jason went to Russet's apartment to pick up Brandon a man whom Jason did not recognize answered the door. He looked like a hippy with his long, shoulder-length black hair, long-sleeved shirt and dark glasses. Russet introduced him as her "friend" Curt Diamond, "a poet like her," who she said was "a sweet guy, and very nice to Brandon."

Curt was deferential to Jason, and seemed to be genuinely concerned with Russet. He kept close to her, and bent down, listening intently to her every whispery word. Jason left with Brandon and an aching heart. *Well, I guess that's that for any continuing partnership, much less a reconciliation. Jesus Christ she could've done better than that creep, a fucking student hippy, no class at all.* Jason's stomach sank. *But who am I to judge? So long as he doesn't hurt Brandon, how can I complain? Thank God she's got someone to take care of her.*

Nonetheless, the queasy feeling Jason had about Curt lingered, and Jason had him researched by a local private investigator. Nelson Pickard was in his middle 50s with close-cropped salt-and-pepper black hair. A rangy man, he had been a CIA operative and had the cool savvy manor of a man who had seen and done everything.

"Curt Diamond," Nelson said, "is an alias for a person named 'Daniel Richmond,' who has a mile-long criminal record in New Jersey," Pickard said. "Curt is a heroin addict wanted by the FBI for drug trafficking in New Jersey and in Ann Arbor, where The Tower Suite is the drug Mecca of the town."

"Does the FBI know about him?"

"Probably."

"Are they going to arrest him?"
"Probably we're waiting for him to lead us to bigger game.
"Dammit."
"Watch out for him, Mr. Adams. Curt's a dangerous guy."
"How dangerous?"
"Very."

Jason's 1972-1973 teaching appointment at the University was for one year. In those days, American universities, unlike most European universities, did not hire their own Ph.D. graduates until they had taught elsewhere for several years. But because of his high value, the University had hired Jason two years in a row contrary to policy.

"But," the Department head told him, "the policy exception had come to an end." Jason was going to be without a job shortly. He was concerned about how he was going to survive, much less finance a custody battle he imagined might be heading at him like an August thunderstorm. The bottom had fallen out of the college teaching market. There were, Jason learned, 120,000 Ph.D.'s out of work. The one job interview he did get, at Elmira College in New York State, fell through because of the torrential rains and disastrous floods that hit the area in the spring of 1973.

Other job interviews outside of academia ended up in Catch 22 scenarios that were like a broken record that always went, "Sorry, you're not suited to this position."

"Why not? I mean, I can certainly write. I teach people how to write."
"You've got a doctorate, don't you?"
"Yes."
"You're way overqualified for this position and you're a bad risk because once a teaching job comes along you'll grab it and leave the company."
"There are no teaching jobs out there."
"Sorry."

In desperation, Jason started to look for full-time jobs as a pianist, and got lucky. Jim Kally had hired another full-time pianist at The Falls, but in August, Jason signed a contract with the manager of The Campus Hotel, for a renewable six month period to perform in the dining room of the ritzy hotel six nights a week, and on Wednesdays for the weekly luncheon fashion show.

The hotel catered to dignitaries visiting at the University. The dining room was luxuriously appointed in gold and silver and had three mammoth glass chandeliers hanging from its 20-foot ceilings. Jason knew he'd make good tip money at the job. It fitted his needs. It paid more than teaching. The question of Brandon's custody still hung in the air. Jason knew he was not going to leave town without Brandon, given the uncertainty of Russet's health, and her strange new association with Curt Diamond.

He couldn't leave Brandon; it was unthinkable because it would leave Brandon empty inside the way Jason had felt and did feel empty inside without his father in his life. He would not do that to Brandon. Leaving town alone was not a viable option, period. There was no retreat. Jason stood his ground, and waited, hoping against hope, for Russet to get better and come back to her senses.

II

Jason's hope disintegrated when Russet fired the opening round of the war with a Complaint For Divorce in June of 1973, asking for and getting temporary custody of Brandon based on Jason's alleged 'desertion' of her and Brandon. The 'Complaint' was an outright lie--but normal in the Byzantine world of domestic law, Jason was to learn.

He interviewed several attorneys, finally hiring Bruce Hamlin, who practiced in Ann Arbor and who had an office in Ypsilanti. Bruce was a married man in his early thirties, a muscular former football linebacker, with broad shoulders, straight blond hair and wire-rimmed glasses. There was a straightforward, no-holds-barred manner about him that, combined with his 'facts only' style, made Jason feel he was in the hands of a man who knew exactly what he was doing.

The walls of Bruce's office were lined with law books, the furniture solid, polished oak, and the phones in the outer room rang incessantly while they talked. Bruce seemed genuinely concerned about Brandon and did not throw legal terms at Jason the way the other attorneys he'd interviewed had. Jason wrote out the retainer check, signed the contract, then looked over the desk at Bruce.

"Ok, counselor, where do I go from here?"

Bruce looked at the check, folded it in half, and put it in his shirt pocket. "Don't make waves."

The metaphor stumped Jason. "What does that mean?"

Bruce shrugged and put an open hand in the air. "Just lay low. We'll get the property settlement out of the way, first. We'll handle the matter of custody later."

"What property?"

Bruce looked down at the legal-sized yellow pad where he'd written his notes. "Well, there's your cottage up North, the $174,000 worth of stocks and bonds your father-in-law gave you two that's in your trust fund for Brandon. The cars, your piano and library. Material possessions of that sort."

Something felt wrong to Jason. His aching gut warned him of how humiliatingly little he knew about law and divorce and custody cases.

"Is that how it's done? I mean, it seems to me that the matter of custody should come first."

Bruce folded his hands together in front of him. "Trust me. I'm the attorney. I told you. I've done these kinds of cases before."

Jason scowled. "Have you won by not making waves?"

Bruce leaned smugly back in his chair resting his hands on his stomach. "Making no waves is a simple matter of presenting the right image to the Judge. I think, for starters, you ought to shave off that beard of yours, stop wearing those Beatnik hippy turtlenecks, and wear a suit and tie to court-- look more like a businessman."

Jason was perplexed. "Hold it. I play rock 'n roll piano--I'm not a businessman."

Bruce ushered him out of the office. "That's a bad image to have in a custody suit, Jason, believe me. A word to the wise."

'Reality', as Jason had understood it, disappeared. Several months later in the hallway of Bruce's Ypsilanti office, Bruce strode up to Jason, grabbed him by the wrist, and said.

"How much do you want for him?" Jason was dumbfounded. He shook his head, not understanding. "What?"

Bruce smiled and looked apprehensive. "How much money do you want for your son? The other side wants to make a cash offer for him."

Jason felt like he been kicked in the groin. He glared at Bruce."You want me to sell my own son?"

Bruce shrugged and put both of his hands in his pockets. "That's their offer. It's done sometimes in these kinds of cases."

"You've got to be kidding. I can't believe that's coming from Russet. She knows me better--far better--than that."

Bruce shrugged, exasperated. "It's their offer."

Jason was floored. "Do men actually do this?"

Bruce shrugged again. "Some do."

Jason felt nauseated. *Brandon as chattel? Selling Brandon like a slave?* He glared at Bruce. "Bullshit. Not this father. Tell them--whoever the hell they are that said this to you–tell them they can sit on their fucking thumbs and spin. My son is not for sale at any price, period."

Several weeks later Jason, still dressed in a turtleneck shirt and still sporting his goatee, sat across the desk from Bruce. Jason had spent hours wracked in anguish leading to a decision. He had carefully weighed the likelihood of Russet's health ever improving against the likelihood of her getting sicker as time passed. He had weighed his memories of her from nine years before, when they met in the poetry class, against the Russet who was now living with a junkie in a drug hotel. The comparison was stunning. He had made up his mind.

"Bruce, I've decided we should go for custody first, then worry about the property settlement later. It's the only thing that makes any logical sense to me, and I think I can--and should --be given custody of Brandon."

Bruce leaned back in his large executive chair and loosened his blue silk tie. "Ok. I have to inform that you don't have much of a chance going that route. Remember. it's a winner-take-all proposition. You either win custody or you don't. There's nothing in between. You don't have much of a chance."

Jason's stomach went empty. "Huh? Why not? I'm his father."

Bruce wagged his head. "True. But that doesn't mean you'll win custody. Being his father isn't much of an argument."

It made no sense to Jason. *Fathers weren't important?* Jason scowled. "What?"

Bruce leaned forward and rested his elbows on the desk. His coat sleeve slipped down and revealed his gold Seiko wristwatch. He sighed wearily, the way parents sigh when dealing with an unreasonable child. "As your attorney, I'm duty-bound to warn you that fathers sometimes have a lot of trouble winning custody these days. It's not like in the old days when fathers literally owned their children. The tide has changed." Bruce looked over Jason's shoulder towards the rows of scarlet-red law books on the wall. "And winning custody is expensive--very expensive."

"Why?"

"Why? Because of the amount of time I have to put in preparing the case."

"What are the odds?"

"The odds for you--or any father--winning custody are about ten to one against you."

Jason's stomach cramped. What Bruce said seemed unreal. It made absolutely no sense. "What? Why in heaven's name should fathers have trouble winning custody of their own kids?"

Bruce sat back and started to file his nails. "Oh, the judges seem to think that a father's job is making money; a mother's job is raising the kids. And the new feminists have some pretty nasty things to say about men, much less men raising children. Everybody knows that raising children is a woman's job, a job for which they are uniquely qualified by nature, whereas we men are good at sports, wars, making money, and protecting our women folk. At any rate, I know that's how Judge Dunning--our Judge – thinks. He's a good Catholic boy, you know."

Jason felt insulted by Bruce's old-fashioned picture of reality. "Bullshit--those are outlandish conventionalized images of women and men. Pure stereotypical garbage–the stuff I heard years ago from my parents. There's at best only a shred of reality in those stereotypes."

Bruce sighed, and leaned forward and clasped his hands before his chest. "It's the way Dunning thinks, Jason, like it or not. Who raised you, your father or your mother?"

What is this? Jason thought, *an inquisition?* "They both did."

Bruce folded his fingers together and smirked. "But it was mostly your mother, right?"

Jason ground his teeth and snarled at the indignity of Bruce's assertion. "My father worked--he had to work to support the family. But he was home a lot and played with me and did tons of things with me and would have done tons more, but he got killed in an accident. He could have easily raised me had something happened to my mom."

Bruce forced a smile and said nothing.

Jason stood, put both hands on the desk, and leaned forward. "This makes no logical sense. I think I should have an awfully good case according to the 1970 Child Custody Act in Michigan you showed me, Bruce."

Bruce stopped filing his nails and met Jason's intense gaze. "Why?"

"I've told you. For one thing, Russet's unpredictable health. One factor of the act reads. 'The mental and physical health of the parties involved,' right? I should be able to win my case hands down on that factor alone."

Bruce put away his nail file in a desk drawer and shook his head. "Logic and realities, eh? What matters is who best fits the image a particular judge has of fathers and mothers--that's what rules the world of the court system."

Jason's face suddenly felt like a crumpled paper bag. "That's bullshit--that's undiluted mindless bullshit."

Bruce's patience with his rebellious client was wearing thin. Bruce threw his hands up in frustration and growled. "It's reality. Better learn to live with it, like it or not. You're the father, get your ass out there and make some money. You've got to appear to be able to support your son."

Jason sat down and shook his head. "I can support him. I'm a professional musician, and have a Ph.D."

"So does Russet."

What the hell is going on? I'm fighting with my own attorney, why? He should be on my side Why the debate? Why are we arguing, why this war within the custody war?

"But she's not a professional musician and she's sick all the time. Her disease sometimes makes her into–what would you call it?--a mental case, too. Those suicide attempts aren't the acts of a rational mind."

Bruce smiled grimly to himself. He had an immature dolt on his hands that knew nothing about the real world, much less the realities of law. "The judge may order alimony for her because of her illness. He's going to feel very, very sorry for her, and figure you to be a bastard for leaving her."

Jason jumped up, put his hands on his hips, and shouted. "Wait just one fucking goddamn minute, Bruce. First, I didn't 'leave' her. She left me. And second, she left Brandon--who is now almost four years old--with me--not the other way around. You've got it backwards and inside out." Bruce shrugged. "Maybe. But no one's going to believe you. Just doesn't fit into the usual picture."

Jason seethed. "Fuck usual pictures. This isn't a usual situation. I'm telling you the truth, damnit."

Bruce gritted his teeth, shook his head and smirked. "The truth is what you can get people to believe, Jason. Understand?"

Jesus Christ, Jason thought, *something's insane, something's all wrong, something's gone totally haywire, something's totally wrong with these ideas. This feels like I have been somehow transported into another dimension in another universe run by utter maniacs.* "And I gave her money to live on until her job started in August."

"You shouldn't have done that."

Jason grimaced. His pianist's hand became gnarled fists. "Why?"

"That shows your willingness and ability to pay her alimony--that's why."

Jason threw his hands up in the air. "Hell, Bruce, she was broke and needed the money. I did the right thing."

Bruce sighed. "In this business, Jason, doing the right thing can get you into all sorts of trouble."

"Huh? Wait a second. If I hadn't given her money, I would've been labeled a bastard and a piker. What is this game, 'heads I lose, tails I lose'?"

Bruce shrugged and studied the backs of his hands. "Jason, toughen up. There's rough waters ahead."

The skirmishes began. Through their attorneys, Jason and Russet exchanged interrogatories about property. Their attorneys wrote each other letters. There were interviews with the Friend of the Court worker about who had worked during the marriage and who had cared for Brandon as an infant—namely, Jason on both scores.

Jason explained Russet's uncontrollable diabetes to the worker, an old woman with a wrinkle-lined face, gray hair, and a mouth full of chewing gum, who nodded her head as he spoke, but took no notes. The worker recommended that Russet be given total custody of Brandon. To make things worse, Jason's boss at The Campus Hotel said that Jason's contract there would terminate on Labor Day. "Another career down the drain," Jason moaned on the telephone to Ariadne, his friend and drinking buddy. "It's not been a good year."

"What are you going to do?"

Jason began to scribble on the yellow legal pad by his phone. The line began at the middle of the page, towards the top, wandered around until it intersected itself, then went on around the page, aimlessly. "Keep a stiff upper lip and fight on, as my dad used to say."

"You can't pay goddamn bills with upper lips. What are you going to do?"

He let the point of his ball point pen go its way towards the right side of the page, then back towards the center, then up, then back down through itself into a tight knot. "Get another job, fight for Brandon."

"You're not going to win, you know. That's the way society is. Mothers always get custody. And the judges are goddamn assholes. I know. I'm divorced now, remember, and my husband got screwed in the property settlement. If we'd had kids, I would've won custody."

Jason doodled. "My case isn't about money. This is a custody case."

"I know. But you can't win–there's no goddamn way you can win."

He grabbed the pen in his fist and dug it into the page watching it draw a tornado shape in the midst. "I've got to fight for him. Who the hell else in the universe is going to do it? And I am going to win. I always win--I always fight for what I want, and I never give up until I get it. My father got killed and I worked and won fellowships to put me through graduate school and made tons of money playing piano in joints; I love Brandon terribly. I want to be his parent. You just can't beat a love that deep and powerful."

"Love? What does love have to do with reality? The goddamn odds are all against you. You told me that your asshole attorney said the odds were ten to one against you, didn't you?"

"Yes. But there's got to be a way."

"What?"

He put his pen down. "I don't know. But if one doesn't exist now, I'll create it."

"Jason. Forget the goddamned dramatic stuff. Go get a job."

"Doing what?'

"Hell, I don't know. Just do it."

He put the phone down, looked at the confusion of lines on the pad, and felt the kind of terror he had felt, years ago just before he jumped off the high dive on a raft in the middle of a lake. It had been a ten-foot jump, but had looked like 30 feet before he jumped, off balance, twisting awkwardly in mid-air, and smacking into the water sideways. He had hurt for days after that foolhardy leap, and had sworn to himself that never again would he attempt to do something dangerous he didn't know how to do. It was just as stupid as the time he'd stood up on his bicycle seat and let go and crashed, chin-first on the sidewalk. Foolishness. But now, he had no choice whatsoever. He was going to jump into the war for Brandon, knowledge or not, and take whatever pain and punishment he had to take to get the job done.

The Friend of the Court recommendation infuriated Jason. Two months before, there had been a Referee's Hearing at the Friend of the Court on the matter of Brandon's custody. Jason had prepared Bruce for the hearing with a monograph of arguments and documents.

The combatants squared off on either side of a long table in a small room with bare ash-gray cinder block walls. The Referee and court reporter sat at one end on Jason's right. Bruce nodded to the transcriptionist and looked directly across the table at Russet, who was seated next to her attorney, Sally Golding, an attractive woman in her early 30s with streaked blond hair.

Russet was sworn to tell the whole truth so help her God and Bruce started. "You alleged in your Petition for an Ex Parte order, did you not, Mrs.

Adams, that your husband had 'never' cared for his son?"

Russet's face was impassive. She wore no make up and willed herself to appear innocently confused and defenseless.

"I believe my attorney wrote that."

Bruce saw through the guise. "No doubt. But it is just as true that you signed them."

Russet said nothing.

Bruce pulled some papers off the desk. His tone of voice was matter-of-fact. "May I introduce for the Referee and the record these Polaroid photographs, apparently taken by you, Mrs. Adams. Would you please identify these? I believe your handwriting is on the back of them, identifying the date and times of these photographs showing Mr. Adams bottle-feeding Brandon. Would you please verify that you took these photographs and that it is your handwriting on the back of them?"

Bruce handed the photographs to Russet. She looked at them briefly, then began to shiver slowly, and then violently, as if she was having an insulin reaction. The Referee and Russet's attorney moved quickly to her assistance, and the Hearing ended without Bruce and Jason presenting to the Referee the rest of the evidence regarding Russet's ill heath that Jason had assembled.

Bruce had the ashen look of a man who had just seen a cadaver. "What was that? What happened to her?" he asked Jason in the hallway.

Jason stared back. "It looked like an insulin reaction."

Bruce shook his head, trying to process the conflicting information. "You say 'looked like.' Are you implying that it was something else, like, say, a heart attack or stroke?"

Jason shook his head. "No, Bruce. It's hard for me to believe, but I think she may have faked it."

Bruce's jaw dropped. "Faked? Sure was effective. Are you sure? I mean, how could anyone fake that?"

Jason put a hand on Bruce's shoulder, wondering how the bizarre reality of diabetes manipulated by a brilliant mind could be logically explained to anyone. "She's terribly bright--and terribly sick. Sometimes, it almost seems as if she uses her disease to control people."

Bruce put a hand to his cheek and scratched. "Hmm. That's interesting."

"What the hell does that mean?"

"Well, it's possible but, I'm afraid, rather fanciful."

Jason grabbed Bruce's shoulder. "Jesus Christ, Bruce, listen to me. She can't control her body because of her insanely unpredictable diabetes. But ironically because of the unpredictable diabetes she can have enormous control over the people in her life. Everyone wants to protect her, everyone wants to rescue her and she knows it."

"Including you?"

Jason flinched. The truth stung. "Not any more. The only person who needs me to rescue them is Brandon, period."

Bruce looked off down the hall at a small crowd of people huddled around Russet. "Sure was effective."

Jason leaned back against the cold wall. "Yeah, I know--believe me, I know."

The referee refused to reschedule the aborted hearing and recommended that Russet be granted full custody of Brandon. The Friend of the Court followed suit and recommended that Jason's visitation be changed from every other day to every weekend, Friday night through Sunday evening "so that the Defendant might attend his employment."

The wheels of justice had turned.

Jason fought back, raided a retirement account, and bought a home, a modest three-bedroom gray ranch built on a slab near Bahr Park, in a neighborhood of similar homes. An infinitely more preferable place for raising Brandon than Russet's apartment in downtown Ann Arbor.

On his weekends with Jason, Brandon played on the playground equipment at nearby Bahr Park or with a boy about Brandon's age named 'Andy' on Andy's next-door swing set, or in Jason's back yard. The yard had a miniature crab-apple tree and bushes and trees around it for hideouts. When the weather was bad, Brandon played in his room with an erector set and other toys Jason bought him, or listened to his father play piano in the living room.

Jason simultaneously relished and was terrified by his power over a vulnerable child. Everything was a discovery for Brandon, everything seemed important to him; and everything had meaning for Brandon that Jason's adult mind couldn't fully understand.

Jason reached back into his childhood for the experiences he remembered sharing with his father—playing catch, playing tag, playing hide 'n seek, singing silly songs—and added his own style to the memory thereby reliving his own childhood in his own way, and soothing old wounds.

Jason sat on his bed mulling over his perplexing role as Brandon's father, waiting for Brandon to come into the bedroom to say good night. "Being a parent is a second chance to grow up--right?" one of Jason's psychology teachers had once said and Jason wondered if he could really somehow change the child inside himself by raising Brandon. It was a mystifying psychological proposition.

At that moment Brandon appeared by Jason's side with an armful of stuffed toy animals, ran back into his bedroom and returned carrying more. Brandon climbed over Jason's knees, lay down in the large double bed, looked up expectantly at his father.

Jason guessed at the thought lurking behind Brandon's unblinking brown eyes and grinned down on him and the zoo of stuffed animals in a pile at the foot of the bed. "Ok, you can go to sleep here, but—by magic--you're going to wake up in your own bed," Jason said.

"'K," Brandon said, and snuggled down next to his father's pillow. Jason caught himself ready to repeat the bedtime prayer of his childhood---"now I lay me down to sleep, I pray the Lord my soul to keep. If I die before I wake, I pray the Lord my soul to take"—and stopped himself. Death? Sleep and death somehow related? Why scare Brandon with Jason's childhood prayer? Instead, Jason reached down to the end of the bed and grabbed Mumbo, the fat, blue elephant with the knee-length floppy ears, rolling him up on his flat feet. Like a puppeteer manipulating Mumbo's limb, making Mumbo slowly lumber—"a-thump, a-thump, a-thump" Jason said --up Brandon's covered legs, over his stomach and chest to land, trunk-first—"thump!"--right on Brandon's hysterically giggling face.

This is great fun—no threats of death and dying here, Jason thought.

Next came Boom-Bam the Bear, who rumbled laboriously up Brandon's torso and lurched heavily forward, plop, right on Brandon's right cheek, Jason saying "Grrrrr, Grrrrr, Grrrrr!"—as Brandon howled with joy.

Next came Petula, the Pretty Pink Parrot, who wobbled—"screech! screech! screech!"-- high above Brandon's head, then fluttered down to perch momentarily on his elfin chin before pecking him----"rata-tat-tat!"—on his tiny red lips.

Last Rudy the Rocking Reindeer rose up on hind legs at the base of the bed, pranced about over and around Brandon's legs, bounced merrily off his stomach, fell down, rolled over on Brandon's chest, righted himself and sauntered into Brandon's face, rubbed their noses together, Jason laughing "nose-nose-nose," as they did.

Brandon laughed, and laughed, and wanted more. Finally, Jason kissed him goodnight on the forehead, and Brandon fell asleep next to Jason hugging Rudy the Rocking Reindeer.

Later, Jason picked Brandon up and carefully carried him next door, to his own bed.

When the divorce began, Russet and Jason stopped cooperating and Brandon was the loser. During the week while Russet worked, Jason discovered that she left Brandon at a childcare center in the dirty, junky, basement of a Presbyterian church in town, an understaffed and slovenly program.

Jason called her on it. "Hey, Russet, there are much better daycare centers in town than the one you've got Brandon in. If it's money, I'll help."

Her attorney had warned Russet about such interference with her custodial authority. "No."

More interference.

"Why?"

The soft edges to her voice vanished and in their place there was substituted a cool, metallic quality. "Just no. I have temporary custody. His care is my responsibility; your responsibility is to visit him and pay your child support. It's my decision to make, my attorney says."

Jason's temper flew into his mouth. He had had it with strangers pushing him around."Fuck your attorney. Brandon is our son, We make decisions for him, not your attorney."

The phone went dead.

Something was wrong. Jason went to the daycare center one day, unannounced, and discovered that it was Curt Diamond who was providing the 'day care' for Brandon.

Jason called Ariadne.

"What's up?" she said.

"Nothing's up. I'm down, way down.."

"Huh?"

"Russet's boyfriend is caring for Brandon every day."

"Well, I guess that's better than a stranger, isn't it?"

"You're missing the point. Please understand this. I now know that anyone on the street--even a stranger--has more right to be with and care for my son than do I. I mean, there he is, my only son, right in front of me, and I am not allowed to care for him? It's absolutely insane. Russet's boyfriend has more right to be with Brandon than I do? What? Where's the justice in that? Where?"

"Sounds awful."

Jason slammed his fist down on the night table..

"It feels almost as if I have been, somehow, just erased from Brandon's life, as if I have no rights as his father, as if somehow the world views me as *persona non grata*--a human being no one wants to exist in the world anymore."

There was a long silence. "Come on over, my friend. I'll buy you a goddamn beer. You can cry on my shoulder. I owe you one."

"Jesus, Ariadne, I'm not going to be good company at all. I mean–I mean I can't–I can't explain this feeling–it's--."

"Just come on over."

"And do what?"

"We'll see. Just come on over, lover."

He stood up and cocked his head. "Huh? I'm not your lover? We agreed to be friends."

"That was months ago. You're an important person to me. Just come on over."

They drank many beers together on the front porch, got drunk, and came inside. Jason sat down next to her on the couch in her small apartment living room. After her divorce she had rented the apartment to be closer to the campus and her part-time work as a departmental secretary. They occasionally met there to drink coffee and commiserate, as friends, over the miseries of their respective lives.

But this night was different. Clearly, Ariadne was drunk and wanted more than just friendship. She rubbed his leg, put her arm around him. She said that her bedroom was just behind the wall behind the couch. Her face was close to him. He smelled her D'Orforio perfume and felt the heat of her desire. He turned to putty inside.

"Hey, Ariadne, you're a beautiful woman and you—you've been a terrific friend to me all these months, but you've gotta understand that I'm not free. Not really free."

She sat slightly back from him, but kept her hand on his leg.

"Because you're still in love with the goddamn redhead?"

"No."

She turned her head and looked up at him from under her eyebrows, her green eyes watery and searching.

"Because I remind you of her because she and I were–used to be--goddamn friends?

Jason didn't move.

"No. Because of Brandon. He comes with me, and I don't think you want to be his mom and get into that bag, right?"

She jumped up, lost her balance, and fell back down next to him on the couch. Her face was florid and there was spittle at the corners of her mouth "Goddamn you, Jason, you're a fucking romantic asshole with not a fucking shred of common sense."

Jason stood, pointed at her, and screamed. "And you're a drunken sot with no heart."

She broke down and cried.

He wobbled out the door. They never saw each other again.

III

The financial tide turned. In August Jason landed a job selling life insurance with New York Insurance Company, that let him play out his contract at The Campus Hotel. Meanwhile, Jason shifted gears and learned how to sell life insurance. As was his style, he was an exceptional student, and by December, 1973, he had sold more than $1,000,000.00 of face-value life insurance. About half of that million was for cash-value life insurance on the lives of the two children of Addy Svengal, the woman who was later to become Jason's second wife, whom he had met at a New Year's Eve party the year before.

The invitation to the party came out of an accidental meeting. Melanie, a black-haired, buxom waitress at The Falls had come up to him on the street the week before New Year's, 1972. Melanie looked at him knowingly, as if he had been a lover.

"Hey, Jason, what's new? The scuttlebutt is that you 'n your wife have split--that you threw 'er out on her ass."

How do I fight this nonsense? Jason thought, *How the hell do I kill a rumor?* He stood in front of Melanie and looked as innocent as he could.

"That's not true--I mean, we've separated, but I didn't 'throw her out.' She walked out under her own power with a check from me in her purse." Melanie clasped her hands together.

"Well, you know, I mean, that's the story."

"Believe me, I know that's the story."

She had heard him play piano many nights at The Falls, and admitted to herself that she had fantasies of him doing the beautiful things he did to the piano to her body. She adjusted her bra, and gave him a come-hither look.

"Oh well. Hey, look, I'm havin' a little New Year's get-together at my pad. Why don't you just drop by next weekend. Ok?"

He watched her full breasts settle back into their bra cups.

"Who's gonna be there?"

"Oh, people, you know. . . folks. You ain't got nowhere to go."

"What the hell, why not?"

Jason arrived at the party and got a drink and chatted lamely with people he didn't know about politics, the weather, and sports. He looked around Melanie's red-draped apartment with second-rate paintings of nude women. He thought about polite ways he could leave.

A brunette, brown-eyed woman, stylishly dressed like a New York fashion model, locked her eyes on his from across the room. He returned the look, guessing her to be a few years younger than he, then went back to chatting with the somewhat inebriated man next to him. Then, out of the fog of his somewhat drunk vision to his left, she came up to him, sat down next to him, smiled warmly, and extended her hand.

"Hello there, handsome, my name's Addy Svengal."

She had a monstrous ring full of diamonds on her left hand that flashed in the dim light of the room like night lightning far out at sea. Jason stared at the ring.

"Jason Adams. Pleased to meet you. That's a gorgeous ring."

She beamed at him and lingered on his hand. "Thanks. It was my mom's. She passed away last year."

"Sorry."

Addy's light brown eyes glistened with curiosity in the shadowy light. To her Jason was boyishly charming, new to her, and she found herself magnetized by his presence. "Where're you from?" she asked.

"The East coast. You name it, I've probably lived there. I came here as a graduate student in 1963 and taught English at the University after I got my Ph.D. in 1970." She nodded, keeping her eyes on his.

"A brain, eh? I used to teach grade school English. Years ago. A bummer. You still teach?"

"No. I'm now making my living as a pianist. I play at The Campus Hotel."

She kept glowing at him, beckoning him. "Oh, really--a piano player?"

"Yup. A piano player."

She pulled both hands along her sides up towards her ample breasts, clasped her hands together and traced the outlines of her ring.

"Do you like French food?"

"Huh?"

His response seemed to delight her and she laughed. She beamed at him. "I love to cook, and I like men who like food. Do you like gourmet food?"

"I like food. As a matter of fact, I also enjoy cooking."

"You do? Groovy. Do you play bridge?"

"Not really. Hey, am I am being interviewed for something here?"

Her eyes continued to fix on his

"Maybe. I think we have things in common."

Jason lit a cigarette and tried to shift the level of conversation. He was not happy talking with a married woman who was clearly interested in him.

"You still teach school?"

"No. Quit years ago. I told you. "

"So, what are you doing now?"

She pointed over her shoulder.

"Philip--my husband--he's sitting over there talking with Melanie--my husband and I run a party store over on Elm Street. We just bought it. It's a crummy business and we're having a shitload of trouble with our advertising people. We can't seem to get them off their dead asses."

Jason heard the distant sound of a cash register.

"What kind of advertising are you talking about?"

"Oh, some direct-mail stuff."

"That's the kind I sorta did once in high school. A push over."

Her eyes remained fastened on his.

"Maybe you could help me write it?"

"Maybe. Besides playing piano, I do have the doctorate in English, like I said."

She sipped at her red wine, never taking her glistening eyes off him. There was something boyishly alluring about him, about the way he laughed, the way he cocked his head, the way he talked.

"So, when do you play?"

"Monday through Saturday, 7:00 to 10:00 in the evenings. Do you like rock 'n roll?"

"I guess so. Can I come by to hear you, maybe show you the crummy advertising crap we've got, on your breaks?"

What the hell, Jason thought, as he glanced over at Phillip, who was bug-eyed drunk.

"Sure. Any night."

Addy struck Jason as a paradoxically sophisticated yet rough-hewn, gorgeous and earthy, probably more intelligent than most women and as sensual as the Biblical Jezebel. For some reason she was more than mildly interested in him. But he reminded himself she was married. There being no other 'free' women there besides Melanie, who was a hooker, Jason excused himself, left the party early and forgot the encounter.

Addy did not. A few weeks later, she showed up at The Campus Hotel and collared Jason at the bar at the end of his job. She was smartly dressed in an expensive Saks Fifth Avenue brown business suit; her hair tied up in a stylish bun. Her eyes glistened. They sat together at the polished bar facing rows of liquor bottles and an ornately rimmed mirror.

She riveted him with her eyes and reached out her hand, showing off the gigantic diamond ring.

"Remember me? Addy Svengal?"

"Yes."

"I filed for divorce. Will you buy me a drink? I'm a mess."

Jason rested both elbows on the bar.

"Oh-oh. I think I've heard that song before."

She laughed.

"Then you know I'm ripe for the pickin'. Let's have a belt and shoot the shit about the good old days. Ok, Tarzan?"

"Ok, Jane," Jason played along. He knew with the certainty of the setting sun that the night had just begun.

He was right. It was the early 1970s, the era of the pill and abortion on demand. They were both at moments in their lives where saying 'no' to one another or playing cute courting games was silly. An hour or so later they wound up in a nearby Holiday Inn hotel for the night.

The next morning Addy called room service for coffee before he woke. Dressed in her bra and panties she bent over him and nuzzled his cheek and woke him up.

"Grrrr," she purred, "up 'n at 'em, tiger. We've got java."

"Mornin'," Jason said. He rolled over, sat up, reached for his cigarettes and brushed her breast with his arm. He foggily took in the bland, brown-walled room with its prosaic tan drapes and Formica table tops, and foggily remembered how he'd gotten where he was.

"Mornin' lover," Addy chirped, "Whatta we doin' today?"

"Weeell," Jason groaned, "I should go back to my apartment, pay some bills, and then go get Brandon for a visit this afternoon."

She grinned at him.

"How old's Brandon?"

He reached over to the night table and took a sip of his coffee from the plastic cup, and glanced at Addy's long, shapely legs.

"He's almost four. His mother left me about a year ago, and we're not divorced yet. A damned mess."

She put her hand lightly on his shoulder.

"She left you? Is she crazy?"

"No. Confused, physically sick, but not crazy."

She stretched her arms above her head.

"I've got custody of my kids--Andria and Bobby. Went to court last week with my attorney, filed and bam, it was over. Phillip didn't stand a chance."

Jason took another sip of his coffee and took a deep drag on his cigarette. A vague picture of bug-eyed Phillip flashed through his memory.

"Is he a boozer? I mean, he sure looked four sheets to the wind at Melanie's party."

She frowned.

"Booze is his middle name. Night and day. But there's a reason. Poor guy. His family was once one of the richest families in Lithuania and they freakin' lost it all."

"Huh? What happened?"

"The Nazis took the country and killed his parents. He spent part of his childhood in concentration camps."

Jason grimaced.

"Jesus. He lost his childhood. Not pretty. No wonder he drinks."

"He drinks all the time, like I said."

Jason brushed some of his long, dirty-blond hair away from his eyes, sipped at his coffee. He was slightly hungover and his mind wasn't functioning yet.

"So, what'd you think of my piano boogie-woogie last night?"

She put a hand to the side of her head and looked off somewhere.

"Fabulous--just fabulous."

Oh-oh, Jason thought, *a teenybopper disguised as a major movie star. She makes no sense. This broad is pushy--how the hell did I get myself in this mess?*

He rubbed the stubble on his cheek.

"Thanks. Look. . . I didn't bring my razor with me, and I feel sorta grubby, so. . . ."

Addy laughed, reached into her purse at the foot of the bed, and handed him a packaged razor blade and can of shaving cream. "I'm way ahead of you. You've got to learn how to plan things ahead, lover. Boy do you ever need a woman."

Jason went into the bathroom, shaved, showered, and returned to the lukewarm coffee at the bedside.

Addy had gotten dressed in a rich brown-green-yellow plaid business suit and was standing near the dresser putting her lipstick on.

He stood by her, buttoned his shirt and looked at her eyes in the mirror.

"So, want to grab a quick lunch?"

She shook her head.

"No time today. I've got to get to the store after noon to take care of it. My mother--even though she's dead as a doorknob--would kill me if I didn't. It was her loot that bought the place."

Jason put his wallet into his pants pocket, and slipped on his wristwatch.

"What did you mother do for a living?"

Addy kept dabbing on her lipstick and checking it in her mirror.

"She--like her mother--never worked a freakin' day in her life. She was a, you know, heiress to the family fortune."

"What does your father do?"

She put her mirror back into her purse, looked up, smiled at him, and sat down on the bed.

"He's a brilliant man, and a university professor like you. He loves the loot he inherited when my mom died, 'specially when the stock split three ways."

Jason stood, yawned, and glanced at his wristwatch.

"Three ways? Wow. So, you're *nouveau riche?*"

Her smile was polite.

"I guess you could, you know, say that. Whatever it means."

She suddenly started to cry.

Jason put his arms around her.

"What's wrong?"

Addy blew her nose and lit a cigarette. He kept his arm around her.

"I was, you know, miserable in that marriage. Were you miserable in your marriage. too?"

"No. And yes."

"Huh?"

He kept his arm around her.

"I loved--and in a way still love--Russet. But she's got a disease–diabetes--and the damn thing is eating her alive, day-in, day-out. It's the disease that made me miserable, not her."

Addy got up from the bed, looked towards the door to their room, and turned to him.

"Phillip has a disease too. He's a drunk, and I hate him for it. But I love my two children, Andria and Bobby, deeply. Do you love your son?"

"With all my heart."

She turned to him and put her hands on his shoulders.

"Would you like to meet my kids?"

"I–I don't. . . ."

"Phillip's long gone. Moved his ass out. He won't be there. Want to come to my house and meet my kids? Won't be any trouble, I promise."

"Well–Ok. Sure."

She wrote down her address on the back of one of her business cards and handed it to him.

"And meet my father?"

He took the card from her and put it in his wallet.

"Sure. . .I'd like to meet your kids and your dad."

Jason looked at Addy's full breasts, light brown eyes, and remembered their soft night of passion with an odd mixture of expectation and depression--like the feeling you have when you realize that the train in which you have just settled down is headed at breakneck speed to the wrong destination and there's nothing to do but wait for the next stop.

"I'll be there," he said at the door.

Jason and Addy gradually became a couple, although neither of them really knew why they had been drawn to each other and why it was that there seemed to be no way for them to go but straight ahead. They went out to dinner every Sunday, sometimes with the three children, sometimes not. They took turns sleeping together at each other's homes. They drank beer and wine together. They went dancing. They went for long car rides looking at houses, pretending to dream of a future.

"I wanna get married again, do you?" Addy said as they drove along in Jason's 1973 AMC Gremlin sedan.

"Maybe. Why?"

"To have a home again, a place to call home."

He glanced over and grinned.

"And a white picket fence?"

"Oh, come on! Ride with me on this one. Ok?"

"Ok. Just for the hell of it."

"For the hell of it."

"Look at that," Jason said, and stopped the car on the dirt road in front of what looked like a new, two-story home sitting back from the road. There was a 'for sale' sign on the manicured front lawn.

Addy looked.

"Sure looks big."

He scowled and did some quick calculations.

"Probably--oh, 3,000 square feet, wouldn't you say? And probably costs mucho bucks."

She moved over and put her head next to his and looked out the window with him.

"Easy. But I like it. It looks down to earth and not snooty like the dumb-ass palace my father blew a wad on after my mom kicked the bucket."

"Down to earth--like you," Jason grinned, and patted Addy's knee.

She traced the inside of his leg towards his crotch.

"Betcha it's got a big master bedroom."

He ran his fingertips across the top of her hand. She grinned at him.

"And at least four bedrooms. I'm gonna give the realtor a call."

"You're kidding."

She squeezed the inside of his leg.

"What the hell. Why not?

The trial for the custody of Brandon, now five, was in August, 1974 and lasted three days. On the final day the courtroom was empty except for the Judge, the Bailiff, the clerk, the court reporter, and Jason, Russet and their two attorneys.

The trial cost Jason every cent he had for attorney fees and for the expert medical testimony of several physicians the preceding two days and, most particularly, that of Jason's final expert witness, Dr. Marsh.

"Call your final witness," Judge Dunning said, and Dr. Marsh was sworn in..

"Good morning, doctor," Bruce smiled, flashing his white teeth.

"Good morning," Dr. Marsh replied, expressionless.

"With regards to factor 'g' of The Michigan Child Custody Act, namely, 'the mental and physical health of the parties involved,' the Plaintiff, Mrs.

Adams has a chronic illness, does she not?" Bruce smiled.

Dr. Marsh looked from side to side in the empty courtroom. Clearly uncomfortable in his role as witness. He cleared his throat.

"Ahem. Mrs. Adams, has a form of diabetes called 'juvenile-onset diabetes."

"Please explain to the court," Bruce said with his back to the witness stand, "what juvenile-onset diabetes is." Bruce said.

Dr. Marsh adjusted his navy blue bow tie, glanced at Russet, clearing his throat several times.

"Ahem. It is a. . .a particularly virulent form of sugar diabetes. . .a metabolic disturbance, contracted before age 30. The Isle of Langerhans in the pancreas still secretes insulin, but does so in an unpredictable fashion."

"How is it monitored, er controlled?"

"Essentially, the disease is monitored with urine tests and is controlled by diet and U-80 Lente insulin injections."

"And food? Is food dangerous for Mrs. Adams?"

"Mrs. Adams must be careful about what she eats and drinks."

Bruce spun around and faced Dr. Marsh.

"What can happen if she does not watch her diet and insulin intake? Please be specific in your answer."

Dr. Marsh looked towards the ceiling and fiddled with his bow tie.

"The metabolic balance of her system may be disrupted."

Bruce smiled. He was a heavyweight boxer ready to strike.

"What kind of specific disruption can occur? Please be specific, doctor."

Dr. Marsh held his hands up before him and counted on his fingers.

"She may either suffer insulin reactions or their opposite. If she has an insulin reaction. . . an overabundance of insulin in the blood stream. . .she'll need carbohydrates immediately. . .a candy bar, a glass of fruit juice. If she does not get those carbohydrates in her blood stream she might drop into a diabetic coma, and could be dead in approximately 24 hours."

Bruce moved a step closer.

"What about the opposite?"

"If she built up too much sugar?"

"Yes. Please be specific."

Dr. Marsh looked directly at Bruce.

"She could be dead in about 48 hours if she is comatose with ketoacidosis and it goes untreated."

"How is this. . .keeto. . . ."

"Ketoacidosis."

". . .condition treated?"

Dr. Marsh studied the backs of his hands.

"She must be hospitalized and be given carefully monitored intravenous dosages of pure insulin and pure carbohydrates to bring the system back in balance."

"Are these two extremes of her disease predictable and thus controllable?"

Dr. Marsh looked up at the ceiling, away from Russet.

"Somewhat."

Bruce stared at Dr. Marsh.

"Somewhat. Does the disease negatively affect the thought processes of the diabetic?"

Dr. Marsh's face froze into an vacant mask.

"Sometimes it would appear so. But this is just like you and I getting short-tempered when we're hungry or groggy when we've had too much to eat."

Bruce took another step towards Dr. Marsh, and stopped.

"Or have had too much alcohol to drink?"

Dr. Marsh gave a quick, neutral, nod.

"It is possible. Too often diabetics in an insulin or acidic coma are mistaken for drunks and not given the medical treatment they need. Often, they die on street corners or in alleys because of this failure.'

Bruce took another, calculated step, towards Dr. Marsh, coming within striking distance.

"Could the unpredictable qualities of this disease represent a threat to the well-being of the child if your patient is out of control, Dr. Marsh?"

Russet's attorney, Sally Golding, was a tall, attractive woman with streaked blond hair in her early thirties. She jumped up from her seat and shouted.

"Objection. Calls for speculation."

Sally Golding, Bruce had told Jason, was one of the new 'gender feminist' attorneys who held that 'all the troubles in the world had been caused by men, were being caused by men, and would in the future be caused by men'. It had been clear to Jason from the contemptuous looks Golding had leveled at him from the beginning of the trial that she saw Jason as the very incarnation of her anti-male doctrine.

Bruce's face darkened.

"Your Honor, there have been two documented suicide attempts by Mrs. Adams. The child was with her and. . . ."

"Objection." shouted Ms. Golding, shaking her streaked hair up and down, her face florid, "calls for privileged doctor-patient records."

"There are also police records," Bruce countered, "if it please the court. . ."

Judge Dunning cupped his hand before a yawn and nodded.

"Yes, counselor. . ."

". . .we could subpoena those police records and I will be happy to brief the circumstances under which the doctor-client privilege can be waived. . ."

"Objection, Your Honor," Golding said, "That waiver obtains only in criminal cases. and this is anything but a criminal case. Furthermore, I believe. . ."

Judge Dunning's right eyebrow twitched, the ceiling light shone off his baldhead. He leaned forward and wagged his finger at Bruce.

"This court is not interested in unwarranted mud-slinging, counselor. Court time is expensive and we have already spent a fortune on this case without getting into tricky legal technicalities. Besides, we've had ample testimony that both parties are morally fit to be parents of their—ah--how old is she? How old is the child?"

"He," Bruce corrected. "He's four years old."

Judge Dunning's eyes clicked open with relief.

"Under 12 years old?"

"Yes, Your Honor. But I should respectfully remind the court that the Tender Years Doctrine went off the books in this state in 1970."

"Hm," Judge Dunning murmured. The trial ended five minutes later after a flurry of objections and counter-arguments with Judge Dunning announcing that because of 'docket pressures' the 'case was temporarily adjourned for judicial consideration'.

There were no more trial dates available, Golding was committed elsewhere, and Bruce's demands for considerable amounts of additional money crippled Jason into accepting an out-of-court settlement.

"Don't worry," Bruce assured Jason. "This is the deal most guys get with a specific provision for your particular case."

Three months later the judgment arrived. Russet was awarded full custody of Brandon. Jason was awarded 'reasonable' rights of visitation every other weekend, alternating holidays, six weeks in the summer, the obligation to pay child support, and a provision that anytime Russet was hospitalized Jason would have the first-choice care of Brandon. Jason was ordered to turn over the entirety of Brandon's trust fund and its management, to Russet. No alimony was ordered.

"It's over," Jason said to Addy as he read the judgment in the front room of his house. "Time to sell this place and get on with my life, such as it is. It sure looks like I won't have Brandon with me, like I dreamed."

Addy looked. Jason's face was palpably gray. She gently rubbed his back and sighed.

"That judge is an asshole, Jason. He's dead flat wrong. But maybe someday you'll get Brandon."

Jason glanced at her, then looked away.

"Someday. When's someday? Next week? Next year? Two thousand years from now?"

She rubbed his back.

"Soon. Let's sell your house and go in together on that house we looked at and shove it down their throats. There's no way Russet and her bum boyfriend can afford a place like that. Hell, let's buy the damn thing."

At the closing on Jason's house at Henry MacVicart's downtown Ann Arbor office, Sally Golding appeared, dressed in a navy-blue business suit with a white scarf around her neck. She waved some papers in the air.

"I have a court order here sighed by Judge Dunning that awards one half of the proceeds go to Mrs. Adams."

Jason felt liked he'd been clipped at the back of his head. He looked up from the desk.

"Why?"

Golding's face was blank. Her eyes were ice-cold.

"Her dower right to one-half of your lands and estate."

Jason shook his head no and sneered.

"Bullshit. She promised me when I bought the house that she wasn't going to do that."

Golding smiled contemptuously at him.

"She's changed her mind."

Jason slammed his hand on the desk and shouted.

"But we're divorced."

Golding handed him a packet of legal-sized papers.

"Here's the order. Read it. This portion of the property settlement was reserved in the Judgment of Divorce."

Jason read the papers, realized he'd been had, and wrote out a check for $5,000 from the profit he had just received for the sale of his home. It was financially crushing. He and Addy had planned to buy the home with a two-car garage on an acre of land in Victor Township. That dream was gone.

Addy had to pay the down payment on the new home herself.

Russet and Danny Forge used the $5,000 as a down payment on a ranch style, two-bedroom home two blocks away from Mandermetz Park. They moved Russet's furniture from her downtown apartment, bought new curtains on sale from Sears, and moved in together six months after the sale of Jason's house.

At the housewarming, Sally Golding was one of the invited group cramped together in the modestly furnished living room. Golding looked directly at Russet and Danny, beamed her best professional smile, and proclaimed. "Certainly is comfy, isn't it? I'm quite confident Brandon will just adore living here with you two love birds—away from you know who."

"The liar, ya mean?" Danny grinned.

"The so-called 'artist'?" said Armanda, a 35-year-old divorced woman who felt desperately sorry for Russet and venomously hated Jason, whom she'd never met, for what he'd done.

Mary Lou sat directly across from her daughter, Danny, and Golding. Mary Lou nodded her head approvingly and sipped at her tea. Brandon glanced over from the floor in front of the television set where he'd been seated all morning watching cartoons, said nothing, and went back to watching 'The Road Runner'.

Mary Lou glanced to her right at Brandon, nodded, and addressed Danny, whose crewcut, white shirt and blue jeans looked virtuous to Mary Lou. She smiled at Danny.

"Children should be seen and not heard, don't you agree?"

Danny grinned to himself, patted Russet's knee and smiled politely at his future mother-in-law.

"That's how I were raised, right at the bottom a that pile, and it sure dint hurt me. Just at the right plate at the right time, like they sezs."

Russet's face looked pale and drawn in the morning sunlight. She lifted her glasses and squinted over at Brandon, glanced at her mother, and then at Danny.

"'Place,' Danny dear, not 'plate.'"

Russet forced a smile at her mother—the woman who Russet was convinced had killed Larry.

"Danny's the youngest of eleven children."

Golding smiled to herself, her head held high. and focused her eyes on Mary Lou, who had signed all the checks for Golding's weighty legal fees.

"A good Catholic boy, just like our darling judge."

Mary Lou bowed her bun of gray hair and said nothing.

Danny, who was genuinely as naïve, patted Russet's hand and looked adoringly at her, the way choir boys look at statues of the Holy Virgin. His heart went out to her, for he believed that Russet was the sweetest woman in the world, an innocent victim of a violent man who had thrown her out of the apartment into the cold winter night with a little baby in her arms. That's what everyone else said, and that many people couldn't be wrong.

"A good Catholic boy," Mary Lou reiterated, and returned Golding's knowing look.

Brandon briefly wondered what it meant to be a good Catholic boy, thought it sounded like a good idea, better than a 'liar,' and went back to watching the roadrunner outsmart his antagonist once again

On the other side of town, Jason and Addy lay in bed together after dinner at Abby's house. The kids had gone to bed, the sun had set, all was quiet.

Jason's stomach ached like he'd eaten green apples as the enormity of the custody decision once again ate at his guts. His insides were being sliced, then chopped, then minced into tiny bits of bloody flesh flecked with bone. He stared at the ceiling and fought an impulse to scream. He gritted his teeth and suddenly sat up.

"I am going to fight back with an invisible counterattack. No matter what the court system tries to do to me and Brandon, I'll beat the system at its own phony scam by not playing the court game of attorneys and motions and pleadings and petitions and depositions and endless arguing, but by slowly, silently, creating the decent world of justice behind the scenes that Brandon deserves."

"How are you going to pull off this invisible gimmick of yours?" Addy asked and sat up next to him. .

He looked out the bedroom window into the merciless night.

"I don't know for sure. I just know I'm going to do it somehow."

Addy shifted in bed and put her head on his shoulder.

"Look. I'm not the brain you are, but I've got smarts."

Jason put his arm around her shoulder. She felt warm and soft, and smelled of her pungent hair spray. He pecked her on the forehead.

"I find you to be a very intelligent woman. That's one reason I'm here."

She pushed her soft body against him.

"And my boobs."

He squeezed her shoulder.

"Yes, your beautiful boobs. And your good heart and quick mind."

She looked at him. Her eyes were unblinking and intense.

"Whatever. I look at it this way. You're smart and you can write and play piano and you know a lot about insurance and arty things I don't know, right?"

"I. . . ."

She put her fingers lightly on his lips.

"Sssssh. Hear me out. That's one part. Another part is that my kids think you're the greatest thing since sliced bread, and you have a magic way with them I've just never seen, ever. You just know how to play with them and get them to behave and do what you want them to do and you don't smack 'em and shout or go bonkers like I do. And, for another part, Brandon and my kids get along just fine and they play together and told me they didn't understand why we all didn't just be a family together and be like the rest of the families in the world. Do you follow me?"

He looked at her.

"What's the point?"

Addy stood, bent over him, and laced her arms around his neck and her nose inches away from his.

"No point. A deal."

"Deal?"

She did not move her face. Her forearms were heavy on his shoulders.

"That's right, a deal. Here's the deal. You help me with the store and play piano gigs at night. You take care of Brandon and my kids like you've been doing. We live together in the house we wanted 'cause that asshole bitch attorney of your ex-wife screwed you. So, we make a family to shove up the asses of those highfalutin assholes in the court system. Between us, there's no way Russet and her asshole boyfriend can compete and, finally, you get custody of Brandon. That's how I see it, Jason-- practical, down-to-earth nut 'n bolts little' old me."

He returned her gaze.

"There's something missing out of your deal."

She unlaced her arms, stood back and looked confused.

"What?"

He turned his head away from her. The air was suddenly thick with stinging static electricity.

"There's not a chance in the world of me getting custody of Brandon or of us having a family unless we're married."

She beamed at him and put her hands slightly on his shoulders. She grinned radiantly at him, the way women smile at times when their world is about to actually transform into the dream of happiness they have sought since childhood.

"Right."

"Right?"

"Right, so--will you marry me?"

Jason stared at her.

"I don't have any money left to marry anyone, Addy."

She mussed his hair and ran her index finger down his nose.

"To hell with money. You'll make plenty of money once you get back on your feet and, anyway, I'll sure pay you for helping me with the store. Forget money. I've got plenty of that."

He looked her straight in the eyes. His ears rang; his mouth had gone dry, his heart palpitated the way it did when he was about to go on stage to perform.

"And love?"

She smiled at him, the way mothers smile at their suckling infants.

"Love? To hell with love. You married Russet for love, I married Phillip for love, and where the hell did that romantic crap get us? Jason, we been together for a couple of years now, screwing and loving and drinking and eating and laughing together. We're already married, so far's I'm concerned. So, there's the deal. It's a winner. Take it or leave it."

"No love? Just sex and friendship?"

She smiled at him, beatific.

"The love will come. Not a bad deal, my friend, not bad at all--no?"

Jason and Addy married in July of 1976, at the home that Addy, true to her word, had purchased. It was a split-level home, with five such levels, on two acres of grassy land, out in the country, about five miles from the downtown business section of Ann Arbor. The house sat on a secluded dirt road that ran around their rectangular block of upper-class homes, two acres apart, all of different, and costly, designs, in which doctors, architects, professors, and engineers lived with their wives, dogs, cats, and children of different ages.

Jason found himself magically bequeathed with a prefabricated new family--replete with two children, Andria, age eight, and Bobby, age four.

"The kids wanna call you 'daddy,' Jason," Addy said one night upstairs in their bedroom after dinner. She was posed at the long mirror doing her hair in the double-sink powder room that connected their bedroom with the toilet and shower, and she could see his reflection in the mirror before her.

Jason sat down on the side of the bed nearest her, untied one shoe and threw it over to the floor on his side of the bed where it landed with a loud thud.

"No."

She glanced over at him, paused, and went back to her hair.

"Why not? Phillip never comes to see 'em, and never pays his child support. They love you. They need a, you know, need a real father."

Jason untied his other shoe, threw it over to the floor on his side, and shook his head, thinking *the idea is insanity poured on top of insanity, fire on fire, and will only cause more problems, not cure them.*

"They have a father, Addy. I won't confuse them like that. It's not only unethical, it's dead flat untrue. I am not their father."

Addy turned her head and glared at him.

"You mean that you won't do to them what Russet and her crummy scuzball boyfriend are doin' to Brandon, right?"

"You'd better fuckin' believe it."

She stood, walked over and anchored herself before him.

"Suppose you adopted them?"

He looked up at her.

"That's an entirely different story. But I'm really going to have to think about that. Really think about it."

And think about it he did. For days.

He agonized over his motivation. *Would it be right for me to adopt Andria and Bobby just because they–and Addy–wanted me to? No. The decision was mine to make, and I could honestly take the kids to my heart, and love them as my own flesh and blood. Was that an ego trip? After all, they are Phillip's flesh and blood, not mine. Wasn't it utterly arrogant for me to assume that I can somehow magically become something I am not?*

And what is Addy's motivation? Does she secretly want me to adopt the kids so that she can get back at Phillip for being a drunk and a brute? What do I do?

Then, one lonely night, he formed a complicated plan of emotional balancing and ethics wherein he believed everyone–including Phillip--would win by Jason's adoption of Andria and Bobby. Within months, the adoption took place.

The room at the Probate Court was small, the size of a high-ceilinged two-car garage. The judge sat above them behind a raised desk with the gold seal of the State of Michigan mounted on the wall behind him. Facing the Judge were four rows of polished wooden seats and two small desks. Addy and Jason sat at one desk; the other one was empty.

Andria and Bobby were outside in the hall with a court official, waiting. They knew–and didn't know–what was happening inside the room down the hall. They had been told that 'there was nothing bad' happening, and to 'be yourselves and just wait for the news'.

The clerk looked over at Judge Winslow, an old man with white hair and a bushy gray moustache, and read from the docket paper before her.

"Matter of Adams, Your Honor."

Judge Winslow looked down at Addy and Jason.

"This is an adoption of– who's children?"

Addy swallowed and raised her right hand.

"Mine. My two children, your honor."

"Please stand," Judge Winslow said and pointed to an empty space on the floor before him.

Addy walked to the point the Judge had indicated and looked up at him. She held her hands together in front of her, out of her element, like a child at her first communion.

Judge Winslow smiled down at her. His voice was mellow and baritone, the voice of experience.

"Now, Mrs. Adams, let me explain how this matter of adoption works. First, you understand that the biological father of these minor children has signed off his parental rights, do you not?"

Addy nodded.

"Yes, your honor, I do understand that."

"And that in signing off on his parental rights he has surrendered forever the right to see, talk with, or otherwise interact with his children until such time as they have attained the age of majority. In other words, as of this minute, your children have essentially lost their biological father, and cannot inherit from his estate."

Addy looked up. Her eyes were unblinking.

"Yes, your honor."

Judge Winslow leaned forward.

"Now, as of this moment, the children are in my custody, and in yours. To effectuate this adoption, it will be necessary for you to relinquish your parental rights to these minors and give them to this court, at which time only this court will have custody of the minors. Do you so agree and so stipulate?"

Jason saw Addy's knees falter and then lock. The tone of her voice was scratchy and tearful.

"Yes, your honor, I understand, and I so state–agree and stipulate."

The court reporter handed Addy papers to sign, then gave them to the Judge.

Judge Winslow smiled.

"Thank you. Now, is there a person here present willing to assume the legal position and responsibility of the biological father for these minor children, and in so assuming, stand accountable to this court for the health and well being of said minors?"

Jason stood.

"I am, your honor."

Judge Winslow stroked his chin.

"And you are Mr. Adams, the husband of Mrs. Adams?"

Jason's ears burned. They had been married in Las Vegas the week preceding.

"Yes sir, I am."

"And do you understand that if this adoption is approved by the court, your name will appear on the birth certificates of these children as their biological father?"

Jason glanced at Addy and then up at the Judge.

"Yes, your honor, I understand."

Judge Winslow wrote on some papers and handed them to the clerk, who beckoned to Jason and Addy to come to the desk beneath that of Judge Winslow, where they signed the adoption papers and had their signatures notarized.

"By the power vested in me," Judge Winslow stated, "I now give the two of you the two minor children and grant the adoption of same by Mr. Adams."

Andria and Bobby ran up to Jason and Addy in the hall. Their eyes were wide open and their mouths agape.

Addy held both of their hands, and then pushed them gently towards Jason.

"Here, kids, meet your new father."

Jason knelt down on the floor and Andria and Bobby rushed into Jason's arms.

"Now," Jason said, "you can call me 'daddy."

Jason hugged them both. Andria cried and Bobby looked confused and embarrassed by all the fuss. Jason breathed a sign of relief. Now, he was at last, someone in his new family, someone real, not a charade any more. He was the father of Andria and Bobby, the father of Brandon, the father of all three kids.

Just like that, Jason thought, *with the stroke of a pen, I'm legally the father of these two kids? That simple? What kind of utter insanity is this? I'm fit enough to adopt another man's children but not fit enough to have custody of my own son?*

Two weeks later Jason sat in the family room on the long, charcoal-brown couch facing the stone fireplace. There, appeared the first challenge to his new station in life.

Blond-haired Andria, dressed in her white blouse and shorts, came up to Jason and sat down next to him on the couch.

"What's your fav'rite?" she asked and batted her eyelashes at him the blameless way only little girls bat their eyelashes.

Jason was taken aback.

"Favorite what?"

She looked up at him, her smooth brow tight with anxiety.

"Fav'rite, y'know, fav'rite."

Jason patted her tiny hand.

"I don't know what you mean."

She focused her sky-blue eyes on his.

"Y'know, fav--rite."

Jason felt stupid.

"I honestly don't know what you are talking about, Andria. Sorry."

She grabbed his finger.

"Me?"

"You what?"

She wagged his finger back and forth in her hand.

"Am I?"

"Are you what?"

She looked downcast.

"I think it's Brandon, that what I thinks."

Jason finally figured out what was going on. It was a crisis—a real kid crisis. It was a showdown, a test, a turning point, and he had to figure a way out of the dilemma.

He put his arm around her.

"Hey, Andria, I love all three of you kids the same, only differently because you are all three different people. Do you understand?"

She pouted.

"No."

He caught her under the chin with his fingers.

"Call Bobby and Brandon, tell them to come down here, and I'll show you what I mean, Ok?"

In a few minutes the three, small, children stood before Jason. He bent, wrapped his arms around all three of them, and picked them up simultaneously in a huge bear hug. He kissed them all, one at a time, and then let them down.

"Now, do you understand what I mean, Andria?"

She giggled and ran off upstairs. Bobby and Brandon shrugged their shoulders and ran off after her.

Jason watched the three children play hide and seek in the back yard, a location some five miles from the room in which Judge Dunning had nonchalantly taken Brandon from Jason. *This is all unreal,* Jason mused, *but as fleeting as it is, it's all I've got, and their childhoods are vanishing before me. As absurd, as much of a bizarre fantasy as this all is, I'm nevertheless going to do something about it to be remembered as their father, and the court system that gave me another man's two children and gave my only son to a sick and dying woman be damned.*

Thus Jason set about creating an ideal childhood in his own perfectly just world for the three children. By creating the ideal childhood, he figured, everyone would win, no matter what the court system, the judge, or the world thought of him--and he'd rebel against their insanity without them having the slightest idea of what he was doing. He would become the ideal father, a father so superlative that damned Judge Dunning would someday be put to shame for his asinine decision, and the whole court system would stand when he, Jason Adams, walked into any room, at any time, any where. He Jason Adams, was going to create a childhood so fair, so decent, and so wonderful that no one in the world would ever be able to match its wonder and purity. It would be a childhood constructed out of pure, absolutely pure, love. Someday, those jerks around town and those assholes in the court system would realize how stupid and destructive they were and beg for his forgiveness.

It was the master plan for his invisible attack on the system.

So it was that he dreamed, and the plan was launched and began its journey into reality.

"You kids wanna go for an ice cream at The Dairy Queen?" he shouted when they had stopped running around in the back yard.

"Yea." they screamed, and jumped up and down. They dashed to the car.

First fatherly achievement. Get kids to want to wear their seat belts.

Jason had seen the three kids spellbound by reruns of 'Star Trek,' with its original, and abysmally crude sets. The kids clearly believed that show, the blatant unreality of its sets aside. If they believed that, then surely they'd buy what he had in store for them.

"Do you kids want to play 'spaceship'?" Jason asked all three of them as they sat together in his Khaki green 1973 AMC Gremlin.

"Yeah." they yelled, *en masse,* piling into the car, oblivious to their fate.

None of them put on their seat belts.

"Gonna put on your seat belts, kids?"

Silence.

"You want to play space ship, right?"

"Yeah!" the kids reiterated.

Jason inserted and jiggled his key ring full of keys in the steering column igni*tion* lock.

"Oh-oh. The spaceship won't start without everyone's seat belt on because of the lock interlock ignition system."

There was a moment's silence.

"What?" Andria asked.

"Can't blast off without the lock/interlock ignition system on. That means that all seat belts have to be in their lock position for blast off."

"Click" went Andria's seat beat.

There were no corresponding 'clicks' from the back.

Jason jingled his keys again, turned his key slightly into the contact range of the ignition, causing a brief shudder of the starter..

"Oh-oh—missing two interlocks," Jason said, hoping the hint would register.

Andria turned her head around towards the back seat.

"'Boys!" she shouted."Click" went Brandon's seat belt.

Jason jiggled his keys again.

"Click" went Bobby's seat belt.

And the spaceship's six-cylinder engine roared into life.

Jason backed the car slowly out onto the dirt road.

"This is the Captain speaking. Prepare for blastoff. Ready?"

"Ready."

Jason started and then all counted down.

"Ten--9--8--7--6--5--4--3--2--1 – BLASTOFF!" they counted and shouted together.

The AMC Gremlin's wheels spun briefly on the loose dirt and then the ISG—'The Imaginary Spaceship Gremlin' was aloft, cruising at blinding speed in space.

"Ok," Jason said, as they moved slowly down the dirt road, "this is the Captain of the ISG speaking. Our mission is to find and help lost space monsters on our way to Space Station Dairy Queen. So, watch carefully out there for any monsters that might need our help."

Within seconds, the first lost monster appeared.

"Captain, me sees a lost space monster," four-year-old Bobby said.

Jason reached up to his left, pulled down an imaginary intercom microphone, and put it to his lips.

"This is the Captain speaking. What color is the monster?"

"Him is black 'n red 'n gots a zillions yellow horns."

"Whew. And what is the monster's space-identification number?"

"What dat means?" Bobby asked.

"What are the numbers you can pretend to see on him," the Captain replied..

"One--2--6--7--3--8--9--4." Bobby stated, showing off his vast knowledge of the Arabic number system.

The Captain, who had allegedly been flying ISG for years, was quick with a knowledgeable response.

"Hm. Sounds like he's from the Zadire galaxy. What's the monster's problem?"

Silence. Bobby tried to remember what the word 'problem' meant. Then, he suddenly saw the answer.

"He hongree, he say."

The Captain was prepared to handle that problem on the ISG, which had been equipped with every imaginable kind of restaurant.

"Well, bring the monster on board, and we'll feed him."

The ISG docked at its destination that day and, over the months and years that followed, evolved into a superbly equipped super-machine designed to help all lost space monsters everywhere in the mega-verse. It had restaurants serving every imaginable kind of food; it had a hospital, with doctors and nurses; it had a dentist's office. It also had ray guns, but no monsters were killed because the lost monsters, most of which, it turned out, were usually just hungry, never attacked the space ship. Furthermore, the spaceship crew was protected by an invisible shield, as was true of their home, which was–the Captain assured the crew–'in the monster-free zone'–namely, the zone controlled by Jason, not the monsters of the court system and their minions.

Their home and neighborhood was a child's amusement park. Underneath the living and dining rooms, adjacent to Jason's music and hi-fi studio, there was a wine cellar and a host of other amusements, including a room with an air-hockey game, pool table, and dartboard. Next to this game room, through a waist-high door, was the wine cellar or, as the kids called it, 'the hideaway,' where the kids played on rainy days.

On good weather days they played outside down at the end of the dirt road they lived on at what they called 'the graveyard' where they had once found the skeleton of a bird. Or they fished at a pond in the backyard of a house at the end of the road that paralleled their road. Or they went across the street and stood at the fence and tried to talk to and make friends with the farmer's horses and cows. Or they played in the shallow creek that ran under the road in front of their house and along the boundary of their land, chasing and catching miniature fresh water lobsters they called 'crawdads.'

Jason tried to turn their play into learning experiences as well. Each day he gave Andria and Bobby--and Brandon when he visited--three choices of what they could do. Two of the choices were harmless and roughly equivalent; the third choice was always foolish and in the beginning the children wisely avoided it.

As they grew they began testing limits.

"You can either go to the park, or you can play croquet, or you can walk in the creek with your new shoes on," Jason announced to the three children one day.

The three looked at each other and, wordlessly, the rebellion was born.

"The creek. Walking in the creek!" Andria announced. The other two, younger, children nodded their assent, following the wisdom of their older sibling.

Ok, he thought, *they're testing the limits. So be it.*

"Sure," Jason said, and watched them scramble off towards the creek.

Jason thought it was a rebellion in word only.

At that moment, Addy and Jason were in the kitchen, preparing dinner.

The stockpot had been simmering all day creating the base for the lamb gravy; the lamb chops were lined up and dusted with fine breadcrumbs, ready to be broiled, and the potatoes were nearly done baking. The aromas of Addy's wonderful food had wafted through the house all day, and dinner promised to be splendid indeed.

Addy skimmed the last thin lines of fat off the stock, smelled it, and turned to Jason.

"I'm shocked by the freedom you gave them to make choices. You know, they're just dumb kids, Jason, they don't really know what the hell they want. They'll run all over you, you know."

Jason turned and handed her a plate full of pared and thinly sliced carrots to be steamed.

"With all due respect, Madame Chef, how else are they going to learn to make real choices unless they actually make real choices?"

Addy wiped her hands on her white kitchen apron, took the vegetables and arranged them in the steamer pot.

"Jason. Come down to earth. How can they know what the, you know, right choice is? I mean, they're just kids."

Jason sighed. Time to teach college again.

"The amount of calculation varies inversely with the amount of evidence. The more information you have about a given decision, the easier it is to make the decision. The less evidence you have, the more difficult it is to make the decision. This is true in science, it's true in business, and it's true in law."

Addy threw her stirring spoon into the sink and rinsed it. She turned to Jason, who was fumbling for his cigarettes in the pocket of his blue sports shirt.

"Oh, God. You expect the kids to understand that air-head shit?"

Jason kept fumbling at his shirt pocket, and realized he had left his cigarettes elsewhere. He stood his ground.

"I'm trying to let the kids come to understand how to make choices by having them make fairly innocuous decisions."

"Humph,´ Addy snorted, "Not likely," and she went back to her stock pot.

A few minutes later, Jason called the kids in for dinner and they arrived, at the back door, their shoes sodden and lathered in mud.

Addy exploded.

"Before you have any freakin' dinner," she cried, her arms folded resolutely across her chest, "you're gonna clean up those goddamn shoes so they look brand new."

"Not fair," Andria cried.

"Wa–why?" Brandon wailed.

"NO," Bobby screeched.

"That's what sometimes happens when you make a bad choice," Jason said, and glanced triumphantly at Addy.

After that, the children matured and avoided the third choice like the plague.

In the spring, of 1977 Andria was going on ten, Bobby had just turned six, and Brandon was seven and a half.

It was a period of bitter ironies. Jason was a full-time father to Andria and Bobby and a visiting father to Brandon, who was ostensibly being raised primarily by Russet, when she wasn't in the hospital. It made no sense--the world of the three children and their biological fathers seemed mindlessly fractured and distorted by the intractable mindlessness of the court system.

Nonetheless at times, for Jason, the world was in balance and a place of joy.

Jason's role as their father had been solidified, and the three children called each other brother and sister to each other and friends. Jason consciously tried to think of adventures for them that would allow them to bond and minimize the daily sibling disputes, in particular between Andria and Bobby.

One such adventure was born at a lunch Jason had with the kids at Marty's Steakhouse. Jason asked them what they wanted to do for the summer project that year when, as a university professor he had the entire summer free.

Brandon looked up from his Coke.

"Ca--can wa--we build a na--nature wa–wa-watch?"

He's coming apart inside, Jason thought, as he heard Brandon struggle with the words. *The stuttering's getting worse. Why the hell is he stuttering?*

"A sand box?" Andria asked, and batted her eyelashes.

"I wanna tree hut." Bobby yelled and knocked a potato chip off his plate.

Lightning had struck.

A tree hut. As a little boy, Jason had always wanted a tree hut, but had never had one himself or had one built for him. Here was an opportunity to simultaneously create a missing childhood memory for himself while giving his children an experience of love and togetherness to take into their adult lives.

Jason drew a loose sketch of a tree hut on the back of the paper place mat, showing a platform resting on two tree limbs with the tree trunk growing up through a round hole in the middle.

"Like this?" he asked, and showed the children the sketch.

"Neat--o." they shouted.

That summer they built the tree hut in the large maple tree behind their house. The tree hut was large and sturdy enough to hold 10 or 12 adults safely, but used no nails in its construction, and no nails were put into the tree.

The floor of the tree hut was bolted to double-thickness supports and rested on two of the larger tree limbs. Wood struts extended from the railing down to the tree hut floor. Hence, it was impossible for anyone to roll off the floor in their sleep and fall seven or eight feet to the ground. Jason made a wooden ladder. The floor of the tree hut and its supporting wood structure were stained. Finally, it was ready to go.

"The tree hut is finished," Jason announced to the three children. "You got your nature watch, sand box, and tree hut all in one place. I now give it to you three kids. It's yours. Remember that it has to be cared for and only you kids can play in it unless either your mother--Addy--or I say it's Ok for a friend to play there with you, Ok?"

Jason's gift almost instantly created realities of its own.

Andria, Bobby and Brandon proceeded to invent an imaginary kingdom, 'El Sat' that invisibly surrounded the tree hut. Brandon was the President, Bobby the General, Andria the Chief Justice. They then officially banned all adults from the kingdom and the tree hut, including Jason although they later decided that it was possible for him to perhaps get a special dispensation to perform repairs.

El Sat had a mathematics of its own wherein all computations resulted in a 0 answer,- a mathematics that kept the kingdom forever broke. The kingdom's financial difficulties were a source of endless high-level political discussions between the three of them. each of whom had redoubtable powers. Brandon, as President, had the only veto power, Andria, as Chief Justice, was the only one who could declare an idea unconstitutional, and Bobby, as the General, was the only one who could declare war.

High-level governmental meetings took place at the circular kitchen table in the El Sat world of government, a mere five miles away from the courthouse in downtown Ann Arbor where the futures of the El Sat government leaders had been decided once, and would be decided again.

Brandon started the meeting into session with a slap on the table, tried, and failed, to look his fellow leaders in the eyes.

"Wa--We are bro--broke a—again. Wa--wa--we'll have to t--tax our 'lowances," Brandon announced.

Andria jumped up. She raised her right index finger in the air and waged it back and forth in front of the faces of the confreres.

"That's unconstitutional. I declare it unconstitutional."

Bobby slammed his fist on the table, and adjusted the holster of his plastic ray gun. "I's gonna declare WAR if we gots taxed."

"It's Constitutional for us to go to war to make the money," Andria announced, and fastened both hands to her hips.

Brandon raised his thin hand in the air.

"I wa--veto the wa--war."

And so the high-level conferences went, day-in, day-out, with great verve, solemnity, and no material results whatsoever, a mirror image of the Ann Arbor court system a few miles down the road..

Jason also found some practical usage for El Sat and the tree hut.

The tree hut was El Sat's fortress and the vantage position for the kids to use exclusively in another one of Jason's inventions, the annual summertime 'Great Water Gun War' between the children, Addy's father, Roy Spangler, and a friend of the family's, Henry MacVicart, a childless local realtor, who had sold Addy their house.

The first family conference regarding the rules of the war was convened in the downstairs family room before the fireplace. Jason, as the creator of the war, headed the conference. He was preposterously dressed in his ugly bright red turtleneck shirt, blue jeans, and yellow sneakers. He stood before the fireplace and looked straight at the three children who were seated on the couch directly before him, dressed—at Addy's command—in their oldest play clothes.

Jason cleared his throat.

"Ahem. Attention!"

The room fell silent.

"Kids, don't you think it's only fair, since Roy and Henry are real old, that they be given the fort to hide in?"

Andria raised her hand.

"What fort?"

"The sheet metal shack that the tractor goes in over by the tree hut. You could shoot down at them from the tree hut," Jason said, grinning.

Addy grinned also, then frowned.

"They're also gonna need a large bucket of water in the fort for filling their water guns. Fair enough?"

That was fair, the kids silent nods seemed to say.

Henry, in his late sixties and balding, wore thick glasses, and had a little potbelly. He nattily dressed in green pants and striped yellow shirt. Henry grinned, and said "And at least one cocktail."

"Two," added Roy, seated in the easy chair to Jason's right.

"Ok," Addy said relishing the torment she was inflicting on them both, "the rules are that you two old jokers, you know, can't be shot inside the fort, but the freakin' second you leave the fort, you're dead meat."

"Not fair," countered Roy, "We're outnumbered."

"Ok," Jason said, "to be fair you're going to get the tractor as a getaway vehicle."

Addy laughed. "But it's gonna to be parked several feet away from the fort, minus its ignition key. If you can figure out how the hell to hot wire it without getting soaked, it's all yours."

"These aren't exactly fair rules," Roy grinned. "As a matter of fact I think they're loaded against old age."

"That's the American justice system at work," Jason quipped.

"Can they be shot fillin' their water guns at the faucet?" Andria asked and smiled cherubically at the two older men.

Jason straightened up, at attention.

"Of course they can. They're wonderfully vulnerable at that moment.".

"What are the penalties to the, ah, non-family person who tries to steal the tractor?" asked Henry, scanning the room around him.

"They get kicked out of the war," Jason suggested, and blew on his fingernails.

"Isn't that a little stiff?" Roy asked, lighting his pipe for the fourth time since the beginning of the meeting, and not looking particularly threatening, given his frail 70 year-old body.

"This is serious business," Jason replied, "with serious consequences."

"Ca-can we fill our wa-water guns in th-he ha-house?" Brandon asked, and looked longingly at the heap of plastic water guns on the coffee table inches away.

They took a vote on the issue and decided yes, but only for the first fill-up. After that, only at the outside faucets, was the consensus of opinion.

"Can we use the tree hut if we capture it?" Henry grinned.

"Unconstitutional." said Andria.

"I--I wa-veto it." stuttered Brandon, who tried to focus his wandering eyes on Jason, and failed.

"Dat's grouts for WAR." Bobby shouted, brandishing an imaginary gun.

"In other words, hell no," Addy concluded.

Aunt Dot opened the sliding glass door to the right of the fireplace. The sunshine splashed onto her sixty-year-old, wrinkled, oval face.

"The faucet-filling station awaits," she announced. The kids came as one, grabbed their multi-colored plastic water guns and scurried over to the doorway.

Jason walked upstairs into the kitchen and filed a stockpot full of water and lugged it out to the fort. Addy followed with a gin martini for her father and a Manhattan for Henry.

Jason and Addy stood at the entrance to the fort. Jason looked each man in the eyes as he received their drinks from Addy.

"Inside the fort, here, you're safe," Jason said, "outside, you're fair game. You gentlemen—and here I speak very loosely--are now on your own," Jason said and Addy marched backwards, in lockstep from the fort to the two-seat couch on the patio, some 15 feet away.

The three kids, who had earlier devised their a plan of attack, stood before Aunt Dot loaded water pistols hanging from their hands. All eyes turned to her. She raised her glass of Chablis in the air; Jason hoisted his can of Budweiser in the air; Addy raised her glass of Merlot; Ray and Henry, crouched under the roof of the fort, raised their cocktails in the air; the three kids cocked their pistols under their chins.

"Let the war begin!" Dot shouted.

Andria, Brandon and Bobby peeled off in three different directions like attacking fighter planes, screaming and firing copious streams of water in the opening of the fort as they flew by their antagonists, who left the cover of their fort to return fire only to be considerably damaged.

The kids retreated and regrouped, according to plan. Bobby climbed the ladder into the tree hut perching himself at the corner overlooking the entrance to the fort. Andria and Brandon positioned themselves at the corners of the entrance to the fort.

"Cow-erds!" Bobby shouted.

As the kids had planned, both Ray and Henry took umbrage at the insult to their manhood, emerged from their fort and fired up at Bobby only to be ambushed on either side by Brandon and Andria. The water from their counterattack on Bobby rained back down on their upraised faces.

"We gotta get outta here," Henry groaned, water dripping from his nose as he looked at the cherry-red 16 horsepower tractor glistening in the sunlight four feet away from the fort. Ray followed his companion's longing gaze, wiped his wet brow and cursed the droplets of water inching down his back under his white dress shirt.

"It's a treacherous trap," Ray observed. "No keys."

Whereupon the three kids appeared out of nowhere emptying their pistols on their aging and outclassed, antagonists.

Relief, however, was on its way.

Andria and Brandon squeezed mightily and fruitlessly at their empty water gun triggers.

"We 'na-need sa-some ma-more wa-water!" Brandon shouted and ran headlong to the outdoor faucet, followed by Andria and Bobby.

Reloaded, and seeking targets, the three soldiers stood before Jason and Addy.

Addy raised her hands in the air.

"Shoot me and no dinner or dessert," she declared.

Brandon aimed his green water pistol at his father.

"Hey, " Jason protested, "I'm innocent and I'm not armed!"

The three kids looked at one another, poised for action.

Meanwhile, Henry tiptoed to the tractor and begun to fiddle with the ignition wire. He found himself suddenly surrounded by the three water gun warriors, who proceeded to douse him head to foot and similarly saturate poor Ray, who had mistakenly come to his compatriot's rescue.

Jason sipped his beer, smoked a cigarette, and quietly admired the fruition of another one of his hair-brained dreams.

The kids were mercilessly soaking Ray and Henry despite cries for "Mercy! Mercy!"

Doubled-over with laughter, Addy looked imploringly at Aunt Dot, The Keeper of the Rules, for assistance on behalf of the beleaguered older generation.

Dot caught the pained look in Addy's eyes, noted the slaughter in progress a few feet away, and looked at her wristwatch. Ten minutes had elapsed.

"Time!" she shouted, "The Great Water Gun War is over!"

The kids complained loudly but fell silent when Addy announced dinner was served. The annual Great Water Gun War propagated yet another component of the Adams family.

Just before the second Great Water Gun War began, the kids decided to adopt Henry, a widower with no other family than the Adams. Jason prepared the adoption papers. Besides being forced to swear he would stop stealing peanuts from Addy's store, Henry had to swear to abide by the rules of the family, which Jason wrote, and handed to Henry to read out loud.

Henry stood before the fireplace, adjusted his glasses on his nose, cleared his throat, and read.

The Rules

1. Since growing up is HARD to do, and growing down is easy to do, growing down is forbidden.
2. The rules apply equally to kids and grownups alike.
3. Promises are to be kept.
4. Anyone, at any time, can call a family or personal meeting with one other family member or the whole family; all family members must attend a family meeting and contribute to that meeting.
5. Stealing anything is not allowed.
6. ALL family members MUST participate at the top of their lungs in any hooray given by any other family member who has eaten all of his/her dinner, regardless of whether or not the participating member will him/herself get a hooray. (Hoorays are not allowed in restaurants.)

Henry let the paper with The Rules on it slide down in front of his chest. He looked cherubic, smiled at everyone.

"These are damnably hard rules, awfully tough," he said.

"Those are the rules, like it or not," Jason growled, "You either abide by them, or no booze and no Great Water Gun War. What's it going to be, sir?"

Henry grinned and signed his name.

"You are now officially adopted," Addy beamed, "You must now abide by all of our rules. All of them, and that includes no stealing peanuts from my store!"

"Done," said Henry, a grin stretched across his face.

"Done," said Jason, and winked at Henry.

"Yeah!" the kids yelled and bounced up and down.

Henry radiated joy.

"It's a deal. I now have a family!"

Over the years, the rules expanded from almost nightly family meetings about such critical matters as how much food one had to eat to get dessert (the rule became 'one-half of what you served yourself'), to complicated issues of privacy, truth-telling, tattle-taleing, sharing the upstairs bathroom, bedtimes, dating, use of the car, and on.

"The Rule About The Rules," Jason explained, was "that some day The Rules will go away and you'll have to make up your own rules for yourself. "Which, in part," Jason explained to Addy, "was also the reason for the existence of The Rules."

"Which is?"

"To give them practice in making up cooperative rules agreeable to themselves and to all others. Essentially, the rules are based on the Constitution."

Addy sneered.

"Like the blessed court system?"

"The way the court system is supposed to be, not the corrupt club it has allowed itself to become ."

Eventually, each of the kids, when they took a junior high school civics course, figured out that 'the rules' were based on the Constitution of the United States of America and The Bill of Rights, translated into kid-ese.

"When one lives in a participatory democracy," Jason said to Addy, "one should be raised in a participatory democracy and the children will hopefully be so raised by us. Agreed?"

"Agreed. But it's sure as shit a hard way to parent."

Jason threw his hands up.

"So what? Democracy is a hard way to govern, too."

Jason had only vague ideas of how Brandon was raised by Russet during these years. Jason knew from what Brandon said that he watched television every day, and had a 'treat drawer' which held candy given to him as a reward for being 'good'. Clearly, the care he received was poor. As the years passed, Brandon deteriorated both physically and mentally.

"He's a mess," Addy said, "He's a freakin' mess."

"I know," Jason replied "And there's got to be some way to get him fixed."

Brandon was scrawny and ate ravenously when he visited them. He stuttered incessantly and his hands grabbed frantically at the air as he stuttered. His eyes were off-center and the left eye continued to 'wander'. He had no depth perception and he could not make baskets or see an antagonist clearly in a fight. His teeth were crooked and, Jason guessed, probably cavity-filled because of the candy he was allowed to eat out of his 'treat drawer' as a reward for being good.

"He stutters all the time," Addy said to Jason on one of the early evening walks they often took.

Jason kicked a small rock as they rounded the first corner and dodged four oncoming grade school bicycle riders.

"Yeah, and I know. . .or think I know. . . what is probably causing the stuttering."

"What?"

"He's being vastly confused by that son-of-a-bitch asshole, Danny Forge."

Addy reached over and took Jason's arm.

"Her new husband?"

"Yeah, her new acolyte and yes-man."

"When were they married?"

"Can't forget that date. October 27, 1975. Same day as my mother's birthday."

Jason glanced over to his right. Their next-door neighbor's wife, Julie, was an artist who did her oil paintings in the garage..

"How is Danny confusing him?"

Jason glanced at Addy then glared straight ahead.

"Danny's pretending he's Brandon's father."

"Well, he's Brandon's, ah, you know, step-father, isn't he?"

Jason's blood boiled.

"Hell, no. I did legal research on that at the law Library. A stepfather is a man who marries a widow, and then legally adopts the child or children, or is a man who marries a woman whose husband relinquishes his parental rights so that the man can adopt the kid or kids. Exactly what I did with Andria and Bobby. But Danny's situation with Brandon is neither of these."

Addy blushed.

"I didn't know that. And I'm adopted."

"Law aide, who the fuck does he think he is? He knows I am and wants to be Brandon's father! The utter arrogance of the son-of-a-bitch!"

They rounded the corner where Dr. Mason's immaculately trimmed bushes and rose garden greeted them. The doctor could be seen every night bent over his beloved roses, pruning, watering, and spraying his brood, just as Jason's father had done years ago

Jason felt a twinge of nostalgia and scowled at Abby's lack of knowledge.

"What do you mean you didn't know? That's what had to be done for me to adopt Andria and Bobby. Phillip sighed off on them. How the hell could you forget that?"

Addy counterattacked.

"He did that because he owed a fortune in child support."

"That was just money. You're missing my point–the point. There were more important things at stake. Incredibly important things."

She stared at him, her mouth agape.

"Your father thing? Is that why you put him and the kids in therapy afterwards?"

Jason marched straight ahead.

"Phillip's their father. He had a right to know them, they had a right to know him. That relationship is sacred. The adoption was a tactical move to give me the power to do good, that's all."

Addy missed his point again and grabbed his arm.

"Now they've got two fathers, Jason. Your name's on their birth certificates, you know."

Jason ignored her hand, grimaced, and kept walking

"Yeah, it's awkward--but it was the right thing to do. They decided to call me 'dad' and Phillip 'pop' to end the confusion."

"You sure they're Ok with that mess?"

"They were happy when they told me about it--and rather proud that they'd figured out such a complicated adult problem."

Addy sighed.

"Ok, that's sorta two kids down. Back to Brandon's confusion. . . ."

Jason stopped, lit a cigarette, picked up a rock and hurled it at a tree across the road that stood tall in the field next to architect Morrison's home. On the east side of the home there was a pond that Morrison stocked with fish and invited the neighborhood kids to fish in, for free, and for the unannounced reason that Morrison's son, for whom he created the pond, had died of leukemia as a child.

The reflections of the sun hurt. Jason squinted and pulled on Abby's hand as they turned the corner. He glanced over at her, and sighed.

"Brandon's probably also getting confused by Russet's constant hospitalizations. I believe –and I have every reason to believe that unless I get custody of him, his problems will only get worse. It's driving me insane to see him suffering so much for no goddamned reason. None."

They walked on, wordlessly, for several minutes.

The shadows lengthened as they walked under the overarching line of elm trees near the end of the block and the woods that contained what the kids called the 'graveyard'.

Addy squeezed his hand.

"Why don't Russet and Danny help him?"

The tone of Jason's voice was bitter and he spoke rapidly.

"Why? Russet can't take care of herself, and Danny is 10 years her junior, a weasel of a guy not much taller than Russet--she's 5' 2"--and is vastly her intellectual inferior. He's Russet's lap dog, or her choirboy–shit, I don't have any idea what the hell his game is or why the hell he married a woman who is sick and dying. There's no one except me to help Brandon."

"How smart is Russet?"

"She told me her IQ. was 168, and I believe it."

"If she's so smart, why'd she marry a jerk like Danny?"

Jason thought.

"Poor Russet. She needed someone to take care of her, not entertain her with intellectual challenges, There's no way Danny can think at her level. And he's gutless."

They turned the corner four houses away from their home. A car full of teenagers inched by them and pulled into the driveway of Dr. Landon's spacious ranch home with its fenced-in yard and backyard deck and swimming pool. The card radio was blasting the Beatle's "Can't Buy Me Love" hit, and Jason ground his teeth.

Addy tapped him on the shoulder.

"Why gutless?"

"Why? This is why. After Danny married Russet I invited him to meet with me in a local restaurant to discuss how he and I were going to work together as sorta two father figures–one real, one pretend--with Brandon--but our conversation quickly turned sour."

"How?"

"We sat down together and ordered coffee. 'Well,' I said, 'you know Russet's sterile, can't have any more children, don't you?' and Danny said that he 'knew that.' I asked him if Russet's sterility didn't bother him because he was a young guy and didn't he want kids?"

"And he said?"

"He looked at me smugly, his blue eyes blank with conceit, and said, "I want what Russet wants."

Addy moaned.

"My hero."

"I said, 'Danny, you know that Russet might not make it past age 40.' He just smiled at me contemptuously, like I was some kind of moral leper to even mention that. 'She's getting better all the time,' he said, and seemed convinced of the supreme morality of his own delusion. I ignored his adolescent bravado and again asked him about kids, and again he said that he wanted what Russet wanted. He was mindless putty, a nice doggy, a Momma's boy, I figured."

"And?"

"Well, that ended it. He got up suddenly from our table and said that he'd had enough of my intellectual shit and that he was gonna fight me all the way, and walked out."

IV

The torture went on.

Russet refused to get Brandon any help for his stuttering and Danny refused to even admit that he stuttered. Brandon 'talks with his hands' Danny said. Not one of the several licensed child therapists Jason called or met with would take the case because Jason did not have custody of Brandon.

Obsessed with and dismayed by Brandon's deterioration, Jason pressed on and in the fall of 1977 he found a pastoral minister with a Ph.D in psychology and counseling. David was a dark-haired, slender married man in his mid-thirties with children. He said he would work with Brandon on his stuttering.

"I don't have custody of him," Jason said.

"I don't care" David said matter-of-factly.

"My ex-wife has custody."

David smiled, and his smile exuded confidence.

"No she doesn't."

Jason was taken aback.

"I don't understand. Why do you say that?"

David smiled again and touched Jason on the arm.

"God has custody of him. God's my boss, I do what He, not some Judge, wants me to do."

Ohmygod, Jason thought, *a real human being.*
"How much for your services?"
David shrugged.
"Whatever you can afford. This is a church, not a lawyer's office."
"Why don't you tell Russet you're taking Brandon to Dr. Hurtler?" Addy asked over lunch.
Jason toyed with his French fries and sipped his Coke.
"I'm threading a tiny needle. My bet is that if I told her she'd tell Golding, and I'd be back in court because I don't have a court order to do it. That's also why I don't tell Brandon that he can't mention his visits with Dave."
Addy pushed around her salad with her fork, and scowled.
"Huh? I don't understand."
Jason's face was blank, like that of an attorney.
"No matter what happens, Brandon is going to win."
Addy's face darkened.
"Huh?"
Jason drained his Coke and looked for the waitress.
"Ok. If Brandon says nothing, he sees Dave, and gets help; if he says something to Russet or Danny, maybe they'll do something to help him, to spite me."
Addy wiped her mouth, lit a cigarette, and scowled.
"Including hauling your ass into court."
"Including hauling me into court. But it will cost me nothing. I'll represent myself. There's no law involved here. The issue is a father's love for his son, and that's not against the law, dammit."
"Do you think it's really goin' to work?"
Jason stood.
"It's better than the nothing that has been happening so far."

The plan worked. Brandon apparently told his mother about his 'worry doctor', and Russet put Brandon into a therapy program at Children's Hospital for, so Jason thought, his stuttering.
When Jason told David what had happened, David smiled and said, "God works in strange ways. Be of good heart, and may the Lord bless you and your son."

Brandon's therapist was a divorced and childless social worker named Rachel Payne. She worked in Children's Hospital in a small office with a tiny desk and two chairs opposite one another. She was an attractive woman in her late twenties with black hair, chocolate-brown eyes, and a creamy complexion.

In their first meeting Payne wore a low-cut dress and she sat across from him in a large, beige chair with her legs pulled up under her.

Jason sat down across from her. Ms. Payne looked him over, head to toe, the way women study men in bikinis at the beach. She looked him straight in the eyes. The tone of her voice was flat, void of feeling, her words precisely enunciated. "Turtle necks are out of style."

Not when you hate buttoning that top shirt button, Jason thought. He stared at her and said nothing.

She sat back and looked down her nose at him.

"Goatees went out of style in the 19th century."

Not when you've got the kind of scar I've got on my chin, Jason thought.

"I thought I was here to discuss my son's speech therapy with you."

She glared at him, stone-faced.

"Quite. What would you like to discuss?"

"I just told you that I expected to discuss his therapy to find out what's wrong with him."

She threw her head back and looked at the wall to her right.

"I know what's wrong with Brandon."

Jason was taken aback.

"Really? You've tested him? A speech therapist has tested him?"

She smiled at him smugly.

"No. I did not need to do that. It wasn't required. I'm a professional. All that was needed was a brief case history."

Jason scowled.

"That doesn't seem right to me somehow."

Payne looked at him.

"It's quite simple. He's seeing too much of his father."

Jason's spine turned into an iron rod. He stared, incredulous, at the pretty social worker.

"Where the hell'd you get that?"

She raised her chin slightly and looked down her nose at him.

"Oh, you're one of those guys who don't get it."

Don't get what? Jason thought, *get what?*

"Don't get what?"

She straightened her back.

"The new reality of the 1970s, that's what."

Ohmygod, Jason thought. S*he's one of the new feminists who hate men! Better face the damned issue head-on.*

"Ok, I need enlightenment. That aside, where'd you get the idea that seeing too much of me is causing Brandon's eyes and teeth to go physically crooked and his mouth not to physically work when he tries to speak?"

She reached over to the small bookshelf to her left, and held up a copy of Gold, Froud, and Solning's book, Beyond The Best Interests Of The Baby.

"Here."

Jason had read and analyzed the book. It was shortsighted, sexist, and dangerous because of the stature and reputations of the authors.

"That book is malarkey, Ms. Payne, I daresay. Just for openers, the authors say it is best to legally order things so that non-custodial parents--90% or so of whom are fathers--have no rights at all to visit with their child, so that the custodial parent has the exclusive right to decide whether or not it is desirable for the child to have such visits. There is no evidence that setting things up like that is going to have demonstrably positive effects on anyone, especially the child. It's an insane invitation to utter tyranny."

She shrugged nonchalantly, as if his criticisms were those of a child.

"It's a fine book, the latest and most important theoretical text we use here at CH." She smiled politely, put the book back on the bookshelf next to a stack of Ms. magazines, and leaned over towards him.

Jason was furious.

"There's no psychological evidence to support their absurd proposition that a single parent is preferable to two parents, Ms. Payne."

She threw her head to the side and daintily curled her hand into a cylinder before her mouth.

"It's how we work here."

"What's here? Some kind of medieval prison?"

"That's how we work."

Jason ground his teeth and took a deep breath,

"Ok, that's how you work. But there is nothing in that book about juvenile diabetic mothers or the effects of that unpredictable—and terrifying—disease on their child or children.. Don't you know Russet's medical history?"

Payne curled up in her chair, put her legs tightly under her, revealed her white panties, and smirked.

"I don't think she's that ill."

Jason's jaw set.

"Wanna bet? I can prove it. I've got over 200 pages of medical evidence showing the severity of Russet's illness."

"The evidence from the custody trial?"

"Yes."

Payne shook her head.

"That's water over the dam. What's important now is the single parent-child bond between Russet and Brandon. That's what is most critical to Brandon's mental and emotional health at his age."

Jason stared.

"You're totally ignoring the fact that Russet has been constantly hospitalized for a multitude of problems--two more emergency room hospitalizations last year I just learned, for example--and is not raising him. Danny Forge, myself, and an assortment of baby-sitters hired by Russet, are."

Payne studied her fingernails.

"I haven't seen her being sick at all."

Jason leaned forward in his chair.

"Russet's sick all the time, Ms. Payne. For Christ's sake, she's chronically ill—as a matter of fact, she's very, very seriously ill—so ill she probably won't live beyond her fortieth birthday.."

Payne leaned over towards Jason, and waved her finger at him.

"She's not sick 'all of the time' and, when she is, which I'm told is rarely, there's someone there to care for him."

Jason ground his teeth and snarled, "Who told you that?"

"Danny. Her husband."

"And you believed him? Christ, he's her puppet."

Ms. Payne tossed her head and sighed.

"I had no rational reason not to believe him. I found him, ah, rather charming."

Jason took a deep breath and tried another tack.

"Then, when she's 'rarely sick,' as you so quaintly put it, why not me taking care of him?"

She smiled politely and leaned over towards him, displaying her inviting cleavage.

"I told you. He's seeing too much of you."

Jason kept his eyes fixed on her eyes.

"The Court Order is that I care for Brandon when Russet's sick, Ms. Payne."

Payne interlocked her fingers and studied the backs of her hands.

"Well, we're not the court here."

The frustration and rage crested. He shouted.

"It's an order of the court. It's the law!"

Payne continued to scrutinize the backs of her hands.

"I don't care. That's not my job."

Jason took a deep breath and tried yet another line of argument.

"Russet's only sibling, Terry, died when she was very young. Russet has no experience raising kids."

Payne pulled her legs under her, shrugged, and said nothing.

"Payne, I've taught kids how to play the piano. I taught 4th through 6th graders creative writing in the Recreational Department. I have two adopted kids roughly Brandon's age. I have tons of experience interacting with children. Russet has virtually none."

Payne said nothing.

"Will you meet with my adopted kids, Andria and Bobby? They are the best examples I have of my parenting skills."

Payne shook her head.

"That would be against our hospital policy."

Christ, she's a bigot, Jason thought.

"Your policy makes no sense--none at all. Do you think Russet is a good parent?"

Payne positioned her open hands carefully before her, fingers raised.

"Well, she's not a great parent, but I can teach her how to do it."

"How?"

"I got an 'A' in my Developmental Psychology course in the M.S.W. program."

Jason stared at her, bit his lip, got up, and left.

"Look, Ms. Payne," Jason said to her at another session, "Danny and Russet are telling Brandon to call Danny 'daddy Danny'. Don't you find that rather cruel and confusing to Brandon? A child only gets one father, and he must be vastly confused at his age--he's only seven and a half, you know."

"I find nothing wrong with the 'daddy Danny' practice of Russet and Danny. They are trying to be loving parents to Brandon, I believe."

Jason's clenched his teeth.

"Then why does he stutter?"

Payne pulled her legs up under her.

"I told you. He is seeing too much of his father."

At another session, Jason pointed out to Payne something Addy had perceived.

"Addy has pointed out that Russet and Danny are 'copycatting' us. More confusion for Brandon. It's like having double vision."

"What do you mean?"

Jason consulted the list Addy had prepared.

"In 1973 I bought an AMC Gremlin, then Russet bought an AMC Gremlin; I bought a home, then Russet bought a home; I found David Hurtler, the minister with a Ph.D. in counseling, who helped Brandon with his stuttering and a month later, after Brandon had apparently mentioned that he has a 'worry doctor,' he's suddenly a patient of yours. It goes on and on."

She frowned.

"Well, what you call--what your wife called--the 'copycatting' is, I admit, perhaps more than coincidental, but I'll take care of it if it will make you happy."

"How?"

Payne's lips pulled over her teeth in the semblance of a smile.

"I'm the professional; you're the patient. I know what I am doing."

Jason cringed and changed the subject.

"Brandon has nightmares every night, Ms. Payne."

"How do you know that?"

"He told me."

"And what did you say to him?"

"I told him that nightmares were worries that he needed to talk about."

"With whom?"

"With me."

"You? You're just a piano player. I'm the professional. I'll take care of it."

Jason lurched forward in his chair.

"I'm also a Ph.D. and his father, dammit, Ms. Payne. What about the copycatting and the 'daddy Danny' crap?"

Her jaw muscles knotted.

"I think you're being too sensitive about the so-called 'copycatting,' and 'daddy Danny'--way too sensitive."

In March of 1978 Payne submitted an affidavit to the Court in which she stated that it was her 'professional opinion' that visitation of Brandon and Jason 'should be reduced,' and said that this opinion was her own and that of the 'entire psychiatric team' at Children's Hospital.

"The Court," Judge Dunning said after he'd read the affidavit, "rules that visitations be reduced from two times a week to one eight-hour period per week, with no overnight visits, and from six weeks in the summer to two weeks in the summer. Child support remains the same."

Jason met with Payne for one last time. He was furious about the affidavit and the ruling.

"What the hell are you trying to do to Brandon and me?"

Payne sat back in her chair.

"I want you to sign off on Brandon so that Danny can adopt him."

The world disintegrated before him and Jason's fell open in disbelief.

"My God, are you insane? He's my son."

Payne's face was impassive.

"It's in his best interests that you sign off on him."

"Let's put that on tape," Jason said, and turned on the hand-held tape recorder he had concealed under the jacket on his lap.

Payne's brown eyes popped wide open. She raised her voice.

"Turn that off or I'll call security."

Jason's nostrils flared. He wanted to beat her unmercifully.

"If you won't go on the record, then you and I are through talking, period."

Payne raised herself straight up in her chair.

"I don't work like that."

Jason could taste the fury in his throat.

"You haven't the slightest fucking idea of what you're doing. You have absolutely no idea of how downright destructively dumb and uneducated you are. None."

Payne jumped up out of her chair, and screeched.

"I'm calling security."

"See you around, little girl," Jason jeered, walked out, and never saw Payne again.

Weeks passed.

Jason stomped into the kitchen, where Addy was stirring a sauce.

"I am losing my own son," Jason said, "It's driving me fucking crazy. No matter what I do, I lose. I feel like some idiot dog in a 'learned helplessness' experiment jumping from one side of the cage to the other to escape electric shocks, and never succeeding."

"You said that before,"
"Sorry."
Addy bent over, tasted her sauce, and looked up at him.
"Why the hell do you think Russet's doing this?"
Jason gritted his teeth.
"It's not Russet. She's not really the one doing this to me. It's the mass of dumb, 'morally superior' people who blindly think well of themselves for 'protecting' her against their image of me as some kind of horrendous monster. She's a very, very sick woman, physically. Her diabetes screws up her perceptions of reality. She sees monsters when there are none, but doesn't know she's demented until the diabetes is under control. She's far sicker than she's ever been. Her hair's almost totally gray, her skin's dried up like parchment with wrinkles everywhere. She's not even 37 years old. Why the hell can't these dumb people who are protecting her see that?"

Addy looked up and over at him. Her face was rigid with despair.
"Maybe she'll just die and it'll be over for you?"
"I can't really wish her dead, Addy. I just can't do it."
Addy turned off the burner under her sauce, and sighed.
"You still love her, don't you? Fine. I'll do the damned wishing for you."

V

"Addy's Party Store" was a long, rectangular liquor store that also had a full line of groceries and a Deli area.

From 1978 on Jason managed and worked at the store. He wrote the employee manual, wrote and designed the direct-mail advertising and handled the insurance. He did much of the cooking in the catering business and sometimes bartended at catering jobs, as well as working behind the counter at busy times and closed the store at night.

When he didn't work at the store or at parties, Jason wore the same khaki, paint-smeared and stained Bermuda shorts, torn, dilapidated sneakers and a ripped gray sweatshirt that he'd worn during the construction of the tree hut. He knew he looked like a bum, but by then he had become embittered about the world and didn't care any more what other people thought.

He also wore the ragged shorts shopping.

"I'll give you a hundred bucks for those goddamn berms," Addy said in front of their house as they unloaded the week's groceries, "$100 to get something besides that rag."

"No thanks."

"You're freakin' losing it, Jason. You live inside your hermit's world over how to get custody of Brandon and your brainy world of legal books, not the real world."

Jason balanced the second bag of groceries in his arms.

"What's the 'real world'?"

She shook her head as she reached back into the trunk.

"Money, power, manipulation, greed, back-stabbing. Exactly the shit that's happenin' to you."

He held on to the grocery bags and sulked.

"No thanks. I flatly refuse to join that moronic club of middle class assholes. That's not my world at all."

They took the groceries inside, put them away, Addy began dinner and Jason walked outside and down the dirt road that ran around the block.

So long as I keep myself occupied, he said to himself, *I will function. The minute I'm unoccupied, the nightmare my life has become returns with a vengeance and I think of nothing other than possible ways I can get Brandon the help he so pitifully needs and deserves. There is absolutely nothing rational or just about these assholes in the court system or, for that matter, the mealy-mouthed feminist assholes like Ms. Payne with her big tits and head full of doctrinaire man-hating crap. I now know what it must've felt like to be black in the south before the civil rights movement of the 60s.*

"Some day, Jason," Addy said when he returned, "Russet's going to croak. You told me that. When that happens, you'll automatically get custody, right?"

He leaned against the refrigerator and looked at the dinner of sautéed chicken breasts simmering on the stove

"I assume so. But what the hell kind of brutalized, twisted shape is Brandon going to be in by then? The only thing he's got that they can't mangle is his memories of the parks, the Great Water Gun War, the tree hut, the Imaginary Spaceship Gremlin and me. There's no way they can rob him of those things, is there?"

She pulled the dinner plates from the shelves above the sink and slammed them down on the counter next to the stove.

"Shit. How the hell do I know? Let's talk about somethin' else."

VI

Things got worse.

In December of 1978 Addy and Jason went out to dinner at the Country Club they belonged to. Afterwards they went for drinks at a tavern in Stansburg, Michigan, called Big Momma's Den, to hear a couple of Jason's old musician friends play. Jason drank four bourbon Manhattans, and Addy matched him with glasses of Grand Marnier liqueur.

Going home they were pulled over.

"Wast the problem, Officer?" Jason asked the face behind the flashlight beam in his driver's side window.

"Please get out of the car, sir. You were driving erratically and without your headlights on."

Jason spent the night in the Stansburg jail. The police drove Addy--who was as drunk as Jason–home, where she slept it off and returned to get Jason out of jail the next day.

After lunch with Addy, Jason went to see Vincent Wilcox, a local attorney whom Addy recommended. Vincent was a married Catholic man in his fifties with thinning brown hair, who had five children, had never divorced, and was a man whom Addy said handled drunk driving cases. He was dressed in a dark-brown, freshly pressed 3G suit. His shoes glistened; and his office reeked of money with its polished wood floors and walls covered with framed law degrees and community awards.

"I think we'll probably get the DUIL ticket reduced to impaired driving," Vincent said after he'd heard Jason's story and observed the unshaven face and blood shot eyes of his potential client.

"What's 'DUIL' mean?"

"'Driving Under the influence of Liquor.'"

"And 'Impaired'?"

"A lesser offense--a first time offense. There'll be about a $300 fine, a requirement that you attend alcoholism classes, and six points on your driver's license. The record of the offense will stay there for life."

"Ouch."

"Well, that's the law."

Jason retained attorney Wilcox, started out the door, and stopped in the doorway.

"Ah, do you handle child custody cases?"

Wilcox looked up from some papers on his desk.

"Yes."

"Do you have a minute?"

"Yes. Please have a seat."

Jason told attorney Wilcox his story.

"The Judge is Dunning?"

"Yes."

Wilcox shook his head and spoke in a low, carefully controlled courtroom voice.

"You might have difficulty. He's part of one of the old families here in town. The Dunning name is everywhere. They're old money. Real old money. He's rather conservative, shoot from the hip kinda guy, particularly after he's had his luncheon martinis. My advice to you is to give up the custody fight-- you can't win."

Jason was appalled.

"Give up on my own son?"

Wilcox smiled politely and nodded.

Jason looked Wilcox steadily in the eyes. Addy had told him Wilcox was a staunch, conservative Christian.

"'For God so loved the world He gave his only begotten son'?"

Attorney Wilcox smiled smugly to himself and looked up towards heaven.

"There's nothing better that has happened to the world."

"A God who killed his own son?"

Attorney Wilcox nodded and beamed beatifically..

"You're fired," Jason said, retrieved his check, and walked out.

Jason hired another attorney, and the drunk driving charge was reduced to 'impaired' at a later hearing.

"I am a complete failure," Jason said to Addy in their bedroom the next morning. He sat on the edge of the bed, facing the large double-sink connection between their bedroom and the shower.

Addy looked up from one of the woman's fashion magazines she usually read while she did her hair, nails, and make up, and snarled.

"Huh? Come on, get off it," she snapped.

"Brandon's counting on me to teach him how to grow up and be a man, and where the fuck am I? Thrown in jail for drunk driving. A bum. Despite my Ph.D., my skills as a pianist, the immense success of our store and catering business, I am a horrendous failure. You've said that I'm bright. Ha. Some brightness. I can't figure out how to outsmart the unabashed bigotry of Ms. Payne and CH and the mindless court system and gain custody of my own son."

Addy put away her nail file, and sighed.

"She's gonna croak someday, Jason. Just wait."

"Wait? What the fuck for? It's been almost seven years now since Russet left me and this whole nightmare began. Wait for Brandon to dry up and die a stuttering, cross-eyed idiot?."

He headed downstairs to the kitchen and their liquor cabinet.

For about three months Jason lost himself in the bottoms of bottles of Lauder's scotch. He thought of killing the judge, or himself, or of disappearing somewhere, so that the nightmare would end.

Addy watched Jason deteriorate and despaired. Then she saw a way out that astonished her with its utter simplicity. She became obsessed with the idea of making a long-distance call to an old high-school friend who was a junkie and Viet Nam veteran. He was a hit man who everyone in the liquor business knew and feared. No doubt he'd be interested in the job. Addy looked over at Jason.

"I can get a hit man," she said in the kitchen after Andria and Bobby had run outside.

"You're kidding. You haven't actually. . . ."

Addy brushed her hair vigorously and talked to the mirror.

"No. I haven't called. I just know who he is. It will be an accident. It will look like an accident."

The idea was fascinating in its gruesome way, and Jason thought Addy might be putting him on for some unknown reason.

"An accident?"

"Yeah, accident. Otherwise the goddamn finger's gonna be pointed straight at us."

Jason sat down on a kitchen chair and sucked deeply on his cigarette.

"I see. What kind of accident? She doesn't drive. She's legally blind."

"The less we know, the better. Her being blind is the entry. It will somehow be used to cause the accident."

Jason looked straight at her.

"You're not kidding, are you?"

"Not really. I've had it with all this bullshit. We've all had it up to here. This is the quickest and easiest and most cost-effective way to fix the problem."

Jason mulled over the idea the way that he wrangled with the meaning of obscure poetry. Then the reality hit him and he felt sick to his stomach. He shook his head.

"I can't do that–I just can't do that."

She looked over at him.

"Why not? I've heard it only costs about ten grand. We can get the freakin' money, you know. We can skim it in a couple of months."

Jason snapped his head back and forth.

"No-no-no. It's not the money, Addy, it's not the money at all."

Addy's upper lip curled.

"You still love the bitch, don't you?"

Jason stood and looked out the window towards the tree hut.

"Part of me will always love her, but that's not the point."

Addy shouted. "What the hell is?"

Jason's stomach ached.

"The point is that I just realized that if I went through with it, some day I'd have to tell Brandon I had his mother killed, and I felt deathly sick about the whole insane thing. Let's drop the fucking idea."

"Morality?"

"Love. Brandon's love for me. It's precious. I won't destroy it."

Addy stood .

"You're never going to win this stupid war, Jason. You've got to learn how to be a, you know, kick-ass son-of-a-bitch."

"Perhaps."

She whirled around and planted both hands on her hips.

"Where the hell has this 'love' shit gotten you?"

"Gotten me? Well, let's see. I feel helpless, like I once did years ago looking into the eyes of a dying kid staring at me."

"The kid who got hit by the car?"

"That's the one."

Addy went back to the sink and rinsed her dishes.

"Who's the dying kid now? You or Brandon?"
Jason looked down at the glass of scotch in his hand.
"Both of us."

One Saturday in February 1979 there was a knock on the door. It was a female process server who served Jason with a motion to further reduce visitation. The motion claimed there had been drinking and a verbal fight between Addy and Jason. Clearly, Brandon had told Russet and Danny something about a fight.

And there had been a fight--over Jason's obsession with winning custody of Brandon to the exclusion of caring for Addy. Two weeks before, while Brandon was there, Addy and Jason had been drunk. There had been shouting and swearing, and threats of divorce.

Jason re-read the papers, and thought: *Danny's intention is to adopt Brandon. Brandon blithely informed me that he had 'decided ' that he wanted Danny 'to be his new daddy,' stating this as if it were a fait accompli. Ms. Payne mentioned the adoption scheme point-blank to me in our last session together, and my bet is that Brandon is being interrogated after his visits in the hopes of finding some kind of damning evidence that would force me to give up the custody war.*

Jason re-read the motion. The fight between him and Addy was the final nail in the coffin he'd been slowly lowering himself into over the years. Legal nail after legal nail; motion after motion; loss after loss; failure piled on top of failure, the way dirt is shoveled into a grave.

He had lost. It was over. He had buried himself alive.

Addy went upstairs to put on her make up while Bobby and Andria sat down to watch television.

It was almost noon. Brandon was due any minute for a visit and something in Jason collapsed with the finality and hopelessness of a fallen tree. He went up into the kitchen, got out the half gallon of scotch, sat down at the kitchen table and poured himself half of a water glass of warm, straight, Lauder's Scotch, chugged it, and gagged. He poured another half glass of scotch, threw it down, gagged again, and ransacked his mind for a last ditch strategy.

By the time Brandon got there Jason was drunk, and had a plan that had struck him as brilliant. *I am going to kill Brandon's love for me. That way, the interrogations of Brandon will end, the war will end, Brandon will have "daddy Danny" and his mother, and the world will be at peace. I am going to give up the fight, do what Russet, Danny, Ms. Payne, Judge*

Dunning, and the rest of the fucking world, goddamn them all, want me to do. I am going to sacrifice my love and myself to save Brandon from this nightmare. There's no other way out.*

He finished his glass of scotch and poured another.

Brandon came in the front door and made his way into the family room.

"H-Hi," he said.

"Hi Brandon," Andria said.

"Howdy," Bobby said, imitating the language of the western movie he'd been watching.

"I wanna call a family meetin'," Jason cried to Addy and the kids.

They all went downstairs to the music studio. Brandon, Andria and Bobby sat to the left, at the far end of the room, on the bright yellow sofa, and Addy sat at the other end of the sofa next to Jason's record collection, record player, hi-fi equipment, and tape recorder. Jason squatted on one of the bottom steps of the small flight of stairs leading down into the music studio, directly across from the bank of sound equipment next to Addy.

"Turn on the tape recorder, Addy, please. I wanna record all of this," Jason said. He looked over to his left at Brandon.

"Brandon, you're a goddamned tattle-tale, an' thas against the rules here, you know--a- against our rules, dammit."

Brandon cowered, and Jason saw the tears start to flow.

Jason ignored the tears and willed himself to attack Brandon.

"Do you really want Danny to be your dad?"

Brandon's lips trembled. He started to fidget rapidly with his hands, putting one on the top, and then the bottom, of the other, all the time trembling and staring teary-eyed at Jason.

Here comes the unvarnished truth, kid, Jason thought, and took a swig of scotch.

"Have they told you--has your mom and Danny told you that for Danny to adopt you I mush sign off on you?"

Brandon looked wide-eyed at his father, and shook his head from side to side, his lips trembling the way baby birds tremble.

Jason raised his voice.

"You don't know?"

Brandon shook his head from side to side. Clearly, neither Russet nor Danny had told Brandon the truth. *Ok,* Jason thought, taking a heavy hit of scotch. *I'm going to educate him about the truth of adoption, by Christ.*

"It mesh--means no more tree hut, no more Addy, no more Andria and

Bobby, no more Great Water Gun War, no more Imaginary Spaceship Gremlin, no more times together in th' parks wish me 'cause it means that I will never see you again, ever."

Brandon's jaw worked right and left, tears flooded his eyes, and his shoulders quivered violently.

"Is that whash you want? Do you really want me to sign off on you?"

Brandon stared, tears pouring down his face, sobbed and shook uncontrollably and didn't answer.

Jason wobbled to his feet, pointed his finger, and shouted.

"You do, don't you? Ok, if thash what you goddamn want, kid, then I'm going to fucking sign off on you!"

Jason's words came at Brandon like a bullet aimed at his heart and he jumped to his feet and screamed at the top of his voice, his body shaking from head to toe, his fists clenched and thrashing in the air in a futile terror.

"Nooo!
Nooo!
Nooo!
Nooo!
Nooo!
Nooooooo!"

Jason looked down at his shrieking son, the child he loved more than any one or anything in his life, and was sick. He knew instantly that he didn't mean a word that he had said. He realized that Brandon didn't have the slightest idea of what Danny's proposed 'adoption' of him, in reality, meant, and didn't know because, until that moment, Brandon had not been told that adoption by Danny was to be accomplished by the loss of Jason, forever. Brandon was just a kid. He probably thought that, like Andria and Bobby, he could have 'two Daddies'.

He had been brainwashed.
Why?
Revenge?
For what?
Brainwashed by whom?
Danny?
Mary Lou?
Why kill Brandon's love for his father?

Two weeks later, when he saw Brandon again, Jason was sober. He took Brandon out in the back yard to the tree hut, sat him down under the shade of the elm tree on the 'sandbox' rim, and knelt down in front of him.

"I want to say something important, Brandon. Ok?"

Brandon's red hair looked patchy from the shadows of the tree leaves. He nodded.

Jason spoke softly, and kept his head eye-level with his son.

"Brandon, what I said to you about signing off on you wasn't true. I was drunk and I was stupid and cruel to you and I broke all the important rules of our family about growing down. I'm ashamed of what I did and said, and I'm terribly sorry that I hurt your heart. I want to apologize to you for what I did. I love you more than life itself, and never, never, ever will I sign off on you, and that's a promise."

Brandon squinted and tried to focus on his father's eyes.

"O-k-kay."

"Will you forgive me?"

Brandon stared at his father, seemed to see tears in his eyes, and was scared, but of what, he knew not.

"Y-y-yes."

Jason hated Lauder's scotch, had never liked it or any other scotch before, hated the way it tasted, hated what it did to him, and got scared that he was becoming an alcoholic. As part of the penalty for the impaired driving ticket, he was supposed to attend classes on alcoholism locally.

"That doesn't strike me as a wise public relations thing to do for the vice-president of a party store," he said to Addy during one of their walks around the block.

The setting sun was in her eyes and she shaded them with the palm of her hand.

"You've got to go, you know. The Judge said so."

Jason's gaze was straight ahead, unblinking.

"All he said was that I was to attend classes on alcoholism. I'm going to put myself into the Winton Grove to dry out and get some help."

"When?"

"In March I called them, and set it up. I want some time to myself, away from you, Andria, Bobby, and Brandon, to think."

Addy took his arm, her voice was raspy with anger.

"Jason, you are obsessed by this damned custody fight. I don't think you can win it--everyone's against you, you know. I am, frankly, sick and tired of it."

He glanced at her and kept walking.

"I don't blame you, but I am absolutely horrified by the smug, doctrinaire, wrong-headed imbecility of Ms. Payne and the appalling dumb-headed stupidity of the court system--not to mention my own fucking asininity in response to them. I've got to think this damned madness through. Somehow I'm going to beat those bastards, all of them and get Brandon out of this fucking insane world he's been sentenced to and is being held hostage in."

Addy stopped walking and glowered at him.

"Oh? Really? What the hell are you going to do?"

His eyes were focused on a point somewhere ahead of him.

"First, I'm going to dry out."

VII

There was no alcohol in Jason's blood stream when he registered in the morning at Winton Grove and had a physical examination. He attended all his classes dutifully and saw Addy and Andria and Bobby on 'visitor's day'. A court order, petitioned for by Golding, prevented Brandon from visiting.

Jason was desperate. He talked to everyone he could at Winton Grove about Brandon's and his plight, including the physicians and therapists, who thought he was, at best, depressed; at worse, a paranoid psychotic. "Nothing like his story could be anywhere near the truth," he later learned they wrote in their reports.

He did as he was instructed in his classes, and took inventory of his life. One night, sitting on the side of his bed he had a fantasy. Someone was talking about him, in a courtroom, to the judge. "Jason Adams," the person said, "is a brilliant man, a highly talented man, who's got to be the toughest guy alive, given what he's gone through trying to get his son."

Suddenly, Jason stopped the fantasy. It felt good to have it, but there was something dark, something painful, lurking behind the bright, egotistical surface. He'd had fantasies like that one, he realized, many times, for years. Why? *Confusion.* he said to himself, *there's some kind of nightmare hiding* behind that ego-trip, something that is forcing me to repeat it over and over again, something terribly painful that happened to me once, or several times.

He kept looking at the bright light of the fantasy, and kept trying to allow himself to feel what was hiding behind the light. Then it hit him: *I am imitating my father's self-glorifying dinnertime 'guts' story about his heroes: Teddy Roosevelt, Ty Cobb, Sergeant York. How he was like them in his days of glory playing basketball with his body racked in pain in the championship games, and he fought on, anyway.*

And as a kid, I worshipped my dad. I bought it all.

The poor guy. Life certainly dealt dad some bum cards--but, somehow, he always delivered, always kept his promises, and has always somehow been there when I really needed him. He was there when I had that car accident as a teenager, was there when I joined the same fraternity he had been in, was there at my piano concerts in high school. He was always there at the crunch times.

I'll be damned, Jason thought, *I haven't been seeing him as a whole man for all these years. I've just been seeing the negative phony hero side of him so that I could go on my self-pitying ego trips, imitating him.*

I got it.

I got what that fantasy means.

And, he thought a few minutes later, *maybe I can finally see my dad as a whole man, a man, like me, with assets, and liabilities. Just a guy and, on balance, a good guy who, as best he could, loved me.*

Then he realized where he was, and what he'd done to Brandon.

Can Brandon see me that way? Will he ever be able to see me that way?

Jason came home from Winton Grove resolved to fight for Brandon with the last ounce of strength he had in his body.

It was a crisp November afternoon when he got home and Addy and the kids surrounded him in the living room, their eyes expectant, sitting quietly before him.

"I'm Ok kids. I'm all better now. I missed you; I missed all of you, and Brandon too."

"'The judge wouldn't allow Brandon to see his father," Addy said.

"I hate the judge," Andria said.

"Me too," echoed Bobby.

Jason leaned forward towards them.

"I am going to win this war for Brandon, period," he announced, "No matter how much money, or how long, it takes. Under no circumstances will I give up on Brandon."

"Yea." Andria and Bobby yelled for their dad. He was going to be a hero, just like on television.

Addy told the children to go outside and play. Which they did immediately to catch the warmth of the sunlight.

She stared at him.

"Win the war? That's going to be really, really, tough. You're labeled as an 'alcoholic' now that you put yourself in the hospital to dry out. You really shouldn't have done that, you know."

"I don't give a shit. I'm going to win this thing, period."

Addy frowned and handed him some legal-sized papers.

"Maybe. This came in the mail the other day."

It was a legal documented titled "Petition for Order Prohibiting Release of School Records Pertaining to the Minor Child (Brandon Adams) it read. Sally Golding had filed it, and Judge Dunning had signed it while Jason was at Winton Grove.

"Why the hell didn't you show this to me before?"

Addy looked guilty--and afraid.

"I didn't know what was in the envelope. It was addressed to you, after all."

Jason slapped the paper down on the coffee table.

"Judge Dunning had no business sitting as judge in this case--and I don't give a damn that he's a friend of your father's."

Addy's face wrinkled up.

"He's not a friend of my dad's, Jason."

"I thought he played poker with him?"

"No, that's Judge Dunning's brother, Harry."

Jason threw a hand up in the air.

"Fuck it. Well, he--Judge Dunning--should have disqualified himself long ago."

"Why?"

He stood up.

"Just a second."

Jason ran upstairs to his study where he kept all the legal documents of his case and returned downstairs to Addy.

"Here," he said, "read."

"What is this?"

"A portion of the transcript of the last day of my custody trial for Brandon. My whole case was based on Russet's diabetes."

Addy looked at the paper.

THE COURT: All right, you asked me to view this under the Act, to weigh both parties. We have gone into this thing for three days, and the disease of the plaintiff has certainly been before us. All the doctors agree that it is severe in and of itself. I know this, I have personal knowledge of it. I have a brother-in-law who has juvenile diabetes.

Addy looked up.

"It's true. I know his brother-in-law."

Jason glared at her.

"Tell me. How could Judge Dunning explain to his brother-in-law that he had ruled against a juvenile diabetic?"

Addy shrugged.

"Oh, he's a judge. He'd find a way."

Jason walked around the family room a pacing white shirt on a merry-go-round..

"Up his. He's now found a way to prevent me from seeing Brandon's schoolwork. Jesus Christ. What the hell have I done? I'm paying my child support. I adopted Andria and Bobby in 1977. I have never physically hurt them or Brandon. I am cold sober. And I am being treated as if I were some kind of a psychotic child abuser. This is insane."

Addy looked at her interlocked fingers, and smiled to herself.

"No. It's the justice system. It's a reality. You attacked a sacred cow and you're paying the price."

Jason stopped in his tracks and stared at her.

"What 'sacred cow'?"

Addy scowled.

"You, with all your brilliance and knowledge, don't know what the sacred cow is?"

"No."

Addy looked down at the piece of paper in her hands.

"Motherhood, you asshole, motherhood."

VIII

Days, hollow with failures to secure more visitation, went by slowly, creeping, as time had crept for years.

In late April, 1979, Jason pulled into his driveway after having posted advertisements at the University Law School asking for law students to help him do research work on child custody cases. The car radio was on and Hal Young on the WCR 'Spotlight' show was interviewing a professor of American history named Howard Stein.

"The court system is sexist to the hilt," Dr. Stein was saying. "Fathers lose custody 90% of the time, even in situations where they are clearly the better parent. They spend years and thousands of dollars trying to get custody of their kids, or even the right to see their own children, and lose almost 100% of the time. That's pure prejudice. It's as primitive as running the gantlet."

Host Young played to his middle-class audience.

"Excuse me, doctor, but—for us uneducated yahoos—what's a 'gantlet'?"

"'It's a form of military punishment or initiation into manhood in certain Indian tribes. A man runs between two rows of people hitting him with clubs, beating him unmercifully each step of the way—in the American Indian tribe—towards manhood. In the court system instead of clubs, it's words, court orders, financial punishments and whimsical judgments as the brutalized litigant struggles to achieve justice."

Young, a notoriously conservative interviewer, whose father had been a prominent attorney in Detroit, was quick to defend the status quo. And, after all, he knew Stein had lost a custody fight for his children.

"Aren't you being a bit over-dramatic and self-serving, Dr. Stein? I mean, isn't all this a matter of law? I mean, we have some of the finest attorneys and law schools here in Michigan."

Dr. Stein fired back with the haughty contempt for the uniformed typical of jaded university professors.

"Attorneys? Law schools? Mr. Young, it might interest you to learn that law students get taught nothing about domestic law, nothing about clinical psychology, and nothing about developmental psychology. Law students cannot major in domestic law—in Michigan or, for that matter, in any other state in this country. Not one. When students get their law degree and get involved in divorces and child custody cases and say they are 'family law attorneys' they are, to put it plainly, outright liars. It's a scandal of massive proportions. In reality, the attorneys you seem to so admire might as well be barbers performing brain surgery. It's evil, evil in itself."

Young felt personally, and unfairly, under attack. Stein was clearly a communist, or a seditious traitor, or both.

"All evil? What about judges? Certainly they have special qualifications."

"They're know-nothing attorneys with robes on, period."

There was a pause. Young regrouped. His voice was high and nasal.

"Clearly you appear to have an ax to grind. Tell me this: why don't divorced fathers pay their child support?"

Stein took umbrage at what he considered to be an outrageously unfair and untrue statement, and raised his voice in indignation.

"For your information, Mr. Young, and to set the record straight, they do pay support–91.4% of them pay, on time, and the correct amount when they see the child or children for whom they're paying support. The business of 'dead beat dads' is a feminist—sexist--hype job--it's a hate crime like calling a Negro person a 'nigger' or a Jewish person like me a 'Kike."

Young's trained voice was strained around the edges.

"I guess wa-we have different figures, Mr. Stein."

"It's 'Dr.' or 'Professor Stein,' Mr. Young. And we undoubtedly have different figures. Mine come from the Census Bureau of the United States government, yours undoubtedly come from the Feminist Fiend of the Court."

Young was clearly becoming frustrated with his belligerent guest.

"You mean 'Friend of the Court,' don't you, Professor Stein?"

"No, I meant what I said, Mr. Young. We send our child support payments in envelopes addressed to 'The Fiend of the Court."

"Why? That seems, ah, unusual, does it not?"

"Because that's what they are: fiends from the hell called 'greed.' They're a collection agency, pure and simple—and that's all they are. They are certainly not friends of fathers or of children."

"What do you mean, a 'collection agency'?"

"They routinely recommend that custody go to the parent least capable of paying child support so that the support-payer is the non-custodial parent. The Fiend of the Court gets a percentage of every dollar they collect, Mr. Young."

Young figured he had a radical extremist on his hands, and had no choice but to challenge the upstart on the facts.

"Oh? Who pays this so-called percentage?"

Professor Stein had done his homework.

"You and I and every other law-abiding tax payer. The percentage program is a governmental program out of Washington, D.C., called 'Incentive Payments to the States.' Ask your congressional representative. It's a public document.'"

Young refused to be confused by the academic nonsense.

"So, I take it you think that fathers should just automatically get custody and mothers should pay child support?"

Professor Stein seemed unperturbed.

"Not 'automatically,' Mr. Young. We are working on putting together a 'Joint Custody Bill' with the legislature at the Capitol, just as they're now doing in California. We want to keep fathers in the lives of their kids, and vice-versa. Without a father, a hole forms, and the demons rush in--kids rot inside and drift, like ships without rudders. They become juvenile delinquents, criminals—after all, some 85% of the inmates in Federal Prison are fatherless kids gone bad."

Young's boiling contempt for the Professor finally spilled over.

"And what do you think the chances are of this so-called 'Joint Custody Bill' actually passing?"

"If California does it, we'll surely do it. It will be a first for the country if it passes in California, and we think it will."

There was a strained silence.

Finally, Young spoke, almost in a sneer.

"Tell us, Mr. Stein, what, in your opinion, is a father? The kind of man who wines and dines one little woman after the other and then and parades around the streets disturbing the peace--as I am given to understand your group of malcon---er, men has recently done?"

There was another weighty moment of silence.

"You want me to define the concept 'father'?"

Young's tone of voice was pure contempt.

"Yes. If you can."

"Fine. Here it is. Imagine an endless universe of tenderness, stretching forever in every direction, at the center of which there is a tiny, almost invisible, point. Imagine further that tiny point to be made of pure resolve. And, finally, imagine further that this point of resolve has been fused from and is a dangerously fissionable synthesis of pure love and pure aggression. That is what a father is. Watch out."

The professor's complex formulation struck Young as fanciful and not worth pursuing; besides, the time for the interview had expired.

"Thank you, Mr. Stein. And what is the name of your organization again?"

"Dr. Stein."

"Professor Stein."

"Well, Mr. Young, we're tentatively calling it 'Equal Rights for Men,' a non-sexist organization of men and women devoted to ending the discrimination against men by the sexist court system. Men are being financially raped and unconstitutionally deprived of their children, and we are going to do something about it."

"And our listeners can reach you at the telephone number earlier announced?"

"Yes."

"Thank you Mr. Stein for your, ah, interesting views."

Jason turned off the radio and the car, ran into the house to the telephone, called the radio station and two hours later hooked up with Howard at his apartment. They talked for almost an hour–about the court system, about Howard's case, about Jason's case–and they arranged to meet with several other men that weekend at a Howard Johnson's restaurant in Summerville.

There were four men at the meeting: Jason, Howard Stein, Walt Laurel, and Bill Stilton. They sat down at a booth to the back of the restaurant, introduced themselves, and ordered coffee.

Jason had the inescapable feeling that in some way the meeting was historic--like the conspiratorial early meetings of the men who were later to write the Declaration of Independence but warned himself that he had the tendency to sometimes exaggerate the importance of events. He resolved to remain calm and objective, and listen.

Walt Laurel sat directly across the table from Jason and was first to introduce himself at Howard's suggestion. Walt was dressed in a dark blue sport shirt and jeans. He was a short man with a pudgy face and watery brown eyes. In his late twenties, he was divorced with three children that he was rarely allowed to see. He was enraged by what he called the 'Gestapo brutality of the so-called justice system'.

"They jailed me for non-payment of child support," Walt said, visibly clenching his coffee cup, his eyes unflinching, "Even though I was laid-off from work and had no damned money at all--I was livin' with my folks--and then, when I got out of jail--I mean the goddamn second I got out--the goddamn bastards arrested me again."

Howard shook his head and muttered "bigots."

Bill Stilton was an athletic-looking man in his early forties, an electronics engineer, dressed in a gold, pullover sweater. He sat next to Walt and looked baffled by Walt's report.

"Why? You'd served your sentence, hadn't you?"

Walt glanced to his left at Bill, then looked back across the table at Jason and Howard.

"They told me that I'd run up another goddamn arrearage while I was in the goddamn jail. How the hell is a guy supposed to get back on his fuckin' feet when they do shit like that on him?"

"Nazis." Howard growled. Howard was a huge man in his mid-forties, about 6' 6" tall, weighing some 260 pounds. He was balding, worn glasses, and had dark brown, intense, eyes.

"What's your story, Bill?" Howard asked.

Bill swallowed his coffee with an audible "gulp," and looked, wide-eyed and innocent, at Howard.

"It's unbelievable. Judy--my wife--just filed for divorce and before I knew it, I was kicked out of my house."

"By whom?" Howard asked.

"There was a court order."

"Signed by whom?" Howard pursued, leaning forward.

Bill shrugged.

"By the judge in an Ex Parte hearing without me present. They ordered me out of the house, bang! Just like that. It makes absolutely no sense to me, none."

"That's unconstitutional," said Walt, his lower lip curled downward in contempt.

"Are you a lawyer?" Bill asked, his eyes wide.

Walt pumped his closed fists.

"No, paralegal. But every goddamn school boy knows that all Americans are entitled to due process of the law--it's the 14th Amendment to the Constitution--and it sounds to me like your goddamn due process rights were fucked with all over hell and gone. Demand a re-hearing."

Howard shook his head and toyed with a sugar pack.

"Ok, my turn. Here's my story. I haven't seen my children in over four years. I kept going back and back into court, trying to get the court to force visitations, and have spent a small fortune on attorneys. Finally, a couple of years ago, I took a leave of absence from the university where I'd taught history for fifteen years, shut every blind in my apartment and went into a black depression for two years."

"Did you drink?" Jason asked.

Howard smiled inwardly and shook his head.

"I'm not a drinker. I just cried. Endlessly. And raged. Endlessly. Then, I got angry, real angry--furious--at myself, at the Nazi system, at the Pogrom of fathers the system was conducting,. and came out fighting."

"Pogrom? What does that mean?" Walt asked with a mischievous grin in his eyes.

"Annihilation. The massive extermination of fathers," Howard sneered.

"Glad you decided to fight," said Bill, and reached across the table to shake Howard's hand.

"You guys haven't heard anything yet," said Howard. "Jason has been fighting to see his son for about--what--eight years? Jason, tell them your story."

Jason told his story. The men shook their heads, seemed to either not believe or be numbed by what he told them.

Jason looked around the table at each man, one by one. No one said anything.

"So," said Howard at the end of the meeting, "what are we going to do? I'm dead certain that we aren't the only fathers out there who have been and are being screwed by this sick system. We've got to get this thing organized, make some kind of public demonstration like the Boston Tea Party that preceded our Revolutionary War."

My God, Jason thought, *This meeting is historic.*

"The feminists burned their bras years ago. How about us burning our jocks?" Walt jeered.

"How about a jock burning right at the court house?" Bill added.

"With television coverage," Howard said. "To symbolize what? The feminists claimed that their bras were symbols of male oppression, of how men had held them down. What would a jock burning symbolize?"

"Being de-balled by the bitches and bastards in the court system?" Bill asked.

Jason tried to find the right idea.

"Being without support in divorce and child custody cases?"

"No," Howard growled, "burning the jocks will be an act of utter defiance that takes place right at the court house in front of the nation on national television."

"Who's going to watch that? I mean, who in the television business gives a shit about us?" Walt scoffed.

Howard leaned against the wall of the booth, to his right, then swung around to face all three men.

"I've got a friend at CBS and another one at NBC who have worked with me on Public Broadcast system programs about American history. Both are divorced. Both lost their homes, huge slabs of their wealth, and custody of their children. I'll call them tomorrow, and get back to you guys sometime next week."

They got up to leave.

"Boy, am I glad to have met you guys," Jason said, "For years I thought there was no help out there, none at all."

Howard stood at attention.

"There's a reason for that feeling of being hopelessly stranded, and it is that because until now there was no help at all out there for fathers. None at all."

It took about a month to put together telephone calls to friends to gather support for the demonstration, the parade permit and permission from the fire department for a kettle filled with burning wood—a kind of pep rally with a new twist.

The front steps of the courthouse were cordoned off Police in riot gear stood just outside the lines. It was a chilly night, with a dark, clear sky. A noisy crowd of some 30-odd men wearing warm clothes milled about inside the cordoned-off area.

On the plateau just before the top step leading into the courthouse, was an iron garbage barrel the demonstrators had filled with wood, set on fire, turning the barrel into a roaring torch. Sparks flitted in the glowing air above the barrel like escaping fireflies, and smoke billowed from the fire like specters towards the front of the court house and its roof, some four stories in the air. The television trucks with antennas like giant insects on their roofs, police vans with emergency lights flashing, and a milling crowd of spectators surrounded the agitated men carrying placards that pronounced, "Fathers Are People, Too, No Visitation, No Support, and Kids Need Fathers, Not Visitors."

Jason approached Howard.

"Private Adams reporting for duty," Jason said grinning, lifting his jock strap high in the air. "Armed with one empty supporter and plenty of balls."

Howard's huge body stood before Jason like a black statue against the flickering orange background of the fire, Two television reporters stood to either side of Howard with their microphones pointed at him. Jason, heart palpitating, stood to Howard's right, facing forward, and waited. To their left were two hand-held television cameras pointed right at Howard and Jason and from behind the cameras a spotlight suddenly popped on. .

A man appeared in front of Howard and Jason.

"This is Cameron Jordon, ABC news, reporting," said the gray-haired reporter opposite Howard, "and I am talking with Professor Howard Stein, who we are told is the head of the group you see gathered here on the courthouse steps in Summerville, Michigan. Professor Stein, would you please tell our nationwide audience what this is all about?"

Howard took the reporter's microphone, and looked directly into the camera lens.

"We are here to protest the wholesale sexism of the court system that deprives divorcing men of their homes using the unconstitutional ex-parte order. This illegal court order strips men of their life's work and blindly awards custody of children to women 90% of the time in divorce cases, regardless of how fit they are to be parents."

Jordon smiled at Howard.

"So, you're anti-traditionalists?"

Howard's face was expressionless as he looked straight into the camera.

"The only thing we're against is the bigotry of the judges and their lackeys. We are a group of men and women, particularly second wives, who have seen our children stripped from us as if we were common criminals–all because we are simply loving fathers whose wives decided to divorce us. Aspiring lawyers can't major in domestic law in any law school in this country or, for that matter, take cognate courses in developmental or clinical psychology. Hence, the court system has neither the training nor the brains to deal with the contagion of a 50% first-marriage divorce rate, and the system is destroying us, our children, and our country just as did the filthy practice of slavery before the Civil War."

There was applause and loud cheers from the crowd surrounding Howard and Jason. Several police shifted nervously nearby and adjusted their plastic riot visors.

Howard glanced at Jordon.

"And lest you think this is just a sour-grapes personal campaign of mine, I want you to hear the story this man, my friend and fellow professor, Dr. Adams."

Jason tossed his jock strap into the roaring fire, and turned to Jordon, who took note of Jason's goatee and turtleneck shirt under his red and green plaid coat.

"So, Dr. Adams, you're also a professor like Mr. Stein?"

"Yes. But social status has nothing to do with my case."

"So, what is your case about, Dr. Adams?"

Jason had thought long and hard about the short speech Howard had asked him to make on national television. But it evaporated when he realized that Judge Dunning might be watching the newscast.

"The judge in my case is a sexist bigot. His name is Dunning. He listened to three days of expert medical testimony regarding my now ex-wife's terminal illness, totally ignored this scientific testimony, and awarded custody of my then four-year-old son to a sick and dying woman who spends more time in the hospital than all of us here have spent hospitalized--added together."

Jordon's jaw dropped. He stared briefly at Jason, figured him to be a bizarre malcontent, and turned the microphone to the lines of men waiting to burn their jockstraps in the cauldron.

The television segment ran in primetime in all 50 states, and the telephones at Howard and Jason's homes rang steadily for days. There were weekly meetings to plan further demonstrations and map strategies to get laws changed to make them gender neutral. The membership of the newly formed Fathers For Equality swelled to some 500 dues-paying members.

Addy applauded Jason's performance and the goals of the new group, whose meetings she often attended. On the other hand, neither Russet nor Danny said anything to Jason about his newly acquired notoriety. However, there were no more surprise court dates, and the hostilities seemed temporarily at a standstill, as if they were merely waiting for Jason's next move.

I'm finally in control of this war, Jason thought, and on a steaming hot day early in August, his plaid sport shirt and pants soaked in sweat, Jason went to pick up Brandon for his court-ordered visitation at the Ann Arbor home where Brandon had been living with Russet and Danny since their marriage. Jason parked at the curb, went to the front door of the green-shingled ranch, rang the bell, and waited.

No one came.

He rang the doorbell again, this time several times.

No response.

A cold shawl seemed to settle around his sweat-soaked shoulders.

He walked over to the front picture window, and looked inside. The house was totally empty.

He stared at the deserted inside of the house.

The world around him was unreal—an illusion void of all sense and meaning.

A motion to change custody was only a few days away. All his ducks were in a row. His remarriage in 1976, the adoption of Andria and Bobby in 1977, and the continuing poor health of Russet—all the necessary ingredients of a successful lawsuit to change custody.

Now, all that seemed another empty hope.

He went home. Addy was watching a television movie with Andria and Bobby in the family room. He said "hi" to the kids, who remained glued to their movie, and he told Addy what had happened.

She stared at him.

"What the hell are you going to do now?"

He slumped down on the couch next to her.

"The only thing I can do. Wait and let my anger simmer at this boiling point."

"Boiling point," Addy echoed.

"Boiling to explosion," Jason added, and lit a cigarette.

A couple of days later, in the mail, Jason got a one-sentence note that read, "We have moved to Mason, Michigan."

"What'd she have to say?" Addy asked him.

He handed her the note.

"She? This note is written by someone other than Russet. It isn't her writing. I don't know who wrote the note, but it looks like she's moved home up north, out of reach. I'm screwed."

"You're giving up?"

Jason bit down on the filter of his cigarette.

"No way. Brandon is counting on me, and I can't and won't fail him–I'm his dad."

Chapter III

Showdown

Jason told himself that his only hope was to push onward and wait for something dramatic to happen to Russet's health, something serious enough to reopen the custody case. Otherwise, years might pass before he could do anything to help Brandon's deteriorating mind and body, and when the time finally came to begin the repairs, it might be too late.

The phone rang next to him.

"Hello?" Jason answered.

"Hello Jason," a soft, airy voice replied.

Jason was astonished.

"Russet?"

"Hi, Jason."

"Wha-where, ah how are ya---"

"Do you ever play that song you wrote?"

"The song I wrote for you, 'Song For Russet', Ya—yes, of course, but why—"

The phone went dead.

He looked at the silent phone receiver in his hand.

What did the call mean?'

Why had she called? Had she, finally, miraculously gotten better and come to her senses?

He shook his head, and hoped the miracle had finally happened

He told Addy about the call.

"The bitch," Addy cursed, and dropped the subject.

And then the attack came.

On a Saturday morning in March Jason trudged through dirty gray snow in front of his house to the blood-red mailbox at the end of the driveway.

Among the bills, there was a letter to him postmarked March 28, 1980, from Sally Golding. He trudged through the heavy snow back to the house, the icy cold air burning his ears and stinging his cheeks. He threw his winter jacket on the back of a chair, sat down at the kitchen table, and read.

He couldn't believe the words before him. According to Golding, he was thenceforth to obtain visitation with Brandon—somewhere--by writing a letter to Russet in Mason containing specific information, namely:

1. A statement of your desire for visitation.
2. The specific day and hour you wish the visitation to commence.
3. The specific day and hour you wish the visitation to terminate.
4. The proposed activities to take place during the visitation.
5. The proposed location of the visitation.
6. The telephone number of that location.

Golding went on: "When a request is received which complies with these requirements, Mrs. Forge will of course consult with Brandon as to his wishes, as the court order calls for her to do."

Jason read Golding's letter twice, threw it down on the floor, and screamed.

"Insane! This is fucking insane! How the hell can I take him to Mandermetz Park, or any other park? There aren't goddamn telephones in the parks. Golding is outta her mind. And how the hell can Brandon make such choices? He's just a kid."

Addy came downstairs in her bathrobe.

"Hey Jason, the kids are still sleeping--what's all the noise about?"

He slumped over in his chair. He turned around and handed her Golding's letter. His eyes were wild and bloodshot and stung with tears.

"This is insane. I'm beginning to feel like 'K' in Franz Kafka's novel, 'The Trial'."

Addy sat down at the table next him, looked down at the papers in her hand and cocked her head.

"K?"

Jason remained slumped over. He looked at and spoke to his clasped hands before him on the table.

"He's the main character. He's arrested one morning for an unnamed crime, then is shuffled around like a lost letter from one court bureaucrat to another. He never finds out what crime he's committed–and by the end of the novel, he's ready to die for the crime he may, or may not, have committed, whatever the hell it was. It's pure paranoia."

Addy read Golding's letter, and shook her head.

"And what's your crime?"

Jason gritted his teeth and shrugged.

"Beats the hell out of me. Loving Brandon? Being a man? Being a father? Being me? Whatever it is, I'll bet that no matter how hard I try to comply with Golding's insane conditions, there'll always be something wrong with my request."

Jason's bet was on target. All of his written requests for visitation were denied for 'lack of specificity'. Resigned but not defeated, Jason continued to telephone Brandon every Sunday and tape-record their conversation in the hopes of discovering something–anything--he could use in court. But he never found anything he could use to end the war.

Another year crawled by, inch by inch, empty weeks highlighted by Sunday calls to Brandon, each one recorded on the equipment in his music studio.

Jason came upstairs and shuffled over to the couch in the family room after one such Sunday telephone call to Brandon. He plopped down, sighed, and stared at Addy. His voice cracked.

"It's wonderful to hear Brandon's voice, wonderful to listen to him and Andria and Bobby babble and giggle about everything but when I hang up that phone, the world freezes over and what's left? An empty cavern full of despair, that's what."

Addy was sick of the whining. She stomped back upstairs.

"How poetical. So? To hell with it. If it's so damned painful for you, why don't you just give up?"

He snarled at her back.

"Can you give me one fucking moral reason--just one--why I shouldn't love my only biological son?"

She was at the top of the stairs.

"No."

He shouted.

"Then I'm going to keep on fighting no matter how goddamned miserable it makes me."

Jason hired Steve Rhodes, a constitutional attorney Jason had met at one of the Fathers For Equality meetings. Steve was a 30-something black man with an athletic, oval face, sinewy, with a rugged jaw and a cold logical mind. He had never married or divorced, but had seen his two younger brothers financially destroyed in their divorces. Two years ago the youngest brother, Gerard, whose wife had moved out of state to California, had gotten drunk and hanged himself in his garage.

Steve told Jason the story of his brother's suicide as they met in The Java Pit, a hole-in-the-wall luncheonette on the first floor of the courthouse that served fifteen people at the most and smelled of stale cigarettes, coffee, and burnt toast.

"I don't want what happened with my brother to ever happen to anyone again," Steve said smiling at a dark reflection in his coffee. He brushed a fleck of lint from the lapel of his blue-black stylish Italian suit.

Jason looked up from buttering his Danish.

"That why you're in this business?"

Steve gritted his teeth.

"You got it."

The attack continued. Three months after Golding's letter arrived, Steve and Jason were back in court to fight another Golding motion, this time to discontinue all telephone and postal contacts between Jason and Brandon. The clerk called their case. Golding announced she was there to litigate a particular letter Jason had written to Brandon.

"What letter is this?" Steve whispered to Jason.

"Not absolutely sure, but I think I know," Jason whispered back.

Judge Dunning yawned and nodded his head to Golding. The court went silent.

"I want to read this horrible letter into the record, Your Honor," Golding said, the fire in her eyes echoed by the white streaks in her hair.

Judge Dunning nodded.

"Go ahead."

Jason whispered in Steve's ear.

"I don't know which letter this is, but my recent letters to Brandon were coded, two-cushion shots, so to speak. I really wrote the letters to Russet, Danny, and Mary Lou Brockton. I knew they'd been intercepting and reading my letters to Brandon, and I wanted to let them know I knew what they were doing, damn them all."

Golding adjusted the white scarf at the neck of her black business suit, held a sheaf of papers before her, cleared her throat, and read.

"Brandon--

Here is the letter I said I would write to you on the phone Sunday night.

You will not be able to understand this letter because (a) most of the words and comments are far beyond your nine-year-old's educational and maturational status (do you understand that sentence?) and (b) even if it were within your educational and maturational grasp the external 'brainwashing' pressures of your environment would make comprehension difficult indeed.

I am aware that your mother and Danny and Mary Lou and Golding all read my letters and all, *en masse*, attack me because of them. They no doubt teach you to scoff at the letters and me, and you will perhaps be taught to feel more hate for me than you have already been taught to feel. But never forget that right now you are a kid and can do little to help yourself against the 'brainwashing' you are experiencing. Try not to believe all they say to you."

"How long is this letter?" Judge Dunning interrupted.
"About fifteen single-spaced pages." .
Judge Dunning waved his thin, white hand in the air.
"We don't have the time to read the whole thing into the record. Just give it to me."
"Can I read the last page?"
Judge Dunning was fed up with Jason and Jason's endless litigation. The judge tossed his head to the side and yawned.
"Well, Ok."
Golding turned the pages.

"The voice I heard on the phone last night--your voice--was half-dead and half-alive. In one week I will call you to see if, as you--the Voice--seem to think, if you know what my decision will be about trying to see you up there. I predict that neither you or anyone else who reads this letter knows what my decision will be, and this is because the people who are cruel enough to invade your privacy and read my letters to you are people so hopelessly confused by the combination of their sympathy for and terror of your mother's sickness that they think doing her every wish and believing her every word, performing her slightest whim and thereby disguising from her their healthy desire to be done with her forever--are therefore incapable of loving themselves, each other, or the real person, not entirely dead, I named Ellis Brandon Adams."

Golding handed the letter to Judge Dunning, whose normally cherubic face darkened like a black thundercloud. He looked Jason straight in the eyes.

"I am putting what attorney Golding correctly called this 'horrible letter' in my appeals file."

"Thank you, Your Honor," Jason snarled, "That is exactly what I wanted you to do. It's about time you did something remotely resembling intelligence."

Judge Dunning lurched forward, pointed his finger at Jason, and shouted.

"One more word out of you, Mr. Adams, and I will find you in contempt."

Steve grabbed Jason by the arm and pulled him out of the courtroom. Outside, in the hall, Steve sat Jason down on one of the polished, brown wooden benches, and stood above him.

"You can't talk to judges like that, Jason."

Jason looked up and snarled.

"Watch me. I have absolutely no respect for him, period. He's a Momma's boy asshole. He doesn't have half my education, and has no respect whatsoever for my civil rights."

Steve sighed, put both hands on his hips, and shook his head.

"Probably so. Still, that's not how you get things done in court, Jason. That letter is damned near self-destructive, you know. Why the hell did you write it?"

Jason looked down the hall at Golding, who was talking wide-eyed and rapidly with another attorney and glancing at him.

"I was--and am--furious beyond reason at the utter injustice of this so-called justice system. I wrote it on purpose, and in desperation, before I hired you to somehow generate an appeal. I was somehow going to go to the Court of Appeals on the issue of my constitutional right to visitation with my son, and on the issues raised in that letter. I want you to draft the appeal."

Steve shook his head and looked despondent.

"I'm not sure we can win it."

Jason studied his feet.

"The father-son relationship is a constitutional right, dammit—*Stanley v,. Illinois*, right?."

Steve put his hand on Jason's shoulder and looked him straight in the eyes.

"That's true, but the political atmosphere at the Court of Appeals in Michigan is against fathers."

Jason ground his teeth and wailed.

"Fuck politics. I have nothing to lose, believe me--I have nothing to lose. My son is drowning and I've got to rescue him. I promised him I'd never give up on seeing him and that I'd never sign off on him. He's counting on me, dammit, he's counting on me."

Steve's face was racked in sympathetic pain; he shook his head and rubbed Jason's shoulder.

"You're like a wounded dog who's biting its wound to feel better. Stop it. You're desperate."

Jason stood and looked down at Steve.

"You'd better believe it. Brandon's heart and mind are being destroyed while Dunning and Golding play their lunatic legal games--and I'm going to stop it, dammit."

"How?"

Jason curled both hands into fists.

"How? I'll keep biting until the pain stops, that's how."

In April, Steve Rhodes and Jason were back in court on a motion for visitation. Russet wasn't there and Sally Golding said she didn't know where Russet was or that there was a hearing scheduled for that morning. It made no sense. Russet had never missed a court date before, and Steve knew that Golding had been properly notified.

"What the hell's going down? What new piece of treachery now?" Jason asked Steve, who looked perplexed.

"I don't know."

Jason's lower teeth jutted up over his upper lip. He pointed his index finger at Steve's chest.

"Find out."

"I'll try."

II

It was May. Steve had not been able to find out anything from Golding's office. Sally Golding was not there. Her staff knew nothing. No more motions had been filed against Jason.

Addy and Jason were in the kitchen at home packing food into cardboard boxes for a catering job.

The phone rang. It was Addy's former next-door neighbor and partner in the original catering business, Martha Smith. She was calling from the Mason area, where she and her husband had a summer home.

"Jason," Addy shouted, when she'd hung up the phone, "that was Martha Smith. She said that there was a death notice for Russet in the Mason paper."

Jason's back was toward her. His head snapped around.

"Was Martha sure?"

"Absolutely. 'Carol Forge, formerly Carol Brockton, died April 30, 1980, in the Intensive Care Unit of the University Hospital in Ann Arbor, Michigan.' Martha read it to me and I wrote it down."

Jason felt the blood suddenly empty from his face.

"Jesus Christ. No wonder Russet wasn't in court the other day."

Addy came over and put her hand on his shoulder.

"Are you Ok?"

Jason swallowed. His knees were rubbery and his head airy.

"I think so. Things like this don't always register right away."

Addy watched him stare at the floor. She took a breath, and whispered.

"What would her death mean?"

Jason shook his head violently and tried to think. He sat down on a chair at the kitchen table. He felt dislodged, the way one feels when accidentally missing a step on a flight of stairs.

"Ok. Let me think. If Russet is dead, then the custody case is over and done with. As Brandon's sole surviving parent, I am a shoo-in to get custody of him."

Addy put her hand on his shoulder.

"What about Danny?"

Jason clenched his teeth.

"Danny Forge doesn't stand a chance."

Jason stood, spun away from the table and went to the downstairs telephone in the family room. Addy watched him go.

"Who are you calling?"

"The Intensive Care Unit at the hospital. It's the one sure way to find out if Russet's dead. "

"Huh?"

Jason dialed the hospital. Addy stood upstairs in the kitchen and looked at him over the railing separating the kitchen from the family room.

"Hello, this is Dr. Adams," Jason lied, "I am the family physician for the

Forge family, and people keep calling me and asking me if Russ--Carol Forge is dead but I have no idea what to tell them. "

"Yes, doctor," the female voice replied, "She died April 30, 1980 at 10:30 A.M., of a myocardial infarction, right here in the Unit."

"Thank you very much," Jason said, and hung up. He looked up at Addy.

"She's dead. Finally, the disease got her. That's why she wasn't in court last week."

Addy felt her stomach do a flip-flop.

"Now what?"

In a flash, Jason knew what he had to do. His heart pounded in his chest. He stared at Addy.

"I'm going up there to be with him--now. Have one of the people at the store help you with this catering job."

"But--."

"I've got to get to him. His mother is dead. I'm his father--the only family he's got left."

Jason got out the telephone directory, looked up 'private airlines', booked a flight to the Harbor Grove Airport and reserved a rental a car at the airport. Addy went back to packing the food for the catering job, her stomach doing somersaults, her heart pounding against her ribs.

Jason raced upstairs, packed an overnight bag, raced back downstairs and called Danny, who answered the telephone in his boyish voice.

"Hel-lo?"

"Hello Danny, this is Jason."

"What do you want. Russet isn't–"

"–there. I know. This is a courtesy call. I'm on my way up to be with and comfort Brandon--."

"He's outside, I--."

Jason controlled himself. His voice was calm and matter-of-fact.

"Look, Danny, don't play games with me. I know Russet's dead. Brandon needs me. I'm his father, remember? I'm coming up to be with him."

"That is not advisable," Danny snapped, feeling wise and heroic, and hung up.

What the hell does that wimpy son-of-a-bitch mean by that? Jason asked himself, then ignored his own question. He kissed Addy good-bye, drove over to the Saunder's Creek Airport, and hopped in the single-engine puddle jumper for a nerve-wracking two-hour flight. At Harbor Grove Jason jumped into his rental car and headed for Mason.

The road before him turned into a black and white blur racing underneath him. The gray, overcast world of the last eight years was gone. *His heart sang. It's over. It's finally over. It's a beautiful day, the war is over. Russet is at peace. I can bring Brandon home. Brandon and I can live a normal life again with Addy and the kids, together at last, and I'll be a whole man again.*

He turned right into Mason. Brandon lived in a group of small colonial houses across the street from the elementary school his mother had attended years before. As Jason made the right turn off the main highway he wondered at his own lack of grief for the death of a woman he had loved more than any woman in his life, and realized that the woman he had so loved, years before, had been long dead.

He pulled up in front of Brandon's home. *I'm glad her suffering is finished, glad she's dead—for her, for myself, and for Brandon, because her death ends all of her, and our, suffering.*

For the first time in years, he was at peace. The war was over, life could began anew.

Jason got out of his car, and strode intently over to the front door.

He was met not by Danny, but by Allen, the brother of Russet's mother. Allen was a dark-haired man in his late fifties, a career diplomat, a man Jason had met several times. Allen did not open the screen door to Jason.

Something was wrong.

"Hi, Allen," Jason said, "I'm here to comfort Brandon."

Allen was embarrassed. He did not wish to send the wrong message. He did not open the door. He kept his voice cordial but neutral.

"He's not here."

Jason squinted through the screen door.

"Where is he?"

Allen was expressionless.

"I don't know."

What the hell is going on? Jason thought, *something's all screwed up, something's weird here. What the hell is going on?* He leaned closer to the door.

"Where's Danny?"

Allen did not move.

"I don't know."

Jason moved closer to the door, put his face almost flush with the screen, and looked Allen straight in the eyes.

"What the hell's going on, Allen?"

Allen smiled faintly, stepped back, and closed the door gently in Jason's face.

III

The sky turned a pale blue-gray, the color of ashes, as Jason returned to his rented car. He drove into downtown Mason, rented a Holiday Inn room, and called Addy. His heart pounded in his chest and his mouth was dry.

"Hi, Addy, this is Jason. I--."

Her voice was swollen with cheer.

"Hi. How goes it? Got Brandon there?"

Jason shook his head. *She won't believe this.*

"It looks like he has been hidden away somewhere."

There was a pause as Addy processed the news.

"Huh?--that makes no freakin' sense."

"It's insane. I need some fire power."

"What do you want me to do?"

Jason lit a cigarette, sucked the hot smoke into his lungs. His voice in the telephone earpiece sounded unreal to him, the way one's voice sounds when you first hear it on a tape-recording.

"Call Steve Rhodes and have him get to court fast tomorrow and get me an emergency order of custody."

Pause.

In the background Jason heard Andria yell something at her brother.

"I'll call Howard Stein, too. Give me your phone number and some directions. We'll be there as soon as we can."

Addy and Howard arrived the next evening with a custody order giving Jason temporary custody of Brandon, signed by Judge Dunning. There were dark circles under Addy's eyes and Howard looked haggard, too—even his gray three-piece suit was wrinkled, as though slept in.

They drove over to Brandon's house and stood at the front door, court order in hand.

Allen remained shielded behind the screen, his obscured face a smoky mesh. He insisted that Brandon wasn't there.

Howard was suspicious. He leaned over Jason's shoulder.

"May we come inside?"

"Not at this time," Allen replied, turned his head around and closed the door.

"I smell a rat," Howard said.

"Just one?" Addy said, her voice full of contempt, "I smell at least two--Danny and some crummy shit-ass attorney."

"Let's go," Howard growled, "We need a judge."

They went back to the car. Howard sat next to Jason in the front; Addy sat in back and smoked one cigarette after the other; no one spoke.

Jason drove down to the Mason Court House, an old brick building in the center of town with a weathered brass nameplate on its front, and went to the desk of the Clerk of the Court, an ancient man with thick glasses and trembling hands. There were no Circuit Court orders regarding Brandon, he said and pointed.

"You could give 'er a try in Probate Court--it's just down that hall in this building, 'round the corner," the clerk croaked.

Jason, Addy, and Howard marched down the hall silently, court order in hand.

The Probate Court clerk was a heavy-set woman in her fifties with a pinched mouth who looked like she'd forgotten how to smile. She looked over the three well-dressed and manicured strangers before her: they looked proper, deserving of service.

"Yes, there's a case filed," she murmured. "I'll go get it for you."

She went into a back room, returned, and dumped a pile of legal-sized papers on the counter before Jason. Howard and Addy huddled around Jason and read over his shoulder.

What had happened, they read, was that the day before Jason had arrived in Mason, Marylee Abrams, a Protective Services Worker of the County Court system, had petitioned the Juvenile Division of Probate Court to award the guardianship of Brandon to Danny Forge and Mary Lou Brockton. Abrams wrote that Russet had died, that Brandon "was without proper guardianship" and that "the natural grandmother and the step-father, Danny Forge, are both willing to accept custody."

Jason couldn't believe what he read. He shook his head and glanced back and forth between Addy and Howard.

"She's intimating that I'm not available to care for Brandon, or not a suitable person to care for him? Shit. She doesn't even know me. I've never talked with her."

"She's doing what the local politics tells her to do," Howard snapped.

Jason's hands trembled. Nothing seemed real. He turned to the next document.

Probate Judge John T. Murty had awarded Danny Forge and Mary Lou Brockton temporary custody of Brandon, and the document stated that Jason 'should be notified' of the case filed against him.

"Were you notified of any trial, any case filed against you?" Howard asked over Jason's shoulder.

"No."

Jason turned to the next sheet of paper. On the same day an attorney named Gregory Jordin was appointed 'guardian ad litem' of Brandon. Jason held up the order to Addy.

"Why the hell does Brandon need a freakin' attorney?" Addy asked, and put her arm around Jason's shoulder.

"I have no idea," Jason replied.

"I betcha this son-of-a-bitch Jordin knows where the hell Brandon is," Howard sneered. He backed away and paced around the hallway smacking his right fist into his left hand.

"Come on, let's go," he said.

Jason got Jordin's telephone number from the Court Clerk, drove back to the motel with Addy and Howard, and called Jordin at his office. Addy and Howard stood at Jason's side. The fading afternoon sunlight dribbled through the motel window, washing out the already dull tan walls and brown bed covers of the room, casting a yellow pallor on all three of their faces as they huddled around the telephone.

A voice answered at the other end of the line. Jason swallowed. Addy and Howard waited.

"Mr. Jordin, my name is Jason Adams. I understand that you are my son's guardian ad litem."

Jordin's voice was that of a young man.

"That is correct."

Jason glanced at Addy and Howard, and nodded his head.

"Well, I'm here in Mason, and I have a court order giving me custody of Brandon. I flew up to be with him, and comfort him about his mother's death, and for some reason I can't find out where the hell he is. Do you know where he is?"

"Yes."

"Is he all right?"

"Yes."

Jason's stomach relaxed.

"Thank God. Will you tell me where he is so that I can go see him?"

Out of the corners of his eyes, Jason saw Addy and Howard visibly relax.

"Not at this time."

"Why the hell not? I'm his dad--he needs me now."

Jason felt Addy and Howard's bodies stiffen.

Jordin cleared his throat.

"We will arrange a time for you to visit with him."

Jason snapped forward in his chair, as if he'd been elbowed in the stomach.

"Visit? What the hell are you talking about? I have an order of custody for him."

"We will arrange a time for a visit."

Jason stomach turned into a flaming ball of rage.

"I just told you, you son of a bitch, I have custody of him."

Jordin's voice was toneless, his words were crisply enunciated and void of feeling.

"We will arrange a time and a place for a visit."

"When?"

"Give me your telephone number. I'll call you when I know the details."

Jason did as directed, put down the telephone, and told Howard and Addy what had just transpired.

Howard scowled.

"We've got a conspiracy on our hands. These people are trying to steal Brandon for some crazy reason. Christ, they're trying to legally kidnap him."

"But why?" Addy yelled, "why?"

"This is insane," Jason cried, and banged the heel of his fist into the tabletop near him.

Addy lit a cigarette and sat down on the edge of the bed.

Howard paced around the small room like a huge bear trapped in a cage then came to a halt near the end of the bed.

"Let's think this through," he said, "The Probate Court records showed that Russet was buried in Mason on the morning of May 3, 1980, sometime before Addy received the telephone call from Martha Smith, right?"

"I guess," Addy said.

Howard shouted.

"Well, that's it. There's gotta be a probate court record of the death and her estate. Let's go back down there, to see what we can see."

Back at Probate Court, they discovered that in Russet's Last Will and Testament, she left everything she owned--a small estate of some $10,000-- to Danny Forge, her mother, and charity. She left nothing specific to Brandon.

Jason stared at the simple will before him. Like everything else that had happened and was happening, the will made no sense.

"Nothing at all to her only son?" Jason said.

"Hell hath no fury like a woman scorned?" Howard said.

"It makes no sense," Jason replied. He stared at the will as if by doing so a different text would somehow emerge, like letters written in lemon juice emerge under candlelight.

Addy was appalled. He face wrinkled in disgust.

"But she left nothing for Brandon? Nothing at all?"

"Oh, yes she did," Jason answered.

Addy stared at him.

"What?"

Jason wobbled his head slowly from side to side, like a ball coming to rest on the ground.

"Me. She left me behind."

The next day Howard sent himself off an a reconnaissance mission and caught Danny behind his little house and served him with Judge Dunning's Custody Order, but it took until May 6, 1980 for Jason to get a hearing and from there an order for visitation.

Jason saw Brandon the next day. The meeting took place in a back room of the Mason Courthouse. An armed bailiff stood guard outside, and ushered Jason into a small, barren, room with one folding metal chair and a small brown couch.

Jason sat down in the chair, faced the door, and waited. A man in his mid-twenties with sandy brown hair and a thin Ronald Coleman moustache, entered. The man did not smile, and leaned his head slightly over his right shoulder in the direction of the door behind him.

"I am attorney Jordin. Here's Brandon. You two can visit undisturbed. I will return at the appointed time."

Jordin left and closed the door quietly behind him.

Brandon was dressed in a brown, short-sleeved shirt, blue jeans, and sneakers. He had grown taller. He was pallid and skinny, his eyes still off center; his teeth were crooked, and his stuttering unchanged.

"H–he--hello," he said.

The atmosphere between them seemed opaque and impenetrable, the way the air seems in a heavy fog.

"Well, hello stranger, how are you?" Jason said, realizing as he said it, how awkward and insincere his language sounded. How much, in fact, that he and Brandon were strangers. He reached out to Brandon to hug him.

Brandon backed away and sat down in the brown, two-seater couch directly across from Jason's folding chair.

Jason sat down.

"So, how's school?" he began, bewildered by the awkward reunion.

Brandon's hands shook and fluttered when he talked, as if he was trying to grab words out of the air that he couldn't produce with his mouth.

"F--f--fine."

"What are you studying now?"

Brandon looked at his fidgeting hands.

"Ma--Math, En--English 'n st--st--stuff."

"Do you like school?"

"Ya--yes."

"A lot? A little?"

"I--I like it, f--fine."

Jason smiled.

"Addy, Andria and Bobby all said to say 'hi' to you, and said that they missed you a lot."

Brandon did not return his father's smile, but kept looking at his hands as they clawed and grabbed at the air.

"Uh--huh."

Brainwashed, Jason thought, *He's seeing a monster and not me.*

"I'm teaching at the University and playing piano professionally again."

Brandon's eyes popped wide open and, for the first time, he looked at his father.

"Ya-you a--are?"

Jason smiled and cocked his head.

"You sound surprised. Why?"

"I--I d--da--din't kno--know."

Something was wrong.

"I wrote that to you in one of my letters. Didn't you get it?"

Brandon looked down at his feet and grabbed both hands together.

"Na--na--no."

Jason frowned.

"Have you gotten any of my letters? I've written you every week since you moved up here. I sent them certified mail, 'addressee signature only.' Didn't you ever go to the Post Office to get them?"

Brandon nodded.

"Oh, ya--yes. I ga--got tha-those."

"Ok."

Both of Brandon's hands jerked upwards and clutched at the air.

"Wa--wa--why did ya--a--you come up ha--here, da--daddy?"

Brandon's sudden movement and his bizarre question threw Jason off balance.

Something was wrong, very wrong.

"Didn't Danny tell you I was coming?"

Brandon bowed his head.

"Da--Danny sa--said ya--you wa--were ca--coming up ha--here ta--to k--kidnap me, wa--we wa--wa--were hiding fa--from ya--you."

"You're kidding."

"Na--no."

Jason moved his chair a half-inch nearer Brandon, and spoke slowly, trying to get Brandon to look at him.

"Brandon, I came up here to be with you after your mother's death, not to 'kidnap' you."

"Uh--huh."

Jason lowered his voice, and tried to sound quietly reassuring, the way ministers sound at funerals

"Besides, I'm your dad. I can't kidnap you. Only a stranger can kidnap you. You know that, no?"

Brandon sat on his hands.

"I--I didn't know tha--that, I--I tha--thought, I--I ma--mean, I--I tra--trusted Danny. I ha--had ta--too."

Jason was nauseated.

"And he said that I was coming up here to kidnap you?"

"Ya--yes."

You sonofabitch, Danny, Jason thought, *you miserable sonofabitch. You abused a kid's trust in me at the time when he most needed me.*

Jason then realized that Brandon had feelings for Danny, vulnerable kid's feelings, and carefully drained the rage from his voice.

"There must have been some kind of mistake, some kind of misunderstanding. I telephoned Danny, and I told him I was coming to be with you and comfort you, period."

"Da--Danny sa--said--"

"Yes?"

Brandon's hands popped out from underneath him and jerked violently in the air before him. His eyes seemed to shrink and disappear inside his skull, as if looking somewhere inside himself at a world long distant from the room he was in at that moment. His boyish lips trembled; tears rimmed his sunken eyes.

"Wa--wa--why da--did you ka--ka--kill ma--my Mo--mother?"

Jason felt he'd been kicked in the groin. He leaned forward in his chair and reached out his hands towards Brandon.

"What? Who the hell told you that?"

Brandon's eyes were dark with pain and horror.

"Da--Danny."

Jason reached forward and lightly touched Brandon's arm.

"For God's sake, Brandon, she died in the emergency room at the University hospital. How could I kill her in an emergency room? I didn't even know she was there. I found out about her death by accident."

Brandon's hands fluttered. His jaw and lips worked furiously against one another, and his brow furrowed, but he could not produce any words.

Greg Jordin opened the door.

"Meeting's over," he said, "You've gone over your time limit, anyway."

Jason stared at Jordin.

"Jesus Christ, Mr. Jordin, we haven't seen each other in almost three years. We've got a lot to talk about."

Jordin put his hand on Brandon's shoulder, took Brandon's arm, and pulled him towards the door. Brandon resisted Jordin's pull briefly, then gave in to the adult man's superior strength and authority.

Jason stood and watched helplessly as Brandon was led away. He crushed his fury and tried to sound nonchalant and cheerful.

"See ya later, Brandon. We'll talk some more later, Ok? I love you."

Brandon disappeared from view.

Jason went back to the motel. Howard was watching the noon news on television in Addy's and Jason's room and looked up when Jason entered.

"How did it go?"

Jason turned off the television and sat down at the foot of the bed, next to Howard.

"Jordin stopped our meeting after only about five minutes."

Howard looked over his bifocal glasses at Jason.

"I thought it was supposed to be a 15 minute meeting."

"That's what the court order said, and we would have done fifteen minutes if Jordin hadn't stopped us."

Howard shook his head.

"What happened with you and Brandon?"

Jason grimaced and looked straight at Howard.

"It's insane. That cub scout asshole Danny apparently told Brandon that I had somehow killed his mother, for Christ's sake--and told Brandon that I had come up here to kidnap him."

Howard's jaw dropped and his bulbous, bloodshot eyes squinted behind his glasses.

"What?"

"That's what Brandon told me."

Howard jumped up and began to pace furiously around in the small space between the foot of the bed and the television. He stopped abruptly, faced Jason and raised his hand.

"That's child abuse."

Jason sat on the bed, bewildered, slowly shaking his head from side to side. He felt sick to his stomach.

"I'm afraid it's just one, just one of the horrors, going on, Howard. Just one."

Addy came in from the bathroom, still in her blue bathrobe with her still-wet brunette hair in curlers. She sat down on the chair across from Jason that Howard had been sitting in a moment earlier and lit a cigarette.

"That damned shower nozzle doesn't work right," she said, and ran the bathroom towel lightly across the top of her head.

"That's the least of our problems with things that don't work right," Jason said. He told her what had happened in his meeting with Brandon.

She continued to lightly rub her damp hair.

"Holy shit. How'd he look?"

"Skinny."

"His eyes still screwed up?"

"Yeah, they're kinda of crooked, don't really look at you."

"Weird. Does he, you know, still mumble and stutter?"

"Yes."

Addy put out her cigarette, lit another and put the towel down on the bed. Howard paced back and forth and mumbled to himself.

Addy scowled.

"Are his teeth still screwed up?"

"Yes, Addy, he probably needs a couple of teeth removed, and braces. What are you getting at? The poor kid's mind has been really screwed up. Who cares what the hell he looks like?"

The exchange between Addy and Jason made Howard nervous.

"Excuse me," he said, "I've got to go next door and make some phone calls."

Jason turned to Addy. His world was spinning out of control. He needed her at his side, but she seemed to be pulling away from him. He looked her in the eyes.

"Why were you asking me all those questions?"

She looked down at her cigarette.

"I'm just worried, you know, about all the bullshit that he's in for in school from the other kids, you know. I'm bent about the freaky fucked-up way he looks, worried about, you know, all the work that has to be done to put him back together, you know."

Jason lit a cigarette.

"You're assuming I'm gonna get him."

She looked surprised.

"Of course you're going to get him. You're his father. I'm worried about what's going to happen after we get him home."

Jason jumped to his feet and pointed his index finger at her the way revivalist ministers point at their congregations of arrant sinners.

"Hey, look, Addy, shape up. If I get him, I'll fix him--what the hell am I saying?--when I get him, I'll fix him so that you won't have to be ashamed to be with him in public. He's been neglected and horribly emotionally abused, for Christ's sake. He needs love and understanding, a lot of love and understanding. I'm going to love the hell out of him. He'll be fine."

Addy took heed of the lecture and cocked her head.

"What'd you say Danny did to him?"

Jason didn't move his feet and put both hands on his hips.

"Danny told Brandon that I somehow killed Russet and that I had come up here to kidnap him."

Addy's upper lip curled.

"Jesus-H-Christ."

"And God only knows what else has been said and done to him, poor kid. He's only nine years old, you know."

A few days later Jason met with the Friend of the Court, Madeline Byrd, a sparrow of a woman with bleached blond hair and sunken brown eyes. She sat behind the low counter just inside the front door of the small Friend of the Court Office. A plastic nameplate with her name in white sat in the center of the counter surrounded by brochures in pastel colors on either side. There was a lone, black, rotary phone placed next to a register of numbers.

He introduced himself and held up the court order from Dunning.

"Ms. Byrd, I have a court order here from Judge Dunning, and I'm asking that it be honored."

She glanced at the papers and looked down at her tiny feet. She'd heard about Jason, and knew she'd have to soft-pedal things to keep him under control.

"You teach University, don't you?"

"That's right."

"What education do you have to have to do that?"

"Do you mean what degrees do I have?"

She glanced at him and again looked down at her feet.

"What do you have to have?"

"You mean what degrees, right?"

She nodded her head and looked over his shoulder not to offend.

"I have a Bachelor's degree in English, a Master's degree in English and a Ph.D. in English Language and Literature. Why?"

Ms. Byrd shook her head from side to side.

"All them educashuns," she mumbled, "all them educashuns."

"Ms. Byrd, I have this order. . . ."

"You play the pi-an-o, too, right?"

"Yes. I'm a professional musician. Anyway, I have this order. . . ."

She looked at her feet.

"You can't take 'im with you now. He's in school into June, sometime."

Jason held his custody order in the air between them.

"I know he's in school. What I want is to have this legitimate court order giving me custody of him honored and entered here. I'll take him home after he has finished his school year up here."

She looked down at her feet.

"All them educas--, all them educashuns," Ms. Byrd mumbled, and then looked up at Jason.

"I can't do it."

"Why not?"

"I just can't. I don't have authority."

"To enter a legitimate court order?"

She smiled meekly.

"Only the judge can."

"Which judge? Let's go see him."

She wobbled her head.

"He's on vacation, I think."

"You only have one here?"

She bobbed her head once and looked quickly around, the way birds do seated on a power line.

"That's right. You got other children, right?"

"I have two other children whom I adopted. I am married. We own a beautiful house in the country with a room in it for Brandon. We own two businesses--a party store and a catering business--I'm a professional musician and have a doctorate. My wife is a former schoolteacher; and I have a court order granting me custody of my biological son as his sole surviving parent. What the hell else do you want?"

She looked down at her feet.

"Well."

"Well what?"

"Just well."

Jason's patience vanished. He rested his weight on the balls of his feet and leaned downwards towards her, the way boxers lean forward before they plant an uppercut on their opponent's jaw.

"Will you honor this damned order, Ms. Byrd? Yes or no?"

She shrank back and looked down at her feet.

"No. I cannot because of no authority."

Jason put both hands on his hips and shouted.

"Then, find someone with the authority to--."

She turned, disappeared into the door behind her and never came back.

Two days of further inquiries yielded nothing. No one else was available, or willing to, enter Jason's order of custody. Finally, after consulting with

Steve Rhodes, Addy, Howard, and Jason left for the comparatively friendly territory of Ann Arbor, empty-handed and despondent.

At home, Jason launched a barrage of telephone calls and letters in a vain attempt to understand what had happened in the Mason court system. Steve Rhodes subpoenaed more documents than those Jason had seen, but failed to uncover anything to explain how it was that Jason had been so inexplicably overlooked as the only surviving parent of his son.

They were at a standstill for no known reason, victory in sight but out of reach. The barrage of phone calls and letters continued, with no results whatsoever.

IV

Two months later, Gregory Jordin telephoned to say that he had recommended that there be limited visitation that summer between Brandon and Jason in Westin Township, and Glosson had sighed the Order.

"Brandon's coming home" Jason shouted to Andria and Bobby when he hung up the telephone in the family room where he and Addy had been playing Monopoly with the kids.

"To stay?" Andria yelled, and bounced up and down.

"Hooray," shouted Bobby, looking confused about what had happened.

Jason rejoined them on the floor before the Monopoly board.

"You mean he's here for a visit," Addy said.

Jason nodded.

"For at least a couple weeks."

Addy threw her cards on the floor beside her.

"Bullshit."

Jason scowled.

"Jesus Christ, Addy, it's more than I've seen him in months."

The next day while Addy and the kids were down at the store, a court order arrived specifying that during the time of the visit Danny was to take Brandon to see Carl Welsh, a psychiatrist from Children's Hospital, and have a psychiatric evaluation done of him and 'all relevant parties'.

Jason was furious. He went down to his music studio and called Mr. Jordin.

"This is contrary to what I insisted on and the other side had agreed to, namely, that we submit the names of three clinical psychologists to do the evaluations and we'd pick one from the list. I have major problems--with CH."

Jordin paused.

"It is a proper order. Madeline Byrd went to Judge Glosson before you got here and got him to sign the order to have Welsh do the evaluations."

"Without notifying me or my attorney?"

"There was a reason."

"What?"

"Apparently, there was an incident at Brandon's summer camp just after your former wife's death. You called him at camp, did you not?"

"Right. That was before I knew Russet had died."

"After your phone call to him, I believe the fact is that Brandon screamed 'I hate him. I hate him.' referring to you, Dr. Adams. Byrd went to the judge and the Order was signed."

Jason's teeth were on edge.

"Did anyone ask him why he 'hated' me?"

"No. It was unnecessary."

"What?"

"It was clear what he meant."

Jesus Christ, Jason muttered, and hung up.

Brandon arrived, on schedule. He was clearly nervous about his return to Ann Arbor and Jason's home. Jason, Addy, and the kids were tentative also. They talked, played a few board games together, ate Addy's sumptuous meals, and went swimming. Slowly, the edge of the nervousness wore off. Several days into the visit, Jason took Brandon to the back yard, under the tree hut, and asked: "Why did you say that you 'hated' me after I called you at your camp?"

Brandon fidgeted with his hands and shuffled his feet.

"I--I--tha-ought tha--that you ha--had ka-killed ma-my ma--mother."

"What Danny told you, right?"

Brandon bobbed his head up and down.

"Ra--ight. So did ma--my grandma--ma--mother."

"Your grandmother told you the same thing?"

"Ya-yes."
Jason rested his hand gently on Brandon's shoulder.
"Did anyone at your camp ask you why you 'hated' me?"
Brandon looked confused.
"Na--no."

The court order required Jason to see Dr. Welsh.
Dr. Welsh had his luxurious office on the top floor of The Tower Suites, the downtown apartment/office complex where Russet had lived. He was in his early forties with black hair, glasses, and was exceedingly soft-spoken.
"Doesn't Ms. Payne live on the floor below here?" Jason asked as he walked into Welsh's lushly appointed office. Besides the usual mounted degrees on the wall, there were potted plants, an aquarium with exotic fish, and polished wooden furniture tastefully arranged around the large, rectangular, room.
Dr. Welsh did not visibly react to Jason's pointed question and, instead, matter-of-factly, said: "Yes."
"Swell."
Dr. Welsh sat down on a couch opposite the softly cushioned chair he had motioned Jason to. Jason noticed Dr. Walsh kept moving his head around in a tiny circle as he talked, first, about his fees. Then, still rotating his head, he said:
"So, how do you see your problem?"
The question bewildered Jason.
"My problem? Do you mean with getting custody of Brandon?"
Dr. Welsh stretched out on the couch, rested his right hand on his abdomen near his crotch.
"No. Your personal problem."
"My personal problem with what, Dr. Welsh?"
Dr. Welsh lay motionless with his right hand near his crotch, and kept his expressionless eyes steadily on Jason.
"With, let us say, getting work. You have a doctorate, don't you?"
Jason glared at Dr. Welsh. Jason suddenly disliked him.
"That's--the Ph.D.--only one of the problems with getting work. In the early 70s the bottom fell out of the college teaching market. I was too 'over-educated' for the job market, and my work as a pianist dried up when the nightclubs quit hiring live music and went to disco. On top of that I was fighting over 50 separate petitions, motions, etc., filed against me. I was having

my son stripped away from me, when all along I was by far the superior parent."

Dr. Welsh's head kept moving around in tiny circles, his right hand remained near his crotch.

"How were you the superior parent? You weren't working."

Is this an evaluation or an inquisition, Jason thought, and felt his dislike turn into a kind of icy acidic rage.

"First, I was in good health, physically; second, because I was in good physical health, I was in good mental health. Third, I had remarried and gone through the ordeal of adopting two kids, and I could offer Brandon a sister and a brother and a beautiful home with a healthy woman, my wife, Addy, in it. Besides, finally, I was working. I was working in our store and in the catering business as well."

Welsh did not move from his position on the couch.

"You're working in your field now?"

"Yes. I'm teaching again at the University. I'm also playing piano professionally."

Dr. Welsh stood, went over to the desk behind the couch, and returned deliberately to the couch, one slow step at a time. He handed Jason a Xerox copy of the letter that Golding had called 'horrible'.

"Hm. Did you write this letter to Brandon?"

Jason looked at the letter.

"Where'd you get this? It's a court document, I believe."

Dr. Welsh pursed his lips.

"I am the court-appointed psychiatrist and have access to such documents. Now, did you or did you not write it?"

You slimy, pompous ass, Jason thought.

"Yes, I wrote it. I was hoping to generate an appeal to the Court of Appeals with it."

Dr. Welsh's head rocked side to side like the pendulum of a clock.

"Do you think this an appropriate letter to send to a nine year old boy?"

Here we go again with this pompous morality crap..

"It wasn't really written to him. It was written as a slap in the face for Russet, Danny, and Russet's mother. I knew that they'd open Brandon's mail and read it—Brandon told me they opened and read my letters to him before he did. They've been doing that for years. It's absolutely unconstitutional to do that."

Dr. Welsh was not impressed.

"But, you do admit that you wrote it. And it was addressed to Brandon alone, was it not?"

"Yes."

Dr. Welsh nodded his head, stood, and pointed towards the door.

"Thank you very much, Mr. Adams. That's all I wanted to know."

Dr. Welsh sent his report in the form of a letter to Judge Glosson in October, 1980. Dr. Welsh wrote.

Dr. Adams is clearly an intelligent, well-educated man, as well as a talented performing professional musician (pianist).

It is clear, however, that over the past eight or nine years, Dr. Adams has been functioning far below his intellectual capacities. He has been devastated by something, or a combination of things, which one can only speculate about but which it is extremely difficult to speculate about without including some concern of serious mental illness on his part—a syndrome often seen in gifted individuals.

This illness is also suspiciously localized. It seems not to affect his relationship with his two adopted children; but the illness appears to manifest itself only in his relationship to Brandon, his son, who reported to me shortly after his mother's death that he is deathly afraid of his father, although he gave no reason to me why he felt that way."

Dr. Welsh went on to recommend that Danny Forge have custody of Brandon, then added.

"If any, even small, holes in the custody arrangements are left, Dr. Adams will pursue them. As is true of individual with psychotic tendencies, he must be made to understand that he has no recourse left before he can permit himself to give up the battle."

Jason read the report and exploded in the kitchen in front of Addy.

"Nowhere in his fucking report does Welsh address the issue of Russet's terminal illness, her two apparent suicide attempts, her blindness, her constant hospitalizations, or the cause of Russet's death--the entirety of my case. It's a smear job, for Christ's sake."

Addy picked up the report and thumbed through it, waiting for Jason to cool down.

"I betcha I know why," she said, finally.

"Why?"

A peculiar, knowing smile brushed across her face.

"I thought he was a jerk, too. He really pissed me off, the asshole, and I hated being ordered to go see him. So I told him that you were gonna to sue Ms. Payne and Children's Hospital for malpractice."

Jason stared at her.

"And so he's heading me off at the pass?"

"I guess he's setting you up as a loony tunes madman, to kill the malpractice suit."

Jason smacked his right fist into the palm of his left hand.

"I'm not going to let him get away with this character assassination of me, dammit."

Jason spent a month writing a 30-page, single-spaced analytic response to Dr. Welsh's evaluation. Jason sent a copy of the response to Judge Glosson in Mason, then called Howard Stein, who in turn referred Jason to Dr. Fred Shelling, a psychiatrist and a psychoanalyst.

Jason called Dr. Shelling.

"What I want from you, Dr. Shelling, is to give me whatever is your standard psychiatric examination and then, once you have formed your professional psychiatric impressions of me, for you to read Dr. Welsh's evaluation of me, and express your psychiatric opinions of that report as well."

"It sounds fine to me," Dr. Shelling said.

Dr. Shelling was a distinguished man in his early sixties with wavy brown hair, wore glasses and was of medium build. He shook Jason's hand strongly, told him to sit in the chair opposite Dr. Shelling's large desk. The wall behind the desk was filled with framed degrees in medicine, in psychiatry, and in psychoanalysis, and the office was decorated with what looked to Jason like primitive African sculptures.

Jason felt immediately at ease with Dr. Shelling and went to the point.

"Do you personally know Dr. Welsh?"

Shelling nodded.

"He's a former student of mine in the Michigan Psychoanalytic Institute. He was studying to become a psychoanalyst, and quit."

"Why?"

Shelling kept his gaze steadily on Jason, seemed to be absorbing Jason's every movement, word, and tone of voice.

"To become a psychoanalyst one must, first, be psychoanalyzed oneself. He apparently shied away from that requirement, and quit the program."

"Quit? Why?"

"I do not know. Perhaps he found it too expensive and too exacting--as do many students."

Jason and Dr. Shelling met four times. Dr. Shelling sent his evaluations of Dr. Welsh's report and of Jason to Judge Glosson, and sent Steve Rhodes and Jason a copy.

Dr. Shelling had found little to admire in the psychiatric report of Dr. Welsh's report. In the opening section of his evaluation, Dr. Shelling wrote:

"Dr. Welsh's report does not contain any of the obligatory features of a report of a psychiatric examination of Dr. Adams. It contains sweeping generalizations, misinterpretations, innuendoes and absolutely no medical-psychiatric objectivity. It appears that Dr. Adams is being done in by innuendo."

About Jason's mental health Dr. Shelling wrote:

"There is no evidence of psychosis. There are no ideas of reference, or obsessions of any kind. He had a reasonably normal childhood, is heterosexual. I find him a man with a mixed character of obsessional and hysterical traits (the most benign of the neuroses), and see no psychiatric evidence of a serious mental illness, contrary to what Dr. Welsh appears to have insinuated."

"In addition to drawing a conclusion as to Dr. Adams's pathology, it would be useful to say something of his positive features, his assets and his capacities for being a father. He has much to teach the boy. He appears to have extremely acute and sophisticated psychological insight when it comes to understanding what he feels has been the 'brainwashing' of his son's mind. Dr. Adams is an honest and sincere man who respects and treasures his values. He is certainly persistent and determined to be a father. Many men would have abandoned this effort a long time ago. This action has all but exhausted his financial resources. He wishes to do well by his son. He is a man of many talents, high intelligence, and excellent goals and aspirations. He should have a great deal to offer to his son. Most of all, he is the biological father, the child's surviving parent."

"Finally, we're getting somewhere," Jason cried to Addy after he read Dr. Shelling's report, "Finally."

V

When Dr. Shelling filed his evaluation of Jason with the Ann Arbor court, Judge John Dunning disqualified himself. He said that he feared he would be "less than neutral" towards Jason, and added:

"The Defendant in this case, Mr. Adams, and myself have not always seen eye to eye--that's probably one of the greatest understatements of the twentieth century, if not of all time."

Judge Dunning therefore surrendered the court's jurisdiction of the case to the Mason court up north..

Jason and Addy read the notice of the disqualification and the transcript in their bedroom. Jason exploded.

"Shit. I'm not going to get any justice up there--Judge Glosson is somehow biased against me."

"Why?"

Jason went into their bathroom and splashed cold water on his face and on the back of his neck. He smacked his face with a hand towel and returned to the bed.

"Why? In January Judge Glosson ordered my visitations with Brandon reduced to one eight-hour period per month located in Mason, Michigan, approximately 240 miles from here. The order required that Brandon undergo psychological examinations before and after each visit."

"Bullshit. What did you do?"

"I wrote Judge Glosson a scathing letter lambasting the visitation order. I said I thought that such an order was cruel and inhuman to Brandon, and that I would not do that to my son."

"Did you hear anythin' back?"

"Not a blessed word."

Another agonizing eight months went by.

In January, 1981, attorney Gregory Jordin, the *guardian ad litem* for Brandon, filed a report in the Ames County court. Jordin recommended that Danny Forge be given custody of Brandon

Steve Rhodes mailed Jason the recommendation without a phone call or comment.

"I can't believe this," Jason cried, after he'd read Jordin's report. "I can't believe what's happening. What the hell's wrong with these people? This is total madness. Are they being bought? Steve Rhodes is fired. I've got to get a killer attorney, and blow those bastards to kingdom come."

In February, Addy and Jason went into Detroit to meet with attorney Gerry Bruer, a man in his fifties with closely cut black hair and deep blue eyes. They met in The Caucus Club, a swanky downtown restaurant, and Jason told Gerry the story of the custody war.

"Will you take the case?" Jason asked.

Gerry thought silently for several minutes, then looked up.

"Yes."

"And your retainer?" Addy asked.

"One-hundred thousand dollars," Bruer replied, glancing at Addy's diamond ring.

Jason's stomach sank.

"I don't have that kind of money."

"That's my fee," attorney Bruer replied.

"Thank you for your time," Jason said, and he and Addy left.

On the way home in the car Jason struggled against waves of helplessness, and then a huge clearing suddenly appeared in the thick fog that had blinded his mind for months.

"I don't usually think in terms like this--I think in terms of literature, in terms of music--but I think I know Danny's motivation."

"What?"

"It's like a real bad grade 'B' movie plot--it's so blatantly and viciously evil that it's unthinkable. I asked myself 'what could the most evil motive in the world be for what's happening to Brandon,' and then it hit me."

"What?"

"Money."

Addy laughed.

"People will do anythin' for money. What money?"

Jason glanced over at Addy and back to the moving shapes and lights before him on the road.

"I'd forgotten about this for years."

"About what?"

"You know the trust fund I wrote for Brandon? Well, a long time ago Larry Brockton, Russet's dad, asked to see it. Russet and I drove up to Mason with Brandon. Larry told Russet and 'mommy'--that's what Larry called Mary Lou--to leave with Brandon, to go shopping or something, and as soon as they had left, he asked to see my trust."

"And?"

"Well, he sat there in his blue velour bathrobe smoking his Kool cigarettes, right across from me, and read. I was afraid he'd find something wrong in it and waited for him. After about a half an hour or so of reading, he looked at me over his thick glasses."

"So?"

Jason slowed down, and moved over into the slow lane on the highway.

"He shook his bald head, grinned at me, and said that my trust was 'just like' the trust he wrote for Russet, 'mommy' and Brandon. 'Dern close,' he said."

"And? So what? Get to the damned point, Jason."

He slowed down and stopped the car on the shoulder. Other cars whizzed by and the reflections of their headlights flashed and dissolved on the windshield before him. He turned and looked at Addy, whose facial lines kept disintegrating and criss-crossing into one another as the cars on the highway passed.

"I asked him if I could see his trust, and see if in any way his and my trust fund might conflict. He said 'no,' that's what he was looking for, that there was no conflict at all between the two trusts."

Addy's face loomed before him.

"Jason. What's the damned point?"

Jason swallowed audibly.

"My point is that if Larry's trust is like mine, then whoever has custody of Brandon has access to the monies in the trust."

"And that's it? Money?"

Jason hands gripped the steering wheel with the cool ferocity of a strangler.

"What else? Danny knows I'm not crazy now. He knows we're married and have a beautiful house. He knows we're both working. He knows I adopted Andria and Bobby. He knows that there's no good reason why I can't have custody of Brandon. He sure as hell doesn't love Brandon. Look at what he's been doing to him all these years. What else is there?"

"Jesus, Jason, what the hell's the point?"

Jason slammed the heel of his right hand on the dashboard.

"This. My bet is that Brandon is the sole surviving heir to his grandfather's estate. There's got to be enormous greed. There is no other reason except greed--none."

VI

When they got home, Jason called Howard Stein and told him about the trust theory.

Howard's response was instantaneous.

"Sounds like a federal lawsuit to me."

"Great. I have no idea who can write a federal lawsuit."

Howard knew.

"Matt Demming can."

"Who's he?"

"Matt's a Massachusetts-based engineer. He came home from a business trip to an empty house with his wife and seven children gone. He learned constitutional law and took his personal case into Federal Court--but, I've got to warn you, he's not at all easy to work with."

"Neither is the court system."

"He's a patriotic perfectionist."

"I don't give a shit. Dealing with a perfectionist who's on my side may turn out to be a welcome change of pace. What's his telephone number?"

"Ok, I'll give it to you. But watch out."

Jason was enraged by the idea that Danny was acting out of greed, ignored Howard's warning and called Matt and told him the story.

Matt's voice was raspy, and his choice of words deliberate, the way judges choose their words when delivering a verdict.

"I will require a precise chronology of events, and copies of all the legal paperwork filed, in exact chronological order."

Jason wrote down this homework assignment.

"Will do. Do you think I have a case?"

"There appears to be little question that constitutional law has been violated. The other parties have attempted to alienate your son's affections from you, and have conspired to gain--and may have gained--control of the grandfather's trust fund for Brandon."

That's it, that's it. Jason thought.

"And you'll help me write a federal lawsuit?"

"Get me the materials requested and some money."

"How much?"

"My fee is $20 an hour. I do not know how many hours it will take."

"The sooner the better."

"I will work on it as soon as I get the materials and a check for, say, $300."

"They're both on their way."

In early June Jason made a copy of Dr. Shelling's report and sent it up to the court in Mason, requesting it be included in the file of his case. Clearly Dr. Shelling's credentials, which were far superior to those of Dr. Welsh, would turn things around in Jason's favor.

"Heard anything from the court up north on Shelling's report?" Howard asked one night on the phone.

"Not a word."

"Doesn't surprise me. Has Matt finished the Federal suit yet?"

Jason swallowed his disappointment and his optimistic tone sounded shallow, even to himself

"No. But I'm certain it's on its way and that all hell is going to break loose up north when I file it."

VII

Danny Forge called Brandon into the living room of their Mason home.

"I want you ta call my new wife 'mommy', 'cause now she and I got married, your Momma's dead, and we's a family again, a new family again, Ok?"

Brandon nodded his head obediently.

"And you calls me 'dad' now, not 'daddy Danny,' no more, Ok?"

Brandon bobbed his head, being a good boy.

O-O-ka-k."

"And Minnie's your sister now, so you calls her 'sis' even though I's not her real dad, Ok?"

Brandon nodded his head.

"Ah-O-Ok."

Danny lowered his voice and glared at Brandon.

"And there's somethin' else."

Danny sat down on the couch with his head in his hands, his eyes red with worry, and looked up at Brandon.

"I dunno what I can do, Brandon. I's tried everythin' I can ta stop 'im, but he just keeps on a comin', just hurtin' us and hurtin' us all."

Brandon heard the urgent appeal in Danny's words, and tried to look at Danny's blue eyes. They seemed pleading and intently focused on him, but Brandon couldn't see them clearly.

Brandon looked again. There seemed to be tears in Danny's eyes.

"No matter what I does, your--Jason--jus' keeps on a comin'."

Brandon shrugged, and sat down next to his trusted friend Danny, who surely loved him and tried very hard to be his buddy. Danny cooked spaghetti dinners for him almost every night and showed him how to paint pictures of lions by using colors matched to numbers and helped him practice his lessons on their miniature piano.

"Wa--what ca--can we do?"

Danny put his arm around Brandon's thin shoulder and hugged him warmly.

"You can end the war, ya know. I've told ya that, your mother told ya that, for years. The decision's yours."

"Ma--me?"

"Yes."

"Ha--how? I'm ja--just a--a ka-kid?"

Danny turned his head and looked down into Brandon's left eye.

"There's more on it. We been livin' together, now, for a real long time, you 'n me, 'n your mom with us when she's still alive, before the war your--Jason--started over your custody put a strain on her heart, 'n killed her last year, right?"

Brandon shook his head 'yes', and felt sick to his stomach: *His own father had killed his own mother: he was a kind of orphan with only Danny and his grandma to take care of him.*

Danny put his hand on Brandon's scrawny shoulder.

"I told ya that before, right?"

"Yeah, ja--just after she d--died. So d--did grandma."

Danny put his other hand on Brandon's free shoulder.

"And ya know I work in a hospital everyday wit' doctors, 'n other medical people, right?"

Brandon nodded. He was trying to understand what Danny was saying, but couldn't grasp where the conversation was going.

"Right, I g--guess you know things a--about medicine n' stuff."

Danny nodded and kept his hands on Brandon's shoulders.

"I have ta. it's ma job."

Brandon nodded. Danny knew about these things.

"Yeah. You wa--wear a white coat, too, wa--work with those machines n' stuff."

Danny gave him a quick hug.

"Right. And in your mom's Last Will and Testament she said that she wants me, not Jason, ta have the custody of you, wants me ta be your daddy, 'n we can't do nothin', you 'n I, ceptin' what she says she wanted us ta do, right?"

Brandon nodded. He had never seen his mother's Will, but knew he had to trust Danny. Brandon thought he understood Danny's words, but he didn't know for sure what they all meant put together.

Danny turned his head down to Brandon, and looked him in the eyes.

"Outta respect fer the dead, like I told ya. It wouldn't be right, right?"

"I--I guess sa--so."

Danny stood, walked over to the television set, turned on a cowboy movie, came back to the couch, sat down, and started watching the show while he talked.

"I've earned the right ta be your daddy--I mean, Jason don't see ya no more, he don't pay no child's support, he plays psychologic games on ya, confuses you wit' all his fancy words, is a drunk, 'n told ya one time he's gonna sign off on ya, 'cause ya told me 'n your mom the truth on his drinkin' 'n his fightin', right? He's hurt ya 'n all of us a awful lot."

Brandon remembered hearing most of those things, but also remembered other fun times with his father. It was all very confusing, all very hard to understand.

"I--I ga--guess sa--so."

Brandon leaned his head against Danny's shoulder as Danny hugged him affectionately.

"You--'n only you--can end this damn war, Brandon. Only you. Here, read this order of Judge Glosson. It says ya can refuse ta see Jason, if ya want to."

Danny handed Brandon several sheets of legal-sized paper, and pointed out one paragraph titled 'VISITATION'.

"Here, read," Danny said. "See? It's up to you."

Brandon read the paragraph several times and tried to understand what all the words meant. He looked at Danny, who kept watching the cowboy movie on television.

"Ma--me? Ha--how?"

Danny kept his eyes on the television screen and spoke calmly, in a matter-of-fact way one speaks when ordering a meal at a restaurant.

"By callin' Jason, tellin' him that ya don't wanna see him no more. Be a real man, do it for me, 'n for your family. I mean, end it. Only you can do it. I's tried every move I can figure on ta do, 'n it's costin' your family a mint."

Brandon wondered how much was a 'mint', but was too frightened to ask.

"It ah-is?"

"Sure is. He keeps haulin' us back inta court, over 'n over, costs a fortune. Are ya gonna do it, do the right thing, what your mom wanted? Yes or no?"

Brandon thought quietly about doing the right thing he had been told he had to do. He felt lost and lonely; his neck felt all cold and tingly, his stomach seemed to be gnawing on itself. He bit his fingernails, stood, went into the shadowy kitchen, to the telephone, a few feet away from where Danny sat watching television, and dialed his father's telephone number.

"Hello?" Jason answered.

"Hello, tha--this is Brandon."

Brandon? Brandon calling me? Jason thought. *He's never once called here before. What the hell is going down?*

"Hi, Brandon, ah, how are you?"

"Ok, you know that tha--thing?"

"What 'thing'?"

"That court thing that you come up and ta--take me down?"

"No, there's no such thing."

"Yeah, there is."

"That I take you down?"

"Yeah, you come up here and get me and then ta--take me down."

"Down where?"

"Oh, I was wrong. You just ta--take me for the day."

He's talking about visitation, Jason thought.

"What about it?"

"Y--you said the only way, ah, you said that I couldn't go down is if I absolutely refuse, and I absolutely refuse."

Jason's face and hands and body instantly froze.

"Who told you that you could absolutely refuse?"

"No body. I wanna ah-absolutely ra--refuse."

Something clicked in Jason; he felt like he had years before when Russet was going into an insulin reaction. His thoughts raced. *This can't be real. This is madness. I've got to reason with him somehow.*

"Well, somebody had to tell you that you could 'absolutely refuse'."

"Yeah."

"Well, who told you that?"

"My own eyes. I read the ca--court order."

He's lying, Jason thought, *There's no way a kid can understand the legal language of a court order.*

"You read the court order. I think that's a stupid court order, Brandon."

"I da--don't."

"You don't think it's a stupid court order? It only gives us a one eight-hour period per month. You don't think that's stupid?"

"No."

Negotiate, buy time, Jason's heart said. *Delay him somehow before he disintegrates and is lost forever in this insanity.*

"Well, I don't see how we could really talk, ah, to each other, ah, for that short a period of time, and we have a lot of things to talk about."

"But we aren't ga--going to."

"Why not?"

"Cause I don't wa--want to ever see ya--you again."

The guilt came flying out of the past and kicked Jason in the gut. *I can't believe this. Is he getting me back for that scene in the music studio years ago?*

"You don't want ever to see me again?"

"Yeah, you've hurt ma--me an awful lot, ya--you know that?"

"How have I 'hurt you an awful lot'?"

"You know, I da--don't even have to go into it."

"Well, I think that, ah, there are a lot of things, Brandon, that you don't know."

"Maybe sa--so."

Buy time, buy some future, Jason repeated to himself.

"And those things are things you really should know."

"Like wa--what?"

"Well, they will come out. They--you haven't been told those things by me, or by any one because of how much they would hurt you and, ah, hurt a lot of other people, and, ah, I have for years not said anything about them, because, ah, you were way too young to even understand. It was very difficult for me."

"You ca--can tell me now."

"No, I can't. Certainly not on the phone, Ok? And certainly not long--distance, Ok?"

"Ok."

Jason relaxed a bit and lit a cigarette.

"Ok. So we'll have to work on that matter, and I'm working on it. And as far as me coming up there, you seeing a psychologist before you see me and after you see me, I think that's cruel to you, and I simply won't do it to you."

"You wa--won't have to."

"I don't have to do a damn thing, Brandon."

"I didn't sa--say you did."

"I know you didn't. At any rate, we'll be talking, Ok?"

"Hey wait, tha--this court order is about ma--me, you know."

Oh-oh, lost him, Jason thought, *try to delay, try to keep contact.*

"Yes. But, Brandon, you've got to understand something. You're only 10 years old--in about three weeks you're going to be 11, on November 24th, right?"

"Yeah, three wa--weeks."

Jason plotted. *Try rationality; try to appeal to his desire to be grown-up; be respectful–very respectful of him.*

"That means that you are a minor, you're not 18 years of age, and the law is very strong about that, Ok--."

"Ok."

"And there's a considerable amount of question whether anyone has any right to be doing what they're doing to you with the court order you say you read, and I don't think they do have the right to be doing it to you, and I think it's cruel to you, and I think it has been cruel to you for years. Eight years to be exact--since your mom and I got divorced."

"Just--j--just get to the point."

"Brandon, you're not old enough to make decisions like this--that's the point."

"Maybe so, ma--maybe I'm not old enough to do anything."

Now be his dad, Jason's heart urged, *Be his dad.*

"I respectfully disagree with that idea, Brandon. You're old enough to go to school, to learn, to have fun, to play, and so on. But to make a decision like this, which would affect the rest of your life, in such ways that you could not possibly understand--."

"But I've ba--been told--."

"It's Ok, Brandon, I understand."

"They told me--."

There it is, Jason thought. *Who told him what?*

"I know. You have to understand, Brandon, that I love you a lot, and that I have always loved you from the time you were born."

"I know ya--you do."

Jason kept reminding himself: *Be his dad, be the dad he doesn't have right now.*

"And you don't kill that kind of love. You just don't kill it--no courts, no jury, no government can ever kill that love, under any circumstances. It doesn't go away, it stays, and it lasts as long as I live and even after I die."

"Maybe so, but look--every time you talk to me I ga--get confused."

"It's Ok, Brandon, I understand you're hurting pretty badly--it's Ok, I understand."

"But, you have a way of fa--forcing me into things."

Here comes more of the brainwashing, Jason thought, *Somebody's putting bullshit ideas into his head*

"How do I force you into what things?"

"Oh, I don't know--I can't explain it--but you have a way of forcing me into tha--things."

"That's difficult to understand. I think you have been forced into a lot of things, but not by me. To begin with, I don't see you that much, to force you into things. And that makes it pretty hard, wouldn't you say?"

"You have a way of forcing me into things wa--with words."

"With words?"

"Yeah."

Brainwashing, Jason reminded himself. *Deal with the brainwashing, not the self of the poor kid.*

"I ask you questions, but I don't see how--but, see, that's something we could talk about. That seems pretty complicated to me."

"Well--."

"I don't really understand what you mean--I would have to ask you a bunch of questions. I don't want you to feel that way."

"But the thing is you're doing it ra--right now."

"How am I doing it?"

"Y--y--you been listing all these things that we could talk about, and the same wa--way is trying to force me to wa--want to go down."

Be careful, Jason thought, *be careful. This is a bomb that can go off unless you defuse it*

"I'm not doing that at all. I'm saying the truth to you. It's awful hard when two people don't see each other very much--excuse me. It's easy to misunderstand what the other person's saying--even between two adults, Brandon. It's tough when you haven't seen a person for a long, long, time."

"Yeah."

"Now, do you feel I'm forcing something on you?"

"Well, maybe not forcing something on me right now. But you have a Ph.D. and all this sa- stuff."

Let him talk now, Jason thought, *hear him out. At least that way he and I are communicating.*

"Yeah."

"A--and you know all that stuff and fancy words, and I am only 10 years old and in sixth grade and I'm da-doing alright in sca-school."

"Yeah."

"If I wa--were to be forced to do something by one of my friends I could tell--I ca--could do something about it. But the thing is you're a lot older than ma-me."

"Sure am. By about 31 years."

"So, you know wa--ways of forcing me into things."

"Well, it's pretty hard to force anybody at 240 miles away, Brandon."

"Maybe that's wa--why you have a Ph.D.."

"I'm lost."

"What do ya--you have a Ph.D. in?"

"English Language and Literature."

"And English deals wa--with words and that sort of thing, doesn't it?"

"Ah, sure."

"A--ah--and so at 300 hundred miles away you have a Ph.D., you know, you could rather easily force somebody into something."

"I don't know where you get that idea. It's a strange idea to me. I've never heard it before, Ok?"

"It other words, you're smart enough ta--to think of wa--ways in which to force somebody into things."

"Ah. I'm not smart enough to figure out ways to force somebody into things. Forcing is done with a gun, or with police officers, and so on. You can't make people feel anything."

"Wa--wa you can force somebody to do something with guilt, right?"

"You can try to do that."

"Wa--what?"

Agree with him, support his rationality, Jason directed himself.

"You can try to make people feel guilty, that's true."

"Then, fa--force them into things."

Keep it open. Jason warned himself, *Keep the door into the future open.*

"Yeah, I think that's something I'd really love to talk to you about."

"Not only that, ah, there's tons, ah, for every feeling there's a wa--way behind it that you could fa--force somebody into things using that fa--feeling."

Right now, right now, Jason thought, *put your foot in the door and keep it open to the future.*

"Gosh. How? That's strange to me. Maybe. Brandon, I'm sorry, but I've got to go down and close the store now; we can continue this conversation later, Ok?"

"Ok, ba--but--."

"I heard what you said, Brandon, and I think I understand, but you can explain it better when we see each other again, Ok?"

"Ok."

"I love you. Bye."

"Bye."

Brandon put the telephone down, and went into the next room where Danny, who had listened to the conversation on an extension telephone, had quickly returned to watching the white-hat hero dodge an Indian arrow and blaze away with his two six-guns on the television.

"I da--did it," Brandon said, standing near Danny's right leg.

Danny watched his television show, did not look at Brandon, and said nothing.

"I did it. I ta--told him," Brandon repeated, bewildered that Danny didn't reply.

Danny's eyes did not move from the action on the television screen, almost as if Brandon had vanished and simply was not there in the room.

Brandon turned, and went upstairs, took of his clothes, and went to bed. He felt hugely confused and almost sick to his stomach, as if by doing the right thing to please Danny, he had not pleased him at all and, to make things worse, by doing what Danny told him to do, had just done the most horrible thing he had ever done in his life. But he couldn't understand why he felt that way or why he started to sob like a little baby for what seemed to be endless hours before sleep came and rescued him.

VIII

After hundreds of hours of work, the Federal suit was ready in late December, on a day where the sun was smothered behind a thick, white early evening fog.

"We are ready to file," Jason said to Addy in their bedroom as they got dressed to go down to close the store.

Addy looked over from the room-length mirror where she was doing her makeup.

"You sure?"
Jason tied his shoelaces.
"Yes."
"Who's gettin' sued?"
Jason picked up the lawsuit from where it lay on the bed.
"Everyone and his brother. Here, look."
Jason handed Addy the lawsuit. She stared at the formidably official first page.

UNITED STATES DISTRICT COURT
FOR THE WESTERN DISTRICT OF MICHIGAN
SOUTHWEST DIVISION

JASON ADAMS, an individual and JASON ADAMS, an individual and JASON ADAMS, an individual and JASON ADAMS, an individual
BRANDON ADAMS, a minor child, by his father, next friend, and natural Guardian,
Plaintiffs,
vs-
DANNY FORGE;
MARY LOU BROCKTON;
HARRY FORGE;
JOHN A. DOE AND JOHN B. DOE, State Officers acting under the color of the law of the State of Michigan;
SALLY GOLDING, DAVID BERNS, and GREGORY JORDIN, individually and as attorneys at law acting under the color of the law of the State of Michigan;
RACHEL PAYNE, individually, and as a Social Worker of the State of Michigan;
MARYLEE ABRAMS, individually and as a Protective Services Worker of the State of Michigan;
JOHN T. MURTY and MARTIN GLOSSON, individually, and as Judges of the Probate and Circuit Court of Ames County, Michigan;
MADELINE BRYD, individually and as the Friend of the Court of Ames County, Michigan;
THE COUNTY OF AMES, MICHIGAN, and
NORTHERN MICHIGAN SUBSTANCE ABUSE SERVICES, INC., a corporation.
Jointly and Severally Defendants

Civil Action No:_____

Jason Adams and Brandon Adams
Pro Se
COMPLAINT AND JURY TRIAL DEMAND

She thumbed through the next 14 pages, then put the document down, and looked, wide-eyed, at Jason.

Jason picked up the papers.

"You don't have to read the whole thing. Read just this one paragraph," Jason said, pointing:

That on or about October, 1971 A.D., after Carol Brockton, now deceased, became ill, the defendants, acting in concert, conspired under pretense of their authority to inflict severe and lasting emotional stress and damage to the plaintiffs, to deliberately destroy the father-son identification to the point of antagonism and thereby terminate plaintiff Jason Adams's parental rights and cause an alienation of affections of said plaintiff from his son, Brandon Adams, to cause the plaintiffs to be deprived of their mutual care, company, love and affection, conspired to gain, and did gain, control of certain trust funds of which plaintiff Brandon Adams was the beneficiary, by denying plaintiffs due process of law and the equal protection of law, and conspired to limit, and limited, the liberty of the plaintiffs to be with each other and share each other's care, company, love and affection.

Addy's-smile was half-frown. She looked at him in the mirror.
"This is what you said in the car coming back from Detroit."
He smiled at her image in the mirror.
"Yes."
Her right eyebrow was raised.
"That's where you were this mornin'--I mean gettin' this copied?"
He saw himself nod in the mirror.
"Yes, and having ten copies made."
Visions of endless lawsuits materialized like rolling white waves in Addy's mind. She twisted around and faced him.
"Jesus Christ," Addy said. "A shit-load of people are goin' to be pretty pissed when they get served with this."
Jason grinned, and relished the sense of cruel revenge that rushed through him.
"You bet. And they're going to be served by Federal Marshals, to boot."
Addy swung her head slowly from side to side.
"It's gonna hurt Brandon, you know. What the hell do you hope to get out of dropping this bomb?"
Jason turned to the end to the 'relief' section, and handed the lawsuit back to her.

"This. Here, look."

DEMAND FOR JURY TRIAL

That pursuant to FRCP 38(B) and the Seventh Amendment of the United States Constitution, the plaintiffs demand a trial by jury on all issues so trialable.

WHEREFORE, plaintiffs request this Court:

A. To impanel a petite jury, and award plaintiff, Brandon Adams, the sum of One Million ($1,000,000.00) Dollars in punitive and/or exemplary damages from the defendants, jointly and severally, and award plaintiff Jason Adams the sum of Five Hundred Thousand ($500,000.00) Dollars in compensatory damages and the sum of Five Hundred Thousand ($500,000.00) Dollars in punitive and/or exemplary damages from the defendants, jointly and severally.

B. Permanently enjoin the defendants, and their employees, agents, associates and successors, from further action under the color of state law, or privately, from interfering with, harassing, intimidating, harboring, or otherwise preventing the plaintiffs from living together, as father and son, as is their right.

C. Award plaintiffs their costs and disbursements in this action, and legal fees, or a reasonable sum in lieu of legal fees.

D. Declare the actions of defendants Murty and Glosson, judges of the Ames County Courts, null and void, and with no effect, and to be stricken from the records of the Ames County Courts, and that the only legal and actual parent and guardian of Brandon Adams is the plaintiff, Jason Adams, and that any further interference with the father-son relationship will be considered contempt of Court; and

E. Plaintiffs may have all such other and further relief in the premises as to this Honorable Court may seem just and proper and as should be agreeable to the equity and good conscience of this Court.

Respectfully submitted,

by:_____
Jason Adams/Pro Se/Plaintiff
and as father, next friend

*natural guardian and sole parent
of Plaintiff, Brandon Adams*

Jason picked up the papers, put them on the bureau, and turned to Addy. The sorrow in his gut was fused with his fury at all the people who, over the years, had neglected and mismanaged and emotionally brutalized his son.

"He's being hurt already. He's being destroyed. I'm certain that Brandon's heart is being mangled. That phone call in which he said he never wanted to see me again just reeked of brain-washing."

Addy put her lipstick away in her purse and faced him.

"I repeat. What are you gonna to do with this thing?"

Jason sat down on the bed, rested his elbows on his knees, and leaned forward.

"I have a plan. I have more or less laid low during this year--have been a good little boy, and made no trouble for anyone. For some reason Danny Forge has agreed to send Brandon down for a post-Christmas visit. Thus, I will have physical possession of Brandon, which I need to file the lawsuit in Federal Court with a Petition asking for an Emergency Ex Parte Order of Custody and pending the outcome of the case, I will not return Brandon back up north."

Addy stood.

"You could blow any chances of ever getting him, you know."

Jason stood and looked out the window at the ashen sky.

"I know. I have no choices left. He's being destroyed. Everything that's sweet and decent in him is being destroyed by those rotten people. It's my last chance to get him out of the nightmare that is drowning him. It's a risk I have to take. I have no choice--none."

She walked over and touched his shoulder.

"Scared?"

Jason looked down at the floor. His hands, his back, his gut, trembled.

"I'm scared shitless--terrified beyond any experience I've ever had in my life."

Addy scowled.

"It's not going to be easy. It's damn near a suicide mission."

Jason's heart seemed to stop, and, for a moment, turn into a block of ice.

"I know."

Addy shook her head, looked at the back of the head of the man she loved and smiled to herself.

"Go get the bastards, Jason, go get 'em."

On December 30, 1981, Walt Laurel, the paralegal from the original meeting of Fathers For Equality, and Jason drove to the Federal Court in Kalamazoo, and filed the suit, then drove back to the Westin Township home.

"Want a beer?" Jason asked Walt who, dressed as he was in jeans and a plaid wool shirt, looked more like a day laborer than a trained, educated, paralegal.

"Sure, if you're goin' to have one."

Jason ran up to the kitchen and came down to the family room with the beers.

"Where's Addy?" Walt asked.

"At our store or out somewhere with the kids, no doubt."

Walt took a slug of his beer.

"What now?" Jason asked.

Walt looked intently at Jason, the way doctors sometimes look at ill patients.

"If I were you, I'd take Brandon and get the hell outta here. All hell is going to break loose when all those people get served by Federal Marshals with a $3,000,000 Federal Lawsuit. You could have cops swarming all over you."

"Cops?"

"Yeah, cops or killers. There's no telling what those damned crazy people will do. Remember, they don't give a flying fuck about what's right or wrong, what's legal or illegal. They don't give a shit, Jason–they're ruthless."

The next morning Jason called Fred Newman, a friend and member of the Westin chapter of Fathers For Equality, of which Jason was then the president. Fred, a World War II veteran, was a grade school mathematics teacher, a rail-thin man with a long, white beard. He had served in the Merchant Marines during World War II, and had been torpedoed and sunk, he told Jason, seven times. Jason had helped Fred get custody of his son from Judge Dunning, so Fred owed Jason one.

"Fred? This is Jason Adams. I've filed a $3,000,000.00 dollar federal law suit, Brandon is with me, we're on the run, and I desperately need your help."

Fred didn't blink an eye.

"You got it."

Jason ran upstairs and grabbed Brandon by the wrist.

"Come on. We've gotta get outta here."
Brandon was baffled.
"Wa-why?"
Jason took a deep breath and tried to sound calm.
"Just to play things a little safe."
"Wa-why?"
"Because I just filed a very tough lawsuit against a bunch of people and we've got to wait for the judge to make a decision. Until he makes his decision some people could get mad and do bad things. So we're gonna sorta play a game of hide 'n seek, Ok?"

Brandon didn't understand any more than when he asked his first question, but the idea of playing some kind of game with his father didn't sound too bad, and so he said:

"O-Ok," he said.

Jason drove to Fred's farmhouse out in the country and put the car far in the back of the large garage behind Fred's house. They covered the car with a brownish tarpaulin and bales of hay. There was no way anyone could see it from the road.

Jason and Brandon stayed at Fred's old, 19th century home, furnished with antique pottery and farm implements, walls of books, and Fred's World War II mementos, including his medals mounted on a stained and polished wooden wall plaque. They watched television, talked with Fred, his teenaged son, Jimmy, Fred's wife, Amelia, jumped when the phone or doorbell rang, and waited for the Federal Court to act.

A week went by. Jason was in his bed on the second floor unable to sleep and kept thinking: W*hat's going to happen if the Federal court dismisses my case? That means the case will be back in Mason, in front of Judge Glosson, who is antagonistic to me because of what he earlier did to me and Brandon with the once-a-month 'visitation' order, and because I'm an 'outsider' in Mason. I've got to get rid of Glosson. But how?*

Then it hit him. He got up and hand wrote Judge Glosson a letter.

"Dear Judge Glosson:

As you are a defendant in the Federal Lawsuit I have just filed against you and several other defendants, it is my opinion that you will not be anything but less than neutral towards me in any future legal matters regarding the custody of my son, Ellis Brandon Adams.

I hereby respectfully request that you disqualify yourself from my case.

Jason Adams
Defendant Pro Se

Fred sent the letter off the next day for Jason, certified mail, "addressee signature only." And they waited.

Days went by.

Several days later, Addy called Jason at Fred's home. A letter had arrived for Jason from the Mason court.

"Open it up, please," Jason said, "and tell me what it says."

"Judge Glosson has disqualified himself." Addy said a couple of seconds later.

"Hooray." Jason shouted, "We'll be home in a flash."

"What does the letter from the court mean?" Fred asked at the front door. Jason scowled.

"The disqualification means, I figure, that jurisdiction is now in Federal Court and, for the time being, Brandon and I are at least temporarily home free. And just in time. I am the opening musical act for the new owner of the Penthouse in four days."

Brandon and Jason went home, had some lunch with Addy, Andria, and Bobby, and relaxed.

The telephone rang.

"I'll get it," Addy, who was in the kitchen, said.

She peered around the corner at them all seated at the dinner table. Her expression was sour.

"It's Danny, he wants to talk with Brandon."

Jason ran downstairs to his basement music studio where a friend had rigged a telephone recording device. Jason turned it on, flipped the monitor switch on and listened as Danny spoke.

"How are ya? Everything Ok? Ya want to stay down there? Is that where ya want to stay? Yes or no?"

"I da--don't know."

"Sorry, but ya gotta give me a decision, I mean, do ya want to stay down there, to stay?"

"I da--don't know."

"Are ya afraid?"

"I am a--afraid."

"You don't want to stay down there, do ya? I don't want to push ya to do that."

"I da--don't know wa--what to say. I am sc--scared."

"Are they listening? Yeah?"

"I am afraid to sa--say yes or no."

"Are ya afraid of me not loving ya?"

"I am afraid, p--p--period."

"Do ya want to live up here?"

"Wa--what da--do you mean?"

"Do ya want to live up here? If ya want to live down there, there's nothing for me to do. I can't decide a thing unless ya tell me what ya want."

Addy, who had also been listening on the bedroom phone, broke in.

"Danny, I am listening. Brandon turns to pieces because no one compromises. It's not fair, it's not right. You cannot goddamn tell him, 'You make a decision now.' When he has to make that kind of decision, you tear him to pieces. There's no way he can win because he feels guilty about rejecting someone. For God's sake, stop hurting him. Stop goddamn tearing him up. He's a child. No matter how it feels, why not let him come home?"

"What's a home?"

"This is his home, here, with his father."

"I guess I won't let him go down there no more."

The phone went dead.

Four days later, two armed police officers carrying a court order signed by Judge Glosson--before he disqualified himself--appeared at their house. Somehow, they managed to slip past Addy when the door was ajar and she wasn't looking as she talked with Jason over her shoulder, and suddenly, out of nowhere, there they were.

The two officers positioned themselves to Jason's right, next to the black couch in the family room. Jason had just finished talking to Daniel Richards-- a friend of Walt Laurel's and another paralegal--on the telephone trying to figure a way out of the plight he and Brandon were in. Jason heart pounded in his chest. He kept grinding his teeth. He felt breathless, as though he had held his breath too long underwater.

The senior officer looked down at Jason.

"We are here to enforce a court order of Judge Glosson. You have to surrender Brandon to us." He was armed and made leathery creaking sounds when he moved.

Addy stood up in the kitchen with Bobby and Andria clinging at her side, and watched.

"Tape those bastards," Daniel said in Jason's ear, "Get it all on tape."

"Just a second," Jason said to the officer, and ran upstairs. He grabbed a copy of the Federal Lawsuit, and the notice of Glosson's disqualification and a portable tape recorder, brought them all downstairs, and began recording.

Jason knew it was useless, but handed the papers to the senior officer anyway.

"Glosson has no jurisdiction. The case is in Federal Court. Here is Glosson's disqualification and the Federal lawsuit."

The officer glanced at the papers in Jason's hand, shrugged his shoulders and looked Jason straight in the eyes.

"We have a court order dated before the disqualification."

Jason waved the papers in the air.

"That order is nonetheless invalid. Jurisdiction is in Federal Court."

Brandon came over and sat next to his father.

"Wa--what should I d--do, dad?"

Jason picked up the telephone.

"Dan, what the hell can we do? The cops won't do anything about the Federal suit."

There was a pause while Dan thought.

"The only thing you can do, is to have Brandon fight them, tape record it, and use it later in court," Dan said loudly on the phone.

Jason's stomach sank. How the hell could Brandon win a fight against two armed cops when he couldn't even see his hands clearly before him? He couldn't. But they wouldn't hurt him either. They were men. They were trained. He was just a kid. Jason turned to Brandon.

"The only thing you can do is fight them, Brandon."

"Come on, kid, let's go," the senior officer said, grabbed Brandon's arm, and pulled him off the couch.

Jason made certain the tape recorder was on and running.

Brandon slumped to the floor, and squirmed and kicked against the officer. The other officer joined the fray, and the two of them hauled Brandon, kicking and fighting them and screaming "Daddy! Daddy!" towards the front door.

Andria screamed "No! No! No!"

"Bye Brandon, b-bye Brandon," Bobby sobbed from the kitchen.

"You fuckin' bastards!" Addy shouted.
"I love you, Brandon." Jason shouted as the front door slammed shut.

Danny called a few days later.
"If ya drop the federal suit, then I'll let Brandon go--let him come and live with ya."
Jason knew Danny was most likely lying. He also knew that the Federal Court would most probably not hear the custody case claiming it did not have sufficient personnel to adequately handle such domestic cases. He had hired a federal lawyer, William Luckin, with money borrowed from Addy's father, had told him. The situation was desperate. It was a shot in the dark. Betting on Danny's immaturity and fear of further litigation Jason said: "Ok. I'll drop the suit. But I warn you, man to man, that I fully expect you to keep your end of the bargain and return my son to me."
Within a few weeks, as Jason had asked attorney Luckin to do, the Federal suit was dropped 'with prejudice'.
Jason called Danny.
"Ok, the Federal suit is dropped with prejudice to no one. I've kept my end of the bargain, When are you sending Brandon down here?"
"He's changed his mind," Danny replied, and hung up.

That was in March, Jason didn't talk with Brandon again until late April. 'He didn't want to talk' or 'was outside' or 'was at a friend's house', and so on Danny said.
After Danny's call, Jason and Addy went on their usual evening walk around the block. It was sunset, the air was cooling but still tinged with the warmth of the day.
"I almost rescued Brandon, so near and yet so far," Jason said to Addy.
" I know, dammit. It's been that freakin' way for years, Jason."
"But, now, there's a difference."
"What?"
Jason squinted against the rays of the setting sun and looked away.
"I've got their number. I know why that son of a bitch Danny has been poisoning Brandon, and I have a pretty damned good idea of why Mary Lou doesn't want me free to someday tell Brandon the story of his uncle's death. My frustration and bitterness is focused now. They can't stop me now, not in a million years."

IX

Jason cashed his last check of the semester, and paid the entire amount to Walt Laurel for research and a legal brief arguing that as the surviving natural parent under Michigan law Jason was the presumptive best parent for Brandon. The brief was filed at the Mason court.

Walt, Daniel, and Jason went to work writing a mammoth set of 2,000 'interrogatories' and a 'List of Admissions' which they sent to Mary Lou Brockton and Danny Forge in Mason. The interrogatories were almost exclusively aimed at uncovering the contents of the trust fund of Larry Brockton. Some of the Interrogatories were also aimed at the death of Russet's brother, Terry, and the brutal list of admissions targeted the death of Larry and medical and other documents related to the death.

Jason and Walt sat on the floor surrounded by the documents piled next to them on the floor. They had finished proofreading in the basement music studio at Jason's home.

"Why all these interrogatories about Terry?" Walt asked.

"Because I have every intention of having an attorney grill Mary Lou Brockton--or threaten to grill her--about Terry's death. Any woman who would purposefully hurt her own son is not fit to be a parent of my son or, for that matter, of any child."

Walt got up from the floor and sat down with a grunt on the piano bench.

"What does that have to do with the trust?"

"I don't know. But I suspect Larry Brockton also included something in that trust that held Mary Lou responsible for Brandon--something to the effect that if she killed Brandon, or lost control of him somehow, she got no money. I suspect Larry detested her for killing his son."

Walt lit a cigarette and frowned ferociously at the floor.

"There are two parts to this case, then: Danny's greed and Mary Lou's guilt?"

Jason got up and stretched.

"Three."

Walt frowned and tapped his cigarette in the ashtray.

"Three? What's the other one?"

"The rank lack of judgement and stupidity of the judges and the court system itself."

"You're going to need an attorney pretty soon, you know, Jason," Walt said a few weeks later, after the interrogatories had been sent.

"Any ideas?"

"Well, you can start with Don Pader in Detroit. He specializes in domestic law."

Pader's office was on the 18th floor of the Detroit Towers building, a downtown office complex. Pader's lobby was filled with people reading magazines, looking anxious, silently waiting to be called. Jason arrived on time, and waited 45 minutes before his name was called.

Don Pader was a man in his mid-forties with blond hair, glasses, chestnut-brown eyes, and the clear, healthy complexion of a golfer. His office boasted sleek, modern, furniture and walls covered with golden framed degrees and multiple awards printed in Old English typescript.

"How may I be of service, Dr. Adams?" Pader said after they shook hands and Jason sat down at the polished desk across from him.

Jason told Pader the outline of his and Brandon's story, and gave him a copy of the federal lawsuit.

"I know where you're at," Pader said, after he had scanned the Federal Lawsuit. "It's a rough business--child custody cases. I know. I've been through it myself. Unfortunately, I didn't win my case. Had a rotten attorney."

"Who?"

"Me."

"Is that how you got into this business?"

"Yes and no."

Jason waited.

"I was in law school when Ruth--my then wife--filed for divorce. I was looking forward to becoming a corporate attorney for one of the automotive companies once I'd finished law school and passed the bar exam when she hit me with the divorce. Thus, I studied domestic law to defend myself."

"Did you have any children?"

"One. A son."

"Did you fight for custody of him?"

"Yes. I lost. She took him with her to France after the divorce was finished and she had cleaned me out financially."

"When was that?"

"Oh, ten years ago."

"How's he doing? Do you see him?"

Pader looked out the window.

"I never saw or talked to him after the divorce."

"Why not?"

Pader kept staring out the window.

"I never knew where he was."

"Do you know where he is now?"

Pader continued to stare out the window to a place far away from where he sat.

"He's dead."

Jason's stomach sank.

"Dead?"

Pader sighed, turned around, and faced Jason.

"He committed suicide last year. Hung himself. Look, I'm going to introduce you to a colleague of mine, attorney Jim Haroldson, who may be able to help you. I can't."

"Can't?"

"I just can't take another custody case for a man's son."

Pader picked up his phone and said something Jason couldn't hear..

A few minutes later the office door opened and a man walked in who Pader introduced as, 'the attorney you need'.

Jim Haroldson was in his early thirties, with a stocky build like a football linebacker, and a burly way of shaking hands. .

Jason repeated his story.

Haroldson scanned through the federal lawsuit, and told Jason that he knew about diabetes. His son was diabetic. Jason described Brandon being hauled out of his home and handed him copies of various motions he'd filed.

Haroldson didn't blink an eye.

"I'll take the case. I'm familiar with the judges in northern Michigan, and feel reasonably certain that we can get the venue changed from Ames County to an adjoining jurisdiction--Chebocken--where for some reason there are ill feelings towards Mason and its Court System. It's a tough case. I'll have to have a $5,000 retainer up front."

Jason's heart sank. That was almost half of what he made teaching.

"Up front?"

"Up front."

"I don't have $5,000--but I'm going to find it," Jason said.

Addy's father had the money. He was a multi-millionaire. Jason drove to Roy's home, went into the office, and made his case.

No deal.

Roy felt that he had loaned Jason enough money.

"You're asking me to throw money down a rat hole. I think you're going to lose. Why don't you just quit, give up the battle? Hell, it's just a kid. You and Addy can make another one, you know. No more money to a losing cause. That's final. Why don't you ask your own father for the money?"

Jason's insides turned to mush. *All these years as his son-in-law and he doesn't remember?*

"My father's dead. He died years ago."

"No more money to a losing cause," Roy repeated, and Jason left Roy's multi-million dollar Ann Arbor home empty-handed.

Jason asked friends to loan him money; they were broke. No bank would loan him that much money without collateral, and he had none because he had exhausted virtually all of his assets over the preceding ten years.

Finally, after hours of arguing and pleading, his mother lent him $2,000. Addy came through, too. One night she walked downstairs to the music studio, where Jason was sitting at the Steinway keyboard, doodling with rock 'n roll licks and racking his brains for sources of money.

"Here," Addy said, "It's all I can scrounge up right now. I tried to sell my mother's ring, but the jeweler wouldn't touch it.'

Before he could thank her, she disappeared upstairs.

What a love she is, Jason thought as he looked at Addy's check. He was still short $1,000, and that thousand dollars seemed to him, at that moment, like all the money in the world.

He wracked his mind looking for money. He could raid his university retirement account but that would take weeks, time he didn't have. He could sell his car, but it probably wasn't worth $1,000. Maybe some local musicians might be interested in buying parts of his music library. Over the years, he had assembled almost all of the chord charts and lead sheets to thousands of pop and rock 'n roll tunes. But even if he could sell those charts, it would take weeks, if not months, to come up to that $1,000.

He looked down at the white and black keys under his fingers and then across the glistening black top of the grand piano. He traced the top edge of the piano top with his fingertips and for a moment, as in a dream, he saw a vivid picture of Russet's face smiling at him over the top of the piano with her collections of poems to him in her hands.

Something inside his stomach went serenely silent, and suddenly he knew exactly what he had to do.

The grand piano was worth at least $1,000.

He stood, gently caressed the top of the piano he loved, a gift of love given him by the love of his life, and said quietly, "Good by, my loves. Thanks for the memories."

John Knight, the owner of Knight's Music, was more than happy to pay Jason $1,000 for the Steinway, and Jason immediately paid Haroldson, who promptly got the venue changed to Chebocken.

It was a new game in a new territory with a new court system and a new judge.

The end was in sight.

August 27th 1982 was one of those hot, humid summer days where the air seemed so thick it had to be swallowed rather than breathed.

The settlement conference was scheduled for the Chebocken courthouse, a squat, cinderblock building with heavy oak doors and an iron fence surrounding it. Mary Lou, Danny, Jason, their two attorneys and a court reporter were to be present. Jason chosen to face final conference alone.

Jason waited in the courtroom hallway chain smoking, his thoughts racing and colliding like cross winds in a hurricane. Inside the downstairs conference room, Jim Haroldson met privately for 45 minutes with Mary Lou, Danny, and their attorney, David Berns, a man in his forties, with a pinkish face that looked like it had been waxed and polished.

Haroldson came out of the meeting, grabbed Jason's arm and headed him towards the side door leading outside to the walkway around the one story courthouse.

There was no breeze to ease the weight of the humid air. Birds twittered sporadically in the bushes and there was scattered automobile traffic in the street. Jason felt bound and gagged by the same kind of powerless terror he'd felt waiting in the hospital for Brandon's birth to be born, not knowing whether his son or wife would live or die.

Haroldson looked straight ahead and marched down the concrete sidewalk.

His voice was controlled and matter-of-fact.

"What Mary Lou and Danny have offered us is physical possession of Brandon to you with joint legal custody of Brandon shared between Danny, Mary Lou, and yourself, if you will stop the proceedings to discover the contents of that trust fund and the other interrogatories and admissions about the death of Terry."

Jason felt like he had been clipped at the back on his head. He tagged alongside Haroldson and kept looking straight ahead.

"Have they read Dr. Shelling's report?"

Haroldson didn't lose a step.

"Yes."

"So they know I'm not a nut?"

Haroldson kept his eyes focused before him.

"I don't think that matters to them. I don't think they ever really cared."

Jason stopped walking and looked at Haroldson's clean-shaven, expressionless face.

"It doesn't?"

Haroldson stopped walking, returned Jason's disbelieving stare, and resumed walking.

"I don't think so."

Jason was amazed. His plan had worked.

"The whole thing is that they're willing to trade Brandon for keeping the contents of Larry Brockton's trust and the details about Terry's death secret?"

Haroldson stopped walking, put his hands on his hips, and looked towards the steeple of a nearby church..

"That's what seems to matter to them."

Jason swallowed the hope rising in him.

"Are you sure it's not some kind of con or trap?"

Haroldson's eyes narrowed.

"My impression is that they're convinced that you'll never give up trying to get Brandon, are ruthless and will destroy them unless you get what you want. They are trying to cover their asses. I suspect–but can't yet prove– that there's been an awful amount of legal hanky-panky that's gone on behind the scenes in this case. An awful lot."

Jason shook his head.

"This is nuts. If I get joint custody of Brandon, if he lives with me, and if the trust fund still exists when he turns 21, he'd see the trust—and the odds are he'll share it with me. What the hell do they think they're hiding from me?"

Haroldson said nothing.

They resumed walking around the north side of the courthouse. Jason was desperately trying to fathom what had happened. He did not want to make a single mistake–not this close to freeing Brandon.

"Do you think Mary Lou killed her own son? Is that what they're scared of?"

Haroldson looked straight ahead, expressionless.

"I don't know. It doesn't matter. What matters to them is the money."

A picture of Larry Brockton's fist full of money flashed through Jason's mind.

"Money? Do you know how much money is in Larry's trust fund?"

Jim stopped walking and scratched his head. They had come full circle. The entrance to the courthouse was before them. Sweat was trickling down Jason's ribs and his brow was beaded with moisture.

"Not exactly. I've seen some of the trust contents--but only some. My impression is that there's lots of money--several millions of dollars. But I don't know the exact amount."

Jason searched Haroldson's unblinking blue eyes.

"Millions?"

Haroldson shook his head 'yes'.

"Millions."

Jason's felt his heart beat in his throat; his teeth ached with rage. His guess about Danny's motivation was no longer a guess.

Jason grabbed Haroldson's arm and shouted.

"Danny did all this cruelty to Brandon for money?"

Haroldson's eyes were locked on the courthouse door.

"A shit-load of money. Millions."

Haroldson took a step towards the courthouse door.

Jason grabbed his arm.

"And they want to trade me a brutalized son for no more interrogatories about the trust and Terry so they can keep their money and guilt hidden?"

"Yes."

"'Is that why the settlement conference and no trial? No press? No people?"

"It will be recorded. There will be a record."

"A private record."

Haroldson nodded, "Yes, I agreed to that."

Jason smiled to himself. The irony was palpable.

"So long as right now I don't have the right to see that trust, I can have Brandon?"

Haroldson kept his focus on the courthouse door.

"That's the deal. You get the kid, but no looking at the trust, and no more questions about the other kid's death. At least until after Mary Lou's death. No look-see and no money. You see, if you don't really know what's in that trust, my guess is that they're betting you'll leave them alone. That's the deal."

Jason's feet wouldn't move.

"Some justice. They love the money?"

Jim shook his head and touched Jason lightly on the shoulder.

"It's not theirs, really."

"It's not mine, either."

Haroldson smiled to himself.

"Right. It's Brandon's."

Jason shook his head. He was now sweating profusely, creating dark splotches under his arms. He still could not believe what he was hearing.

"But the money was what was motivating Danny?"

Haroldson grinned; dollar bills danced in his eyes.

"You're bankrupt, aren't you?"

"Yes. I have nothing but debt and virtually nothing left of any monetary value. I have my books, my clothes, and my beat-up 1974 AMC Gremlin—the ISG."

"The I—what?"

"Never mind—it's sorta a secret between the kids and me." Haroldson's face went blank. He was thinking business. He put both hands on Jason's shoulders.

"I have a plan. We can put them in a corner. We can adjourn this conference today, then file discovery papers and get to the bottom of this property issue, then go after the issue of custody. That way we can recover some of your costs in this action and get the kid, both.

"Any guarantees on this plan of yours?"

Haroldson's face remained a blank.

"It could go either way."

"It's 50/50, right?"

"Right."

Jason turned his shoulders. Haroldson let go. They stopped, side-by-side, in front of the steps leading to the court house side door.

Jason set his jaw.

"Brandon will eventually get the money his grandfather wanted him to have, right?"

Haroldson nodded.

"I believe so. We can go for the money now or later. The decision is yours."

Jason knew what he had to do His legs felt alive .He looked straight ahead.

"The answer is later. Brandon needs me now. Let's go get him."

They went through the side door down a long, steep flight of wood stairs to a small, dim basement conference room. The wall shelves on either side were lined with slate-gray law books with their ruby-red/gold title plates. The long wooden table and chair were dark and polished. The room smelled of linseed oil and stale cigar smoke. A glass pitcher of water surrounded by pale plastic cups sat in the center of the table. Two overhead fluorescent lights drained the room of the little color it had and washed away the normal flesh tones of people's faces so that they looked like bloodless corpses in a funeral parlor.

Mary Lou Brockton, Danny Forge, and attorney Berns were seated opposite Jason and Haroldson at the large conference table. At the left end the table, near the door, a female stenographer with long gray hair and glasses in a dark blue business suit sat in front of a large, reel-to-reel tape recorder.

Jason and Jim sat and faced their antagonists. Jim opened up his black, leather briefcase and looked at them, one by one.

"Are we all ready?"

Attorney Berns nodded his head, the stenographer turned on the tape recorder, and the tape wheels crept slowly and soundlessly around in circles.

Haroldson stood. The low ceiling muffled his voice and he articulated his words carefully.

"Let the record reflect that this is the day, date, and time set for certain depositions in the case of Forge and Brockton versus Adams, those depositions being scheduled pursuant to notice of Danny Forge, and Mary Lou Brockton. Prior to commencing those depositions, there have been extensive negotiations and discussions between the parties hereto relative to resolving outstanding issues relative to the custody of Brandon Adams and other matters."

Haroldson turned over a leaf of paper, and continued.

"A potential agreement has been discussed, and is as follows. Brandon

Adams will spend the coming year through June in Ann Arbor, Michigan, in the primary physical possession of Dr. Adams with reasonable and liberal visitation up here in Mason, Michigan, or such other places as may be convenient to the parties, such visitation to include weekends as agreed between the parties, Christmas holidays, Thanksgiving, Easter, whether for all of those periods of time or a portion thereof to be determined by the parties, and that the change in custody will be evidenced by entry of a consent custody order."

Mary Lou Brockton was dressed in a black 1930's plain business suit with a white scarf wrapped and knotted at her neck. She was as skittish as a squirrel, fiddled with her pince-nez, nodded her head and whispered something to attorney Berns as she looked over at Jason—the man who had brutalized her over the death of her dear son, the man who had violently thrown poor Russet out into the cruel cold of the night, penniless, with poor little Brandon in her arms. It was disgusting to be seated anywhere near him.

Haroldson continued.

"The further aspects of the proposed negotiated settlement between the parties would be that the boy spend the entire school year down in Ann Arbor, Michigan, so that we not be faced with a situation where one month from now, for whatever reasons, he changes his mind."

Haroldson looked directly at attorney Berns whose smooth face seemed to flush ever so slightly in the dim, yellow light.

"However, it is conceived to be the recognition of the parties that this matter is always subject to the jurisdiction of Judge Lipo of Chebocken County. It's further the understanding of the parties that Mr. Forge and Mrs. Brockton will disclose to the extent that they do exist whatever portions of the last will and testament or trust agreements or other such documents do exist for the actual present or contingent future benefit of the minor child, Brandon Adams."

Haroldson paused, and took a sip of the tepid water out of the plastic cup on the table before him.

"It's my further understanding that there are two such documents in existence at the present time, and photocopies of the relevant portions of those documents with irrelevant material magic-markered out, but those portions dealing with the benefit of Brandon will be disclosed to the attorney for Dr. Adams. And I believe that summarizes the essence of the proposed agreement by and between the parties as I presented it earlier."

Berns talked quietly with Mary Lou Brockton, then looked up. His voice was high-pitched and thin, the sound of a metal clarinet. His eyes darted left and right as he talked.

"Thank you. Mr. Haroldson. *Pro forma.* Did you wish to ask anything else on the record?"

"Fine. Why don't we swear Mrs. Brockton?"

"Fine."

Mary Lou was sworn. Jason gritted his teeth, choked down his rage, and stared at the mother of his dead wife and the woman he believed had killed her own son. It seemed impossible. How could such a plain, matronly, petite creature be so vicious and evil? How could she dare not pretend to be other than she was?

Haroldson smiled at Mary Lou.

"Mrs. Brockton, you've been present when counsel and I have described the proposed negotiated settlement between the parties here, isn't that correct?"

Mary Lou's voice was barely audible. She nibbled at, rather than said, her words, and her ears seemed to sting and ache, as if they had been burned.

"Yes."

"And you understand what we've proposed?"

She smiled meekly, and glanced at Berns, who nodded to her.

"Yes. More or less, that is."

Haroldson smiled politely. His voice was low, almost consoling.

"Ok. And do you consent to entry into this consent custody order and the other provisions?"

Mary Lou Brockton looked at attorney Haroldson, and nibbled at her words.

"Well, yes and no."

Haroldson glanced over at Jason and returned his gaze to Mary Lou.

"I see. Do you have any questions regarding the provisions of what we discussed here this morning?"

Mary Lou folded her hands together in the shape of a steeple, and nibbled at the emptiness between her thin lips.

"My one little question was: I do not follow the provisions concerning-- and the chances of it happening are certainly minimal, of course--but supposing little Brandon truly has found it not compatible to stay down there. Do I understand he has no recourse?"

In other words, you monstrous witch, Jason thought, *if you can arrange it, you want to kill another kid--you fucking murderous fiend.*

Haroldson shifted some papers around, and took a deep breath.

"No, that is not correct. What we are attempting to do is to essentially convey to Brandon that this is not a situation like vacation where you're down there for two weeks and then, if you're homesick or you're this or that, you come back."

Mary Lou Brockton adjusted her pince-nez, and kept her tiny eyes fixed on attorney Haroldson.

"I somewhat agree with this, but I don't understand the mechanics of that little option."

Jason glared at Mary Lou.

Mary Lou avoided Jason's eyes and looked straight at Haroldson. She placed a curled diminutive hand to her mouth as if suppressing a cough.

"I would--how it would come about and for what reasons he would decide to change his dear little mind?"

Jason fought an overwhelming desire to leap across the table and shove the belittling words down her throat.

Haroldson smiled at Mary Lou.

"I would expect what would happen, among other things, if he does not convey those problems to Dr. Welsh, he certainly would do so either to you or to Mr. Forge or to Mr. Berns, and then we would presumably be talking again as we are here this morning."

Berns looked at Mary Lou and patted her hand. Mary Lou looked at Haroldson, and smiled meekly.

"Oh, yes, dear me, I quite agree with that."

Berns cleared his throat.

"First of all, I think that you and I maybe ought to talk with Brandon, so that your client doesn't think that we are saying to Brandon, 'Now Brandon, you know--if you don't want to, Brandon--' and that my people think your client's saying 'The Court says you've got to stay a whole year, kid, and there's not a damn thing you can do about it.' Perhaps you and I can go up and talk with him--it's within easy walking distance--and just explain exactly what the deal is."

Haroldson looked at Jason, who nodded yes, then at Berns.

"Fine. I have no problems with that," Jason said.

"Fine," said Berns. "Now, I believe there are certain other matters."

Haroldson turned a page in his notes.

"Correct. Mrs. Brockton. Without going through the extensive examination that I have prepared this morning--briefly are there certain trusts or last wills and testaments in existence in which Brandon is either a present or a contingent future beneficiary?"

The conference room went silent except for the whisper of the moving reels on the tape recorder. Danny ran his hand through his brush cut and studied his fingernails; Mary Lou lowered her head, as if in prayer; Jason stopped breathing.

Mary Lou looked at Berns. He nodded his head 'yes'. Mary Lou's voice was faint, almost a whisper.

"He is a contingent future beneficiary. There's really not that much money there, you know. My husband's little estate was left in trust."

Haroldson checked to make certain the tape recorder was running.

"Is that Larry Brockton?"

Mary Lou swallowed.

"Lawrence Brockton. His nickname was Larry.'

Haroldson checked his notes.

"And are those trust documents at the Mason Bank?"

"Yes. The First Mason Bank, yes."

Haroldson scribbled in his notes and looked up.

"And is it the essence of this provision that at some future point in time after you should pass that the entire estate would pass to Brandon?"

Mary Lou's eyes darted over to Jason, then snapped back to Haroldson, the way rodents peek out of their holes and then vanish.

Haroldson fastened his eyes on Mary Lou. His voice was steady, authoritative.

"I repeat. The entire estate passes to Brandon?"

Mary Lou studied her tiny hands and the foggy reflection of her face in the polished tabletop, and whispered: "I believe that's right."

Haroldson scribbled again in his notes and smiled at Mary Lou.

"And, besides you, there are no other heirs, that is to say, after you pass, Brandon will be the sole surviving heir of the estate of your late husband?"

Jason stared at Mary Lou. She avoided his eyes, and looked at Berns.

Berns gave her a paper cup of warm water. She swallowed visibly and wiped her mouth with a floral handkerchief.

"I believe that is correct, yes. It's just a private little matter, you know."

Haroldson looked down at his notes and then down towards the end of the table to see that the stenographer's fingers and the tape wheels were both moving.

"Is there only one such trust document, which is Mr. Brockton's trust?"

Mary Lou nodded.

"At the present, yes. My own--according to my present will, Brandon will be my beneficiary, you know. I expect to live many years, so. . ."

"And he is not the beneficiary that you're aware of any other last wills and testaments or other documents?"

Mary Lou looked off towards the ceiling with a look of smug self-satisfaction.

"No."

Haroldson turned a page in his notes.

"That's all the questions I have for Mrs. Brockton, but I would have a few questions for Mr. Forge."

Mary Lou sat back in her chair, seemed to shrink down into the seat, and avoided Jason's eyes.

Danny Forge was sworn.

Haroldson checked his notes, glanced sternly at Jason as if to say 'cool it, I'll nail this S.O.B for you'.

"Mr. Forge, you have been present during negotiations this morning, also present during the representations and stipulations that counsel and I have placed on the record, and you've also been present during the testimony of Mrs. Brockton, have you not?"

Danny nodded his head affirmatively, the way he had done in catechism classes.

"Yes."

"Do you understand and consent to the various terms and provisions that we've set forth in this agreement and do you fully understand you have no claim to the custody of Brandon Adams?"

Danny lowered his head and glanced, first, imploringly and then, apologetically, at Mary Lou and Berns.

"Yes. I sorta guess so," he mumbled.

Haroldson leaned forward across the table. His voice was crisp, his words sharply articulated.

"You guess so? Do you have any objections to or specific questions regarding those terms and provisions?"

Danny's face turned to putty.

"No, not really, I, ah, jus' don know much 'bout this stuff."

Haroldson smiled politely.

"Of course you are completely free to convey any such questions you may have to your counsel, who may contact me."

Danny squirmed in his chair.

"Yeah, I understand."

"Are you aware, Mr. Forge, of any trust or will documents in which Brandon may be a current or future contingent beneficiary other than those which have been disclosed by Mrs. Brockton?"

Danny kept fidgeting with his fingers and turning his plastic water glass in circles before him. The question was unsettling: maybe it meant somehow that Danny knew something else that was news to Jason? Danny's eyes were wide open and looked boyishly innocent, a cub scout poster.

"No. I's not aware of any of 'em. There's other income, though."

Harold kept his eyes on the squirming witness before him.

"Social Security income?"

"Yeah, which was his mother's, ya know, that I guess he gets 'til he's 18."

"And what is the sum of money involved?"

Danny glanced at Mary Lou and swallowed.

"Not much."

"How much is 'not much'?"

"Oh, about $1,000 a month."

Haroldson wrote down the figure in his notes, and smiled at Danny.

"You are an inhalation therapist in training, are you not, Mr. Forge?"

"Yeah."

Haroldson looked down at his notes.

"Pays about 12 grand a year right?"

"I guess so," Danny mumbled and looked at Mary Lou.

Twelve grand? Jason thought, *You pathetic opportunist.*

Haroldson put down his papers and pen.

Haroldson nodded and turned to his left.

"I have no further questions of Mr. Forge. I do have a question for my client. Dr. Adams, do you understand the nature of the agreement here described?"

Jason stared at Haroldson.

"What agreement?"

"The agreement that in exchange for joint legal custody of Brandon any and all future interrogatories such as those thus far filed will cease. That is clearly the agreement."

Jason sat on his fury and counseled himself: *Just get Brandon away from them, no matter how much of their crap you've got to eat, just get him out of here.*

Jason stared icily at Danny and then at Mary Lou, and finally, at Berns.

"You want no more questions about the trust. If I stay away from the money, Brandon comes with me, right?"

Berns beamed.

"That, although rather crudely put, is, in approximate essence, the legally negotiated agreement."

Jason fought his fury. His rage and hatred for the people before him was consuming, like the heat in a blast furnace. He wanted to beat them each to death with his bare hands, mutilate their bodies, and incinerate their scraps. He set his jaw.

Burns looked at Jason, and waited.

Danny looked at Jason.

Haroldson looked at Jason.

The stenographer waited at the end of the table, her hand poised over her pad. The reel-to-reel tape recorder wheels revolved slowly, staring down the length of the table at the combatants.

Mary Lou glanced at Jason, looked away, clasped her diminutive hands together before her on the table. She knew how dangerous Jason was, how cruel he could be, how desperate he really was, how evil.

Jason sighed, looked at them all, one by one. Then, without hesitation or the slightest waver in his voice, said "I want my son, now--and to hell with the rest, dammit."

Haroldson frowned and closed up his briefcase.

"Fine. I have no further questions."

Berns stood, and faced Attorney Haroldson. "We are therefore excused from giving the answers to interrogatories, correct?"

Haroldson smiled politely.

"Correct. I think it's time for Brandon and his father to go home."

Berns smiled at Haroldson.

"It's going to have to happen sooner or later, but why don't we make it as late on Saturday as possible?"

Jason stood. Haroldson grabbed his arm.

"Right now," Jason said.

"Right now," Haroldson repeated.

"Now?" Danny asked attorney Berns.

"Now," attorney Berns said to Danny, "the time he leaves doesn't really matter any more. Better go get him ready to go."

"Now means now," Jason said to Danny.

Danny shrunk, like a suddenly wilted flower.

"Give me an hour. He's gonna be ready then, no problem."

Jason glared at Danny.

"It will be advisable– to borrow an eloquent phrase from you--to have him there, on time, and ready to go."

Danny, Mary Lou, and attorney Berns left for their cars, and Jason went outside for a smoke and to wrestle with his rampaging waves of triumph and get them under control.

Forty-five minutes later Jason drove into Mason to Danny's house, and parked in front in the same place he had parked years before when he'd come to comfort Brandon only to find him gone.

He'd better be here, Jason seethed at Danny, *Brandon better be here.*

Jason turned off the engine, threw open the door, and walked up to the house. The front door opened, and Brandon appeared, alone, dressed in jeans, sneakers, and a sweatshirt, his red hair unkempt and falling over his forehead. He looked skittish and confused, as if he had merely been told he had to leave with his father, but not why that was so or how his life had changed so substantially, so suddenly, after all those years.

Jason kept to business.

"Ready?"

Brandon looked up, wide-eyed, at his father, and as if for the first time sensed clearly that he was bigger and probably a lot stronger than Danny.

"I-I-got ta-to ga-get my sta-stuff."

Jason bent down and patted him gently on the butt.

"Just run in and bring it out here to the car, Ok?"

Brandon ran off and returned seconds later with a single suitcase and a large paper bag filled with books and toys, and Jason helped him pack his things into the car.

Jason's heart was pounding wildly in his chest; he fought to avoid making even the slightest mistake.

"Better check inside to make sure you've got everything, Brandon," Jason said, and closed the trunk of the green Gremlin.

"O--Ok," Brandon replied and ran into the house, this time, he noticed, with a strange new spring in his steps.

Jason walked over to the house and waited by the door, his shoulders slightly drooped, a vacant half-smile on his boyish face.

He had changed into blue jeans and a T-shirt that left his spindly arms visible. He stood some 20 feet away, and watched. as Jason slowly walked up to him. The top of Danny's head was level with Jason's cheekbones, and

Jason, who outweighed Danny by a good 30 pounds of pure muscle, stood a right jab's length in front of him.

Brandon ran passed them, sat down in Jason's car, and watched the confrontation of the man who had cared for him for years and the man who had played with him as a baby and as a boy and had apparently come to take him away to an unknown future.

Jason was aware of Brandon's eyes on his back. He lowered his voice so that Brandon couldn't hear.

"Just one question, Danny."

Danny's face turned a pasty yellow color in the late morning sun.

"What?"

Jason kept his eyes on Danny, the way a cat watches a mouse.

"You say you love Brandon, right?"

Danny looked down, smiled to himself, nodded, and avoided Jason's eyes.

"Right. I love 'im."

Jason's body went taut with a fury that had been ripening in his soul for years. He hissed his words through his teeth.

"Then why in the name of all that's decent and good didn't you fix Brandon's wandering eyes, his crooked teeth, and his stuttering?"

Danny flinched, as if he been slapped across the face.

Brandon's eyes widened and he tried to focus and see what was happening.

Danny hung his head.

"Well, ah, we just loved 'im the way he was."

Jason glared at Danny, shook his head, took a deep breath through his nostrils, and walked backwards towards the car where Brandon sat quietly in the passenger's seat. Jason looked back, stared one last time at Danny, closed the car door on Brandon, walked around to the driver's door, and Jason and Brandon left for home.

Chapter IV

Home

"How are you feeling?" Jason asked Brandon once they were on the highway outside of Mason.

Brandon looked perplexed, frowned, and struggled to speak.

"F--fine. H-H-Ha how are ya-you?"

"I feel GREAT." Jason laughed, "I feel like a big dirigible full of pink balloons."

Brandon looked over at his father, who grinned broadly at him.

"Wa--What?"

Jason bounced in his seat.

"Pink balloons."

"Na--no, wa--what's a 'ridgable'?"

Jason glanced over at Brandon.

"A dirigible is a blimp filled with helium."

"Wa--why?"

"Because that's what it's supposed to be, just like you are my son and I am your father."

Out of the corner of his eye, Jason saw Brandon shake his head.

"Na – no. Wa--why pink ba--balloons?"

"Because big pink balloons are light and happy, go high in the sky, fly, and I'm flying."

"You a--are?"

Jason turned his head, and grinned at Brandon.

"As a matter of fact, I am a giantic big blimp full of happy pink balloons. Don't I look like one to you?"

Brandon giggled.

"You're s--silly, dad."

"Ok, I'm silly. You can call me 'Silly dad' if you wish, or 'S--D' for short. Either one's fine with me. You hungry? How about some lunch?"

"Ya--Yes, dad."

Jason pulled off the highway into the parking lot at a 'Bill Knapp's' restaurant located just before their exit to the major highway heading south, and parked the car. They went inside, and sat down across from each other.

"Good afternoon," the young male waiter said, and handed them their menus, "would you like something to drink?"

They ordered two Cokes and asked for a couple of hamburgers with mayonnaise, relish, a slice of onion, tomatoes and lettuce, potato chips, and a couple dill pickles.

"I'm starved," Jason said, "I could eat a house."

Brandon was confused.

"Ya--you mean 'horse,' don't you dad?"

Jason grinned and shrugged.

"Is there a difference? Who cares when the championship has been won?" Jason reached to the center of the table, moved around the salt and pepper shakers, the bottles of ketchup and mustard and the container of sugar, and lightly smacked each to the table with each move. He looked over at Brandon.

"Your move."

Brandon looked puzzled at first, then smiled to himself in silent recognition of the inane game and similarly moved the various items around into a different configuration, whereupon Jason again, this time very quickly and with great intensity, and making growling noises, moved all of the items again.

"There." Jason said, "Game to Dr. Adams."

Brandon moved the pepper shaker and laughed. "Check – ma--mate."

Jason frowned, and looked puzzled.

"I thought we were playing checkers."

Brandon laughed, and shook his head.

"You didn't sa--say it was 'table checkers'."

Jason screwed up his face and tried to look forlorn.

"Hm. No wonder I lost. I was playing the wrong game."

Brandon grinned at his father, and Jason saw the faint outlines of dimples taking hold in both of Brandon's cheeks and thought, for the thinnest of a fraction of a second, that Russet and his son, both, sat there across from him, a family again.

A speck of ancient dust caught in Jason's eye, then vanished.

The food arrived. Jason moved their plates around claiming that he was 'identifying the correct daddy and son portions,' and Brandon noticed he was missing his Dill pickle. He looked at his father and grinned.

"And you s--stole my pickle from ma--me."
Jason threw his hands up in the air and beamed.
"You weren't looking."
Brandon laughed. Something new was happening in his life, something that seemed pure fun, and he liked it. He pointed his right index finger.
"And you ate it, you ate ma--my pickle."
Jason shrugged and frowned, wrinkling his facial lines.
"Aha! Vat kolar vass das pickle?"
Brandon giggled, and shook his head.
"Green. All pickles a--are green, dad."
Jason raised his right eyebrow.
"Prove it. Do I look green to you?"
"Na--no."
"Do you see any little pickle-sized spots on my face?"
"Na--no."
"On my hands?"
"Na--no."
Jason wrinkled his face again and scowled ominously.
"Then how can you prove I stole your pickle. There's no evidence whatsoever?"
Brandon pointed his finger at Jason.
"You st--stole it. I know you stole it."
Jason smirked and shook his head.
"No you don't. You weren't looking."
"That's na--not fair."
"Hold it," Jason said, and reached over the table and pulled Brandon's pickle out of his ear. "Your ear stole your pickle."
Brandon's jaw dropped.
"How'd you da--do that, dad?"
Jason shrugged and pompously puffed out his chest.
"It's magic, just one of the kinds of magic that we dads do, pure and simple. Vanishing and reappearing pickles is only in the improbable range. The impossible takes a little longer–10 years, for example."

II

They got back out on to the highway. In front of them, in the right lane, was an old, gray pick-up truck blowing out a stormy cloud of black smoke and crawling along with what looked like a load of cigar-store wooden Indians lined up in rows in its bed. Jason leaned to his right, pointed over the dashboard at the tribe of bouncing and wobbling Indians.

"What in God's name is that?"

Brandon, for some reason, thought that was hilariously funny, and started to giggle uncontrollably.

When Brandon had calmed down, Jason looked over at him, frowned, and lowered his voice.

"You don't know?"

"Na--no."

God damn this stuttering shit, Jason thought, *it began years ago, when he and I were starting to learn words together in the park, and it's got to stop. I started to teach him words when he was just a baby, and he said his first word to me then. By Christ, if I have to go back to those non-verbal days of pure noise to get him free of his stuttering, then so be it. Right back to the beginning when language was just noise? So be it. Here we go, goddammit.*

"*Moi aussi.*"

Brandon scowled.

"Wa--what does that mean?"

"It's French for 'me, too'."

"Oh. Sounds fa--funny."

"It's a different language, that's why."

Brandon was baffled.

"Ha--how many la--languages are there, dad?"

Jason glanced over, grinned, and went on driving.

"Hundreds."

"Tha--they all different?"

"Yup. But our own language is weird, too. For example, tell me what this cliché means: 'Stones that live in glass people shouldn't throw houses.'"

"Wa--what?"

"You heard me; and remember this, too: 'A hand in the bush is worth two in the bird.'"

Brandon shook his head.

"Wa – what?"

"Ah, the wisdom fathers pass along to their sons. You *capache*?"

Brandon shook his head.

"Wa--what does that mean?"

"Comprehend. It's Italian."

"Wha--what does that mean?"

"Comprehend means understand."

Brandon shook his head from side to side.

"Confused by something Brandon?"

Brandon laughed.

"No. it's just tha--that I think you're c--crazy, dad."

"So I am. But it doesn't matter. *Es kann dir nix g'schehen.*"

Brandon bounced up and down in his seat.

"Wa--what does that mean?"

Jason reached over, and poked Brandon lightly in the ribs.

"It's German. It means 'nothing can happen to me'."

"Ya--you're silly, dad."

"Nopo. Yopu opare soppillopee, notopt mopee."

"What's tha--that?"

"It's a form of Pig Latin called 'Optish'."

Brandon looked straight ahead and pouted.

"Is tha--that a--another language, too?"

"Not really formally a language, but kinda an *ersatz* language superimposed on, in and around English."

"I ca--can't understand--it at all. It's crazy."

Jason lit a cigarette, thought, *he's getting it*, and smiled.

"Not really. It sounds 'crazy' to you because you don't understand the noises I am making, the sounds of words in another language. But that's all spoken language is, anyway--noise."

"Oh."

"So, since language is only noise, it's really nothing to be afraid of. You respect language for what it can do, for good and evil, but, after all, it's just noise, period."

Brandon felt simultaneously confused and enlightened.

"Ok, I th--think I understand."

"But, I do admit to being crazy today. And to prove it, I see that in my hurry to get us on the road and go home I forgot a rather important item."

"Wa--what?"

"Gas."

III

Jason pulled off the highway into a Shell station, stopped alongside the gasoline pumps and turned off the ignition. He turned to Brandon.

"You know how to pump gas and check oil?"

Brandon shook his head.

"Na--no. I'm only ta--twelve years old, you know."

Jason grinned.

"Come on, get out of the car with me. Time you learned. You could be driving any day now, and one cannot trust gas station attendants at all. Sometimes they'll pour oil into your gas tank, gas into your crankcase or your windshield washer tank, just for the fun of it."

Brandon shook his head.

"They da--do?"

"What do you think?"

Brandon smiled at his father.

"I t--think you kidding with me."

Good, Jason laughed to himself, *I'm gonna get to him.*

"You're right. I am."

Jason popped the hood release lever, Brandon and Jason got out of the car, and walked around to the gas pump.

"Ok, Brandon. See, we'll choose the 'regular' gas pump because that's the octane my blue Chevy here uses."

Brandon frowned and squinted his eyes.

"Wa--what's 'octane' dad?"

Jason smiled down at him.

"It's a hydrocarbon, the rating of the chemical balance of the gasoline."

"Oh."

Jason pointed.

"Ok, first, you unscrew the gas cap--right here."

"You wa--want me to do it?"

Jason patted him on the back.

"How else are you going to learn? And, besides, you're the younger."

"Huh?"

"Yes. You unscrew it. Don't count on anything remotely resembling common sense coming out of my mouth today."

"Ok."

Brandon fidgeted with the gas cap, and finally got it off while Jason stood by him and quietly and patiently watched.

"Good. Now, here's the gas pump line. Lift it off where it's sitting and put the nozzle into the gas tank pipe you've just so brilliantly uncovered."

Brandon picked up the gas pump, and jumped.

"It's ca—cold. The handle to the na--nozzle is cold."

Jason smiled.

"It's supposed to be."

"Wa--why"

"Because the gasoline is stored in underground tanks to get it cold so it doesn't explode."

"I sa--see."

"That's why I put my cigarette out in the car ashtray before coming outside. It's not worth it to take that kind of blind chance."

Brandon nodded, and studied the contraption in his hand.

"Now, see the curved mental piece inside the handle of the gas pump?"

"Tha--this?" Brandon pointed.

"Right. That's the trigger. Put the nozzle of the gas pump into the gas pipe in the car, and squeeze the trigger."

Brandon put the nozzle in the gas pipe, squeezed the trigger, turned, and looked disappointed and confused.

"Na--nothing's happening."

Jason laughed, and pointed a finger in the air.

"Aha. Why?"

Brandon shrugged, and looked confused.

"I da--don't know."

Jason laughed again, shook his head, went over to the gas pump, and pointed.

"Nothing happening because we didn't turn the gas pump on. See this, where the handle of the pump rested before you picked it up? We must flip it into the 'up' position, like so--."

The gas line jumped in Brandon's hand.

"Na--now the gas is coming out. I ca--can hear it running and sa--smell it."

"Ok. Keep squeezing the trigger and watch the numbers here on the pump. See the dollar sign?"

"Ya-yes."

"When it starts to get near the $10.00 figure slowly ease up on the trigger--it will slow down--and when you stop squeezing the trigger, the pump will stop."

"O -ka-kay."

Jason leaned against the passenger door, watched his splay-eyed son try to concentrate on the whirling numbers of the gas pump, and jump slightly when he let go of the trigger. *He gets fed decent food and his rotten teeth and crooked eyes get fixed first,* Jason thought, *then the braces to straighten his teeth and then, somehow, I'll get that stuttering fixed, dammit.*

Brandon turned to him, a wide, cock-eyed grin on his face.

"I da--did it."

Jason walked over, gently patted Brandon on the back, and gave him a quick hug.

"Fine job. Now, put the pump back in its cradle, screw the gas cap back on, and we'll go check the oil."

They walked around to the front of the car, Jason lifted the hood, and secured it. Brandon stood next to his father, gazed down into the maze of metal, hoses, electrical wires, and looked baffled.

"Wa--Where do you check the oil, dad?"

Jason pointed.

"Aha. See this little metal pipe sticking up from near the bottom of the engine, next to the octopus of wires?"

Brandon turned to Jason. The sunlight sparkled in his wavy, yellow-red hair.

"What's a, ah, cur--bater?"

Jason pointed his finger.

"That's the carburetor. It mixes gasoline fumes with air, and sends the mixture into the cylinder heads, where the mixture is exploded by an electric spark fired from the spark plug."

"Wa--where a--are they?"

Jason pointed. "Those are the spark plugs."

"Oh."

Jason moved around to the side of the car, Brandon followed, and stood at his side.

"Ready to check the oil?"

"Ya--yes, I--I, guess."

Jason turned towards the gas pump behind them, and pointed.

"First, grab some paper toweling from that box over there by the gas pump."

Brandon walked over, grabbed a paper towel, and came back.

"Ok, now hook your index finger into the little metal circle, here, and gently pull up on it."

"Like tha--this?"

"That's right. Good. Now, wipe the oil stick--it's called a 'dip stick'--off at the bottom with the paper toweling, and slip the dip stick back into where you got it from."

Brandon fished for the hole, found it, and put the dip stick back in.

"Good. Now, pull it out again and look at it."

"Ok."

"What do you see?"

"There's sa--some oil on it."

"See the three little, horizontal lines in the end of the dip stick?"

"Un--huh."

"How far up the dip stick does the oil come?"

"It's b--by the line closest to the top of where the lines are."

"Good. We don't need any oil. Put the dipstick back and close the hood-- never mind, I'll do it. You've done enough grown up work here."

Jason sent Brandon off with a twenty dollar bill to pay for the gas, got back into the car, and waited for him. When Brandon came back he sat down, put his seat belt on, and looked very proud and pleased with himself. Something had changed in the world, maybe changed the whole world, like that one moment in the spring where everything smells differently, buds explode everywhere, and Brandon felt a little like a blooming flower himself. He handed his father the $10 in change.

"Life's sure complicated isn't it, dad?"

Jason beamed at Brandon.

"Yes it is, and you did a fine job. Keep the $10. You're going to need it."

Brandon's chest swelled and his shoulders widened. His father was proud of him, he had $10, he hadn't stuttered, and he had done what grown-up boys do.

IV

Back on the road Jason started cracking jokes, one after the other, and kept it up for three more hours, all the way down state. Brandon laughed at virtually everything Jason said and Jason too, laughed at virtually everything Brandon said.

They drove down the dirt road towards the home where Brandon, Andria, and Bobby had played together for years, towards the home where the tree hut was, where the legendary land of El Sat had ruled, and where The Great Water Gun Wars had taken place.

"Wa--we still have the t--tree hut, dad?"

"Oh, yes. Got a fresh coat of stain a month or so ago."

"Ca--can we still play 'spaceship' together 'n have the Great Water Gun War again?"

"Sure can."

"Da--do you still have your piano?"

"Not the one you remember. A new one. By the way, did I ever play you the song I wrote for your mother, many years ago?"

"I--I don't th--remember."

"Well, I'll play it for you when we get home. Tomorrow, I think I'll write a song for you, a song about you and me, a song about the parks, a song about our secret sound – EEEEYAH--from the parks, a love song of your mom, of you and Addy and Andria and Bobby, and of you and meow."

"A ha--happy song?"

"A very happy, beautiful, song. A concerto in five movements."

"On the piano?"

"No, on the typewriter."

Brandon giggled.

"Ar--are you ka--kidding me again, dad?"

"Yes and no."

They turned into their pebble-strewn driveway, stopped. Jason turned off the engine.

"We're home." Jason shouted, one leg out the driver's door, "We're home."

No one responded.

"Maybe they're grocery shopping or something like that," Jason said as he looked through the garage window at the empty interior of the garage.

They went to the front door.

It was locked.

Jason tried his key.

"That's strange. My key doesn't work. What the hell is going on? I called Addy this morning, told her we were on our way, told her when we expected to be here."

Brandon touched his father's elbow.

"D--dad," Brandon said, "there's a--an envelope on the front d—door. It says your n--name on it."

Jason opened the screen door, peeled the scotch tape away from the ends of the envelope, and opened it up. The handwriting was Addy's.

Dear Jason,

I guess that by now you and Brandon have made it back, and are wondering why we're not home, and why the house is all locked up and why your key doesn't work.

I've changed the lock that's why.

The house is locked because I've taken Andria and Bobby away for a while, so that you can get used to not seeing them everyday, and they can get used to not seeing you every day, for the time being.

Why?

It's real hard to explain. I've stuck with you for all these years in your fight for Brandon because I love you so very much, because you are so wonderful a father for Andria and Bobby, and because you were right to fight for Brandon--against everyone in the world, it sure seemed like at times.

But today, when you called and I realized that you'd won, that you and Brandon would really be coming home, then I suddenly knew that one of the big reasons for our deal of years ago for us being 'us' was gone.

There's a big hole there now, don't you see?

And when I realized that I also figured you'd be off on another one of your stubborn crusades, this time fixing all of Brandon's hurts and ugliness, his eyes, his stuttering, and I knew for sure that there'd be little or no time left in your life for me.

I just can't stand that empty feeling inside.

I'm real scared. So, I guess I'm leaving you. I don't want to, but I have to, to protect myself from being hurt, from feeling unimportant. I haven't filed for divorce yet. I wanted you to have time to think about what I've said, how I feel, so that maybe you can figure out a way for us to work it out now that the horrid war between you and Russet and Danny and Russet's mom has ended.

I can't.

Give me a call next week sometime, after Wednesday, here at home to set up a time when you want to talk, or want to move your stuff out, if that's what you want to do.

I love you,
Addy

Jason sighed, folded the letter, and put it in the inside pocket of his tan sports jacket.

"Damn it all," he said.

Brandon looked up.

"What'd it s--say, d--dad?"

Jason turned, put his arm around Brandon, hugged him, and tousled his hair.

"Just a little more goddamn confusion, that's all."

"That wa-what it said."

"It said it's time for us to have a Coke and a beer, time to have some dinner, and get a hotel room for us to stay in tonight, Ok?"

Brandon jumped up and down and found himself yelling.

"Just you an--and I? Neat."

"Just you and I. And tomorrow maybe we'll go to Mandermetz Park or maybe we'll drop by here to visit the tree hut or maybe we'll go looking for a place to stay after tonight, you and I, alone."

"Wa--What ab--bout Andria and Bobby? Wa--when are wa--we going to see them?"

Jason tousled Brandon's thick red hair again.

"Next week. Come on, hop in the car. Let's go."

Brandon opened his car door, and got in. When Jason was about to start the car, Brandon took a chance.

"Are you an Addy going t--to get a divorce?"

How the hell can I explain this crap to a kid? Jason thought, looking straight ahead.

"I don't know for certain, but at this moment it looks like a crazy possibility."

Out of the corner of his eye, Jason saw Brandon shaking his head from side to side.

"Wa--why? Is it be--because of ma-me, like the other wa--war?"

Jason scowled and looked at Brandon.

"Hell, no. And you weren't the cause of the other war, either."

Brandon scowled.

"I wa--wasn't?"

"Hell, no."

"Wa--what wa--was?"

"Confusion. Same as this mess here. Love is so fragile, so delicate, it sometimes gets confused and gets lost. Love is sometimes like a baby cloud. Sometimes it wanders away, gets lost and can't find its way back home."

Brandon frowned.

"I--I don't understand."

"Have you ever gotten lost?"

"Ya--yes."

"And while you were lost you felt like a part of you was somehow missing from inside of you, and you couldn't find it?"

"Ya--yes, I ca--can remember feeling like tha--that."

"Kinda empty, right?"

"Yeah. Real b--bad empty."

Jason turned, put his arm over the back of the car seat, tousled Brandon's hair and smiled at him.

"Same kind of thing happens to people when they think they've lost someone they love,.or actually lose someone they love--like when your mom died--or, worse, when people are somehow prevented from loving someone that they want to love and be with--they feel lost. When you're lost and find your way back home again, the loving feeling comes back too, and you feel whole again, not empty inside anymore."

Brandon nodded, but didn't look like he'd fully understood what his father had said.

"That's Ok. We've got years to figure it out."

They backed out of the driveway, and started down the road.

Brandon touched his father's leg.

"Are you going to be in another wa--war over Andria and Bobby, D--dad?"

"Maybe--but believe me, if there's a war over them, I'll win it. After you, it'll be easy, like eating a piece of cake."

Brandon watched his hands grab at the air before him.

"Wa--Why?"

Jason beamed.

"Because I'm me again. For the last 10 so years, I've haven't been me, and have been sorta lost from myself because I couldn't be your dad and love you. I was kind of a half-empty shell, a ghost trying to find out who it was. Now, I know."

"Know wa--what?"

"Who I am. I'm whole again, I'm me again."

There was a prolonged silence. Brandon leaned forward, sat back, then leaned forward again.

"Wa--what's going to ha--happen to me?"

Jason slowed down, pulled over to the side, stopped, and looked his son straight in his good eye.

"You're going to be whole again, you're going to be yourself again."

There was a prolonged silence. Brandon leaned forward, sat back, then leaned forward again.

"Wa--what's going to ha--happen to me?"

Jason slowed down, pulled over to the side, stopped, and looked his son straight in his good eye.

"You're going to be whole again, you're going to be yourself again, too."

"Ha--how?"

Jason put the car in gear and moved on down the road, his eyes focused straight ahead..

"I'm going to be your dad and love the hell out of you, Brandon, I'm just going to love the demons out of you, that's how. You see, we're not lost from each other any more. We're home."

Chapter V

Flying

Two years later, Addy and Jason divorced, and custody of Bobby and Andria was awarded jointly. Jason did not remarry, nor did Addy, and they remained friends.

As Addy had predicted, Jason went to work on Brandon's injuries and the demons raging inside his head, a project that consumed hours of work and thousands of dollars—all of which paid off. Eight years later, Brandon's eyes were straight; his teeth were cavity-free and aligned; he weighed 190 lbs of pure muscle; and he no longer stuttered.

After two tries, Brandon got into Wesleyan University, his father's school. The day of Brandon's departure, Jason spent the entire morning composing a letter to Brandon and handed it to him at the airport.

"Promise me not to read this until you are high in the sky," Jason said

Brandon took the sealed envelope and put it in his shirt pocket.

"What's it for?" he asked.

"Something to take with you into the future." Jason said, hugged his handsome, muscular son, and patted him on the back.

Brandon had learned to trust his father again and waited to open the letter until the captain announced they had reached their cruising level of 40,000 feet.

January 13, 1990

Dear Brandon,

I remember once, not so long ago, encouraging you to climb the ladder so that you could come zipping down the park slide into my awaiting arms at the bottom, and pushing you high in the swing over my head, both of us yelling 'eeee-yah. eeeee-yah'--and then we'd go home.

Well, as you read this, you're now flying again, this time alone, high

in the sky to a new destination called your future. But you are the one who must now encourage and push yourself. Quite an adventure you're on, young Icarus.

It's strange. A couple of years ago--even a year ago--I would have felt uneasy if you had then flown away to college. But I don't feel that way at all today. You're ready - you have strong wings, can handle yourself competently now, will be able to meet the considerable and often stormy, windswept challenges awaiting you at college, and hopefully emerge from the struggles stronger yet.

I'm proud of you, of the work you've done on yourself, the qualities you have shown of young manhood, and the promise your life now shows of a terrific adulthood and a splendid, creative, life adventure.

I am proud to have been your swing pusher.

And I am, strangely, looking forward myself to my next life phase also - whatever it is - and while I will always be your father, my calling as your 'parent' has ended, and so I let it fade away into memories that I fondly cherish in my heart. Someday you may choose to assume that role for your own offspring. I pass that scepter on to you with deep respect and in full confidence that should you choose someday to be a father, you will assume that responsibility with integrity and elan.

So, your childhood has ended, my role as your 'parent' has ended, and your young adulthood has begun, as has the next phase of my life.

In endings there are beginnings, in sadness there is always a nascent, bright center of joy springing into being.

Good luck, my son. Fly proud and mighty.

I love you,

Dad

Brandon read the letter several times, with each reading recovering a fond memory of things he had a done with his dad, the things the letter only hinted at.

The letter said nothing about the stupid things Brandon had done that hurt his father. Nothing.

Why?

The letter said nothing of how his father had fixed him.

How did he do it? Brandon asked himself as he read the paragraph about his childhood ending. *How did he fix me? When I came back home I was a mess.*

Then the gift hit him: *My father says he loves me and is proud of me.*

The jet engines purred outside. Brandon reread the letter and remembered the moments of wonder he had experienced as a child with his father, how as a young boy he had been taught to hate him, and how he had come to love him again, this time, as a man.

The letter trembled in his hands. The tears rolled down his cheeks.

Brandon later graduated, with Honors, from the California Institute of Technology and, two months after graduation, with his father standing at his side, Brandon married his college sweetheart.

A year later, Brandon became a father, and the tradition of first-born sons renewed itself for yet another generation of the Adams family.

Printed in the United States
1423000003B/316-321